THE UNQUIET GRAVE

For my sister, Diane,
her enthusiasm and her interest.

Other books by David J Oldman

Looking For Ginger
A Voice from the Congo
On Wings Of Death
A Weapon Of The Bourgeoisie
Dusk at Dawn

THE UNQUIET GRAVE

DAVID J OLDMAN

Papaver Press

Published in 2017 by Papaver Press

Second paperback edition

 British Library C.I.P. A CIP catalogue record for this title is available from the British Library.

First published as an e-book by Endeavour Press Ltd in 2016.

First paperback edition published by Endeavour Press Ltd in 2016.

1

Cocooned in the dark, it came as a shock to see her standing in front of me, larger than life and in the arms of another man. I recognized her immediately, even though they had changed her. Done something with her hair and somehow softened her rather angular features. But they couldn't change her eyes. It was the look in her eyes I remembered most of all.

Friday June 14th 1946

The summer I met Rose Kearney I was living in a cold water flat in Clerkenwell, hidden at the back of one of those old courts just off Cowcross Street. It wasn't much of a place, just two rooms and a shared bathroom down the hall—even if there was no one left to share it with.

Late in the war one of the last V2 rockets to reach London penetrated the maze of railway tunnels beneath Smithfield market and the explosion brought many of the surrounding buildings down into the crater. The building I lived in stayed up but most of the old warehouse tenements around it collapsed. More than a hundred people died—women and children among them, queuing in the market that morning on the rumour of rabbits for sale. But the damage to the building ensured the rent on the flat was cheap and the location was handy for work; two stops by underground from Farringdon on the Metropolitan and District Line to the office my section had been allocated just off Great Portland Street. And living on a bombsite was hardly uncommon in London at that time. Nor, I suppose, was being jammed up against a railway line or a market. At least by then they'd stopped slaughtering live animals there. Even so, none of it gave the address much of a cachet.

The area was close to what had once been known as Little Italy. There weren't as many Italians as there had been before the war—internment and the Blitz had thinned out much of the population—but they had slowly begun drifting back. I daresay swapping sides helped rehabilitate many of Italian descent; we'd all seen the newsreels of the partisans stringing Mussolini up by his ankles.

They'd strung up Il Duce's mistress, too, although watching the film of it I have to admit to feeling a little sorry for her. A case of the wrong place at the wrong time, I suppose. Which ought to be a lesson for us all in choosing the company we keep.

~

I was in Berlin when the war ended, having got there through North Africa and Italy where I received my commission. While waiting my turn to be demobbed, I had expected to spend what remained of my army career riding around the city in a Jeep helping prevent the Russians taking the sort of inch they could turn into a mile. The army hadn't quite finished with me, though, and before my papers came through I found I had been promoted and transferred into a section of the Intelligence Corps under a hard-faced Scot named Jekyll. It had been set up to investigate war crimes and I assumed someone had got wind of the fact that before the war I'd been a policeman. I suppose they thought it might give me some sort of expertise in the matter. It didn't, of course, but I soon discovered that no one else had much expertise in that line either.

To say we were investigating war crimes makes the work sound as if we were personally dropping the sword of justice onto the necks of the Nazi leaders. The truth was our section was just one among many and didn't have anything to do with the big fish being netted for Nuremburg. Our brief was to look into those cases of army personnel who may have been either the victims or the perpetrators of war crimes. And the only things we ever hooked in the piscatorial line were small fry, tiddlers from the schools of cod-faced National Socialists who had "just followed orders"; and some from that swarm of bureaucratic guppies who swam alongside them, handling the paperwork. If it ever looked as if we might get a bite from someone really worth landing—someone involved in camp administration or a regional bigwig—we were supposed to throw them back to the prosecutors higher up the food chain. What this meant in reality was that our job consisted mostly of sifting through files: the interrogation transcripts of POW and Displaced Persons, witness statements, reports dealing with missing persons and accounts of unidentified bodies, where the death might have occurred in questionable circumstances. Trying to marry up the loose ends. War crimes being within the purview of the Army Intelligence Division, cases usually came to us so that we could do the donkey-work before passing on anything of value so that others could squabble over the kudos.

Colonel Jekyll—or Colonel G as we called him—was a short-tempered Borderer with a head of hair like the bristles on a scrubbing brush and a manner just as abrasive. He only had one good eye, which rarely looked warmer than the glass replacement he wore in the other socket, and he used it like a watchful vulture, presiding over other sections besides ours. He'd been an engineer before the war, apparently, used to working within the world of tolerances and pressures, stress and loadings—all measurements he brought to bear upon his subordinates.

Once a week Jekyll would arrive and go over what we were working on. He would take with him anything which he thought others might be more fitted to deal with and, on occasion, leave us with something that had turned up in one of his other units. This meant as a general rule we only saw him on Friday afternoons, although—to keep us on our toes—he was just as likely to drop in unannounced anytime.

We inhabited two stuffy first-floor rooms overlooking Clipstone Street, and were a mixed bunch; it not being immediately clear what sort of military reasoning had brought us together. I admit there was some logic behind co-opting Peter Quince, a lanky lieutenant who had just received his law degree when he'd been called up. To my mind that end of justice always seemed like examining a mummified corpse—hidebound, desiccated remains from which anything recognisable had already been removed. But for some reason it appealed to Peter. He was generally able to pick out the salient points from a situation, like a pathologist separating the vital organs from an otherwise uninteresting carcass. Still looking like precisely what he had been—a bookish law student—Peter was the antithesis of Stan Woodruff, a bull-like NCO who at first glance most would have pegged as a professional boxer. He had the nose for it, slightly flattened by the gloves he hadn't managed to avoid, and also the makings of a cauliflower ear. But he'd acquired these for nothing in the amateur ring, boxing for his regiment. Damage apart, there was still more than a residual trace of the masculine good looks he'd once possessed and, luckily, none of the punches he'd failed to avoid seemed to have made much of a dent in his still sharp brain.

The sole female on our staff was Susie Blake, an ATS—a service arm whose members had once been called, and often still were, FANYs. Susie looked after our filing and most of the routine typing and office work. A vivacious brunette, she gave the office the spark it would have otherwise lacked. Short and bright-eyed, she seemed to suffer from having been issued with a uniform one size too small. It gave her a top-heavy look, but she was good-natured about it and never complained about the extra work re-sewing her buttons might have given her.

Apart from me, that just left my corporal, Jack Hibbert, the man responsible for putting things on and taking things off my desk, and generally keeping the office running. Jack had a thin, bird-like face with a beaky nose that wouldn't support his glasses. He was forever interrupting his typing to push them back in place. He occupied a desk and a typewriter on the other side of the room I shared with him. The other three worked next door.

Jack was sitting at his battered Remington as I got in that particular June morning, picking out the letters with four fingers and a thumb and having to stop now and then to adjust his glasses or untangle the keys where his enthusiasm had got the better of his skill.

He glanced up briefly and said 'good morning' as I dropped into the chair behind my desk, then pushed his glasses back up his nose and went on with whatever it was he was doing. I looked down at what I had in front of me, tried to remember what I had been doing the previous evening, then matched one against the other. Nothing seemed out of place except for a file that lay in the centre of the desk. I opened it and found a letter attached to a report about a burnt-out Bren gun carrier.

I flipped through it then turned to Jack. 'Who's Rose Kearney?'

He stopped typing. 'Rose who?'

'Rose Kearney.'

'Search me. What, some actress or other?'

I waved the file at him.

'What's that?'

'That's what I'm asking.'

'No idea,' he said. 'I thought you'd left it there.'

In the privacy of the office, and in the absence of Colonel G, none of us bothered with the protocols of rank. By then we had all pretty much had our fill of military etiquette.

'Who did you say again?' he came over and looked through the file.

'Not Kearney like in King *Lears*,' he said.

'King Lears? What's Shakespeare got to do with it?'

'Rhyming slang,' said Jack. '*Ears*. I served with a bloke called Kearney. Irish, but from the north. In the south they pronounce it *Karney*, as in blarney.'

'Very apt,' I said. 'How do you know this Rose was from the south?'

He pointed to the letter. 'She wrote from County Wicklow. A Rose by any other name...?'

I took the file back. Jack was fond of the odd Shakespearean quotation although they rarely led anywhere. I read the letter properly then looked through the rest of the file. Kearney was the name of the NCO who had commanded the damaged Bren gun carrier.

'So,' I said to Jack, getting back on track. 'Bren gun carrier. Normandy, July of forty-four. One vehicle, two dead, burned to a crisp, ID through discs. Third member of the crew found with a bullet in the back of the head, which, I presume, is why there's a file. Fourth man—the aforementioned Kearney—sergeant in command, never found.'

'Not one of mine.'

He put his head into the other room and said something to the others about Bren gun carriers and kebabs. Jack had also spent some of his war in North Africa and claimed to know a thing or two about Middle-Eastern cuisine.

Getting no response, he turned back to me and shrugged. 'Got a reference? Want me to look it up?'

I shook my head, tossed the file aside and lit a cigarette. Although tobacco had never been rationed during the war, some brands of cigarettes were difficult to get and I'd recently switched from Capstan Full Strength to Park Drive, finding myself missing the way the Capstan had had of scraping the throat like a rasp. Jack continued to watch me for a moment as if he was thinking of something else, then went back to clattering on the Remington. I pulled on the cigarette for a minute or two and found, if you didn't look, the discordant racket of the typewriter sounded like a tap dancer who hadn't quite mastered his routine. As I watched the smoke curling in a shaft of sunlight coming through our one window, I pictured a fat man in a tuxedo shifting his weight from foot to foot with his face getting redder and redder. Then Susie brought me a mug of tea and I got a picture in my head of something altogether different.

She put the tea down, reached a finger under my chin and raised my eyes to the level of hers.

'I saw Colonel G leaving as I arrived.'

I sat up. 'Did you? What did he want?'

'I was the other side of the road. He didn't see me.' She pouted as if he might have ignored her on purpose.

'Did he leave a message?'

'Not on *my* desk.'

'Oh...*right.*' I put the cigarette back in my mouth, picked up the tea with one hand and pulled the Kearney file back towards me with the other. 'Thanks, Susie.'

'One good turn, Captain,' she replied archly, bright eyes widening and leaving me wondering what she meant.

~

The letter from Rose Kearney was clipped to the top of the file. Beneath it was a sheet headed 43rd Wessex Division, 129th Brigade, and an account of the discovery by D Company of the 4th battalion Wiltshire Regiment of the burnt remains of a Universal Carrier to the south-west of Caen on July 23rd, 1944, some six weeks after the D-Day invasion. The rest of the file was a mix of documents: excerpts from the military records of the carrier crew, a smudged copy of the initial report from the Field Ambulance unit who had recovered the vehicle and bodies, and details of the battalion to which the carrier had been attached. Most interesting of all was a statement dated 22nd August 1944, concerning effects found on the body of a dead SS-Unterscharführer by the name of Vogel following the fighting in the Falaise Pocket.

Rose Kearney's letter was more recent and dated February 3rd of the current year. It informed the recipient that she was Sergeant Kearney's sister. She wrote that she had been told in the summer of 1944 that her brother was missing in action and had heard nothing since. Her subsequent enquiries had not been answered. Since the war was over and her brother had still not returned home—home being a village in County Wicklow, Ireland—she was coming to London to make enquiries. Her Irish address was at the top of the letter and she also supplied an address in Kilburn where she would be staying once in London. She gave no telephone number.

It was a decent letter and Rose Kearney had a neat hand, her loops bordering upon the florid, giving the note an almost artistic air. Reading it made a nice change from deciphering the scrawl that made up the majority of the reports we handled. The letter didn't add anything to the file to which it was attached and I could only suppose that whoever had passed it on to Colonel G had thought it might be worthwhile interviewing Rose Kearney when she arrived in

London. Since she was coming to ask *us* about her brother, though, I didn't see why it should.

The reason a file existed to which Rose Kearney's letter could be attached was plain enough; while two dead men in a burnt Bren gun Carrier, identified only through their ID discs, and a third man missing was hardly out of the common run of things, a fourth with a bullet in the back of his head was another matter. It was the sort of circumstance that our section had been set up to look into—although usually a single death that appeared beyond the code of the Hague Convention wasn't generally of enough importance to warrant the time spent investigating. Besides which, of course, there could also be a reasonable explanation for each of the deaths.

I read all the papers again and decided the most pertinent fact was that found among the effects on the body of an SS sergeant, Otto Vogel, were the identity discs belonging to the missing Sergeant William Kearney. Although Vogel had been killed a month after the carrier had been recovered and at a different location, it was still, on the face of it, a damning piece of evidence. Once again though even this might have an innocent explanation.

I got up and dropped the file on Jack's desk.

'Get on the blower and make sure this Kearney hasn't turned up alive, will you? One of the four seems to have been executed and possibly Kearney too. It's not very likely he survived but there's no point in going to any trouble over him if it's just a clerical fuck-up.'

Jack reached for the phone. 'To be or not to be...?'

'If he hasn't, try his battalion and see what else they've got on him and his carrier crew. And the Red Cross, too. See if his name appears on any of their POW lists. Oh, then see if you can find out if any of Colonel G's other people have seen this file already.'

Jack threw one of his sardonic deadpans over the top of his glasses. 'Anything else?'

'Not unless you can think of something.'

I started back to my desk then turned. 'Yes, the sister. See if she's been in touch since she arrived.'

'Sister?'

'Rose. It's in the letter.'

I left him to it and brewed up another pot of tea for everyone. I ran a very democratic unit.

2

When I first got back to London I found it strangely intact. It might be an odd thing to say but after Berlin it seemed to me as though London had got off lightly. Some parts of the German capital had simply ceased to exist; whole suburbs were little more than a desert of rubble. The centre of London and the docks and the East End had caught it badly, of course, but to me it appeared that beyond these areas the bombing had been random—unlike Berlin where you got the impression that the objective had been to exterminate every living creature.

Having gone through the war to that point without the slightest regard for the fate of any German at all, I had found to my surprise a creeping sympathy for the civilian population. The feeling waxed and waned, of course, depending on things you learned about what had happened, but by then a new villain had already taken the place of the Germans, tailor-made as a substitute once you heard the stories of what the German women went through when the Russians arrived.

Getting back to England was like being able to breathe fresh air again after being forced to inhale someone else's rancid odour. London, of course, was still redolent of coal smoke and fog and the pervasive tang of crushed masonry, but the population weren't wearing that haunted look, that expression of defeat the hunted have when they've finally given up running.

That first impression of seeing the city as relatively untouched soon began to fade. Each morning I became subtly aware of more damage, as if overnight the bombing raids still continued, only silently now. It was an odd sensation and one I kept to myself. In time that faded too as I began struggling like everybody else with the unreliable public transport, food and fuel rationing, and the general drabness of life that manifested itself mostly in shortages of everything you needed and surpluses only of things you didn't want.

~

It took Jack the best part of the day to pull together what I'd asked for, including some material which the battalion said they would forward. This was 7th Hampshires, a territorial battalion to which the carrier had been attached. Sergeant William Kearney was still officially posted as missing, presumed dead, and neither he nor any of the others in the carrier had left any particular impression on those Jack had been able to talk to. But then that was hardly surprising, given the size of battalions and the turnover of men once the Normandy landings had begun. The only fact that anyone could remember was that Kearney had been Irish, hardly a revelation given that his sister Rose hailed from County Wicklow. From what Jack could gather she had been making something of a nuisance of herself, first with the Hampshire Regiment and then with the her brother's battalion commander who until that point had never heard of Sergeant William Kearney. He had shuffled her further along the line and after that she appeared to have been passed from one office to the next like a contagious virus.

'*That*,' Jack said as he returned a thickening file, 'is probably why she ended up on your desk. We were next in line to catch the thing.'

Yet despite what Jack thought, it seemed to me that at some point her correspondence must have caught up with the file on the man who appeared to have been executed. Seen in the perspective of what else had happened during the war, the case might be thought of as small beer. Gravitating towards Colonel G as it had, I supposed it was hardly surprising it had come to us. We, too, were small beer.

~

Moving up through Italy, once we'd got off the beachheads and made some ground, I'd spent a couple of weeks myself in what is properly termed a Universal Carrier. They are tracked open-topped vehicles that on uneven ground pitch and yaw like an Atlantic liner in a gale. Carrier platoons were devised to be small mobile units attached to infantry battalions, usually made up of half-a-dozen vehicles with three or four men in each. Their main armament was a Bren gun and an anti-tank rifle—a Boyes until it was later replaced by the PIAT anti-tank gun. When not ferrying men or supplies or officers around, their job was to move ahead of infantry to secure ground before an advance, hopefully knocking out any tanks or armoured vehicles opposing them. Riding in one, it had dawned upon me what a thankless task that was. They weren't a match for a German tank and the best that could be hoped for was they kept the enemy busy by providing a target while the infantry moved up and found cover. It was the kind of vehicle that often found itself out on a limb, caught as it usually was between the lines. In the case of Kearney's carrier, Jack had a map reference for where the vehicle had been lost, close to a village called Maltot a few miles to the south west of Caen in Normandy.

According to the file, Sergeant Kearney commanded on the Bren, with Private Robert Burleigh as driver and mechanic, Private Joseph Dabs carrying the PIAT and Lance corporal Arnold Poole as the radio operator. As carriers went, Kearney's was well armed; it was just that whatever they had come up against had been better armed. The report said that when the 4th Wilts had come across the carrier they found it by the side of the drive leading to a ruined château. First indications suggested the carrier had been hit by a shell—most likely from a hand-held anti-tank weapon—killing and incinerating the two men inside who could only be identified by their ID discs. They were named as Lance corporal Arnold Poole and Private Robert Burleigh. A third body, that of Joseph Dabs, lay some yards from the carrier. Decomposition aside, Dabs was unmarked except for the bullet in the back of his head. A brief description of the wound was attached but it didn't make a guess at the weapon used or even of the calibre. As there had been no sign at the scene of the fourth member of the crew, a search was made and a shallow marked grave discovered in the garden of the château. The corpse of a man was exhumed, but although it had been partially burned the body was dressed in civilian clothes. Still legible identification papers found on him suggested he had been a French national.

There were no further indications as to what might have happened to William Kearney.

Jack typed up the notes made from his enquiries and I put these with what I was now calling the Joseph Dabs' file. I took it into the other office for Peter Quince and Stan to look at. First I gave Susie the list of the men in the carrier.

'Start a separate file on each, please Susie.'

She looked at the first name. 'Kearney? As in Gene Tierney?'

The film star Gene Tierney was a particular favourite of Susie's. Only a couple of weeks earlier on her recommendation I'd gone to watch a Technicolor farrago called, *Leave Her to Heaven*, starring Tierney and Cornel Wilde, discovering too late I could have better spent the two-hour running time less painlessly hanging by my thumbs. But Susie loved a glossy melodrama. It was the romantic in her.

'Not *Tierney*,' I told her '*Kearney*. As in carny. You know, carnivals?'

'*Carny* is American parlance,' Peter pointed out.

Susie hooted. 'I went out with GI before the invasion. I could barely understand a word he said.'

'He's almost certainly dead,' said Peter, glancing through the file and ignoring her.

'Couldn't say as much for my GI,' Susie muttered. 'He was more than lively.'

I tried to ignore her as well. 'You're probably right, Peter. But we have to consider the other possibilities.'

'Such as?'

'Such as why is anyone interested? The list of missing in the Normandy campaign must be as long as your arm. Dead bodies without names and names without bodies. Why do they want us to look into this one?'

'Because an SS man had Kearney's discs?'

'I'd have thought it was an open and shut case, then.'

'What are you suggesting?'

I shrugged. 'I don't know. I'm just speculating. This Kearney's missing. Perhaps someone suspects he deserted.'

'Wouldn't be the first,' said Stan. 'Have you seen the figures?'

I had and they were alarming. It wasn't something the War Office broadcast but desertion had been endemic. Not so easy in Kearney's case, I would have thought, in France and probably unable to speak the language, with the Germans on one side and the Allies on the other.

'You think he might still be alive?' Peter queried. 'Injured and parted from his ID discs?'

'Happens,' I said.

'Then why hasn't he surfaced?'

'Holed up in Normandy?'

'After two years? Hardly likely.'

'Perhaps he's like Ronald Coleman in Random Harvest,' Susie suggested. 'He lost his memory and Greer Garson found him and—'

'Suppose,' I said quickly so we didn't get the plot of the whole film, 'Kearney killed his mates to cover his tracks? But didn't have time to burn Dabs.'

Peter looked at the file again. 'No, too obvious. If you're planning to disappear you leave your own discs on one of the burnt corpses.'

'Maybe Kearney's not too bright,' Stan put in.

'He made sergeant.'

'All right, Kearney's dead and one of the others switched discs,' I suggested.

'Poole or Burleigh? They had a positive ID on Dabs.' He's the one who got it in the back of the neck.'

'Head,' I said.

'I suppose it's possible. But if that's the way it went he'd need a damn good reason to disappear, particularly if he's going to kill his mates.'

'Comrades. They served together but in my experience that didn't necessarily make them friends.'

Susie was looking up at us. 'Are you serious?'

'I don't know,' I said. 'I'm just wondering why anyone thinks it worth investigating.'

'It appears they do,' said Peter, 'although the chances are Kearney died at the same time as the others. A German unit they ran into wasn't bothering to take prisoners so Dabs caught one in the back of the head. Kearney, too, only his body hasn't turned up yet. What's left of it by now, that is.'

It was the most likely answer, of course, and sooner or later Kearney's bones would surface, turned up by a plough in some out of the way spot. A retreating army is far less likely to take prisoners than an advancing one and, like Joseph Dabs, a bullet in the head and a shallow grave was probably as much as William Kearney got to see of France. Only dabs never even got the grave. Whoever had shot him probably had to pull out before they got the chance to bury him. Either that or they just weren't bothered and left him where he fell. The chances were SS-Unterscharführer Vogel killed them both and took Kearney's discs as a souvenir—or traded for the discs with some other man who actually did it. Small beer except for Kearney and Dabs but, whichever way you looked at it, still a war crime, an act that contravened the Hague Convention. How anyone was going to prove it, I didn't know, never mind bringing anyone to book for it.

Peter handed the file back. 'You saw what regiment the SS man who had Kearney's discs was with, didn't you? 25th SS-Panzer Grenadiers. That's Hitlerjugend.'

Once he pointed it out, of course, the bells started ringing.

'Weren't they responsible for the Ardenne Abbey massacre?'

'That's right. Unterscharführer Otto Vogel was in the 25th. Kurt Meyer's regiment. They were part of 12SS-Panzer Division.'

The Hitlerjugend were SS raised late in the war and formed around veterans from the remnants of 1SS-Panzer Division, the army and the Luftwaffe. Most new recruits came from the Hitler Youth leadership schools, and some were no more than boys of sixteen. 12SS Hitlerjugend, of which the 25th was part, might have been thought of as mainly inexperienced troops who would buckle under Allied pressure. The reverse had been true. What they lacked in experience they made up for in devotion to Hitler and the Nazi cause. They had spent the better part of their young lives immersed in Nazi ideology and were as convinced of its inevitable triumph as other men believe the sun will come up tomorrow.

The Ardenne Abbey massacre had taken place when the 12SS Hitlerjugend came up against the Canadians to the north-west of Caen. There had been a series of particularly bitter engagements in which the Canadians lost nearly three thousand men. The Hitlerjugend, too, had taken heavy casualties and had not taken prisoners. Over the span of a couple of days at a monastery at Saint-Germain-la-Blanche-Herbe, twenty Canadians were executed, most of their bodies not discovered until early the following year. Brigadeführer Kurt Meyer, commander of the 25th SS-Panzer Grenadier Regiment, and two of his officers had been sentenced to hang for the war crimes committed. As far as I was aware they were still awaiting execution.

'Oh well,' I said. 'all bets are off. It doesn't seem as though we have to look far after all.'

'What do you want to do?' Peter asked.

I consulted my watch. It was almost three, the usual time on a Friday that Colonel G appeared for his weekly briefing.

'Use my initiative,' I said, 'and see what Colonel G wants me to do.'

~

We didn't have long to wait. He strode in with his usual air of intent, as if he had decided to shake the place up which always left the rest of us on tenterhooks. He said, 'Good afternoon, Harry,' which was a good start as when he used my surname—or worse, my rank—I knew I must have put my foot in it somewhere. The rest he called by rank and surname, except occasionally Peter who he'd address by his Christian name if he'd done some good work; like the time some bodies had turned up in a shallow grave on the Belgian border near Oost Capel and Peter had managed to identify the German unit who'd been operating in the area during our retreat at the end of May 1940.

There was a general shifting of furniture as we all crammed into the larger of the two rooms and found somewhere to sit. One of Peter's task was to prepare a précis of what we'd been doing all week and Susie had typed it up and had it waiting with the relevant files on her desk. Then she made some tea and passed it round with a few biscuits she had managed to turn up somewhere. Black market, probably, and none too fresh but Colonel G liked a biscuit and always reacted as if it was the highlight of his week. He munched through three or four, dropping crumbs on the files as he read and asked a few questions.

Jekyll was one of those upper-class Scots who'd gone to a public school and had the kind of accent that could cut glass. There wasn't a trace of brogue about him but put him in a kilt and give him a claymore and he'd have been the picture of a Highland terror. Susie maintained he was the laird of some outlandish clan or other but as I've already said she was just a romantic.

'Righto, Harry,' Colonel G said, fixing me with his good eye. 'The file on this fellow Dabs? Had a chance to assess it yet?'

'An execution probably, sir,' I replied, barely pausing, just so he'd know I was on top of the fact he'd been in that morning and dropped off the file. 'And the missing man's ID discs were found on a sergeant from the 25th SS-Panzer Grenadiers, so the chances are we've got two murders. The 25th were part of the 12SS-Panzer Division—the Hitlerjugend. They've got form for this sort of thing. We need to place them in the area, of course, although it's as well not to ignore other possibilities. Jack's pulling the records together for dates and details for the carrier.'

'Where are we talking about, exactly?' Jekyll asked.

'Normandy campaign,' Peter said, glancing at his notes. 'Near Caen. The battalion was 7th Hampshires.'

'Right,' I said, all business. 'Peter, let's see what we can turn up about the German troops in the area. Specifically the Hitlerjugend. Near the village of...'

'Maltot,' Jack supplied smartly, covering for me as I fumbled the name.

'...near the village of Maltot.'

Peter nodded. 'Will do, sir.'

'And Jack,' I said, 'get back on to Kearney's battalion and double check that the identity discs on the two burned bodies had been through the fire.'

Colonel G looked at me as if thinking that no-one swapping discs would be stupid enough to put an undamaged pair on a burned corpse, and I could only agree. But if it turned out later down the line that someone *had* been that stupid, I didn't want to be the one to have to explain to the colonel why we hadn't checked out the fact first.

'The next of kin,' I said to Colonel G while he was still looking at me. 'We don't have anyone for the executed man, Joseph Dabs, but we'll get on to Poole and Burleigh's families. Just on the off-chance...'

Off-chance of what, I didn't know, but as Jekyll didn't pick me up on it I went on:

'There was a letter from the sergeant in command's sister, Rose Kearney. Her brother is the missing man. I can't see as she'll know anything under the circumstances, but it'll be worth having a word if only to put her mind at rest.' I turned to Stan Woodruff. 'Stan, perhaps you can follow that up.'

Colonel G looked over at Stan from where he was sitting behind Peter's desk and sucked air through his teeth.

'We don't want to scare the poor woman, Harry. The sergeant has his uses but consoling widows and orphans isn't one that springs to mind. Do it yourself. The sooner the better. This afternoon, I think. And take Blake with you. Women's touch and all that.'

I thought Colonel G was being a bit hard on Stan, particularly as from what I had seen, getting himself knocked about a bit had only enhanced Stan's appeal rather than damaged it. But I suspected Jekyll was aware that Rose Kearney had become a nuisance and decided it was going to take a visit from an officer to pacify her. Though just why he should want me to take Susie along I didn't know.

'Any particular reason, sir, that you've given us the Dabs file?' I asked.

Jekyll skewered me with the glass eye. 'Do you mean apart from the bullet in the back of the man's head and the SS having a missing man's discs?'

'Of course,' I said quickly. 'But given the number...I mean, since it's just the one man—or two, that is—I was wondering...'

Floundering, I turned to the others for assistance. They turned the other way.

'Normandy,' Colonel G said. 'The area south of Caen? Would that have been Operation Goodwood?'

He raised an eyebrow while we all looked at each other hoping someone might know the answer.

Jack was taking notes. 'As in the racecourse, sir?'

'You were on the beaches, Stan,' I said for the want of something better to say. 'Wasn't your outfit involved in that?'

Stan knit his brows in a scowl. He had been on the beaches but only for twenty-four hours—as he knew I knew full well. He'd caught one in the arm on landing and had spent hours on the beach before eventually being shipped back across the channel again.

'Well,' Colonel G said, standing up abruptly. 'If that's all?'

We got to our feet. Everyone swapped salutes and the Colonel left.

I wasn't sure whether he had dropped the hint about Goodwood deliberately or was boasting because he happened to know the name of some operation in the area the carrier had been found. But if he already had some sort of handle on the thing, I thought I'd better get a grip on it too. And quickly, if I knew which side my bread was buttered.

Not that it went any further than the metaphor. Butter was still on ration and as scarce as contributors to an Adolf Hitler memorial fund. Besides, no one wasted the stuff spreading it on bread these days.

'I know,' Jack said as soon as the door closed on Colonel G. 'Get on the blower and see what I can dig up on Operation Goodwood. You looking for anything in particular?'

I hadn't the faintest idea. 'Something out of the ordinary?' I suggested. 'Why anyone's interested in Dabs...?' But I could tell from Jack's expression that he hadn't any ideas either.

'Does that include military fuck-ups?'

'*Out* of the ordinary, I said.'

3

Fridays I generally liked to wind things up as soon as Colonel G left the office, get a jump on the weekend and have a drink in a club I knew that opened early. This Friday the colonel had got the jump on me and it looked as if the drink would have to wait. I wasn't sure what his rush was but supposed I'd find out all in good time. Until then it seemed wise to make it look as if we were on top of things.

'Peter, you'd better concentrate on the SS. See if we can get a better idea of which units were where at the time. Get hold of a decent map for the area south west of Caen if you can. In the meantime we'll see what we can dig up about the carrier crew, just in case someone believes there's something dodgy about all this.'

'Dodgier than an SS bullet, you mean?' Jack said.

'I just want to make sure we touch all bases, as the yanks like to put it.'

'My yank certainly wanted to touch them all,' Susie remarked as she put on a face before we called on Rose Kearney. 'When I told him I was a FANY he took it *quite* the wrong way.'

I tried to ignore the picture that brought to mind and asked Stan if he had anything on for the weekend. He didn't so I told Jack to draw a rail warrant for Burnley if Stan fancied the trip. He had a brother there he hadn't seen for a while and if he travelled up on Saturday for the weekend, I thought he could call on Arnold Poole's father who lived in nearby Blackburn. If he took the early train Monday he could be back in the office mid-morning. I couldn't really see that talking to the dead men's families was going to be of much use but we had to do something while we waited for all the information we'd requested to come in. And in the army, I've found, it's often appearances that count. Even if you're really wasting time, not *looking* as though you're wasting time is what's important.

'And try and find out if any of the crew spoke French,' I suggested as an afterthought, thinking that if there had been a desertion a French speaker might get a head start.

Then, having sorted Peter, myself and Susie, and Stan out, I suggested to Jack that while he was digging up what he could on Operation Goodwood, he might see if he could find out what had started Colonel G's nose twitching about the business. If there was something, I wanted a sniff of it too.

While Susie finished putting on a face I looked up the street in Kilburn where Rose Kearney was staying then bid my staff a cheery goodbye. I really didn't expect them to hang around much after we left and assumed they'd be gone while Susie and I were still walking around Kilburn in search of Kearney's sister's address.

~

In exceptional circumstances we could have asked for a staff car from the pool. But staff clerks don't rate relatives of missing servicemen as exceptional unless they wear a general officer's insignia or have more than two lines in Burke's Peerage. Somehow I doubted that Rose Kearney's name had ever been mentioned in anything, except perhaps the County Wicklow Gazette—if there was such a publication.

We rode the Metropolitan and District line a couple of stops to Edgware tube station then caught the number six bus through Warwick Station to Kilburn Lane, Susie craning her pretty neck round at the view as if we usually kept her chained in the office.

Sitting on the top deck of the bus offered a good perspective of the area and I often spent my spare time riding around London looking at the damage the Blitz and the later V1 and V2 attacks had done. Seeing those gaps where houses—sometimes entire blocks—had disappeared, I often found myself wondering what all those vanished buildings had been. Even on routes familiar from before the war, I still had trouble remembering what had filled the gaps. Like pulled teeth they left a sense of their own former presence behind, a ghostly flabbiness, not of the gum but of the memory. Time would remove it eventually and from the fifteen-foot high vantage point on top of a bus it looked as though, for many people, it already had.

The previous Saturday I had watched the Victory Parade process through the streets surrounded by cheering crowds as the Chiefs of Staff, mechanized columns and lines of marching men passed us by. Behind them—at least from where I stood between Trafalgar Square and Admiralty Arch—the boarded-up buildings and ruined façades seemed to provide a backdrop that showed the other side of Victory's coin. Or was it just the cost of the coin? For many, perhaps the parade was the full stop that finally ended their war.

From the top of the bus I watched pedestrians hurrying up and down the streets, barely giving their surroundings a second glance. Most people, I suppose, thought life was getting back to normal. But that was only because most people had forgotten what normal was.

I certainly had. The army had changed me, although not through any personal commitment to it. Never having been one to concern myself overmuch with military strategy—and certainly not those grand Napoleonic movements so beloved of armchair generals—I had adopted the only tactic that had seemed sensible. That of self-preservation. Gaining promotion is generally a matter of displaying leadership qualities—staff appointments apart where they seem to play by their own rules. To what I owed my commission, I assumed, was the ability of personally taking control of situations where I thought those issuing the orders didn't have my own safety uppermost at heart. That's a dangerous game to play, of course. I'd been fortunate enough to get away with it and come out with a commission. Despite the obvious direction in which the finger of blame for Private Dabs' death was pointing, the possibility had occurred to me that William Kearney might have tried something similar. Perhaps *he* had taken control of a situation in an attempt to save his own skin, abandoning the rest of the carrier crew to their fate. If he had, Dabs' fate hadn't been a fortunate one.

But none of it was anything more than idle speculation and perhaps Kearney hadn't been any luckier than Dabs.

~

I'd brought my briefcase along with the original report and had Rose Kearney's letter in my pocket. In truth, I was only going to be able to tell her what she already really knew: that her brother wasn't coming back. *How* I was going to tell her was another matter. I could use the same words that everyone she'd already talked to probably had and let her down as gently as I could, or I could show her the report that had been filed after they had found Kearney's carrier. It wasn't pretty reading but that sort of thing rarely is. I don't know if anyone had told her yet that her brother's ID discs had been found on a dead SS soldier. If not, I didn't want to be the one who did. Particularly since the soldier in question had belonged to Kurt Meyer's 25th SS-Panzer Grenadier Regiment.

After they found the bodies of the murdered Canadian soldiers, the story had been all over the news. The men had either been shot or bludgeoned to death over a two-day period. That it had happened more than a month before Rose Kearney's brother had gone missing was neither here nor there—nor that the monastery at Saint-Germain-la-Blanche-Herbe was several miles from where the burnt-out carrier had been found. That distance was no more than a quick run for a Panzer. Whether we could pin Dabs' death on Meyer, though, was doubtful—even if you could put him on the spot. But it *had* been established that he had issued orders to the effect that prisoners were not to be taken. I didn't suppose too many people would quibble if Joseph Dabs' name was added to the list of Hitlerjugend's victims. And—since one of his men had been found with Kearney's ID discs on his body—Sergeant William Kearney's name, too.

I would have been happier if they had found Kearney's remains. But until they did, he'd go down in the book as another unexplained casualty of war. All but two of the abbey massacre victims, Canadians from either the North Nova Scotia Highlanders or the Sherbrooke Fusiliers Regiment, had remained missing until early in 1945—over six months after they had been murdered. Only one body was found in July of forty-four when the ground around Saint-Germain-la-Blanche-Herbe was finally taken, which meant that the remaining body has yet to be discovered. In the Canadians' case there was little doubt as to what had happened. They had all been taken prisoner together and the outcome had been clear. As far as Rose Kearney's brother went, it wasn't.

Despite the obvious need to bring criminals to justice, given the butcher's theatre that the Caen campaign had been, it still seemed a lot of trouble to go to over what was, at most, the death of two men. But perhaps I had become desensitized to this sort of thing. I had spent too much time reading reports of similar cases and the repetition had begun to numb me. Too long looking in the face of war had insulated me against the horror. Perhaps the same was true of that line of men and women—ordinary-looking for the most part—who had been brought to the dock of justice in Nuremburg. They might even have pleaded something of the sort in their own defence. If they had, it hadn't washed. Equally, I suppose, neither should it wash in my case.

Perhaps I shouldn't have even considered trying to shelter Kearney's sister from the nastier possibilities of his failure to return home. Being told what had—in all probability—happened to him might at least persuade her to go back to Ireland. Desensitized or not, one shouldn't shy away from the realities of war. Glory and honour are, after all, little more than a veneer some use to cover what is in truth monstrous ugliness. It seemed to me that to ignore the fact merely risked everyone stumbling blindly into the horror once again.

~

The address Rose Kearney had given in her letter was Claremont Street, a crescent off Kilburn Lane sandwiched between the railway line and the main road. There was severe bomb damage at the eastern end and what buildings remained proved to be a line of shabby terraced housing subdivided into flats. I couldn't imagine it was the kind of place that figured in the dreams of anyone from County Wicklow, but then I hadn't been to County Wicklow. At least these terraces had the advantage of still standing, which was more than could be said for the area around my flat. There had been a plate for residents' names by the front door but no one had bothered to use it and it was now little more than a smudge of rust. I pushed the front door open and we went inside.

The flat was given in the letter as number three which was on the first floor. There was a telephone on the wall in the hall, which made me wonder why Rose hadn't supplied the number in her letter. But perhaps she hadn't known it. Susie jotted it down in case we needed it then looked over the other numbers scrawled on the stained wallpaper beside the phone, as if she might be considering a blind date.

A gloomy silence filled the house as we climbed the stairs, pale light filtering through a grimy window at the turn of the half-landing giving only a hint of the bright afternoon we'd left on the street. The stairs led up to a second floor and, I supposed, an attic beyond, and the door to number three lay down a short corridor. Its once green paint was now peeling and cracked. The frame, too, was chipped and splintered around the lock which suggested it had been forced more than once. That could have been a reflection on the area's crime rate, or simply an indication that whoever lived there was in the habit of forgetting their key.

I knocked on the door. The house was quiet enough for me to believe I caught the sound of movement inside the flat. When no one answered, I looked at Susie who raised her eyebrows as if she had heard a noise, too. I waited a moment longer, knocked again and found myself feeling that if there'd been a peephole in the door, someone would have been looking through it at us. I was considering whether it was worth knocking a third time when the latch clicked and the door opened an inch or two on a chain.

'What is it you want?'

I couldn't see much through the crack but it was a woman's voice and it had an Irish accent.

'I'm looking for Rose Kearney,' I said, taking off my cap and leaning towards the door. 'Sister of Sergeant William Kearney?'

The woman hesitated, then said:

'I'm Rose Kearney. Who's wanting to know?'

As she came closer to the door and I could see her eye flicking from me to Susie, I experienced a momentary sensation of what the Germans call *schadenfreude*—or at least future *schadenfreude*—and relished the thought of Jack's discomfort when I told him how Rose Kearney had pronounced her own name.

'My name's Tennant,' I said into the crack.

'You're from Billy's regiment?'

'No,' I said, 'but I have the letter you wrote to your brother's commanding officer.' I held it up so she might see it. 'Can you spare us a few minutes...?'

She pulled the door wide, almost as wide as her eyes.

'You have news of Billy?'

She was tall, almost my height, and slim to the point of thinness. Her face looked drawn and tired and somehow angular like her body. I put her in her thirties and saw there was no wedding ring on her finger. She was wearing a darned sweater over a cotton print dress, her auburn hair tied back at her neck. The overall impression was one of drabness. Except for her eyes. They were still wide.

'I'm sorry,' I said. 'I don't have any news about your brother.'

The bony shoulders slumped and the spark went out of her eyes. 'Then why have you come?'

'I was hoping you could to tell us something about your brother that might be of help.'

She stepped aside to let us in and shut the door behind us. A cramped hallway led past two closed doors to a kitchen. It held a two-ring gas stove, a sink and some chipped cabinets. A scrubbed deal table and chairs stood in the middle of the room. Rose Kearney slumped into one. Above the sink tattered curtains framed the window and its view of a brick wall beyond. I sat opposite her at the table while Susie walked around to the window and leaned against the sink. Rose Kearney glanced up at her then back at me.

I told her I was sorry again and that her letter had come to me because my department dealt with missing servicemen. I didn't go into details. She listened patiently, her hands resting on the table, the left over her right. I asked when she had last heard from her brother.

'We got a letter from him in early June, nineteen forty-four.'

'And no word since.'

'No.'

'Do you have other family?'

'Uncles and cousins, but it was just me and Mam after Billy left.' Rose Kearney raised a defiant chin. 'The rest of the family took against Billy when he joined the British army. When Mam died in December I decided to come to see what I could find out about Billy. This is our cousin Patrick's place. He's not told his father I'm here but he says I can stay till I get fixed up for myself.'

'You're going to stay in England?'

The thin shoulders rose half an inch as if she thought I might have an objection to the fact. 'There's nothing back home,' she said.

'Your father?'

'He died when Billy and me were kids.'

'What would he have thought of your brother joining the British army?'

Rose Kearney's eyes flashed and she gave a short, mirthless laugh. 'It's just as well he was dead, I'll tell you that.'

I didn't suppose that meant a lot. Thousands of men from the Irish Republic had joined the British army at the outbreak of war, despite the fact their government and many of their fellow citizens saw them as traitors. Almost a quarter of a century had passed since partition and the civil war but the wound was still raw.

Susie asked Rose what her brother had done before the war but she didn't tell us much. There'd been some farm work, she said, then unemployment and Kearney had come to England looking for work. When he couldn't find any he joined the army.

'He wasn't conscripted?'

'Billy joined before the war,' Rose said.

'Did he write often? To you and your mother?'

She nodded. 'Every week, right after church.'

'He was Catholic?'

'And why wouldn't he be?' she demanded.

'Would you have a photograph of him, Rose?'

She reared a bit at that, my use of her first name, then calmed quickly.

'No. We never had any taken back home. There was no photographer in our village.'

'He didn't have one taken here and sent back for your mother?'

She regarded me suspiciously. 'And how would you be knowing that?'

'So he did.'

'Yes, but I buried it with our Mam. It's what she asked me, before the end.'

'It must have been a comfort to her,' Susie said.

But Rose Kearney was having none of that, no hollow-sounding sympathy from a busty ATS in her own flat. She threw Susie one disdainful glance then ignored her.

'Did your brother ever mention any of the men he served with?'

It hadn't occurred to her to bring his letters with her, she said; they were back in Ireland with what few other possessions she owned and would be sent on once she was settled. She did remember Billy mentioning some names now and then though, but couldn't recall exactly who.

'One or two of the officers, maybe. But it wasn't a subject Mam cared to read about, it being the *British* army you understand.' Then she reached across the table and laid a hand on my sleeve. 'No offence meant, Captain. Things being what they are, if you take my meaning.'

I did and wondered—things being what they were—if her brother would have been likely to go back to Ireland given the rest of the family's feeling against him.

'No,' she said when I asked. She didn't think so. As far as she was aware he hadn't any particular plans for after the war.

I'd brought the report I had of the carrier with me, the account of two burned bodies and a third nearby with a bullet in his head. I didn't show it to her. I asked if she could remember her brother ever mentioning Robert Burleigh or Arnold Poole.

'Were they friends of Billy's?

'They were part of the carrier crew. Four of them. The other man's name was Joseph Dabs.'

'Carrier?'

'Bren gun carrier. It's what they call the kind of vehicle your brother commanded.'

'One of the officers I spoke to told me they found some bodies—'

'Burleigh and Poole,' I said.

'And the other man...Dabs?'

'Joseph Dabs. They found his body close by.'

'But not Billy,' she said. 'So there's a chance...'

'That he wasn't killed?' I finished for her. 'It seems unlikely.'

I was about to tell her that her brother's ID discs had been found on a dead SS soldier, but at that moment Rose bowed her head as if the emotion had become too much. Susie sat down and reached a hand across the table but Rose jerked hers back.

'Thank you Captain,' she said, looking at me rather than at Susie.

I gave her a sympathetic look and asked if her brother happened to speak French.

'French?' she said. 'No, not Billy. French wasn't the sort of thing we learned in Ballydrum. He could speak a little of the Gaelic, though even that wasn't encouraged when we was children. Why would you be asking, Captain?'

I told her it wasn't important and that we'd be in touch if we found anything further. Then we left. Once on the street I asked Susie what she thought.

'About her?' she replied, as if she thought I might be asking her opinion of the flat's decor. 'Difficult to say. She didn't like having me there, did she?'

I laughed. 'She probably took you for a wicked girl from the big city.'

'Poor little Irish peasant? I don't think so. I grew up in a village so I know what goes on behind the hedgerows.'

'Do you? You'll have to tell me sometime.'

'And I think Rose is hiding her light under a bushel.'

'In what way?'

'Nail varnish.'

'Really? I didn't notice.'

'Just traces where she'd removed it. You were too busy looking into those big Irish eyes. Where did she get it, I wonder? It's not easy to find these days.'

'Ireland, I suppose,' I said.

'Ballydrum?'

'Why not? It's where she comes from.'

'County Wicklow? Up in the mountains? Is that likely?'

'Do they have mountains? She probably passed through Dublin. Maybe she got it there.'

'Country girl out on a spree,' said Susie. 'And I'll tell you another thing...she wasn't alone, either.'

'Alone? What do you mean?'

'There was someone else in the flat.'

'How do you know?'

'The ashtray on the sink was full of cigarette butts and one had only just been put out.'

'Perhaps they were Rose's,' I suggested.

Susie shook her head. 'If she smoked that much she'd have nicotine on her fingers. There was just the nail varnish.'

'It's her cousin Patrick's flat,' I said. Perhaps he was there.'

'Then why not show his face?'

'Maybe he doesn't care for the British like the rest of the family.'

'Bloody odd place to come and live, then,' said Susie.

'Or maybe she's got a boyfriend and didn't want him drooling over you.'

'Or let him see Rose doing the drooling? *No offence meant, Captain, if you take my meaning...*' Susie mimicked in a bad Irish accent. 'And didn't you think it odd she didn't have to ask what rank you were?'

'I told her.'

'No, you just told her your name was Tennant.'

'People recognise uniforms these days,' I said. 'There's been a war.'

'Not in County Wicklow there hasn't.'

'Well, the Troubles, then,' I said. 'Ireland was full of British soldiers. That's why her family—'

'She'd be too young to remember,' Susie interrupted. 'Unless she learned how to tell one soldier from another at her Mam's knee, of course.'

I was beginning to see why Jekyll had told me to bring Susie along. I had been in the police—the uniformed branch admittedly—but not many of the detectives I'd known had been as shrewd as Susie.

~

It was after six and the pubs were open and I asked Susie if she fancied a drink. She had a date, though, and was going home to get changed. It was Friday and she was going dancing. We took a bus back to Edgware and I put her on the tube.

I'd only been thinking of a drink. I had never made any sort of approach to Susie before—the atmosphere of a small office is claustrophobic enough without adding the complications of extraneous affairs. I knew she'd gone to the pictures once or twice with Peter although didn't know if it had gone any further; they made an odd couple I couldn't quite reconcile. Stan had always shown more of a fatherly interest in her than anything more libidinous and Jack was married with two children. That didn't necessarily preclude interest in other women but I'd met his wife and Jack was too smart a man to upset a woman who looked to be a tougher prospect than the Wehrmacht had ever been.

On a whim I went up the West End and walked around for a while. It was June and wouldn't get dark for another three hours yet. The theatres were opening and so were one or two restaurants that catered for the early dinner crowd. I thought I'd try a pub I used to know in Soho. I hadn't been there since before the war when a detective-sergeant I'd known had used the place to meet his snitch. It had a narrow bar that ran the length of the room with coloured mirrors behind that advertised the sort of beers and tobaccos you could no longer get. There was a small alcove at the back where the DS had used to sit, unseen by the rest of the customers. I wasn't sure it would still be there but I turned the corner into Broadwick Street and saw it across the road.

The place looked shabbier than I remembered, although that was hardly surprising as it now had a timber buttress angling into the road shoring up the wall. Inside felt like walking into the pantry of Sleeping Beauty's castle. Dust coated most surfaces and cobwebs hung in the corners of the few cracked mirrors that still remained. I looked around and then at a barman I didn't recognise and walked out again. After that, it seemed to me that even the lights in the West End had a sort of second-hand glow about them, as if they'd been rescued as a job-lot from the demolition of a far smarter place.

I stopped off at another bar and paid too much for a gin and French, then compounded the folly by having a second. I'd always thought that there were two kinds of drunks: those that were born to it and those who had to work at it, having to practise until they got the hang of the thing. I had tried at times to be the second kind but had never managed it. I had always found that the hour or two of airborne equilibrium drinking gave was never worth the following hours of down-to-earth misery. And it didn't matter how long I practised, I never got past feeling like shit in the morning. So, a couple was as many as I generally had and after those I walked to the tube and rode the train home.

Which was just as well because when I got there my wife was sitting on the stairs waiting for me.

4

I'm not sure which of us was the most surprised.

She looked at my uniform. 'You're a captain?'

My promotion had come through the last time I'd seen her but I'd been in civvies. I walked past her and unlocked my door, illogically hoping that she wouldn't smell the drink on me. She followed into the flat.

I put the kettle on to boil as she stood in the doorway watching.

'I phoned your office.'

I wiped out two cups and put them on the table.

'They said you'd left early to see a woman.'

The kettle boiled and I made the tea, deciding I'd answer if she ever got around to asking me a question. I heard her sigh with exasperation.

'Are you involved with someone?'

I imagined the improbability of my being involved with the dowdy Rose Kearney. Susie would be another matter but I didn't think Jack would have mentioned her. I turned around. Penny had taken a step into the room and had crossed her arms. She'd taken off the jacket she'd been wearing over her jumper and skirt. I thought if you gave her a pair of hiking boots she'd look quite the country girl. She'd been a WREN during the war but had been demobbed over a year and had gone to live with my mother and brother in the Cotswolds. And she *was* looking well. Maybe it was the country air in Gloucestershire, or perhaps she and my mother had latched on to some farmer and had first dibs at his butter and eggs. I wondered which of the two was the more likely, although that probably depended upon the age of the farmer. It wasn't just cynicism on my part; the war had played hell with everyone's morals. I'd seen what it could do in Berlin where some people were willing to do almost anything to maintain a tolerable existence. It hadn't been that bad here, of course, but you couldn't blame people for making the best of things. And after all, perhaps it *was* only the air.

'I saw her to tell her that her brother wasn't coming back from France,' I said.

It wasn't an answer to her question but Penny was never one to bother about details.

'Did you know him?'

'No. Would you like some tea?'

She seemed about to snap out a refusal then sighed again and pulled out one of the kitchen chairs and sat at the table.

'Can't we at least be civilized about this?' she asked.

'When did you come up to town?'

'This afternoon. A friend was driving up for the weekend and offered me a lift.' Adding, just in case I was wondering about the friend, I suppose, 'I'm staying with Aunt Julia.'

'And how is Aunt Julia?'

'She's well.'

We had lodged with Penny's Aunt Julia after we'd married. Perhaps lodged wasn't the right word as Julia had a house in Belgravia. It was where I had met Penny shortly after the outbreak of war, when the blackout afforded all sorts of new opportunities for criminals and Julia's house was one that had been burgled. The street was on my beat and I had been the first to respond. Julia hadn't thought much of her niece taking up with the policeman investigating the robbery. Ours had been one of the proverbial whirlwind romances, owing much to the atmosphere of those days when one didn't know what tomorrow would bring. Our families weren't exactly on the same rung of the social ladder but, unlike Penny's parents, Julia had relented sufficiently after we married to allow Penny and I to stay with her until we got fixed up with a place of our own. On the condition I didn't leave my bicycle on the front steps, that is.

Actually, I knew Julia was well because I'd been to see her after I'd got back. I was concerned that she might have suffered during the bombing. I found her polite, as was the way with her class, but somewhat frosty. She hadn't changed much but I had. The frostiness hadn't bothered me.

'I'm getting a lift back Sunday afternoon,' Penny said.

I considered that, whether it was simply information or if there was more to it.

'There's no sugar, of course.' I put a cup of tea in front of her and she looked up at me.

'I've given it up.'

'Sweet enough?'

'Don't be like that.'

'How'd you want me to be?'

I sat down. I'd only seen her twice since I'd got back and still wasn't quite used to the fact that she looked older than when I'd left for North Africa. There were lines on her face I didn't remember and she wore her hair differently; it was shorter now and waved. I preferred it as it was but then I preferred a lot of things as they were.

'How's George? And my mother?'

She spooned powdered milk into her tea and played with the teacup without picking it up. 'They're well. I'll give them your love.'

'I wouldn't go that far.'

She sat watching me. 'Do you still mean that?'

That made me smile. I couldn't help it. She looked at me uncertainly, as if wondering if she should smile, too.

'You haven't answered my question.'

'Sorry, I've forgotten what it was. What did you want to know?'

'If you're involved with anyone?'

'Why?'

She sipped at her tea, as if she needed time to answer. 'George wants to marry me.'

'Oh? Your idea or his? His, I suppose. At least it'll keep you in the family. Mother will appreciate that.'

'Harry...'

'What is it you want me to do? Arrange something? A dirty weekend in a dirty hotel? Well, if George is prepared to stump up for the private detective and the photographer...I used to know the going rate for that sort of thing but I'm a bit out of touch, I'm afraid.'

She looked at me, a hurt expression on her face and tears starting in her eyes. I should've stopped. I don't know why I didn't. I was quite calm.

'Will he supply the tart as well? Only I don't think Rose Kearney will fit the bill—'

'Rose Kearney?'

'She's the one with the dead brother. Irish Catholic, and I've got an idea they don't go in for that sort of thing. Besides, I only met her this afternoon and I'm not sure how she'd react if I suggested it. We're not on first name terms yet.'

She got up then and left without saying anything else. I stayed at the table and finished my tea. I could have handled it better; I wasn't angry with her—I'd got past that—and I wasn't even angry with my brother George. Who knows, in his place I might even have done the same thing. Perhaps it was in the blood. My mother thought so—if for a different reason. As far as she was concerned I'd done the deserting. Just like my father, I'd gone off to war when I didn't have to. Something in the blood. She'd never forgiven my father for getting himself killed and not coming back, leaving her with two small boys to bring up. She hadn't forgiven me for not doing the same. I'd come back. As far as she was concerned it would have been more convenient all round if I hadn't.

~

Saturday morning, over a breakfast of tea and cigarettes, I went through the notes Jack had made. Robert Burleigh had also left a wife and two children. The address was down beyond the Commercial Docks towards Deptford. I took the District and Metropolitan tube to Surrey Docks. It was still early and mist was rising on the Thames, swirling in the eddies where the current ran round a sunken barge and some moored boats. Through the mist the sun turned from grey to pink and then a primeval red, giving the river a savage cast. A few rusty ships were in, loading or unloading, but there wasn't the bustle there had been before the war. There seemed a lethargy lying over everything like a patient who hadn't yet pulled himself out of a depression. Some shattered warehouses left gaps in the waterfront, tangled shrubs and weeds growing up through the rubble. Barges were moving down Limehouse Reach, their broad prows pushing through water like syrup, the chug of their engines heavy on the morning air.

I had to ask directions and got lost more than once in streets where empty and derelict houses looked indistinguishable from occupied slums. When I finally reached the right road I found a terrace that truncated above a crater like a gravel pit that stretched down to the river. Children were clambering over the rubble, throwing stones in pools of stagnant water. On the other side of the road a terrace stood, bookended by the remains of houses that had gone, plaster, brickwork and wallpaper still hanging in recesses like the flaking skin left by some disease.

Two women stood on a doorstep talking. Dressed in housecoats, one, with a scarf wound like a turban round her head, was thin and rangy and now and then punctuated her conversation with asides bellowed across the road at the kids in the gravel pit. The other woman, the stouter of the two, had a small girl hanging onto her dress and another, an older boy with a grimy face and a mop of dark hair, standing in front of her. He was staring at me as I approached, as if I had just parachuted down out of the blue June morning.

'I'm looking for Mrs Edna Burleigh,' I said to the women.

The thin one looked at the stout one who raised her chin a couple of inches, pointing it at me.

'I'm Edna Burleigh. It's about my old man again, is it?'

I identified myself and she led me into the house, pushing the little girl ahead of her, threatening to trip her mother up. The boy tagged on behind, muttering something I couldn't catch except the word 'mister' that finished every sentence. Edna Burleigh ushered me into a room that held a cheap table on a threadbare rug and two armchairs of faded plush. Dark grease stained the back and arms. A couple of pictures hung on the walls, faded prints of Edwin Henry Landseer's Highland stags in heroic poses. The distempered plaster on the rest of the walls had pickled with damp and turned blotchy where it had been scrubbed clean. The air had the cloying staleness of a cellar.

She must have noticed the expression on my face because she said, 'You can't keep it dry. Goes black. Mould...and the vermin... Pity Jerry didn't blitz the 'ole buggerin' street.'

She pointed to one of the armchairs then beat at the upholstery with her hand as if wanting to knock it into a different shape.

'Sit yourself down and I'll put on some tea. You'd like a cup of tea, wouldn't you?'

I told her not to use her ration on me but she stomped off down the hall anyway and I could hear a clatter of pans from the end of the house. The two kids stayed in the doorway, the girl with her nose running and her thumb stuck in her face, and the boy just staring at me. I smiled at them but it made no difference.

'You a pilot, mister?' the boy finally asked.

'No. I'm in the army.'

I suppose he was disappointed because he didn't ask anything else, just looked.

His mother came back a few minutes later, pushing past them with a battered tray and tea things. She put them on the table then looked down at the boy, saying he wasn't to be cheeky to the officer and gave him a casual clip round the ear on account. Then she told him to bugger off across the road. He gave her a shrug and with a last look in my direction wandered out. Mrs Burleigh poured the tea, passed me a chipped cup and took hers to the other chair. Settled, she hauled the girl onto her lap, wiped her nose with the hem of her housecoat, then looked expectantly at me.

She had a broad, fleshy face with lifeless skin and pale, almost colourless hair. It looked to have been cut round a basin and reminded me of a German helmet. Judging from the age of the children I supposed she might have been in her thirties but looked closer to fifty. I told her how sorry I was for the loss of her husband and asked if she was receiving her widow's pension from the army and if she was managing. She barely was, of course, but I hadn't expected anything else. I asked if she had been sent any of her husband's personal belongings. She shook her head.

'I didn't suppose there was any,' she said.

I said that under the circumstances, with his battalion in action, anything Robert had left was probably mislaid.

'Nicked, more like,' she responded, looking at me.

'Your husband was part of a carrier crew,' I said. 'They were all killed, although the body of William Kearney was never found.'

'He was Bob's sergeant, wasn't he?'

'That's right. Did he ever speak of him?'

'Only to say he was an Irish bastard. Not that Bob had anything against the Irish. He wasn't bothered who he served with.'

'You never met any of his army friends, I suppose?'

'What, Bob bring people 'ere?' She laughed. 'Not likely. Besides, 'e 'ad enough of 'em in the army. Wasn't goin' t'spend his leave with 'em, too.'

'No, of course not,' I said, and smiled at the very thought of it. 'So he never told you anything much about his colleagues?'

'He said the one called Poole was a bit of a bugger.'

'Arnold Poole? In what way was he a bugger?' I tried to look sympathetic, hoping she didn't mean literally.

'Throwin' 'is weight around, mostly, bein' a corporal. Miserable so-an'-so, Bob said. But then, you couldn't blame 'im, could you? Lost 'is wife and kiddies to a doodlebug. Thing like that's enough to get on top of anyone.'

I looked through my notes but there was no mention of Arnold Poole's family having been killed.

'Do you know when that happened exactly?'

'Exactly? No, I don't. Sometime in forty-four it was.' The girl started struggling and Edna Burleigh put her on the ground and she ran out the door. 'How come all the interest in my Bob all of a sudden? Been dead two years.'

'Trying to tie up loose ends,' I said.

I was about to ask if her husband had spoken French when she said:

'Because of the grave, is it?'

'The grave?'

'Like the other officer said. From the Graves Commission, 'e said 'e was.'

'I don't know anything about that,' I told her. 'We're a different department.'

'Cause 'e wanted to know about this Kearney, too. Not that I could tell 'im much.'

'When was it he spoke to you?'

'Couple of days ago. Thursday, it was.'

'Did he give you a name?'

'Hendrix. Major Hendrix.'

I asked her a few more questions and she gave me a photograph of her husband she found after rummaging in the drawer of an old chipped dresser.

'You can 'ave that one. I got others to remember 'im by.'

I took it, then on impulse gave her ten shillings to buy some sweets for the children. I didn't suppose she had much money to spare to spend on her sweet ration. She looked at the note warily for a second. 'For the children,' I said again and she slipped it into the pocket of her housecoat.

~

I treated myself to lunch in a greasy cafe by the docks, a gristly sausage and fried slice. The tea tasted as if they'd brewed it up on VE day and left it to stew and the whole plateful sat in my stomach all the way back to Clerkenwell. I kept telling myself that the bright side was I'd saved on ration coupons and it worked until I got as far the station lavatory and threw the lot up into the stained pan. I wiped my mouth and dabbed at the sweat running down my face and trudged back to the flat. I lay down on the bed waiting for the first signs of food poisoning, then fell asleep before they came. When I woke I felt better. I heated up enough water for a shallow bath and took out some fresh clothes. By six o'clock I was feeling so bright I telephoned Aunt Julia.

5

Saturday June 15th 1946

'Who's this?' Julia demanded when she finally answered the phone. There was a buzz of conversation and the sound of music in the background. She had to raise her voice above the noise.

'Harry,' I said. Then, just to rub it in, 'Your nephew by marriage.'

'But for how much longer, Harry?' was her reply.

'Is Penny there?'

'Somewhere,' she said.

'Having a party?'

'Just a few drinks with friends before the theatre. Sorry, but I could only get a half-dozen tickets.'

'That's all right,' I said. 'If you remember I always preferred the pictures.'

My using the common idiom for the cinema was one of the things about me that had always irritated Julia. The pictures, or the movies was what ordinary people called cinema. And besides, Julia would only watch a film if it had a cultural pedigree. Snobbish, I'd always thought, given the sort of theatrical fluff her beloved West End had been in the habit of putting on before the war.

'If you want to see her,' she suggested unexpectedly, 'you'd better come round and have a drink before we leave. But be quick or you'll miss us.'

The invitation aside, what struck me most about the conversation was that Julia was answering her own telephone, and her unorthodox manner in doing so. She had told me when I had seen her after getting back to London that she was having trouble finding servants, but I had supposed she would find someone soon enough as there were always people looking for work. Before the war she had had staff—only two, admittedly—to screen her from those with whom she did not wish to speak. One, a ladies' maid, was a vivacious Londoner named Lizzie Benson whose GI boyfriend not only survived the invasion of Europe but came back afterwards to whisk her off to Oklahoma, or some other god-forsaken state where

I couldn't picture Lizzie living at all. The other half of Julia's staff had been a man named Lawford, more a major-domo than a butler, and someone who had made it plainer than Julia that the general opinion was that Penny had married beneath her. He had still been of conscription age and when his papers came through in 1940 he'd taken it on the lam, as Lizzie's GI might have said. One morning I got up and found Lizzie struggling to light the stove—Lawford's job—and grumbling that he'd disappeared. Along with Julia's petty cash, I suspected, although she never lodged a complaint. I assumed he had spent the war in some funk hole, keeping his head down, but the warrant is still active and sooner or later he'll surface and I'd cheerfully give a week's pay to be there when they arrest him.

As with so many other people, the war had reduced Julia's circumstances and now she had to struggle through on her own with just a woman who came in twice a week to do the cleaning. An example of the unfairness of life with which, I was sure, Edna Burleigh would concur.

I was quick, as Julia had advised, but even so only reached the Belgravia house a few minutes before the party was due to leave for the theatre. A flamboyantly elongated Bentley was parked at the kerb, of a size I suspected would need a month's petrol ration just to fill the carburettor. Its driver was dressed in chauffeur's livery and was leaning casually on the front wing, smoking a cigarette while he waited. Behind the Bentley was a far more modest Humber, sleek enough as limousines go but obviously only a poor relative.

I rang the bell and a man in a dinner jacket opened the door to me with a highball glass in his hand. He called over his shoulder to Julia who was behind him in the hall and about to go up the stairs.

'Harry,' she said.

'Julia,' I replied.

She was Penny's mother's younger sister and still an attractive woman. The last few years had added some lines to her face that she was obviously trying to disguise, but to my way of thinking they were the kind of lines that enhanced mature looks, not detract from them. She gave me a limp gloved hand to hold and the offer of a cheek to kiss and I dutifully did both.

'We're off in a moment or two, I'm afraid,' she announced, 'but do stay and have a drink. Ronnie will see to it, won't you Ronnie?' and she turned towards the man with the highball.

Ronnie agreed and led me along the hall towards the drawing room. I supposed in the absence of a hired flunkey she had co-opted one of her hangers-on. At least Ronnie looked to be a man who knew his way around a glass and a bottle.

'Nice to see you again!' cried a woman I'd never seen before as we passed.

I realized I was the only man there in uniform; the rest of the company had dressed for an evening on the town except for a few who were dressed more casually in suits. Uniforms were no longer *de rigueur*, in fact had become unfashionable, and the number like myself still bound to wear them was diminishing every day. One of those dressed more casually, standing in front of Julia's Adam fireplace with his back to me, seemed to have taken insouciance to the extreme and was wearing a hound's-tooth check jacket and light grey trousers. And, oddly enough, although I couldn't place him, he looked unaccountably familiar. He stood out even more in that he was talking to a man in full evening dress; a bespectacled and exceptionally tall individual with hair greying to silver at the temples but as black as the devil's soul on top. I assumed it was some kind of toupee until I realized that no one would look that peculiar by choice, and so must have been his real hair. As I got closer to them I heard the tall one say something to the man in the hound's-tooth jacket about being "kept appraised of developments" then caught no more as the man addressed turned around and I found myself looking into the glass eye of Colonel G.

'Harry?' he said, briefly disconcerted.

As surprised as he was—a square peg in a round hole—I stammered, 'I didn't...didn't realise you knew Julia, Colonel.'

Jekyll glanced momentarily at the tall man beside him then extended to me the hand that wasn't holding his glass.

'Our hostess? No, I don't. I came with Sir Maurice. He was...well...' he raised his glass and smiled although his false eye wasn't looking as cordial.

He introduced me to Sir Maurice Coveney, telling him that I was the man handling the business. I might have thought to wonder what interest Coveney had in what our section was doing had I not been a little dismayed by the way Coveney was looking down his nose at me. His face wore the sort of imperious expression I'd see on Roman statuary in Italy. I was used to being on the wrong end of disdainful looks but something about Coveney's colourless face and dead eyes seemed doubly disconcerting.

I pegged him at first as either a businessman or a politician although, since Labour won the election, I'd found the latter tend to affect a sloppily-dressed man-of-the-people air; something this man obviously eschewed. And as for the former, most businessmen I had come across were decidedly more portly than Coveney—fat from the profits they'd made from the war. Coveney, hovering over Jekyll and myself like a praying mantis, had more of the stamp of the senior civil-servant about him.

'You'll be Penny's husband,' he said to me, which I wasn't expecting. 'I'm surprised we haven't met before.'

I didn't know why we should have, and although it was a harmless remark I thought I detected a note of censure in his tone which insinuated the fault was probably mine.

Making light of the fact, I said, 'I've been otherwise engaged,' attempting to make my war service sound like a prior engagement. But it came out sounding more like the defensive snap of a dog who's just been scolded.

'North Africa and Italy,' Colonel G interposed on my behalf. 'Not much opportunity for leave.'

'Hard on your wife,' said Coveney.

'I'm rather afraid it was,' I agreed.

Julia appeared at the door just then and announced it was time for the theatre party to leave. Coveney nodded curtly in my direction then drew Colonel G aside, whispering something into his ear I didn't catch. I wasn't really listening because I saw Penny bringing up the rear of the group, looking at me with a mixture of hesitation and irritation that seemed perfectly to sum up how we behaved towards each other each time we met.

'I just wanted to say...' I began as I reached her, 'About yesterday...'

'Come along Penny,' called Julia from the door, putting on her wrap.

'I've got to go, Harry. You should have come earlier.'

'I know.'

'Come back tomorrow morning. Early.' And she put a hand on my chest and patted me absently, as though I were a purchase that had proved something of a disappointment.

I followed her down the hall and outside and watched as she climbed into the Bentley beside Julia and Coveney.

After they had driven away I turned to see Ronnie on the doorstep, watching.

'So you're Harry,' he said as we went back inside. 'Not what I was expecting, I have to say. You'd better come in and have that drink.'

Since he had taken the trouble to stuff himself into the dinner jacket, I had assumed he was part of the group going to the theatre. Obviously not, he helped himself to another highball and mixed me a gin and tonic. There were still a few guests left but Colonel G wasn't among them. Assuming he wasn't going to the theatre in a houndstooth jacket, I supposed he'd slipped away while I was taking with Penny. It seemed an odd coincidence to have found him there but I didn't know from which direction the coincidence was working—his knowing Coveney or Coveney knowing Julia. Either way, I thought I had detected something proprietary about Coveney's attitude towards Penny. Whether it was fatherly concern or something more carnal, I couldn't have said. I wondered whether I ought to call my brother to give him something to worry about. Knowing George though, he was probably already brooding about Penny spending the weekend out of his sight in London.

'Who's this fellow, Coveney?' I asked Ronnie, tasting my drink and finding it heavy on the gin.

'Something in the Ministry of Something,' he said, knocking back half his at the first attempt. 'Don't ask me what. One of Julia's. Friend of the family, but not one of the set, if you know what I mean. Don't know about the fellow with him. Never seen him before but not Julia's sort. Not in *that* jacket.'

'No,' I said. 'He's one of my sort. He's a colonel.'

And despite what Ronnie thought I rather suspected that if Julia ever got a look at the kilted Jekyll in full dress uniform he might very well prove one of her sort after all.

'I was surprised to see him here myself, actually,' I said. 'The colonel, not Coveney. I've not run across Coveney before.'

'Bryce over there knows all about Coveney,' Ronnie said lifting one of his chins towards a young man in wire-rim spectacles by the window. 'He works for him.' He raised his glass and shouted, 'Bryce, come and say hello to Harry.'

Bryce came over, a vacuous smile pasted on his face. He stuck out a hand.

'Harry was asking about Sir Maurice Coveney.'

'I was just saying to Ronnie that if he's a friend of Julia's family, I'd not run across him before,' I said to Bryce.

'Oh, I don't know anything about that,' said Bryce. 'All I know is he had to work late and asked me to run round to his flat and pick up his evening togs so he could change here.'

I didn't suppose he was Coveney's valet as I couldn't see Julia wasting her alcohol on someone's manservant, but since he obviously had access to Coveney's flat I thought he might at least know what Jekyll was doing with him.

'The fellow in the houndstooth jacket—' I began.

'Haven't a clue, old man,' Bryce said quickly. 'Don't know anyone here. Ronnie told me to stay for a drink even though I don't know him from Adam either. Tell you what, though. I wouldn't mind getting to know the young girl who just left with Sir Maurice. She's a corker.'

'Tennant here's her husband,' said Ronnie.

'Ah,' said Bryce. 'Put my foot in it, have I? No offence, old chap.'

'None taken,' I said.

'Not going with them to the theatre?'

'No. You look as though you're dressed for it, Ronnie,' I observed, wondering if he was miffed at not being invited.

'Didn't fancy it,' he said. 'Not my sort of play.'

I took another pull at the gin to make room for some more tonic, topped myself up and turned to ask Bryce something about Coveney. He'd gone, though. I had another one with Ronnie but he was already drunk and started to ask me awkward questions so I left too. I assumed Julia could handle him if he was still conscious when she got back and he needed handling.

I walked down through Sloane Square and Chelsea Bridge Road to the river, in no hurry to get back to my empty flat. Dusk had fallen and the street lights were on. A novel experience even after a year for anyone who had spent the war in London, perhaps. There was still some river traffic despite the hour, tugs towing lighters loaded with rubble and other detritus to be dumped somewhere down the estuary. I expected in time London would rise like a phoenix from the ashes but she was a very dowdy bird at that moment. The country was exhausted and it showed in the faces of its people. Drawn and haggard, the gaiety they had exhibited in the early years of the conflict and manifested in the impulse to enjoy themselves no matter what, had given way to a realization that they weren't all about to die after all. Now they would have to buckle down and get on with things. The lights coming back were, in that respect, like an artificial dawn, one that heralded a long and uncertain day of hardship and privation.

I was feeling glum and the alcohol hadn't helped. The prospect of seeing Penny in the morning filled me with a sense of trepidation. We had only seen each other two or three times since I'd got back and we'd managed to argue each time. She could hold her end up in an argument but I always felt afterwards that it was my fault. Knowing that never helped me stop it happening again the next time, though. I'd fall into the same trap like a stubborn child who knows he's in the wrong but is too wilful to admit it.

I resolved to phone her early the next morning and make some excuse for not seeing her, not sure if that was cowardice or the bitter part of valour.

Taking the bus back to Clerkenwell reminded me of the ride out to see Rose Kearney with Susie the previous day and that thought led inexorably to her missing brother and his dead comrades. I recalled what I had overheard Jekyll say to Sir Maurice Coveney about my “handling the business” and wondered, if he was talking about Dabs and Kearney’s carrier, what Coveney's interest in the matter might be. A couple of scorched corpses was hardly uncommon in war—an occupational hazard in armoured divisions—and hardly a concern, I would have thought of a civil servant. If that was what Coveney was. There was the way Dabs had died, of course, but as for Kearney, Europe was a continent of missing bodies. All the same, whatever it was about, I thought I had better get abreast of it or find myself on the wrong side of Jekyll’s short temper. In peace as in war it was generally the innocent—like us in the office, or Rose Kearney in County Wicklow for that matter—that got caught in the crossfire. I thought about Rose for a while and then about Edna Burleigh whom I’d seen that morning. Winning the war hadn’t done her and her kids any good and I doubted if she’d get much out of the peace that was to follow, either. Life was hard enough for her as it was without people like me coming round asking questions she didn’t have answers to.

Then I remembered she’d said something about someone else coming round asking questions, an officer from the Imperial Graves Commission. Edna’s husband, Bob, would have wound up in one of the military cemeteries in France, I supposed, and it was hardly out of the ordinary for the next of kin to be notified. Although why he had asked her about William Kearney I couldn’t guess. Of course, it just might be that Kearney’s body had finally turned up and through some bureaucratic foul-up his battalion hadn’t yet been informed. That would hardly be uncommon, either. I’d have to get Jack on to it Monday morning, to double-check with Kearney’s battalion and the Graves Commission. I tried to remember the name of the officer Edna Burleigh had said visited her, but after a couple of Ronnie’s gins it had gone. By the time I reached Clerkenwell I had given up trying.

6

Sunday June 16th 1946

I telephoned the Belgravia house at eight the next morning. Without a flunky to answer her phone and too early for Julia to answer herself, I assumed Penny would be up and waiting for me. But I didn't get Penny.

'It's Harry,' I said. 'Can I speak to Penny?'

'You're too late,' Julia said. And for an odd instant I thought she was sharing some insight she possessed on the state of our marriage until she added, 'She's already left.'

'Left? Left where?'

'Back down to the country, where do you think, Harry?'

'But I was supposed to see her this morning.'

'Were you, Harry? She never said.'

'When did she leave?' I asked, loading my tone with enough suspicion that even Julia couldn't fail to think I didn't believe her.

'Half-an-hour ago. The man who brought her up had to get back unexpectedly.'

'She didn't leave a message for me?'

'No. You could always telephone down there,' she suggested. 'You know your own mother's number, I suppose?' When I didn't reply she said, 'It was nice seeing you again, Harry,' *her* tone conveying enough irony that I couldn't fail to miss that either. Then she hung up.

The exchange left me out of sorts despite the fact I had telephoned to tell Penny I couldn't see her. The desired result had been achieved but I couldn't help thinking I had lost an advantage. I won't term it as the moral high-ground because morals didn't exactly figure too much in our relationship. It was more a case of Penny having done to me what I was about to do to her, and no one likes a dose of their own medicine. I tried to persuade myself that her lift back to the country probably did have to leave early, but there wasn't enough sugar in that to make the pill taste any less bitter.

I idled my way through the rest of the day, which is about all one can do with the barren wasteland that is a British Sunday, and went to bed so early that I was up at dawn and in the office before any of the others.

Jack attempted to hide his surprise at seeing me already in when he arrived and assumed there was some sort of flap on.

'What's up, Jekyll been on to you?'

'No,' I said, 'although funnily enough I did run in to him on Saturday evening.'

'You don't look as if it was funny.'

'He was with some ministry wallah. I got the idea they were talking about our Dabs case.'

'Why would—'

'No idea,' I said. 'We'd better see if we can find out, though.'

Jack dropped into his chair and reaching for the telephone. 'Name?'

'Coveney,' I said, 'Sir Maurice Coveney. Oh, and by the way, *Kearney* rhymes with journey, at least that's how his sister Rose pronounces it.' I'd liked to have laid it on a bit thicker, using rhyming slang, but I didn't know the cockney slang for journey. I suppose I could have taken the trouble to look it up at the library but that would have knocked the spontaneity out of the thing. As it was Jack only looked at me doubtfully and grunted and I couldn't squeeze much *schadenfreude* out of that.

We only had the one telephone line so I made a pot of tea as the others arrived then, between Jack's calls, and before Susie got on the extension, I made one of my own to the Graves Commission. I still couldn't remember the name of the officer who had visited Edna Burleigh, which was beginning to annoy me, so I made some general enquiries to see if there were any plans afoot for the re-interring of Burleigh, Poole and Dabs. The usual practice—given the circumstances of battle and troop movements at the time—would be for the dead to be buried where they fell until such time as a permanent grave and headstone could be provided for them. The clerk I was speaking to wanted to know the area of operations in which the men had died so I gave them the map reference we had. Several minutes later he came back on the line and told me that all the bodies in that area had already been moved to purpose-built cemeteries.

I put the phone down wondering why, if that were the case, a man from the Graves Commission would visit Edna Burleigh. I told Jack about it and asked him to get back onto Kearney's battalion again and double-check that his body hadn't turned up after all, then went into the other room and had Peter show me exactly where the carrier and the three bodies had been found.

Peter said he was waiting for a more detailed map and in the meantime had pinned up a general one of Normandy on the board and stuck a flag into the village of Maltot. It was to the south-west of Caen.

I remembered there had been some sort of argument between the Allies about Montgomery's progress around Caen after the Normandy landings, the Americans operating to the west of Caen accusing the British of a certain lack of resolve. I only heard of the controversy later. At the time I'd been fully occupied in Italy, trying to make an impression on what Churchill had described as the soft under-belly of Europe. Perhaps there had been soft patches but I hadn't found any. Most of the bits I'd had a poke at were as hard and unyielding as a Panzer's carapace and, if a lot of the Italians had been pleased to see us, there weren't many Germans standing by the side of the road waving flags as we passed.

I made a few notes as questions occurred to me but mostly I stood staring sightlessly at the map, running through the different scenarios that would leave two men dead in a carrier, a third man with a bullet in the back of his head, and a fourth who had vanished altogether.

I was still staring at Peter's flag when Stan rolled in. It was too early for lunch but I'd had no breakfast so I took him out to the pub around the corner, found they had nothing on offer that looked palatable enough to eat, and settled for a couple of pints.

'Poole's father's a decent sort,' Stan said. 'There wasn't much he could tell me, though. His wife died and he bought his son up on his own. Turned into a bit of a wide boy is the impression I got.'

'What makes you say that?'

'Eye for the main chance, is how his old man put it. He was a bit worried about him till the army took him and he thinks they straightened Arnie out.'

'Arnie?'

'That's what they called him.' Stan reached into his pocket and took out a photograph and slid it across the table.

It had been taken in Blackpool because I could see the tower and the amusement arcades along the Mile. Arnold Poole was between two girls, his arms linked through theirs as they walked along the front. All three were grinning as if they were having a hell of a time. It looked to me like a works' outing before the war and one of the Mile photographers had snapped them and, I supposed, sold Poole a copy. I took a closer look at him and saw a young man in his best suit, dark hair slicked back under a trilby and with one of those thin moustaches that Flynn and Ronald Coleman had popularized before the war. Despite what Edna Burleigh had said, he didn't look miserable. But perhaps he hadn't cared for the army. He was a good-looking boy and I could tell by his expression that he knew it, and knew the two girls he was escorting knew it, too. Given how he looked at the end, I thought not for the first time that it was as well we don't know what the future holds for us.

'He worked at a cotton mill before he was called up,' Stan said.

'Where?

'Blackburn. Not on a loom,' said Stan. 'Poole was office staff.'

I was puzzled. 'Even a V1 off-course couldn't reach Blackburn. They didn't have that sort of range.'

'V1?'

'Edna Burleigh said her husband told her Poole's wife and kids had been killed by a doodlebug. Perhaps they were in London.'

Stan shook his head. 'Poole wasn't married. Either she was confusing him with someone else or perhaps Arnie was in the habit of making up stories.'

I supposed that was possible if what his father had said about him was true. 'Write home, did he?'

'Postcards to his dad but he did have a girlfriend he wrote to. Met her six months before he left. Seemed serious.'

'Either of these two?' I asked, gesturing at the photo.

'No.'

'Perhaps she was the one who was killed.'

Stan lifted his pint and took a swallow. I waited.

'No,' he eventually said. 'I went to see her. Pretty little thing. Married someone else after she heard about Arnie but kept his letters.'

'Oh? Did you ask to look at them?'

Stan drank some more beer and I could tell there was more to it.

'Poole's dad gave me her address and I went to see her on the Sunday morning.'

'Surprised to see you, I suppose,' I said.

'Yes. So was her husband. She was sort of embarrassed about it, though I could tell she wanted to talk about Arnie. I would have preferred to speak to her on her own, but her husband wasn't having that. Kept interrupting. Belittling her...you know the type.' Stan lit a cigarette. 'Anyway, she didn't know anything about Kearney or Burleigh but she had met Dabs. They'd had some leave and Poole had brought Dabs back with him. He hadn't stayed with Poole's father so he must have had a room somewhere for the weekend.

Ida—that's Arnie's girlfriend—had taken a friend along to make up a foursome and they'd gone out together. She said she didn't care too much for Dabs. Sly, she thought, although she said him and Arnie got on well.'

'Sly's an odd way of describing someone you probably never met for more than a few hours,' I said.

Stan didn't have an opinion on that but he did have more to say.

'As I was leaving, Ida try to slip me the letters Arnie had sent her. Her husband saw them and wanted to know what they were. Upshot is he flies into a rage and starts cutting up rough.'

'With you?'

'With his wife.' Stan looked at me and shrugged. 'I had to teach him some manners.'

'Hit him?'

'Just a clip,' said Stan.

I imagined how much damage a clip from Stan might do.

'She said she'd be all right but I was worried what he'd do when I wasn't around.'

'It's not your fault,' I told him.

'I was the one who went there asking questions,' he said.

'Sounds to me like her husband is the type who doesn't need excuses.'

Later, when everyone got back from lunch I called a meeting. Most of what we were currently employed upon was the routine business that took up most of our time. Given that I was coming to suspect Coveney was putting pressure upon Colonel G over the matter, I decided it would be as well to concentrate all our efforts on Dabs, Kearney and the carrier until we at least knew precisely what it was about.

I'd spent the best part of the previous week ploughing through sworn testimonies taken from a clutch of minor minions in some lower Bavarian backwater. From the version these men had given their interrogators, I was almost convinced that the war hadn't reached that far south in Germany. We were looking for links to a Waffen SS unit active in Czechoslovakia in 1940 and although there was still a healthy stack of interviews left to go through, I knew the odds of finding anything useful in the Bavarian testimonies would be slightly longer than the chance of Adolf Eichmann getting a caution and being bound over to keep the peace should anyone ever lay their hands on him.

Tired of reading the accounts of people who apparently hadn't noticed anything of what was going on all around them, I for one wasn't averse to a change of subject.

We talked about what we had discovered so far over a mug of ersatz coffee and Stan passed the letters from Arnie Poole to Susie to read. I pinned Arnie's photo up on the board by the map and put beside it the one of Robert Burleigh his wife Edna had given me. Burleigh hadn't been blessed with looks as good as Poole's and, in contrast, looked more like a gormless member of the Three Stooges. Thin where his wife was stout, they must have made an odd couple. I didn't think his children had inherited his looks, which might be thought of as a blessing until you considered that he hadn't left them anything else either.

'These are really sweet,' Susie said, looking up from the letters. She was sitting on one of the desks, swinging her legs.

'Heartfelt?' I asked.

She scowled as if she suspected I was being cynical. I wasn't. From the description Poole's father had given of him, Stan had assessed Arnie Poole as being something of a wide boy. I was merely wondering if his letters held any trace of insincerity, any suggestion that he was stringing the girl along. Hardly any concern of ours if he had been, one might think, but it would give some sort of indication as to the way Arnie Poole's mind worked.

'Yes,' said Susie. 'He must have really loved her. They'd been planning on getting married.'

'Then suddenly he was posted to the south coast in time for D Day,' said Stan, as if he'd already got the story from the girlfriend herself.

'But nothing in them about the rest of the carrier crew?' I asked.

'Not yet,' Susie said, reaching for the next letter.

I lit another cigarette, trying to remember what the Capstan I'd switched from used to taste like. Beach tar came to mind, but I was probably just trying to persuade myself I'd made a good decision. I was thinking of cigarettes mainly because I didn't want to think of the letters I'd written to Penny while I'd been away. And, more to the point, whether she had kept them.

'Well,' I said, exhaling a stream of less than satisfactory smoke. 'It was a long shot anyway, but it doesn't look as if we're going to get anything useful from Burleigh or Poole's families—'

'Dabs was an orphan,' Jack put in. 'A Barnardo's Boy, so he's a dead end.'

'Aptly put, Jack,' Peter observed.

'We don't know anything much about Kearney, do we?' said Stan. 'Do you want me to have a word with this sister of his, see what I can get out of her?'

'No,' I said. 'She's got a cousin who doesn't care for the British army, so you'd better keep your hands to yourself for the time being.' This brought a round of raised eyebrows from the others but I wasn't about to explain. 'I'll have another go at her myself,' I told him.

'Would you like me to come along again?' Susie asked. 'In case you need a chaperone, *Captain.*'

'Thanks but I think you inhibited her last time, Susie. Give me that phone number you took and I'll see what she can tell me about her brother without the distraction of having to compete with you.'

'There's gratitude,' said Susie, flouncing off the desk and narrowing her eyes. 'Just you mind that Rose Kearney doesn't become *too* uninhibited, *Captain.*'

I went over the map with Peter again, trying to pin down exactly which German units were active west of Caen. It must have been a confusing campaign, particularly for Bren gun carriers which, by their very nature, operated in advance of the infantry. He had made an appointment with the Hampshire Regiment to go through the official accounts and the 7th battalion's War Diaries. For the moment, though we still had several choices for the units Kearney's carrier had run up against.

I left him to it and went back into my office where Jack was just putting down the phone.

'That was the Provost Marshall's office wanting a word with you. Twelve o'clock tomorrow.'

'What about?'

'Wouldn't say on the phone. Said you'd know.'

I wondered what the hell I was supposed to have done now that might interest the Provost Marshall's office.

'Where?'

'Said he'd call tomorrow and let you know.'

'Who?'

'A Major Hendrix.'

7

The phone kept ringing but no one bothered to answer. I waited, doodling Hendrix's name surrounded by question marks. Finally someone picked up the receiver at the other end of the line and barked a terse, 'Yes?' at me.

'I'd like to speak to Miss Rose Kearney in number three, please.'

'What am I, a bloody doorman?'

I had no idea what he was beyond uncivil, but there was no point in making a guess in kind so I replied as equably as possible:

'I'm really sorry to bother you but it is rather urgent. I would be obliged if you could ask Miss Kearney to come to the telephone.'

He grunted then and said, 'Who's calling?'

'My name is Tennant.'

'You'd better wait, then,' he said and I heard him stomp off down the hall and up the stairs, picturing the receiver left swinging on its cable beneath the set.

Sweetness and light, I had found, will often take the wind out of some belligerent's sails. And even if it doesn't work it still leaves the option of punching them on the nose if one has a mind to. Awkward down the telephone, I admit, but for those with a fanciful imagination like mine some satisfaction can still be taken.

I waited another couple of minutes, wondering how long I should give her. Or if the man who'd answered had just left the receiver hanging out of spite. When he finally came back on he said, 'No one home,' and broke the connection. I listened to the silence for a few seconds before replacing the receiver, contemplating whether it was worth going round to the flat again unannounced or not. I decided there was no rush.

As it happened, Rose Kearney rang the office the following morning and asked to speak to me.

'I rang yesterday,' I told her, 'but you were out.'

'I'm so sorry Captain Tennant,' she replied in that lilting brogue that had more than a hint of allure about it. And, while she explained she had been out looking for work, that fanciful imagination of mine applied a little make-up and did something with her hair. 'Now, I wasn't expecting to hear from you quite so soon.'

'No news, I'm afraid,' I said, before she started to get her hopes up, 'but I was wondering if I might come and see you again.' Adding, as Susie's admonishing image jumped into my head, 'Just a few more questions about your brother.'

'No, well I supposed there wouldn't be any news,' Rose said. 'So what would it be you'd be wanting to talk about, Captain?'

'Oh, just general things,' I told her. 'It helps to build up a picture of the missing men in cases like this.'

'Man, surely,' said Rose.

'I beg your pardon?'

'Man. There's only *one* missing man, isn't there? Our Billy?'

'Of course. But a little background on the man's character can sometimes give an indication about how he might react in a given circumstance...'

'I don't know that you could say Billy had *character*, so I can't think what I'd be able to tell you.'

'No, but—'

'And it might be better if you didn't come here, Captain, what with it being my cousin Patrick's flat and all.'

'Of course,' I said. 'We could meet somewhere else, perhaps?'

'Well, there is a public house not far from here,' she said. '*The Minstrel Boy*, I think it's called. You understand, I'm not in the habit of frequenting public houses, Captain Tennant, and certainly not on my own, but I can see no harm in just this once. Can we say six o'clock, before it gets busy?'

I said six o'clock and she told me the name of the street.

'And will you be bringing your friend with you again?' she asked.

'ATS Blake? No,' I said, 'I'll be on my own this time.'

'Ah well,' said Rose, 'I'm sure we'll rub along without her.'

~

Hendrix did not telephone, so later that afternoon a couple of hours before I needed to be in Kilburn, I rang the Provost Marshall's office and then the Imperial Graves Commission. Neither had a Major Hendrix on their staff. It didn't come as any great surprise. Neither did it tell me who our Major was or who he worked for, and I was curious as to whether he had visited Rose Kearney as well as Edna Burleigh.

As I had time I went back to my flat, having decided to wear civilian clothes to meet Rose. I didn't mention this to Susie as I said goodnight, knowing she'd jump to some erroneous conclusion. The one I had reached was that Kilburn had a growing Irish population—not all from the republic admittedly—but I didn't want Rose Kearney to suffer any adverse attention for being with a British officer. Nor, come to that, put up with any myself.

Successive waves of Irish had come over in the twenties and thirties, escaping the civil war in the Free State and then unemployment. A lot had settled around Camden and with the need for labour for the railway reconstruction many had moved into Kilburn. There was a sizeable Nationalist population now, although I'd yet to fathom why a people that seemingly so disliked us would choose to come and live among us.

My civilian wardrobe wasn't sufficiently extensive to offer much in the way of choice but I found a pair of slacks that held a decent crease, a shirt that didn't, and a jacket that wasn't too worn at the elbows. Clothes rationing didn't look like ending any day soon and there wasn't a great deal in the shops anyway, but I did have a wider choice in ties—even in the middle of a war Italy had still been a good market for ties for those whose taste ran the gamut from sedate to garish. I chose a silk number in pale blue, a colour Penny had once said matched my eyes.

~

The evening was warm and I got off the crowded bus a couple of stops before the street Rose had given me for the *Minstrel Boy*. As I walked, and long before the pub sign hove into view, I hummed the old Irish tune that had given the place its name. The words had been written at the end of the eighteenth century, I'd read somewhere, in memory of men killed in some Irish rebellion or other. Then put to an existing air as was the practice. There was also an alternative hymn using the same melody apparently, although as I supposed it to be Protestant I didn't think it would cut much ice with the republicans. I couldn't recall many of the words to the song but that rarely stopped me singing along whenever the opportunity occurred. It was a propensity that had always embarrassed Penny but she wasn't there to exhibit the sentiment so I merely embarrassed myself.

The pub was like a thousand others in London. A U-shaped bar with a brass foot-rail and stools; chipped tables and shabby chairs; linoleum floor. The pub sign was a representation of a young uniformed boy with a fife marching along a country lane. But if there had been any further military references to the pub's name inside they had long since disappeared. The decor mostly consisted of variations on a theme of nicotine brown. Drab was the adjective that sprung to mind which was probably why I didn't immediately spot Rose Kearney sitting at one of the tables.

She didn't look how I had pictured her while talking on the phone, but at least had done something with her hair, having tied it back into a bunch on her neck. Perhaps in my civilian clothes I was pretty drab, too, because she didn't see me either and I had time to note the look she gave to two men at the bar who had turned towards her. I hadn't reckoned on Rose Kearney possessing a Gorgon stare but it wouldn't have been an exaggeration to say she froze the men where they stood. Not having been turned to stone myself, I merely hesitated in my progress and, by the time Rose saw me, her expression had assumed that of the country girl in the big city again, the look she had given Susie and myself in her cousin's flat.

'Captain Tennant,' she said, 'I wouldn't have recognised you out of uniform.'

'And you've changed your hair, Miss Kearney,' I said, just so she'd know I'd noticed.

She blushed a little and put a hand behind her head, patting it into place.

'It's Rose,' she said. 'You called me Rose before, I remember.'

'I wouldn't have wanted to appear forward,' I said and asked what she would like to drink.

'Just a small glass of beer, if you please. I never touch hard liquor if you must know. It was the undoing of my father and I'm afraid Billy was much too fond of a drop himself.'

The two men at the bar gave me an appraising look as I stood beside them so I thought it only polite I should give it them back. I ordered two half-pints. Since Rose was drinking beer I thought I had better have one as well in case she got the impression I was a slave to liquor like the men in her family. I took the drinks back to the table and Rose smiled at me.

'Do you mind if I smoke?' I asked.

'No, Captain. Please go ahead. Billy was a smoker.'

'Would you care for one?'

'No, thank you.'

I lit up and exhaled the smoke to one side.

'I want to help if I can,' Rose said, 'but I don't know what it is I can tell you.'

'You've already told me your brother liked a drink,' I said.

'Oh well, there's precious few men I've met that don't. And I wouldn't want to give you the wrong impression. I'm not about to suggest Billy was a raging alcoholic.'

'No, of course not. But it suggests to me that he was a sociable man who probably liked to drink in company. Most soldiers like a drink.'

'Well, there you are then,' she said, 'you didn't need me to tell you that, did you?'

I smiled at her indulgently. 'What I mean is, your brother was probably friendly with some of the other men in the battalion.'

She shrugged. 'And supposing he was? Does that help in finding out what happened to him?'

It didn't so I asked her about Hendrix.

'Have you spoken about Billy to a man named Hendrix? Since you've been in England, I mean.'

'Hendrix? The man from the Paymaster General's Office? I think he said his name was Hendrix. A major, he was.'

'Yes, that's probably him. What was it he asked you?'

'He said he was making arrangements for Billy's back pay. He wanted to know if he had a bank account and who his beneficiary was.' She sniffed derisively and lifted her chin. 'Beneficiary! And who did he think was Billy's beneficiary now Mam is dead? Anyway, I told him, who's to say that Billy is dead? Isn't that what I came to England to find out?'

'And a bank account?'

'Now what would Billy be doing with a bank account? Didn't he spend all his pay just as soon as he got it? Excepting the little he sent home to Mam. And he always used the Post Office for that. The rest went on drink, I'll be thinking.'

'So you weren't able to tell him anything?' I said.

'Well aren't I the one needing the answers?' she replied tartly.

'Of course.'

'What made you ask about Major Hendrix?'

'Our paths seemed to have crossed,' I said. 'That's all. He's been to see Robert Burleigh's widow as well. As a matter of fact,' I said, 'I was supposed to meet him today.'

'And Corporal Poole's family? Has he been to see them, too?'

'One of the men in my office saw Poole's father over the weekend,' I told her, ignoring her question as I didn't know the answer. It was something I needed to ask Stan. I should have thought of it earlier. 'He saw Poole's girlfriend as well,' I added.

'Poor thing,' said Rose.

'She married someone else,' I said.

'Ah well,' Rose observed pragmatically, 'there's no point in waiting for a man who's not coming back, is there Captain? She wouldn't want to end up an old spinster like me.'

'You're nothing of the sort, Rose,' I replied, knowing the response was expected.

'The girls marry young in Ireland, Captain.'

'You're in England now,' I reminded her.

'But at least she knows her man's not coming back. They identified *him*, didn't they. I mean, there's no chance that Billy might have been in the vehicle and they made a mistake? Weren't they badly burned...?'

I told her they had been identified through their army ID discs, preparing her for the fact that her brother's had been recovered from a dead German.

She was frowning. 'But the fire...'

'Pressed asbestos,' I said. 'They survive most things.' I glanced towards the men at the bar and unbuttoned the second and third buttons of my shirt. The men were taking no notice of us now and I pulled my own discs out to show her.

She seemed surprised. 'You wear them even when you're not in uniform? I wouldn't have thought you to be a man expecting a violent end, Captain.'

'Habit,' I said.

Rose leaned across the table for a closer look. There were two discs, the main one octagonal in shape and coloured green. Below was a red circular one. They were hand-stamped with surname, initials, service number and whatever the religion the wearer subscribed to. As in most others things, if the holder had no particular religion they were classed as C of E. Rose peered at them and took hold of the red tag

'H?' she asked.

'Harold,' I said, tucking my discs back into my shirt and buttoning it.

ID discs were issued with a three-foot cotton cord although most men eventually replaced this with a leather bootlace. I supposed it was likely that either would have burnt through in the carrier which meant that the discs would most probably have been found lodged on the bodies. On finding a corpse a note is supposed to be taken of the ID and, along with any weapons, the man's pay-book and any other identifying information is normally collected. I doubted that there was much of anything left in the carrier after the fire but it was something else Jack would need to chase up for me.

I should have told her then about her brother's discs but had hesitated so long I felt the moment had passed.

'Perhaps you could tell me a little bit about your brother when he lived in Ireland,' I suggested instead.

'Now why would you be wanting to know that, Captain?'

'Harry,' I said. 'Friends call me Harry.'

'And is that what I am?' Rose asked. 'You an English officer and me Irish? Now there's a novelty for you.'

I sighed and Rose raised her eyebrows.

'We're on the same side here,' I told her. We both want to find out what happened to your brother.'

The Irish and their grievances were no concern of mine. It had been enough that I'd had to contend with Italians and Germans in the last few years without worrying about an Irish contingent back home carrying chips the size of bazookas on their shoulders.

'I've got nothing against the Irish, Rose. I can't see that that they should have anything against me, just because I wear a British uniform. I'd have thought there's been enough of us been doing that recently.'

'You're not one for history, then?'

'Only my own.'

'I'd be interested to hear that, Harry.'

I remembered what Susie had said and reminded her it was her brother we were supposed to be talking about.

'What can I tell you, Captain?' she shrugged. 'Billy was my older brother.'

'How much older?'

'Eight years. There,' she said, coquettish again with her head tilted slightly to one side, 'now you know how old I am.'

I did. According to his service record William Kearney had been born in 1908. If he was still alive he'd be thirty-eight. That made Rose thirty, probably. She had said they'd been kids when their father had died yet either Rose had been very young or her brother had been well into his teens when they lost him.

'When did Billy come to England, Rose?'

'Nineteen thirty-one.'

'Surely that wasn't the last time you saw him?'

'No, he came home now and then to see our Mam and me. When he had the money, that was.'

'So when did you last see him?'

'Before the war, it would have been.'

'But you heard from him regularly.'

'Once a week, regular as clockwork. Until he was sent to France.'

'That wouldn't have been unusual,' I assured her.

'No,' said Rose, 'so everyone else has told me.'

I tried then to get childhood memories of her brother from her but she didn't care to share them with me. When I pressed her she asked me the time.

'Almost seven,' I said.

'Then I'll have to be getting back. Patrick will be wanting his tea when he gets home.' She stood up and began fussing with her handbag.

'What does your cousin do?'

'Clearing bomb damage,' she said, 'and the good Lord knows there's no shortage of that at the moment.'

I offered to walk her back to her flat but she said there was no need. She had the telephone number of my office, but on the spur of the moment I wrote down my home number and address for her.

She looked at it. 'Clerkenwell? Is that a nice area, Captain?'

'Not now,' I said. 'And it wasn't much before the war. But it's handy for work.'

'And you've your own telephone?'

'No. It's like yours—on the wall in the passage. Keep ringing and someone will eventually answer.'

Me, generally. If I heard it, that was. Only two of the other flats in my building were still occupied, the others having been too badly damaged. An old lady who rarely set foot outside the door lived on the top floor, some Samaritan bringing her everything she needed to keep her bones connected. The other occupant—Sam something—lived above me and kept the oddest hours of anyone I've ever met. I'd only ever passed him on the stairs.

Rose put my address and number in her bag and left; walking erect and, I couldn't help thinking, with some degree of elegance. She glanced towards the two men who were still standing at the bar as she passed, but they kept their eyes studiously on their glasses. I waited a minute or two then finished my beer and followed Rose out the door. Once on the pavement I jogged a few yards and ducked into a doorway. Sure enough, a moment later the two men came out of the *Minstrel Boy* and looked up and down the street. After some indecision they set off unhurriedly towards Rose's flat. I let them turn the corner then went in the opposite direction.

8

Tuesday June 18th 1946

The streets around my flat had long since been cleared or rubble. But only as far as the side of the road and onto vacant lots where it had been bulldozed into piles. Successive springs had spread a proliferation of weeds and buddleia and now the gaps between buildings had begun to look like vagrants' gardens. I had no idea when work would begin shifting the mounds of brick, stone and plaster that had once represented homes, although rumour had it that when they did they'd pull my building down first. I think the only reason it hadn't been pulled down earlier was that it had been expected to collapse under its own weight. Judging by some of the cracks in the façade, it hadn't quite given up on the idea. The place had been condemned as unsafe during the war, but somehow the old girl living on the top floor had been overlooked when everyone else had been moved out. Later, after it failed to collapse, people came and went again, more through desperation at finding somewhere to live than any belief in the building's integrity. I planned to stay there as long as I could, but that was through habit rather than sentiment.

I stopped for a bite to eat on the way home. It was still light by the time I got back, the evening dancing on the edge of twilight as it does in early summer. Later in the season, just as one has got used to the light evenings they wane, dusk bringing with it that sense of fading hope. Perhaps the notion is a consequence of a melancholy nature. Yet I wasn't alone. I imagine we had all got used to the war being over and those first feelings of exhilaration going flat. The future we may have suspected we didn't have now seemed full of lost illusions.

Passing the telephone in the hall, on the spur of the moment I put in a trunk call to Penny. I only had to wait five minutes for the connection as, being late in the day the lines weren't busy. I smoked another cigarette to pass the time while tracing the progress of one of the newer cracks from the corner by the front door to the cornice where an opportunistic spider had made its home. When the phone rang with my call it almost took me by surprise. Only it wasn't Penny I was talking to but my mother.

'Why won't you give Penny a divorce?' she demanded without preamble.

'How nice to hear your voice, Mother.'

'Don't be facetious, Harry, it doesn't suit you.'

'I wasn't aware Penny wanted a divorce,' I said.

'Why do you think she came to see you?'

'I thought she came up to go to the theatre with Julia and Maurice Coveney.'

'Maurice Coveney? What's he got to do with it?'

'Precisely what I was thinking. Put her on and I'll ask.'

'She wants to marry your brother,' Mother said.

'I thought it was the other way around.'

'She isn't home.'

'Is George home?'

'Do you want to speak with him?'

'Not especially.'

'Then why have you called?'

'I wanted to speak with my wife.'

'Don't play games, Harry,' said Mother and hung up.

I assumed games didn't suit me either. I held onto the receiver as if giving her the opportunity to reconsider, but the connection was broken and she would have had to call trunks and book another call. That would have been far too much trouble for my mother to go to just to speak to me. I hung up, said goodnight to the spider and went up to my flat. I passed Sam on the stairs, on his way out, and I wondered if perhaps he wasn't a housebreaker just off to work for the evening. If I'd still been a policeman I might have asked.

~

Early on in my army career I had always supposed—given that we'd win the war and I'd get through in one piece—that I'd go back to the police once it was over. Getting a commission changed that and, as the years passed, the prospect looked less and less appealing. For one thing those contemporaries of mine who had chosen to stay with the police rather than enlist would have made progress through the ranks while I would have had to re-enter again as I had left—as a uniformed constable. I suppose having reached the rank of captain in the army might have counted for something eventually, although the thought of taking orders from sergeants and inspectors in the meantime—men who might have only achieved rank through the general lack of manpower—would have stuck in my craw. I had got used to telling others what to do and wasn't sure how long I'd last taking orders from people who, in another service, might well have been serving under me. That left me in the position (depending upon how one chose to view it) either with the prospect of a bleak and uncertain future, or the opportunity to start over with a fresh slate. Being divorced might have looked like part of the freshness of that slate, but being told to do it was something else that stuck in my craw.

~

Peter Quince was sticking new pins into the map when I got into the office the next morning. In addition to the flag that marked the general area where Kearney's carrier had been found, a series of coloured arrows showed how the Allies had moved off the beaches towards Caen. South of the town, there were several new flags flying swastikas.

Peter glanced over his shoulder as I walked in.

'It's not as straightforward as it looked.'

'Oh, why not?'

'The 12SS-Panzers were in Caen. Kurt Meyer took over divisional command when Fritz Witt was killed on June 14th. He held Caen until July 8th then evacuated the city, leaving some elements of the division holding the line between Eterville and the River Orne.' He stabbed a finger to a spot to the south of Caen near Maltot. 'The division pulled out of the line on July 11th and was sent to Potigny, about 30 kilometers north of Falaise, for a rest and a refit.

'That puts them where we want them, doesn't it? Briefly, anyway. Vogel had Kearney's ID discs and he was Hitlerjugend.'

'Except the Hitlerjugend weren't the only Division in the area.'

'Who else was there?'

'Let's start with the other SS units,' Peter said, picking some papers up from the desk.

As far as I was concerned, if it was a war crime you were investigating, the SS was always a good place to start. Experience had shown one rarely had to look any further. The propensity of the SS for atrocities was legend.

Peter pointed to the map again.

'The 17SS Gotz von Berlichingen arrived just a few days after the window we're looking at, part of the ISS-Panzer Corps. That included the 101SS Heavy Panzer Battalion, 12SS Hitlerjugend, 17th SS-Panzer Grenadier Division Götz von Berlichingen, and the Panzer Lehr Division as well as 1SS Leibstandarte. Although it does look as if most of these units arrived too late to be involved in Operation Epsom at the end of June. That's the 26th to the 30th.'

I looked at Peter askance. 'Epsom? Goodwood? Did a bookie help plan the invasion?'

'Actually, Colonel G was wrong. Operation Goodwood was July 18th to 20th and took place to the east of Caen. Kearney's carrier was involved in one of a series of feints Montgomery designed to pin the Germans to the west, away from Goodwood.' He went back to his map. 'I'd assumed Kearney's carrier was involved in Epsom, but they weren't. His platoon was attached to the 7th battalion of the Hampshire Regiment. They were part of 130 Brigade's operation to take the village of Maltot and seize the bridgeheads over the Orne while 129 Brigade was to take the high ground of Hill 112 that commanded the ground between the village and the Orne.'

'Don't tell me,' I said, 'what was that called, Operation Cheltenham?'

Peter smiled indulgently. 'No, Jupiter, as a matter of fact. July 10th. That's when the carrier was lost, along with much of 7th Hampshire's B Company. It wasn't actually recovered until 23rd of July, after Operation Express on July 22nd.' He grinned at me. 'There were two other operations before Goodwood, called Greenline and Pomegranate, if you were wondering.'

I hadn't been. It sometimes seemed that headquarters staff kept a special detachment solely for the purpose of dreaming up names for military operations. For me these last names spoilt the symmetry of racecourse-themed operations and made them more difficult to remember. I hadn't read any of the reports on the battle for Caen and the surrounding country and place names like Orne and Hill 112 didn't mean anything to me. I wanted to concentrate on the carrier.

'All right, the Hitlerjugend were there on the 10th when the carrier was lost. What other units can we definitely place at the scene?'

'Companies of the 21st and 22nd battalions of the 10SS-Panzer Division—Frundsberg. They were holding Hill 112 and the ground east to Maltot and the River Orne. The Hohenstaufen—its sister Division, 9SS-Panzers—was in reserve. It was because they came up into the line that Jupiter didn't succeed in taking Hill 112 and crossing the Orne.'

'But they were all SS, right? And if we're talking racing they've all got form. You said there were still elements of the Hitlerjugend nearby and the Division wasn't pulled out until July 11th, the day after Dabs was murdered.'

'The day after the carrier was lost,' Peter corrected. 'Not necessarily the same thing.'

'Well, if Meyer's 25th Grenadiers were there then as far as I'm concerned they're still the favourite. But just to be safe let's start by taking a close look at the others.'

'That shouldn't be too difficult,' Peter said. 'Although if you're thinking of making a bet, there was another SS unit in France at the time. You might want to make them joint-favourites.' He consulted the papers on his desk for a moment and stuck another flag on the map.

'Who's this?'

'They were in Montauban, north of Toulouse on D-Day, and were ordered to the landing beaches. They were in Tulle on the 9th and the on the 10th reached Oradour-sur-Glane.'

'2SS Das Reich?'

'Right on the money.'

Ninety-nine men had been murdered in Tulle and the next day the village of Oradour-sur-Glane was torched and six hundred and forty-two more were massacred. They were civilians. Given the nature of the fighting north of Caen between the Canadian and 12SS Hitlerjugend, the fact that prisoners were not taken was not exactly surprising; it was even rumoured that the Canadians hadn't been too fussy in their treatment of surrendering Germans. 2SS Das Reich, though, had systematically murdered men, women, and children. If Das Reich had been anywhere near Kearney's carrier I knew who my money was riding on.

'Okay,' I said, 'let's see who we can place where and when. We've got runners with form, let's see if we can put them in the same paddock.'

I left Peter to get on with it and went into my office. Jack was venting his ire on his Remington, stabbing accusatory fingers at several keys in turn. I knew how he felt.

'Did you find out about the condition of the ID discs in the carrier?' I asked when he stopped typing long enough to push his glasses onto the bridge of his nose again.

He pulled a sheet of paper from the pile beside the typewriter.

'Yes,' he said, passing it to me. 'Consistent with going through a fire. What was left of their weapons were also present but pay-books and any other ID didn't survive. They found nothing else, anyway.'

I read through Jack's notes, verifying the facts for myself, then dropped into my chair.

'I don't suppose Major Hendrix rang back?'

Jack shrugged. 'Not while I've been here.'

I got up again and went into the other office.

'Stan, did Arnold Poole's father mention he'd been visited by a Major Hendrix by any chance?'

'Nope,' said Stan, looking up from the pile of papers Peter had dropped onto his desk. 'But then I didn't ask.'

'Robert Burleigh's widow told me Saturday she'd had a visit. This Hendrix told her he was from the Graves Commission. He's been to see Rose Kearney, too. Told her he was with the Paymaster General's office. He rang here the day before yesterday after me with a story about being with the Provost Marshall.'

'Gets around,' said Stan.

'Doesn't he, though? I was supposed to meet him but he never got back to us.'

As I turned back into my office Stan said:

'Ida got a visit from an officer from Poole's battalion asking about Kearney and the others.'

'Ida?'

'Poole's girlfriend.'

'The wife of the man you smacked?'

Peter and Susie looked at Stan and then at each other.

'Whoever it was could only have got her name from Poole's father,' Stan said. 'No one else knew about her and Arnie, she reckoned.'

A thought occurred to me. 'Assuming it was Hendrix who visited her, why didn't she give him the letters?'

'Because her husband was there probably. That's why when I turned up he got so irritated and turned nasty. Someone else talking to his wife about her old boyfriend. I suppose the letters were the last straw.'

'You've read them all now?' I asked Susie.

'Every line,' she boasted. 'Unfortunately our Arnie doesn't mention any of the men he served with. There's the usual sort of stuff you'd expect but mostly he wrote Ida about what they'd do when he got home. Sad really. Since he didn't come home, I mean.'

The phone rang in the other office and a moment later Jack put his head around the corner.

'Major Hendrix sends his apologies.'

'For not getting back to us? Did he say why?'

'Just that something came up.'

'Would that be with the Graves Commission, the Paymaster General, or the Provost Marshall?'

'Didn't specify.'

'He didn't leave a number, I suppose?'

'No.'

Peter and I exchanged a meaningful look and I decided I needed to ask Colonel G if he knew anything about Major Hendrix.

'All right,' I announced while I still had their attention, 'let's keep digging with what we've got. This looks to be straightforward and maybe I'm just suspicious, but something doesn't smell quite right and I'd like to find out what it is before it starts rubbing off on us.'

I went back to my desk and rang Jekyll's number. He wasn't in his office so I left a message with his secretary. Her name was Joan and she had the kind of husky voice that was full of promise. I'd woven a whole series of fantasies around the sound of that voice while studiously avoiding any opportunity I might have of meeting her. I had so few illusions left I was rather miserly about keeping those I still had.

Having apportioned the work among the others, I found myself at a loose end. It was a warm day and stuffy in the office. There had been a wind overnight and dust hung in the air as it had in Berlin after the bombing. Like the other German cities, Berlin had resembled a sea of destruction out of which the few buildings that hadn't been pulverised stuck like the bleached bones of beached whales. Dust had coated everything. It got in your teeth and the balls of your eyes. It left a gritty residue that wouldn't wash off. Maybe it was my imagination but I thought the Biblical accounts of how the world might end had missed a trick. They should have added dust to fire, water, ice and plague. I sometimes thought everything might finally end by being swallowed under a fine accretion of bone-dry particles, choking us all on our last words. Perhaps that's how they had died in Pompeii and Herculaneum; moving up through the Italy I'd never had the chance to investigate. Now I'm glad I hadn't.

I got up, making an excuse to Jack he didn't believe, and walked out of the office onto the street. The air smelt clearer outside but only because petrol was rationed and the few horse-drawn vehicles that had been left on the roads before the war had now disappeared. Perhaps in Victorian London I would have worried about drowning in horse-shit.

9

Wednesday June 19th 1946

If finding the unit responsible for the death of Dabs and his comrades would take some disentangling—given the close proximity of several German SS companies—it wouldn't be impossible. Finding the exact culprits, though, was another matter. If, indeed, culprits there were. We'd been assuming that at least one of the dead had been the victim of a war crime although the burnt-out carrier and the bodies—even the missing Kearney—could very well still have quite logical explanations; it was really only the fact that Joseph Dabs had been found with a bullet in the head that marked the case out at all. The fact that Kearney's ID discs had turned up on a dead German didn't mean the man had killed him. Soldiers were notorious for collecting souvenirs. I had heard from old police colleagues I'd run into that London was awash with small arms now the war was over—some purloined British and American army service revolvers, others German pistols taken as souvenirs. In the far east it had been Samurai swords and gold teeth, pulled from the unresisting mouths of Japanese corpses.

That was the nature of war and if people want to get prissy about it, it behoves them to elect leaders who'll keep them out of conflicts.

All right, I'll admit not everyone has the opportunity to cast a ballot. But Germany certainly had, and it struck me they got more than they bargained for. If you want to make a pact with the devil, however, you're obliged to dance to his tune. Even so, although I wasn't about to admit to having much sympathy with Kurt Meyer and his 25th SS-Panzer Grenadiers, it seemed to me that given the desperate nature of the fighting, had the jackboot been on the other foot and Germany had won the war, the commander of the Canadian forces might well have found himself in the dock. And not a few British commanders alongside to keep him company. Always assuming the SS would have bothered with a dock, that is. Whether those who had sentenced Meyer to hang suspected something similar, I don't know, but since we'd started looking into the circumstances of Kearney's carrier I'd learned that back in January Meyer's death sentence had been commuted to life imprisonment.

Massacres like those committed at Tulle and Oradour-sur-Glane had been a different matter. And yet even they paled by comparison to what was now coming out about the actions of the Special Action Groups—*Einsatzgruppen*—in eastern Europe and Russia.

What I suppose I was wondering was how the degree of what constituted a crime was a matter of perspective. Not just relative to other, greater crimes, but to the victor and the vanquished. Not a very original thought, I grant. It's a cliché—but still also a truism—that the victor writes the history; but he also convenes the court—or erects the scaffold, or merely find a convenient wall to stand his victims against. At base, it's a matter of morality and even then one has to try to pin down morality's shifting parameters. The evidence and consequences of that lay all around me in the results of bombing raids; raids the consequence of which were even more apparent in the German cities. There was plenty of guilt to spare for actions once deemed necessary and, I had noticed, it already seemed some of those who had taken the necessary action were no longer so keen to have the responsibility lying at their door.

~

I walked around for an hour or so then went back to the office. Peter and Susie were out to lunch but Stan was still at his desk trawling through interrogation reports and I could hear Jack's Remington taking a beating in the other room.

Stan glanced up, looking even more dour than usual, as if something was troubling him.

'If you're worried about that woman's husband lodging a complaint over you smacking him,' I said, 'I'd forget it. From what you told me he's more likely to take it out on his wife than go through normal channels.'

'That's what's worrying me,' said Stan. 'Can't get her out of my head, if you want the truth.'

'What?'

'Not like that,' he said quickly. 'Don't get me wrong, she's a good-looking girl. Or was when I left,' he added morosely. 'It's just I feel guilty about bringing her trouble.'

‘People make choices,’ I told him. ‘She married the man. Would Arnie Poole have treated her any better? What was it you called him, a wide boy? He certainly wasn’t above making up stories about himself. It seems to me that those who have mainly their own interest at heart rarely have room for anybody else's. Perhaps she's better off with her memories of Poole than what she might have got if he came back.'

'I can't see that she could do much worse than what she's got,' said Stan.

Not having been there, I couldn't disagree, so left him to brood over it. Jack wasn't doing much brooding but was threading a new ribbon through the Remington, fingers stained with ink.

‘Did you get a chance to ask anyone about Maurice Coveney?’ I asked, dropping behind my desk and lighting up my lunch.

Jack looked at me in his lugubrious way, wiped his fingers on the piece of rag he called a handkerchief, and leaned across the gap between our desks with a sheet of paper in his outstretched hand.

To be honest my main interest in Coveney was his interest in Penny, but given his conversation with Jekyll at Julia’s house which seemed to concern the business we had in hand, at least I had a legitimate reason for wasting Jack’s time in making enquiries. Not that he had needed to do much asking around. The typewritten sheet consisted mostly of the fact of Coveney’s being in the Foreign Office and his entries in Who’s Who, Debrett’s, and Burke’s Peerage. The last two, to be strictly accurate, weren’t entries for Maurice Coveney but for his cousin, Peregrine, who held the baronetcy. It dated from the elevation of their grandfather, John Coveney, who was a mill owner in the 1860s and made his fortune in the manufacture of cotton goods. By now the family had their fingers in other pies—heavy engineering and ship-building on the Clyde—so they weren’t old aristocracy but trade, although I didn’t suppose the fact gave Peregrine dyspepsia. And I didn’t suppose it mattered to Sir Maurice either; he had made his way in the Civil Service and, if his entry in Who’s Who was current, was one of the Permanent Secretaries in the F.O. He had followed the usual upper-class education route—Eton and Cambridge—and had achieved a First in Classics, joined the Civil Service following war service and had married Marie-Louise Pellisier in 1920—one son.

The more I read the more I understood why he had looked down his nose at me. When I got to the bit that said his wife had died in an air raid in 1941, I found I was even beginning to feel some sympathy for his attitude: Coveney had lost his wife while I had thrown mine away. There was just the one child from Coveney’s marriage and Maurice's pursuits were listed as shooting and fishing. On Peregrine's estate, no doubt.

I dropped the sheet of paper on my desk. 'What interest would Coveney have in us?' I said, more to myself than to Jack.

'We could always try asking?' Jack suggested.

I favoured him with what I hoped was a withering look. 'Didn't you learn any tactics in the army? I was hoping to outflank him.'

Jack grunted. 'That'll be why you're the officer then, I suppose.'

~

I tried telephoning Jekyll again at around six that afternoon and managed to find him in his office. I told him what I knew of Major Hendrix. He hadn't heard of the man but said he'd make some enquiries. Then he asked if I was free for a drink. Not having to consult my diary I said yes, and he said he'd meet me in his club at seven.

We'd had the odd drink together before—more than once when he'd been pleased with our work—but that had usually been in the pub around the corner from the office and involved all of us. He had certainly never invited me to his club. That was the Army and Navy in Pall Mall, somewhere I had always thought I would have liked to be put up for if I could have scraped up the provenance. I'd been inside once, early in the war before I'd shipped out to North Africa. Only not for a drink. I had a message for a major in the tank corps that I'd been instructed to deliver by hand. He wasn't at his home so I'd gone to his club. They'd kept me hanging around in the foyer and I'd assumed at the time that corporals weren't encouraged in the lounges unless their name happened to be Bonaparte. The place was all sandbags and broken glass then as an air raid had demolished a couple of the gentlemen's clubs up the road and inflicted some on the Rag—as the Army and Navy was apparently known.

Walking up the street towards it, I saw that the sandbags had gone along with much of its pre-war grandeur. I supposed the last years had taken their toll of its membership, too, and that there were probably now a few vacancies. No longer a corporal but an officer and eligible for membership, I nevertheless suspected that I still lacked the provenance.

A steward led me through the club to a small smoking room where Colonel G was waiting. We shook hands and, as I sank into the soft embrace of one of the Army and Navy's leather armchairs and pulled out my cigarettes, I thought it just as well I'd switched brands and wouldn't be stinking the place up with my old Capstans.

Colonel G was in civvies although he had abandoned the houndstooth. He was wearing a nicely cut suit with creases in the trousers that were sharp enough to shave with. The suit was made-to-measure, rather than the sort of off-the-peg kind I could afford, and I wondered if the Army and Navy kept a maid on hand to press pants at short notice.

'Good of you to come, Harry,' he said. 'What'll it be?'

That's when I noticed the waiter, silent as a doodlebug once the engine had cut, hovering behind me. I asked for a gin and French and Colonel G indicated his empty glass and said he'd have another.

'How's the investigation?' he asked, squinting at me with his glass eye.

There was no one else in the room to eavesdrop and the armchair was winning an easy points decision over the battered settee in the my flat, so I saw no reason to sit on the edge of the seat and whisper. Just to let him know we hadn't been idling away the hours, I told him about my visit with Susie to Rose Kearney and that I'd seen her again since; how I'd also talked to Burleigh's widow and how Stan had seen Poole's father and an old girlfriend in Blackburn. I left out the bit where he'd smacked her new husband as not being relevant to the investigation.

He listened dourly as I went through it all, since what interested him most were any German army units we could identify as being in the area at the right time. Then I told him what Peter had come up with—the companies of the 21st and 22nd SS-Panzer Grenadiers, and 10SS-Panzer Division that had been between Hill 112 and the River Orne on the day.

The waiter returned with our drinks.

'No shortage of suspects there,' Colonel G said.

'No,' I agreed, and having left the best till last said:

'The 12th SS-Panzer Division pulled out on July 11th which means there's a good chance the 25th SS-Panzer Grenadiers were actually on the spot the day the carrier went missing. Actually pinning Dabs' death on them won't be so easy, even though the SS man who had Kearney's ID discs was from the 25th SS-Panzer Grenadiers.'

'You'll find a way,' Jekyll said, making the remark sound more like a threat than a vote of faith in my capability.

I took a slug of my gin. Then, trying to make it seem as though the thought had just that moment occurred to me, asked what Sir Maurice Coveney's interest was in the matter.

Jekyll cocked his head as if he'd caught the faint skirl of bagpipes somewhere in the building.

'What gives you the idea Sir Maurice is interested?'

'I'm sorry,' I said, 'perhaps I'm wrong. Only when you introduced us, I thought I heard you tell him I was the man handling the business. I rather assumed you meant the investigation into Dabs' death.'

'You rather assumed it, did you?'

His brows knitted and he fixed his glass eye on me like an irritable owl sizing up his next meal. I knocked back the rest of my gin, trying to hide the fact I'd started to squirm.

He let me stew a minute or two longer but didn't press the point. Instead, he seemed to become almost indifferent about the business.

'Given the reputation of the SS, I doubt you'll have too much difficulty in pinning the responsibility where it belongs. Let's not waste too much time on this, Captain Tennant. Wrap it up as soon as you can.'

'Of course, sir,' I said, still apparently a captain even though I felt I'd been demoted. I lifted my glass again but discovered it was empty. I should have excused myself and left, but finding myself in a hole felt compelled to keep digging. 'We've not turned up any hard evidence as yet. It's a matter of trawling through all the SS interrogation reports to see if we can find men who served with the units—'

'Exactly the work you were set up to do,' he interrupted curtly. Then he looked at his watch, downed his drink and announced, 'If that's all, I've got a dinner engagement,' stood and abruptly strode off at a pace that suggested he hadn't eaten all day.

The waiter returned immediately to collect our glasses and pointedly neglected to ask if I wanted another. I acted as if I hadn't anyway and, after a wrong turn or two and having to double-back in front of him, eventually made my way out of the Rag.

On the tube back to Clerkenwell it occurred to me I hadn't reminded Jekyll about Major Hendrix and, given how the interview had gone, wished I'd saved myself the trip to Pall Mall in the first place. The only useful thing to come out of it were the second thoughts I was now having about wanting to join the Army and Navy Club.

Coming up from Farringdon station, although it was still light, I found the streetlamps had come on—at least those that were still working. The gaps between and the odd bombed buildings gave the city a snaggle-toothed air, like an old harridan in a children's pantomime. She'd been knocked about a bit but could still cackle with fun if you had the money to pay her. Not that the people passing me on the pavement looked as if they had enough—most seemed merely intent on where they were going, shoulders hunched and heads down. I couldn't help compare the way they were dressed to Jekyll in his tailored suit. Fashion for most people had been on hold since before the war. Many dressed the way they had in the thirties. There hadn't been a lot of money around for clothes then, either. By now, though, the women's dresses and men's jackets and trousers had the look of having been through a hard campaign and in need of being demobbed. My gear hadn't fared too well, either. Penny and I were still living with Julia when I enlisted and the clothes I had left behind had followed Penny down to the country and had probably ended up on my brother's back, covered in chicken shit and cow dung. He had been drafted into the land army, poor eyesight having kept him out of the services. I didn't mind that so much except it left me with a limited wardrobe besides my change of uniform. And, after six years, no one looked so dated as a man in uniform. True, I wasn't spending my pay on anything much and could have afforded a new wardrobe, except that the lack of ration stamps hindered any spending-spree and made hoarders out of everyone. There were other ways—the black market or those out-of-the-way tailors who were busy turning now unneeded uniforms into serviceable clothes. But heavy khaki serge for summer wear seemed somehow even less of an attractive proposition than even pre-war fashions did.

Lost in thought, I reached home quicker than I expected and decided I wasn't yet ready to shut myself away for the evening. It was still relatively early but Clerkenwell didn't offer too many attractions for a man on the town. There were the pubs, of course, and a cinema not too far away, but the main feature would have already started and I didn't want to walk in halfway through the story. I felt I'd been doing too much of that recently—finding myself having missed the beginning and piecing events together from what I could pick up as the story unfolded. Kearney and his carrier was like that. I'd come in on the last reel, long after the characters had been established and their motives worked out. Piecing the story together from the last few scenes was like working out the picture on a jigsaw from a half-dozen pieces left lying in the box.

I was beginning to mix my metaphors and that just shows how muddled you can get when you walk in after the show's begun. I'd been in the show—all over North Africa and Europe—but still I couldn't shake the feeling of having missed it. Most of what was important had happened somewhere else, to someone else, and I had become a bit player. The kind of character who wasn't going to get the girl. That's really what it was all about and for once I could feel it was one of those times when just two drinks weren't going to be enough. I'd already had one at the Rag so I turned my back on the cinema and headed for the nearest pub, someplace where they didn't employ snobs to serve the drinks.

10

Thursday June 20th 1946

I should have known better than to play around with a concept like *schadenfreude* as there appears to be something infinitely amusing for other people in seeing someone else suffering with a hangover. It's akin to watching a man being hit in the balls by a football or a cricket ball—vastly entertaining for all except the poor bugger writhing on the ground in agony.

I wasn't writhing on the ground, exactly, more wallowing in a puddled heap behind my desk. Everyone else in the office was chirping cheerfully around me, being insincerely solicitous and asking if I wanted more tea. Well, not everyone. Stan was looking almost as morose as I was although no one seemed prepared to offer *him* more tea. In those moods he was just as likely as not to take a swing at you. I managed to weather the worst of it and by lunchtime everyone else had gone out to eat, having squeezed as much enjoyment from my condition as I suppose they thought they'd get. Again, everyone except Stan. He stood in the doorway of my office and looked at me like a man bereaved.

'What's the matter with you?' I asked. 'You don't get hangovers so don't come here looking for sympathy.'

'I've got a problem,' he said.

Feeling less than charitable I was hoping he was going to keep it to himself but knew only too well that there was more than a grain of truth in the old adage that misery loves company. Stan pulled out Jack's chair and sat down.

'It's Ida,' he said.

'Ida? Who's Ida?' It wasn't that I particularly wanted to know, just that if one of us was going to expend the energy talking I'd rather it was Stan.

'You know, Arnold Poole's girlfriend. The one I went—'

'Blackburn,' I said. 'Yes, I remember now. What about her?'

'She's here.'

'*Here*?' I sat up so quickly my head began to pound.

'No, not *here*,' he said. 'In London.'

'What's she doing in London?'

'She's left her husband.'

'How do you know that?'

'He knocked her around after I left like I thought he might, so she cleared out as soon as he went to work.' His face hardened and I wouldn't have given Ida's husband much chance of staying out of hospital if Stan could have got his hands on him.

'She's been in touch?'

He mumbled something.

'She what?'

'I said, she turned up at my lodgings.'

'How did she know where you lived?'

He mumbled again then said, 'I gave her my address.'

'So what's she going to do now?'

'She needs somewhere to live. She doesn't know anyone in London and she can't stay at my place. You know what my landlady's like. It was all I could do to persuade her to let Ida sleep on her settee last night.'

'Don't you know anyone who can put her up?'

He sighed and tutted and looked everywhere except at me. 'You know what it's like. Too many people and not enough accommodation. More arriving every day.'

I knew what it was like. Between demobbed servicemen, families who had spent the war in the country or overseas finally dribbling back, and those who had never left but had been bombed out, finding somewhere to live was at a premium.

'Aren't there some empty rooms where you live?' he asked.

'Only because the bloody building's on the verge of collapse,' I replied.

'You live there. And that old girl on the top floor.'

And Sam the housebreaker, I thought. But I wasn't going to start discussing my dodgy neighbour with Stan. He was more civic-minded than I'd lately become and if he thought Sam really was a burglar he'd expect me to inform the police. Particularly if it resulted in an empty flat.

'They're going to knock the place down any day,' I protested.

Stan grunted mirthlessly. 'If the Luftwaffe couldn't do it I can't see the Ministry of Works getting round to it any time soon. Com'on boss,' he said, spotting a chink of indecision in my reply and putting his big boot into it. 'It'll only be till I can fix her up with something better. Temporary, that's all.'

Everything in London was temporary but that didn't stop it still being there when you woke up in the morning.

'All right,' I said, 'but you'll have to come with me when we knock off and take a look. There's nothing worth having now. The scavengers had been through the place before I moved in. There'll be nothing useful in it even if we find a room that's habitable.'

'That's grand,' said Stan, grinning at me and bouncing out the chair as if someone had just taken a bag of cement off his head. 'It'll just be somewhere to get her head down, that's all.'

And his, I thought, and almost warned him against getting too involved with the woman—a married woman. But it was probably too late for that and none of my business anyway. The others came back from lunch and the noise level rose so I took my break and walked all the way down to the river, breathing deeply to try and clear my headache.

Barges were still hauling rubble downriver and what looked like a police launch was heading the other way, making heavy weather against the current. I watched it thinking that might not be a bad job, cruising up and down the Thames checking the odd boat and pulling the occasional corpse out of the water. But I'd seen as many corpses as I wanted to and decided there were probably better occupations to aim for. My brother George, for instance, having developed a taste for chicken shit and cow dung, now had ideas about becoming a farmer. There were opportunities and the country needed to up its production if we were going to get out of the financial hole the war had dropped us in. But I wasn't holding out much hope if we had to rely on people like George to do it. Knowing him as I did, I suspected he thought marrying Penny might be a good move; some of her family had land somewhere up on the Welsh borders and, if they had no more sense than to let him get his hands on it, they deserved him. I pictured Penny in Wellington boots humping bales of hay for the cows to munch and thought what a waste it would be. But, like Stan and Ida, it was probably now too late and none of my business either.

On the way back to the office I stopped in a pub for a sandwich and half a pint and drank it without gagging. I was cured.

~

Stan came back to Clerkenwell with me after work and, climbing out of the tube station and rounding the corner to where my building stood like a badly-balanced cardboard box on end, I saw a woman hanging around the door clutching a battered brown suitcase.

I gave Stan an accusing glance but he just shrugged.

'She's got to look at the place, hasn't she?'

I had called her a woman but, closer to, saw she was really little more than a girl. She had to be in her twenties at least if she had been engaged to Arnie Poole but he must have snared her straight from school and she couldn't have grown much since. The worn coat and dress beneath, the badly-cut shoulder-length dark hair and scuffed shoes said she had been through as much as the rest of the population, even if it didn't seem to have aged her face. What had left its mark was her husband's fist, leaving a dark bruise below her left eye and a half-healed cut on her lower lip.

'Ida,' Stan began awkwardly as we reached her, 'this is my superior officer, Captain Tennant.'

I didn't feel particularly superior and even Ida's attempt at a bob as she shook my hand didn't qualify me for the high ground. Maybe it was the look of the building I lived in, or the lack of enthusiasm that must have been plain on my face, but I could see she was in two minds about the whole idea.

'Oh, Stan,' she said in a broad Lancashire accent, 'maybe I shouldn't have come.' Then her lower lip began to tremble and I thought the cut might reopen and she'd cry and bleed at the same time.

'It's not as bad as it looks,' I said, trying to sound cheerful, aware that in parts it was even worse.

I was going to make us some tea in my flat but between entertaining Penny and stumping up my share for the office I'd used up my ration. So instead I thought she'd better see the worst of the place before the slightly better, and we started at the top where there were some vacant rooms next to the old girl, then worked our way down. The gaping roof at the back of the top floor precluded several rooms there, and some shattered joists where a bath had fallen through to the floor below, another. We did find an iron bedstead in a flat along the hall to me, bolts too rusted to allow disassembly and theft, but there was no mattress to go on it, never mind bedding. Stan said he knew where he could lay hands on an oil stove, some dishes and cutlery, and I had a rolled rug in my flat that I used to keep out the draughts that I said she could have. Her little round schoolkid's face hadn't perked up much, but when we finally went into my flat she suddenly brightened, looking around as if the place had come straight out of *Ideal Home*. I didn't know what she had left in Blackburn but neither word was one I'd have used to describe where I lived. Even despite the state Berlin was in when I left, most of my German billets had been far better than Clerkenwell. And the last time I had lived in London it had been at Julia's, complete with Adam fireplaces, moulded cornices and servants.

'Just till we can find something better,' Stan assured her, seemingly oblivious to the irony that his *superior* would still have to live there after he had taken Ida on to finer things. I was daydreaming about the prospects of Julia taking me back when Stan asked if it would be all right if Ida stayed on my settee until they could fix up one of the other rooms.

Startled, I'd barely had chance to open my mouth when Ida said, 'Oh, thank you Captain. I won't be no trouble,' and then did start to cry.

Stan and his big pugilist's face turned sheepish. He muttered something and I didn't even bother to ask him to repeat it.

11

Friday June 21st 1946

On Friday morning, while Peter was trying to pin down exactly which Panzer Grenadier companies were in the vicinity of Maltot on July 10th, Stan was keeping his mind off Ida by continuing with his self-appointed task of reading through all the files we had in the office. He was looking to turn up anything on an SS-Unterscharführer Otto Vogel, or any other 25th SS-Panzer Grenadier who might have a bearing on the case.

He glanced up as I walked in, a mute question written all over his face.

'I left her sleeping on the settee,' I assured him. 'Poor kid must have been knocked out.'

When our section had first been set up we found a dozen boxes of files stacked outside the office door waiting for us. Mostly smudged carbon copies of statements given by POWs, or verbatim reports of interrogations, I had left them for Stan and Jack to sort through, put in date order and collate. We had planned to index them but before we got round to it found they were of little use if you were seeking a particular reference or geographical location. For the most part they had sat on the shelves against one wall of the outer office ever since, taking up useful space. Now and then one of us might consult one of the files in the vain hope of finding what we were looking for, and it usually proved such a frustrating exercise that more than once I had been tempted to box them all up again and dump them on some bombsite.

Since he'd got back from Blackburn, Stan had been methodically working his way through each file in the hope of finding something on the Hitlerjugend Division. The sight of him blowing the dust off each successive report before opening it had become a feature of office life.

It was while I was brewing up a pot of tea that he grunted with the kind of satisfaction he had probably got back in the days when his right uppercut found his opponent's chin.

I turned to see him scan through several pages of the file he was consulting, and then get up and carefully replace on the shelves the stack of files he had accumulated on the floor around his desk. He was wearing an oddly smug expression that didn't sit particularly well with his bent nose.

'What?' I said.

'I knew these files would come in useful one day. I've found a couple of names.'

He knew no such thing, of course, and had moaned as vociferously as any of us about them cluttering up the office. But I didn't want to spoil his mood so I put a mug of tea on his desk and asked:

'Where from?'

'25th SS-Panzer Grenadiers.'

'Hitlerjugend? I didn't know we had much on them.'

'More than you'd think,' said Stan. 'When the bodies of those missing Canadians turned up at the Ardenne Abbey it seems the Intelligence Corps interrogated any SS from Meyer's regiment they could get their hands on. Meyer had used the place as his HQ so they knew who they were looking for. The thing is, they made copies of everything for circulation and we got some of it.'

'I thought they'd wrapped up the Ardenne Abbey investigation before we were established.'

'Yes, but I suppose someone must have thought their reports would come in handy.'

That sounded to me like a military wrinkle on policing methods I was familiar with from before the war: once you've got your hands on a known villain, peg every unsolved crime you possibly can on him. From the lofty heights of the upper ranks they had seemed to think it a better way of clearing up unsolved cases than looking for the real culprits.

A pragmatic way of dispensing justice, I thought, and one that was a mite too cynical for me. I'd never been entirely happy with that sort of thing, but being on the bottom rung of the force I didn't have an opinion and was expected to do as I was told. It wasn't that I was concerned one way or the other about the known villains, more that I was conscious of the unknown ones getting away with something. Now it seemed to be much the same with the 25th SS-Panzer Grenadiers: once you've given a dog a bad name, one more crime won't make their name any blacker. Jekyll had said he wanted the matter wrapped up quickly and it seemed I was still in the position of being expected to do as I was told.

'Who have you got?' I asked Stan.

He pushed the file towards me. 'An SS-Mann named Werner Richter.'

'Was he at the abbey?'

'No, but that's the point.'

'Is it? Why?'

'Werner kept a diary. When they started questioning him about the abbey, he was able to furnish a day to day account of where he was from the day the battalion arrived in Normandy to the day they put him in the bag. That was the end of August when the Canadians broke through the Falais pocket.'

'The Canadians took him?'

'I know what you're thinking, boss, that the Canucks settled a lot of scores with Hitlerjugend, but Richter was only wounded. He was interrogated about the massacre but was able to show them that when the Canadians were murdered at the abbey he was with his platoon in Caen, not at Meyer's HQ.' Stan consulted the file again. 'Platoon commander was a lieutenant, SS-Obersturmführer Franz Müller.'

'What about July 10th?'

'Whoever wrote up the interrogation wasn't interested in July 10th. They were investigating the abbey massacre.'

'What good is it, then?'

Stan's face turned smug again. 'His diary names some of the other men in his platoon. One of them was SS-Unterscharführer Otto Vogel.'

'Vogel? Well done *Stan*,' I said. 'So, do we have the diary?'

'Not the diary, no—'

'Where is it? Don't tell me they gave it back to Richter...'

'Doesn't say.'

'Have we got anything on Müller?'

'Not a file, boss, no, but we do have this,' and he passed some sheets of paper to me.

There were about a dozen sheets, smudged photocopies of small handwritten pages that appeared to have been taken from a notebook.

'What are they?'

'Copies of excerpts from Richter's diary. At least, the pages that cover the time from when the 12SS-Panzer Division arrived in France until Richter was put in the bag.'

It was barely legible. Smudges, as I said, faint from an over-used photocopier, and worst of all, of course, in handwritten German.

'You can make out the dates,' Stan said. 'There are entries for July 10th and 11th.'

That was about all I could make out. My time in Germany had furnished me with enough of the language to hold up one end of a very basic conversation and to be able to buy a beer or a bottle of schnapps.

'Where's Peter?'

Susie looked up from her desk. 'He's still going through the War Diaries of the 7th Hampshires.'

'Couldn't he get copies? Never mind. When he comes in give him this.' I put the photocopies on her desk. 'Priority.'

Peter had better German than any of us. Not as good as his French, but good enough. Whether he'd be able to decipher SS-Mann Richter's handwriting was another matter. If not, I supposed I'd have to make other arrangements. At least we'd found a lead to SS-Unterscharführer Vogel, the man on whose body they'd found William Kearney's ID discs.

I left Stan to comb through the rest of our files for the five or six other names Richter had given his interrogator and went back into my own office.

'We're looking for the interrogation report on an SS officer,' I told Jack. 'SS-Obersturmführer Franz Müller, 25th SS-Panzer Grenadiers. Don't know what POW camp he's in now but he would have been picked up sometime between July 11th and the end of August forty-four. Stan's got some more names for you, too.'

Jack's shoulders slumped like a man who'd just been handed a hundredweight sack.

'I know,' I said, 'but it's the leg-work that gets results.'

'Wouldn't mind some *leg*-work,' Jack complained. 'Sittin' in this bleedin' chair's giving me blisters on my arse.' He sighed ostentatiously and wrote down the name, then passed me a letter that had come in that morning.

It was a reply from the Red Cross about POWs named Kearney. I took it to my desk and lit a cigarette. Jack had already sorted through the possibles, which left us with just two Kearneys named William, both of whom might fit the dates. Of them, the least likely of the two had been captured at Arnhem following the airborne landings, been badly injured and died of his wounds two months after being taken prisoner. It hardly seemed likely to me, though, that *our* William Kearney would have made his way to Arnhem, seeing as at the time he disappeared—as well as at the time of the airborne landings—it was a long way behind enemy lines. The other Kearney had been bagged during the German Ardennes offensive, their last throw of the dice in the west. He'd been in an infantry battalion and had spent five or six weeks as a POW before being released and repatriated. There was an Edinburgh address for him but no phone number. I thought it was hardly likely that our Kearney would be in Edinburgh—excepting a *Random Harvest* loss of memory and the thought of how Susie would react to that persuaded me not even to contemplate the possibility.

Between his phone calls I irritated Jack further by asking him to check the Red Cross information with the battalions given, and see if he couldn't get some clarification. It was hardly unknown for lost men to wind up in units other than those they had begun with, but that was more common during retreats than offensives. Having said that, though, the fighting in the Ardennes Forest had been so confusing it hadn't been easy to tell who was going which way. A phone number might be enough to sort the matter out or, failing that, Colonel G might arrange for a local man to visit. What I didn't want, was to have to send one of us up to Edinburgh on what was most likely a wild goose chase. Particularly as we now had a possible link to the Hitlerjugend, and in the vicinity of Maltot.

~

Since it was Friday we expected a visit from Colonel G who, no doubt, would be bringing along expectations of our having made some progress. So I spent the next hour preparing a report for him, then I went out for lunch and treated myself to a pint and a sandwich.

When I got back I found to my surprise Jack had already received an answer to his enquiry concerning SS-Obersturmführer Franz Müller. He'd started with the office that had dumped the boxes of files on us when our section had first been established. They told Jack they had had the original file of Müller's interrogation.

'Are they sending it on?'

'No.'

'Why not?'

'Not available,' said Jack.

'What do they mean, not available? Is someone else using it or have they lost the thing? Or perhaps they're worried if they give it to us *we* might lose it. Haven't they got another copy?'

'Didn't specify,' said Jack.

'Well get back to them and *ask* them to specify.'

'Right-you-are,' said Jack.

'Did Stan give you the other names?'

'Still working on it,' said Jack.

'Better still,' I decided, 'find out what camp Müller is being held in if they know. SS-Mann Werner Richter, too. Richter was wounded but unless it was a bad injury he won't have been repatriated yet. Don't know what condition Müller was in. Tell them we want to interview both of them, particularly Müller. Let them know who we are and if a mere captain isn't good enough for them refer them to Colonel G. And I still want to know what happened to the original interrogation file on Müller.'

Barring bad injury, there was a good chance that Müller and Richter were still being held in one of the POW camps. Until earlier in the year, apart from men who had been hospitalized, there had been no repatriation at all of German POWs. There were still tens of thousands of them in the country, working mostly in either construction or agriculture. Repatriation had finally started, but only of those prisoners deemed not to have been hard-core Nazis. And SS would have been rated as hard-core. I was pretty confident that we were going to find someone like SS-Obersturmführer Franz Müller was still kicking his jackbooted heels in one or other of the camps.

Before Jekyll arrived I got everyone together in the front office to make sure we had got our facts straight so as not to contradict each other when the time came.

While I was at lunch Peter had returned from consulting 7th Hampshires' War Diaries. He had also turned up a blackboard and chalk from somewhere and was drawing a diagram of Operation Jupiter on it. He had even acquired a swagger stick with which he planned to point out the salient details to Jekyll. More impressive still was a new map he had managed to get hold of: an *Institut Géographique National* map—the French equivalent of our Ordnance Survey. It was a good scale, 1:25,000, and detailed the exact area west of Caen we were interested in. It had been over-printed by the Intelligence unit of 43rd Division and showed the position of several Panzer Groups and two Divisions. Where Peter had managed to lay his hands on the map I'd no idea but, treating it as too precious to mark, he was using the blackboard for diagrams and would only go as far as sticking pins in his precious map. He was transferring the flags from the old map to the new as I watched.

'The map was overprinted before the Jupiter offensive but turned out less than accurate unfortunately.' He ran a hand over the map's contours. 'German strength was underestimated. That's why breaking out into the open ground beyond the River Orne proved so difficult.'

That hardly came as a surprise. Most armies tend to underestimate their enemy. Two years down the road, though, it was water under the bridge—or maybe down the Orne; what mattered most was demonstrating to Colonel G that we were on top of the job.

'Susie gave me the photocopy of Richter's diary. I've got the translation here.' He rummaged through the paper on his desk.

'You've done it already?'

'You're only interested in July 10th and 11th aren't you? The entries were short, it wasn't too difficult.'

'What does it say?'

Peter peered at his own handwriting as if he found it harder to decipher than Richter's German. 'What was left of the 25th SS-Panzer Grenadiers pulled out of Caen on July 8th,' he said, 'as we already knew. According to Richter, the remnants of his platoon occupied some buildings near Maltot. Somewhere he calls the *Strandhaus*.'

'What's that in English?'

'Translates as beach house.'

'But there isn't a beach there,' I said. 'It's miles from the sea.'

'There's the river,' Stan suggested.

'The Orne,' Peter agreed. 'It must have been somewhere on the river.'

'Is the château near where the carrier was found on the river?'

'I don't think so. Apart from the Château de Fontaine which is some distance from Maltot to the north-west, the only château I've found near the village that was mentioned in the War Diaries is the Château de Maltot.'

'How many châteaux can there be in a place the size of Maltot?' said Stan.

'Quite,' I said, 'and the carrier wasn't actually *at* the château and there's no reason to suppose Richter and the rest of Müller's platoon were there either. It was probably an HQ or command post so they'd probably be nearby.'

Peter grunted in a way I'd come to recognize suggested he wasn't altogether convinced.

'Was there anything else in Richter's diary?'

'Yes. Quite interesting as a matter of fact. Richter says they were ordered to the Strandhaus and that when they arrived they found the owner still there along with two Gestapo officers.'

'Gestapo?' said Jack. 'What would they be doing there?'

'Richter didn't say. The place was supposed to have been occupied by a company of the 10th SS-Panzers but they'd already pulled out. 9SS Hohenstaufen were supposed to relieve them but Müller and his platoon had orders to stay until told to withdraw. The rest of the 12th were engaged with the attack on Maltot. The next couple of entries are pretty brief. They pulled out on the evening of the 10th and Richter notes as they withdrew they met 9SS Hohenstaufen moving up.'

'Nothing about the carrier or Dabs, then?' I said.

'I'm afraid not. Richter made a few notes on how hard the fighting had been and the names of a couple of his comrades who'd been killed, but that's all.'

'Pity,' I said. 'Still, life wasn't meant to be easy.'

'That's usually what people say when they want you to do something nasty,' Jack observed.

'See what else Richter has to say when you've got the time, will you Peter? You never know, one of the later entries might mention something relevant.'

'I'll take it home and go through it tonight.'

'All work and no play...' warned Susie.

'This is Peter,' I reminded her. 'Jack's already a dull boy.'

'I resent that,' said Jack.'

'You'll get over it. Put the kettle on and get it ready for Colonel G,' I said. 'He'll be here shortly.'

~

Susie had managed to lay her hands on some cupcakes and I'd got a half-bottle of scotch in, in case he wanted something stronger than tea. It might sound as if we were in the habit of brown-nosing our superior officer, but we weren't usually that toadyish. It was mostly that after my abortive meeting with him at the Rag, I could see no reason to put his back up any further.

He arrived at three o'clock and found everything set up and all of us waiting. I could tell he was impressed by Peter's map because he strode immediately across the office and began peering with his one eye at the contour lines delineating the country between the Rivers Odon and Orne.

Peter, in his rather ponderous lawyerly fashion, began by outlining Montgomery's objective in the series of operations around Caen; attempting to keep the bulk of the German armour occupied defending the ground to the west and south of Caen, and so enabling the American forces further west to break out into more open country.

After about ten minutes, he got Operation Jupiter under way, getting 8-Corps over the River Odon and taking the villages of Baron-sur-Odon and Fontaine-Étoupefour.

He chalked a fresh arrow on the blackboard. 'Resistance was stiff, particularly at the château—'

'Which château is this?' asked Jekyll.

'Château de Fontaine—between Hill 112 and Éterville. It wasn't much more than a ruin although 10SS-Panzers were well established. Jupiter's first objectives were achieved by mid-morning. The next phase of the operation was to take the high ground here.' He rapped his swagger stick against Hill 112 on the board. 'The enemy was dug in on the rear slopes with Panthers and Tigers. Our Churchills had good armour but poor guns—the M10s, good guns but poor armour. And open turrets, of course. So something of a mismatch—'

I cleared my throat noisily, trying to alert Peter to the fact that Jekyll was getting restive. The only château mentioned so far hadn't been the right one and I wanted to hurry things along. Peter, though, didn't take the hint. He waited a second, assuming I had something to add and when I didn't, continued:

'Hill 112 overlooked the ground not just to the north and the Château de Fontaine, but the villages of Éterville and Maltot...'

'If it wasn't Château de Fontaine,' Jekyll interrupted, 'near which château was the carrier and Dabs found?'

'That would be here, sir, in Maltot,' Peter said, sliding his stick a little across the map. He pointed to a blood-red flag that represented Kearney's carrier. 'The Château de Maltot, between the village and the River Orne.'

He paused for another question but as Jekyll seemed satisfied he continued:

'Early in the morning 7th Hampshires supported on their right flank by 5th Dorsets moved up to Maltot. Unfortunately they found the village to be far more heavily defended than they'd been led to believe. They managed to superimpose themselves on the hamlet but only by leaving pockets of the enemy still in place. The village changed hands several times during the day but by 1300 hours it was a stalemate. 7th Hampshires' B Company to which Sergeant Kearney's carrier was attached on the left flank of the attack penetrated furthest, almost to the banks of the Orne River. Communications were lost, though, and subsequent counter-attacks and flanking manoeuvres from the German positions Hampshires had by-passed almost wiped them out. Those not killed were taken prisoner. Not many men made it back to our lines.'

'Prisoners were taken?' said Colonel G.

Peter, still looking at the map, cocked his head to one side and didn't seem to hear.

'I said,' Jekyll repeated, 'prisoners *were* taken?'

'Sorry sir. Yes, they were.'

'Although Dabs was executed.'

'Well,' Peter replied, frowning and still glancing at the map as if something was troubling him, 'we're not entirely sure he was, are we? After all, there's always the possibility his wound was the result of skirmishing.'

I glared at him but he didn't notice. We hadn't even discussed this possibility. It was just the sort of complication I had gathered us all together to avoid before Jekyll arrived. But before I could repair the damage, Peter was off again.

'By mid-afternoon under the impression that the Hampshires had secured the village, 4th Dorsets were sent to relieve them. They were surprised to meet some units of the Hampshires withdrawing to the northern edge of Maltot. The Dorsets attempted to secure the position and the Dorsets' A Company followed the line Hampshire's B Company had taken and suffered a worse fate. They were lost to a man.'

Jekyll got to his feet. 'You've obviously done your homework, Peter,' he said, spoiling the compliment by looking ostentatiously at his watch. He leaned over the desk towards the map, claiming the last cupcake which had been sitting on the plate in isolation, no one else having the effrontery to take it. 'When was the body of Dabs found?'

Peter had become preoccupied with the flags on his map again so I said:

'Operation Express, thirteen days later. It was found on the drive of the château and according to the diary of an SS private named Werner Richter, we can place at least one platoon of the 25th SS-Panzer Grenadiers close to the Château de Maltot—'

'*Almost* place,' Peter demurred once more. We do still have to verify their exact location.'

'We're not going to quibble just because Richter called it a *beach* house,' I replied irritably. 'Kearney's ID discs were found on the body of Unterscharführer Otto Vogel and he was a member of this particular platoon. It was commanded by...' But in my irritation

I'd forgotten the man's name. I looked to Peter but he was moving his damn flags again.

'Obersturmführer Franz Müller,' Susie piped up.

Colonel G gave her the benefit of one of his rare smiles. 'And this is the 25th...?'

'25th SS-Panzer Grenadiers,' I reminded him. 'Hitlerjugend. The 25th had been Kurt Meyer's regiment. They were the men responsible for the Ardenne Abbey massacre.'

'Well,' Jekyll said, 'if you've managed to put SS from that regiment on the spot I don't see the need to pursue this much further. They recovered three bodies, correct? Which just leaves this sergeant...'

'Kearney,' I said.

'One assumes he wasn't the only missing man?'

'Sir?'

'During Operation Jupiter. You do have a number on missing personnel?'

'Missing as opposed to dead?' I asked, playing for time while Peter sifted through the papers on his desk again.

'Missing,' said Jekyll curtly.

'Only casualties for 7th Hampshires at the minute, sir,' Peter said. 'Eighteen officers and two hundred and eight Other Ranks.'

'I can't imagine this Kearney was the only missing man,' said Jekyll. 'You said 7th Hampshires' B Company was lost? The company to which Kearney's carrier was attached?'

'All but those taken prisoner, sir,' Peter said. 'And a few who managed to get back to our lines.'

'Well, I can't see the point in spending any more time on Kearney.'

'No, sir. I've examined 7th Hampshires' War Diaries, but none of the survivors shed any light on what happened to his carrier.'

'On the other hand,' I said, unwilling to let go of Kearney altogether, 'if his body's found and he was shot in the back of the head like Dabs, we can assume it wasn't the result of Peter's skirmishing and we've got two executions.'

Jekyll shrugged. 'Two killed when the carrier was destroyed...? Dabs executed by the SS. You said Kearney's ID discs found on the body of a dead SS soldier? I think we can already assume Kearney met a similar fate. You're certain the man who had Kearney's discs was in this Müller's squad?'

'According to the evidence of Richter's—'

Jekyll turned to Peter, cutting me short. 'Anything untoward as far as other men missing following this engagement?'

Behind his glasses, Peter looked like a rabbit caught in headlights. 'Nothing reported as far as we're aware, sir. But we're still looking, naturally.'

One might have thought it a natural avenue to explore, but the fact was we hadn't been looking to see if there had been any other incident like the Dabs' shooting. No one had told us to. Nor had it occurred to me that it might be expected. I saw Jekyll glance at his watch again so I asked Susie if there was any more tea, on the principle that giving someone a reason to stay if they're short of time always hurries them out the door.

'Not for me, thank you Blake,' Jekyll told Susie. 'I'd better be on my way. Good work, Peter. Tidy up the details and I think we can put this one to bed.'

He looked pointedly at me so I followed him out the door and down the stairs.

'We've got some likely suspects here, Harry. Vogel had Kearney's discs. Richter puts him there. I can't see any point in looking under every stone.'

'No sir, of course not. It was just that since you specifically dropped the file off...and what with that letter from Kearney's sister, I—'

'Sister?'

'His sister, Rose? I assumed there was a particular reason...' I let the statement hang, wondering whether I should mention Sir Maurice Coveney again.

Jekyll shook his head as if it had nothing to do with him.

'I was merely asked to pass it along to you. Nothing more. A bad business, but that's war.' We reached the street and he stopped. 'That Major you asked about, Hendrix, was it? No trace. You did have the right name? Anyway, I wouldn't worry too much about him. Crossed wires most likely. Square this one up as soon as you can.' He put on his cap, tipped a finger to it and strode off in the direction of Great Portland Street.

I climbed back up to the office. 'That's pretty clear,' I told the others. 'He wants it squared up as soon as possible so we have to pin it on the 25th.'

Peter was looking less than happy. I didn't know if it was the embryonic barrister in him taking exception to the suggestion we should attribute to the SS the murder of a man we weren't even sure was dead, or whether he had taken umbrage because Jekyll had grown restive during his presentation of Operation Jupiter. Had it been the former, I could have told him the Metropolitan Police had never been adverse to pinning something on a likely suspect if the cap fit. So why should we expect the army to be any different? And in my opinion, just about any cap fit the SS as snugly as a Balaclava.

'So what does he want us to do exactly?' asked Stan.

'What officers usually want you to do,' Jack observed. 'Do what you're told and as quickly as possible. And don't get it wrong.'

'For once,' I said, 'Jack's cynicism isn't far off the mark. Jekyll wants us to wrap it up as quickly as we can but he'll also expect us to make it convincing. In that case, let's see if we can't find anything else concerning the SS men we've got names for. Who knows? Maybe one of them kept a diary, too, and we'll get lucky and stick the pin in the proper place.

'First we'll get back to the Dorsets and the Hampshires, just on the off chance there's anything else we ought to be looking at—any other missing men or suspicious deaths. More suspicious than getting blown apart by a Tiger tank, I mean.'

'Right,' said Peter. 'I'll get on to that.'

'Give him a hand, Susie, if you will.' I glanced at the clock. 'Though by now half of those you need to contact will probably have left on weekend leave.'

'Even if they're not,' Susie said looking at me expectantly, 'they won't be keen on going through their files at this time of a Friday.'

'Okay,' I relented. 'There's nothing that won't wait until Monday. We'll start fresh next week. Go on, clear off. You've earned it.'

Jack and Stan looked like a pair of dogs wanting their reward, too; Jack a wire-haired terrier getting a bit grizzled round the muzzle, and Stan a bull-mastiff as likely to take a bite out of you as lick your hand.

'First thing Monday, Jack, start contacting the Barnardo homes and see if you can't find out where Joseph Dabs was brought up. Despite what he said, Jekyll won't thank us for missing something he thinks we should have seen. We've talked to the other families so let's tidy it up for Dabs as well. Did someone say he was a Londoner? Start in London anyway. When you get a hit perhaps you can follow it up, Stan. Some of those kids came up the tough way and they're less likely to bugger you around than the rest of us. Dabs is the one we know least about and apart from his discs the only ID we've got is from a visual, and that almost a fortnight after he died. I don't know how far decomposition had got but it was July and he was shot in the head. Chances are they just took it to be Dabs because of the discs.'

I didn't elaborate, but there were also the animals to take into account: birds, foxes, badgers, stray dogs and cats. Admittedly there wouldn't have been a shortage of bodies for scavengers after Epsom and Jupiter although excepting those blown apart, the bodies were wearing uniforms. Dabs' face would have been exposed. Easy pickings. Not much of a thought to start a weekend on.

Jack began clearing his desk and I shuffled a few papers around on mine before ringing the number I had for Rose Kearney again on the off-chance of catching her. She had seen Hendrix and despite Jekyll having dismissed him as irrelevant, I didn't like loose ends. I thought I might get some sort of description of the elusive major out of her.

Jack said goodnight while I was listening to the phone in Rose Kearney's hallway ring. Finally giving up, I went into the other office. Susie had gone and Peter just leaving. Stan was just hanging around. He regarded me with a thoughtful expression that really didn't suit him.

'What's all this "tidying it up for Dabs" business?' Stan said once Peter had left. 'What can his background have to do with anything?'

I was about to give him some flannel about covering all eventualities and leaving no stone unturned, despite what Jekyll had said. But in the end I simply shrugged.

'Aren't you happy pinning this on the SS, boss?'

'I'm not sure,' I said. 'It's not so much that I don't believe they shot Dabs. Kearney too, probably. It's just I've got this feeling there's something more to it all.'

'Why? Because of this Hendrix bloke asking questions?'

'In part. Jack may be right and Rose Kearney making a nuisance of herself simply meant the file got shuffled along and happened to come to us. Jekyll *says* he was only passing it on, but he's keen on it and for us to reach a quick conclusion. I just don't want to get it in the neck later for not having done the obvious. No harm in making sure we're covered. After all, it's not as if we've got anything else particularly urgent on at the moment.'

'You're worrying about it too much,' Stan said. 'You ought to put in for some leave. Take a couple of days off. Like you said, we've nothing else on and Jack and Peter can handle this business.'

I was about to ask him if this new-found solicitousness for my mental well-being and eagerness to get me out of the way could have anything to do with Ida being back at my flat. I didn't though and said instead:

'I've just been trying to get hold of Kearney's sister...'

'What for?'

'Rose met Hendrix. I thought I might at least get a description of him out of her.'

'Oh well,' said Stan, 'I don't see there's any need for Jekyll to know if we dig a bit deeper. After all, if nowt turns up it's not going to make any difference is it. We can still tell him it was the SS.'

'Exactly,' I said.

'And even if they *didn't* shoot Dabs and Kearney, they certainly shot a lot of other poor buggers we don't know about. If they cop for it, fair enough.'

'Ever thought about joining the police?' I asked.

'Me?' he said. 'Not likely. I can't wait to get out of this uniform, never mind get into another one. I've had a gutful of saying *sir* to every Tom, Dick and Harry with a pip on his sleeve.'

I opened the office door and followed him out. 'I can't say I remember you ever called this particular Harry anything but boss,' I said.

Stan shrugged. 'Well, you're different, aren't you? You're a ranker at heart, just like me.'

There wasn't any ready answer for that so I asked instead what he had planned for the weekend.

'As a matter of fact I thought I'd ride back with you and see how Ida's settling in. If you've no objections, boss.'

'Me?' I said. 'Why should I mind? Us enlisted men have got to stick together.'

~

Although I hadn't said so, Ida had made herself quite at home. Rather than wake her that morning I'd left her the door key on the kitchen table so she could get in and out while she got herself organized. I hadn't told Stan but the evening before I'd made an excuse to go out for an hour and left her to it. When I got home, I found her cooking dinner for me. She said she'd already eaten and while I ate told me she'd acquainted herself with the old girl who lived on the top floor. She'd also met Sam the housebreaker from the floor above.

Grateful as I was for a decent meal for once, my first reaction was that Ida was going to prove something of a problem. But I was wrong and as soon as she had washed up she took a bucket of water into the room she'd chosen down the hall and spent the rest of the evening cleaning and scrubbing. Feeling guilty, I made a half-hearted offer of help which, fortunately, she turned down.

Considering the meagre ingredients I'd had to hand in the flat, she'd turned out a surprisingly good meal and I thought if I picked up a few more things in the morning there might be the prospect of finding dinner waiting for me again when I got back that evening. Luckily, though, it had slipped my mind; finding Ida cooking for me was something I didn't want to have to explain to Stan.

On the tube to Farringdon, I asked him to find out from Ida if the officer who had visited her in Blackburn saying he was from Arnold Poole's battalion was our Major Hendrix again. If he could get a description from her, I might be able to tally it with one from Rose.

Stan, though, had moved on and seemed keener on telling me how he'd already found Ida a mattress and also managed to scrounge some furniture and a stove. He had arranged with a mate of his who had the loan of a lorry to bring them round the following morning. They planned to wrestle the rusted bedstead we'd seen in one of the derelict flats into Ida's room at the same time.

Sensing his enthusiasm, I hoped it didn't squeak.

~

In the hall I picked up my mail and left Stan to it. There was a letter from Penny saying that Julia had told her I'd called round on Sunday morning and apologizing for having left early. She said she was sorry to have missed me and was so reasonable about it I found there was nothing I could take exception to. It seemed that we only wanted to argue when face to face. There was little else of note in the letter except Penny's amusement at the problem Julia was having with her help.

Reading this, I couldn't help wondering if Penny's motive in telling me was because she knew I would also find it funny, or if she was trying to make some more devious point.

Following her demobilization and move down to Gloucestershire to share the cottage my mother had taken after George was conscripted into the Land Army, Penny had done all her own cleaning and shopping. Something that would never have occurred to her before the war, and something with which Julia still hadn't come to terms. Whatever Penny's motive, I noticed she barely mentioned my mother or George, and she ended by saying she would let me know the next time she was coming up to town.

I propped the letter against the saltcellar on my kitchen table and thought it might be a nice touch if I replied. I did pen a few lines but found I wasn't in the mood for letter writing. In fact, the mood to write letters rarely came over me. I wasn't one of the world's best correspondents and though I'd written to Penny while overseas, of course, I hadn't written as frequently as I should have. Even when I did, I usually spent most of the letter making excuses for my dilatory response, pleading the situation...the lack of time...and—not so subtlely—the dangers I was experiencing. Not the most intelligent thing to do I realized later, when picturing Penny and Julia sheltering from falling V1s under the kitchen table or wherever it was they took refuge.

Whether it was the recollection of my own correspondence or something else that had been nagging at the back of my mind, I wasn't sure, but I started to think about other letters, those Arnold Poole had written to Ida. Susie had read them and had thought them touching, and I supposed Susie was sufficiently well-versed in the form to know what she was talking about. Yet I found this difficult to square with what else we knew about Poole. Even his father had described his son as a bit flash...

I dropped onto the settee, suddenly tired. I was over-thinking it. Perhaps Stan was right and I needed a few days away. I felt a sense of *déjà vu*, Jekyll reminding me of the old superintendent I'd had before the war whose only concern as far as police work went was squaring up the paperwork so the division looked good. I'd always thought it was about the people and now it seemed I was falling into the same trap. Perhaps Jekyll was right after all and the sensible thing to do was simply to lay it all at the door of the SS.

But if that was the sensible thing to do, why did it make me feel so uncomfortable?

12

Saturday June 22nd 1946

Despite it being a Saturday morning, I got up early, put on my uniform and left the flat before anyone was about. Ida hadn't used the settee, presumably having found a bed elsewhere and if there was a possibility it was one she had shared with Stan, I thought running into him would be embarrassing for both of us. So I went for a walk, bought some cigarettes and a newspaper and found a café where I could sit over a mug of tea until I thought the time respectable enough to make a call on Rose Kearney.

After an hour or so, I took the tube at Farringdon and changed onto the Bakerloo line, curious to see what the Luftwaffe had done to Kilburn High Street. An age-old thoroughfare and part of what had once been the old Roman Watling Street, I had been fairly familiar with the area before the war. Compared to some parts of London I found it had got off reasonably lightly and, passing the Gaumont State cinema, I was pleased to see that it had survived the Blitz. The place had opened eighteen months or so before war broke out and I'd taken Penny there several times while courting her. It was a big, plush art-deco confection that at the time I thought might impress her. Eight years of the tainted breath of half a million coal fires had stained it black though, and where once it had looked like something out of a Busby Berkley musical it now had more than an air of Fritz Lang's *Metropolis*. It sometimes seemed that the German air force hadn't needed to destroy London—the city was quite capable of suffocating itself under its famous smog. Something I'd forgotten until I got back.

By mid-morning I thought it unlikely I'd catch Rose Kearney in her dressing gown and I made my way to Kilburn Lane. Down towards the junction of Carlton Vale and Albert Road I found some bad bomb damage but turning into Claremont Street it wasn't easy to tell if the German air raids had taken an extra-special toll or whether the place had always been a bit of a dump. Entering the house I caught the tang of someone's burnt toast, walked up the stairs and knocked on Rose's door.

It opened straight away which caught me by surprise—no chain or eye peering through the crack—and instead of Rose I found myself looking at a young man in a stained collarless shirt with his sleeves rolled up high enough to give a good view of a set of impressive biceps. For a second the young man stiffened and I thought I saw a reflex in his right arm. Then he relaxed.

'Patrick, is it?' I asked.

'No Patrick here, mate,' he said, subtlely accentuating the mate.

'I was looking for Rose. Rose Kearney.'

His eyebrows lifted a little higher than his arm had but he shook his head.

'No Rose either. If you're looking for the people who had the place before us, they've gone.'

'When?'

He shrugged. 'We moved in Thursday. Don't s'pose it had been empty long, though.'

'Did they leave a forwarding address?'

'All they left was a bloody mess. Me an' the wife are still trying to clear it up.'

'What about their post?'

He shrugged again. 'Maybe they didn't get any. Friends of yours were they?'

'I'd met her a couple of times.'

'Oh yeah?' He glanced over his shoulder and leaned closer to me, pulling the door to. 'What was she like?' he asked, lowering his voice. 'The woman next door said there was always men in and out of here, all times of day and night. On the game, was she?'

The thought of the Rose Kearney I'd met entertaining clients seemed absurd; plain and dowdy and a stranger to cosmetics, she hadn't been my idea of a tart; but perhaps they did things differently in rural Ireland.

'I'm here about her brother,' I said to put him straight. 'He went missing in Normandy. What about your landlord? Would he know where they went?'

'Doubt it. They scarpered owing two weeks. That's how we got the place, paying their back rent.'

He said he didn't know who owned the property but gave me the address of the agent who collected the rent every week.

'Been out long?' I asked him before I left.

'A couple of months. Signal Corps. How'd you know?'

'You started to salute.'

He laughed. 'Bad habit, that.'

'You'll get over it,' I said.

Walking back towards Kilburn High Street and the address of the letting agent, I passed the *Minstrel Boy*, where I'd met Rose the previous Tuesday. The young man said he and his wife had moved into the flat on Thursday and I wondered if Rose had already left when she rang me, and if that was why she arranged to meet in the pub. The place wasn't open yet although a couple of men were hanging around outside smoking and looking at their watches. Seeing them made me wonder who the men going in and out of the flat had been. This pair looked at me as I passed but they weren't the ones who had been in the pub when I met Rose Kearney there. I thought about asking if they knew her or her cousin Patrick but doubted they'd tell me if they did.

The letting agent's office was on the first floor above a greengrocer's shop. Veg was on display on the pavement outside and although what they stocked wasn't exactly a cornucopia the shop wasn't doing bad business. A plaque on a door to the side advertised the letting agency upstairs. I walked up and knocked on the door at the top.

The room held some filing cabinets, a desk and a couple of chairs and a middle-aged man who was pecking at an elderly typewriter with two indecisive fingers. He looked at me through a pair of rimless glasses and shook his head before I even opened my mouth.

'Nothing, I'm afraid,' he said through the smoke curling up his face from the cigarette in his mouth. 'I do my best for you boys coming back but I've nothing at the moment. Leave your name and I'll put you on the waiting list if you like.'

'I'm not looking for somewhere to live,' I said, and gave him Rose Kearney's former address and said I was looking for her or her cousin.

'Oh, *them*,' he said, giving the typewriter some respite and taking the cigarette out of his mouth.

'The new tenant told me they left owing the rent. If that's the case I don't suppose they left a forwarding address.'

'Hardly likely since they did a moonlight. I had a week in lieu but they owed another. And he wasn't her cousin, either. Leastways I can't imagine it. Catholic, weren't they? Told me they were married.'

'*Married*?'

'Well,' he said, seeming surprised at my reaction, 'I didn't ask to see the certificate. They seemed a decent enough couple at the time. Irish, but there's a lot of them here now.'

'How long had they been there?'

He scratched an ear as if it were an *aide-mémoire*. 'Four months, maybe a little longer.'

'And they arrived together?'

'Far as I know. I dealt with her to begin with. Saw him when he signed the agreement and once or twice when I called round for the rent. Then they took to dropping it out of hours through the letterbox here. Mind you, if they hadn't known the man who had the property before them they'd have had to wait. As it was, he was moving out and they were willing to pay a month in advance. Didn't baulk when I told them the rent was going up, neither. Flats being at a premium like they are.'

I didn't expect he'd told the man from the Signals Corps and his wife he'd had a week in lieu when he asked them to pay the rent arrears before giving them the flat, either, but it was a seller's market.

'You don't know where the friend they took the place over from went, I suppose?' I asked.

'No. He was Irish, too.'

'Did they show you any references?'

'Pay book. The husband had just come out of one of the Irish regiments. And like I told you, I try to do my best for you boys.'

'I don't suppose you remember the regiment?'

I reeled off a few Irish regiments and he said:

'That's the one. Royal Inniskilling Fusiliers. Been a sergeant.'

'I don't suppose his name was Kearney?'

'No, Cochrane. That's what the pay-book said. Patrick and Rose Cochrane. All above board.'

I wondered where he'd got it as I didn't expect for a minute he'd actually been in the Royal Inniskilling Fusiliers. Not after everything Rose had said about the British Army. At least his name was Patrick. She hadn't lied about that.

'What's your interest, anyway?'

I gave him the story about Rose's brother.

'What did Cochrane look like?'

The agent screwed up his face as if the question was a real poser.

'Nondescript,' he eventually said, obviously pleased at being able to use the word.

'Tall, short...dark, fair?'

'Dark, I'd say. Not very big either. Ugly fellow, now you mention it, but in a nondescript way, if you follow.

I wasn't sure I did.

'Surprised me he'd got a wife like that, to be honest.'

'Like what?'

'She was quite a looker.'

'Rose? Are we talking about the same woman?'

He seemed surprised again. 'Nicely turned out, she was. Hadn't let herself go like some of the tenants I get. Didn't peg her as the type to do a flit, if you want to know the truth, but it takes all sorts.'

He dug the rental agreement out of his files to show me and I looked at Cochrane's signature. Rose hadn't needed to sign it. He was going to drop it into his basket so I asked if I might keep it.

'Just wastepaper now,' he said. 'Take it if you want.'

I thanked him and took the tube back to Clerkenwell where I found a lorry parked outside the flat and Stan helping a man off-load a cast iron stove. The three of us struggled up the stairs with it to where Ida was waiting dressed in a housecoat and a headscarf, smudges of dust blackening her pretty face. The bruise around her eye had gone down and the split lip had healed a bit more and she was trying to stand out of the way while Stan manhandled the stove on his own, demonstrating I suppose what a healthy young lad he still was. Looking at the two together, I decided Stan hadn't spent the night with her. Something in the way he was behaving reminding me of a love-struck adolescent. Not a pretty sight in a bruiser like him but there's no vaccine for the virus and it doesn't only target the young. I took a leaf out of Ida's book and kept out of Stan's way, too. There wasn't much point in telling him what I'd discovered about Rose Kearney, as his mind looked to be on other things, and Monday in the office would be soon enough.

Back in the flat, I dropped the rental agreement the agent had given me on the table—the place where most of my paperwork fetched up. I still had some bread and found a little piece of cheese in my larder so I bought myself a bottle of beer at the off-licence counter in the pub and made myself some lunch. Sitting at the table I saw the reply to Penny's letter I'd begun the previous evening, read a few lines, then screwed it up and tossed it into the waste bin. Perhaps seeing how Stan was behaving had knocked some of the sentiment out of me, but looking at what I'd written made me embarrassed to think of Penny reading it. So, instead of thinking about her, I thought about Rose Kearney.

Looking on the charitable side I could see a bit there. To give her the benefit of the doubt, her story of having a cousin Patrick might have been no more than a fabrication to hide the fact she was living with a man. And I suppose she was hardly likely to give her name as Kearney to the letting agent while posing as the wife of Patrick Cochrane. Even all that business about her cousin not liking the British army might just have been a spur of the moment excuse for him not to show his face when Susie and I called round.

Given that then, why wasn't I feeling charitable? For one thing I couldn't forget the letting agent describing Rose as a looker. Susie had sensed there was something about her although, beyond the nail varnish, hadn't been able to put her finger on it. It also seemed suspicious that the two of them—Rose and her so-called husband—had done a moonlight flit shortly after I'd got in touch. Coincidence or something more? It was true that apart from the men supposedly visiting the flat I hadn't been the only one to call on her—the mysterious Major Hendrix had also been there—and so it might have been him who spooked her. Just why, though, I couldn't guess. After all, if she had something to hide, why make enquiries about her brother and give out her address?

I thought about Hendrix again and his careless use of different background stories—Graves Commission with Edna Burleigh, Paymaster General's office with Rose, Provost Marshal with Jack...he'd told Ida he was from Arnold Poole's battalion. Jekyll maintained no one knew him but I wasn't ready to take that at face value yet. We knew Colonel G had sections other than ours digging around in his musty files and, despite his claim that he had "just passed" the Dabs' file on to me, it would be typical of Jekyll to deny the existence of one of his own. Even if I had no idea why he'd do it.

And then it occurred to me that if it wasn't Jekyll, there was still another possibility...

I finished my beer, giving the matter some thought before going off half-cocked. Then I pulled out my old address book. Combing through the telephone numbers, I wondered how many still existed. Most were pre-war and some perhaps little more than holes in the ground now. But the only way to find the man I was after was to start ringing so I dug out all the copper from my pockets, went down the hall to the pay phone, and piled my stack of pennies on top of it.

It was rather like trying to find a way through a maze: wrong numbers like wrong turns until someone I'd known, who didn't know the man but knew someone who might, would send me in a different direction. Often it proved a blind path, leading me back to where I'd started, but finally by mid-afternoon I had made some progress. Like slipping through a gap in the hedge, I was given an office number to call. No names, and when I did there was a flat denial the man I was after even worked there. But they took my number—just in case.

That was the way of Special Branch. But I'd learned a trick or two myself about deviousness since I'd first run into Henry Gifford.

13

I first met Gifford a year or two before the war. I was eager and officious back then and not out of the police college long enough to have learned any better. As I have said, the station to which I was assigned meant my beat was around one of the better parts of London, certainly among the most expensive. There was money, a smattering of titles, and several consulates and embassies. Burglary was the worst problem—at least for a copper at my level—and it had been made clear we were there to protect the property and persons of those within our precinct. And that we had better know our place while we were doing it.

One evening sometime after midnight and towards the end of my shift, I happened to notice a car parked in West Halkin Street, lights off, with two men sitting in the front seat. I was on the other side of the road and I walked on, affecting not to notice them. I circled around the block and came back behind the car some ten minutes later. It was still there, as were the men. Approaching the nearside front window, I got out my torch and shone it inside. The window wound down and a thin-faced man squinted up at me from under a trilby hat.

'Move along, sonny, will you? We're working.'

Being eager and officious I didn't take kindly to being called sonny and was about to ask the man to step out of the car when he flashed some sort of identification at me. I didn't get a good look at it and before I could say anything else the driver said, 'Jesus! He's leaving,' and drove off. Leaving me standing on the pavement shining my torch like a fool after them.

I'd been alert enough to get the car number, though, and when I got back to the station gave it to my desk sergeant who said he'd phone it through to the vehicle licensing department. I didn't think anything more of it until I went on shift the next day and the sergeant told me there was someone waiting to see me in our interview room.

Gifford was there, back to me and staring at the wall as if it was a picture window. He was a tall man, dressed in a raincoat and dark trousers and when he turned around, balanced between a pair of ears designed to catch the wind, I saw a face that might have earned him a living as a professional mourner. They seemed the only mark of individuality about him, the ears and a bristle moustache that put me in mind of the novelist George Orwell.

'Inspector Gifford,' he said, by way of introduction. 'Constable Tennant, is it?'

I was standing as stiff as a broom handle not knowing what to expect.

'You took the number of a car last night in West Halkin Street, is that right?'

I said it was, and had been pleased with myself for being sufficiently quick to do so. But if I had been expecting a pat on the back Gifford's tone suggested he hadn't come to commend me. Although I could think of several reasons why I should have taken the car's number, something told me not to offer them in mitigation.

'You were shown a warrant card, is that correct?'

I told him I hadn't got a good look at it before they drove away.

'They were my men,' Gifford said, 'and they were watching one of the houses. You putting your big boot into it might have ruined the whole operation.'

I apologised and was impertinent enough to suggest that if there had been a surveillance operation in our district it might have been helpful if we'd been informed.

'Tell every beat copper what we're up to?' Gifford roared back at me. 'How long do you think that'll be kept under the helmet?'

I didn't think he wanted an answer so kept quiet.

'Smoke?' he asked suddenly, pulling a packet of Craven 'A' cork tips out of his raincoat pocket.

I declined on the grounds of being on duty.

'Quite right too,' said Gifford, then lit one himself and carefully placed the spent match in the clean ashtray on the single square table, treading on a dozen spent matches on the floor as he reached over to do so. 'Well,' he said, expelling a stream of smoke, 'I don't think we can risk another parked car for a night or two. So what's the answer?'

I wasn't sure if this question was rhetorical so didn't reply. When the silence started to become embarrassing, though, I began suggesting hesitantly that since the house in question was on my beat, if I knew which one he was keeping under surveillance, I could keep a watch out myself.

'This isn't a Buck Ryan cartoon,' Gifford replied sarcastically.

I countered that by saying the residents were used to seeing me walk down the street several times a night, and would think nothing of it.

He seemed to consider the suggestion then told me which house he was interested in.

'Nothing out of the ordinary, Tennant. Don't increase the number of times you pass the place. But if you *do* happen to see anyone enter or leave, a car arrive, or anything else at all, just make a note of it and let me know.' He wrote a number on a card and placed it on the table.

Back to being pleased with myself, I assured him I would.

'And the next time you see two men in a parked car along that street, walk on by even if one of them's dressed like the Angel Gabriel, understand?

'And here,' he said, dropping his Special Branch warrant card onto the table in front of me. 'The next time you're shown one of these, you'll know what it is.'

I didn't see anything happen at the house, of course, and my shift was changed before I had a chance to see the men and the car again. After a couple of months, I'd all but forgotten the incident. It only came to mind after Chamberlain returned from Munich with his piece of paper and over the next few months Special Branch made several arrests of suspected spies. Gifford's name may have been mentioned but whether, at the time I met him, he had been looking for German agents or Russian, I couldn't say. He certainly hadn't. And after the Russians and Germans signed their non-aggression pact in August 1939, just a few days before war was declared, it hardly mattered.

By then everyone knew war was inevitable and, after Dunkirk when it became obvious we were on our own, I swapped uniforms. Of course in Berlin a few years later there was no shortage of spies. And no shortage of Intelligence agents supposedly countering them. I never had much to do with them beyond liaising with the local police if one of them got himself in strife, but we all knew SIS had men on the ground and that *they* were liaising with MI5 and Special Branch back home.

Well, that was the way it was supposed to work, and we were expected to stay out of their way. That had suited me then, but the wheel turns and we either make accommodations or we're liable to find ourselves in a seat at the bottom with no view. Those sitting at the top, of course, can see everything that's going on around them.

And that's how I was beginning to feel—sitting at the bottom of the wheel—and if I was ever going to see what was going on around me I decided I needed to do something about it.

~

I left my door open so I'd hear the telephone if it rang but it was gone six in the evening before it did. I clattered down the stairs to catch it before they rang off and was panting so hard I could hardly hear the man on the other end when he said his name was Gifford. I took a deep breath and told him that we had once met. Before the war, when I was in the police force. Now, I said talking myself up, I headed up a military war crimes unit and was concerned I might be in danger of stepping on Special Branch's toes with my latest investigation. I needed some guidance, I told him, and suggested we meet. He didn't sound keen. I assumed he felt his steel toecaps more than sufficient to protect his toes from the likes of me. So that's when, in the vaguest of ways, I dropped Sir Maurice Coveney's name into the conversation. I said I'd heard the Foreign Office might have an interest in the case I was pursuing. Gifford asked where I was and I told him near Farringdon underground station. He named a pub some half-a-mile from it and said, seven o'clock.

I knew the place although had never been inside. When I got there I could see why. It lay at the dingy end of the spectrum London pubs run and, although the competition down among the sawdust and the dirt and the lack of hospitality can often be fierce, this place must have been in the running for a rosette. I found a few drinkers here and there when I walked in, sitting like islands of depression in a sea of silence. Even the barman didn't speak. He merely looked at me with a blend of boredom and expectancy. I asked for a pint of beer, paid for it and took a sip, soon wishing I hadn't. The other drinkers were avoiding being caught looking at me and none, as far as I could see, fit the idea of what I thought Gifford might look like eight years older. I took a table near the door where I could see anyone who came in and left my sour beer to stew in its own juice.

I knew Gifford as soon as he walked in, a fact I can take little credit for as no one else came through the door from ten-to-seven until twenty past. I didn't know what George Orwell looked like after six years of war but Gifford hadn't changed that much. Bespectacled now and a little stooped, as if catching spies in wartime had been a wearing business, he seemed just a touch greyer than I remembered and perhaps more mournful. He walked to the bar without looking around, bought a whisky and came straight to my table as if he'd known me for years.

'Constable Tennant,' he said with what I supposed for him passed as humour.

'You remember me, then?'

'West Halkin Street, wasn't it? You put one of your big boots into an operation of mine.'

'I hope I didn't ruin it,' I said.

'No, my marks weren't that smart. I had your shift changed though. Just in case. I don't suppose you minded—daylight hours are generally more sociable. Or are you like me and prefer the night?'

He was looking at me as if he was genuinely interested in my answer. Oddly it had never occurred to me that it might have been Gifford who had engineered my shift change. Eager, officious and naïve, it seemed.

I shrugged, as if it hardly mattered. 'A police constable just does what he's told.'

'Not now though?' he asked. 'When did you switch to the army?'

'Nineteen-forty.'

'You could have stayed where you were. Even London would have been safer.'

'That's what my wife said.'

'Going back into the force?' He raised two greying eyebrows and regarded me over the top of his spectacles. Had he worn them when we first met? I didn't think so.

'I doubt it,' I replied. 'I can't imagine myself going back as a copper on the beat. Not after—' What I was going to say was not after having the rank of captain and running my own unit, but I didn't finish.

'There's ways,' Gifford said. 'Don't dismiss it out of hand. Unless you've got something else in view...?'

It struck me that I had very little in view beyond the immediate future. It also struck me that although I was the one who had got in touch with him in the hope of learning something, Gifford was the one getting all the information.

'What I called you about,' I said, getting to the point, 'was an investigation I'm conducting into a dead private and a missing sergeant. I'm finding a man called Hendrix getting everywhere before me. Says he's a major but can't make up his mind in what.'

'What's so special about your two men?' Gifford asked.

Exactly what I'd been wondering myself. Beyond the manner of Dabs' death, ostensibly nothing at all. Since I wasn't aware of anything particularly sensitive about our work—certainly nothing I couldn't say to a member of Special Branch—I told him about Kearney and the rest of the carrier crew; how Dabs was found shot in the back of the head.

'We investigate anything that might possibly be classed as a war crime,' I explained. 'Not the big stuff—concentration camps and the wholesale massacres—more run-of-the-mill incidents. Summary execution of POWs...reprisals against civilians...that sort of thing.'

'And who did you say your section was under?'

I hadn't but since it wouldn't have taken him long to find out I gave him Jekyll's name.

'And this Hendrix, you're sure he isn't connected with another unit who might be looking into the same incident? SIB, for instance?'

The Special Investigation Branch were part of the military police but the equivalent of the CID. They came from all the services but mostly from the army, having been formed early on in the war. I had thought it possible that Hendrix was SIB, but any attempt to find out on my part would have had to go through Jekyll and I had to assume he'd already checked.

'Not according to my colonel,' I said.

'Well he's not someone I've run across. Description?'

For a moment I wasn't sure if Gifford meant Hendrix or Jekyll. Assuming he was talking about Hendrix I said:

'No, afraid not.'

The truth is, until recently, it had never occurred to me to ask anyone for a description. People tend to look at the uniform rather than the man. I told him about the carrier crew and how all the family members we'd interviewed had already been approached by Hendrix. 'And the odd thing is,' I said, 'he tells everyone a different story.'

'Oh, how?'

I explained about the Graves Commission and the Paymaster General's Office. 'When he rang my office to make an appointment he said he was with the Provost Marshal.'

'He rang you?'

'My corporal. I didn't speak to him myself. Then he rang back to cancel. Said he couldn't make it and would call again.'

'But hasn't.'

'No.'

'How would he know who the families of the dead men are and where they live, if it's not official?'

'Not a clue. That's why I thought he might be one of yours. Although I suppose if you've got the men's names there are still ways of finding out. It's what we often have to do.'

'You have access to regimental files.'

'As I said, that's why I was wondering if it isn't official. That Hendrix might have some sort of pedigree.'

Gifford had taken out a notebook and jotted a few things down while we talked. He made another note and glanced up at me, eyebrows raised once more.

'William Kearney? Irish?'

'County Wicklow. A place called Ballydrum.'

'The others?'

'No, although it's always possible Dabs might have been. He was a Barnado's Boy so he could have come from anywhere.'

I thought then that I should have mentioned an Irish connection at the outset. Nothing ever concentrates Special Branch's mind more than an Irishman. They had been chasing Fenian tails ever since Cavendish and Burke had been murdered in Phoenix Park seventy years before.

'What about Kearney's family?'

'Only a sister. Her name's Rose. She came over to find out what had happened to him.'

'You've talked to her, I take it?'

'Yes, but not before Hendrix had. He told her he was arranging her brother's back pay.'

I told him then how Rose and her cousin had left their address owing rent. Only that it turned out he wasn't her cousin. Gifford wanted to know about Patrick Cochrane then and I repeated what the letting agent had told me, that Rose and Cochrane had said they were husband and wife.

Gifford rubbed his thumb and finger down the length of his nose as if I had finally said something to stimulate his olfactory sense.

'And what do you think? Married or not?'

'Unlikely,' I said. 'It was probably just a convenience to get the flat.'

Gifford grunted, closed his notebook and slipped it back into his pocket.

'I'll ask around,' he said, lips curling into the smallest of smiles. 'For old time's sake. I'll get in touch with you. Don't ring my office again.'

He glanced down at his glass, assured himself it was empty, then stood up. We shook hands briefly and he left.

I sat at the table with my untouched pint for a few minutes longer, aware that the only thing we hadn't talked about was Maurice Coveney.

~

Instead of going home I walked back to Farringdon station and took the Piccadilly line to Hyde Park Corner. It was a fifteen minute walk to Julia's house from there and passing Belgrave Square found several people sitting on benches under the trees, enjoying the evening.

I hadn't called ahead to warn Julia I was coming; I didn't want to give her an excuse to be out. She might have been out anyway, of course; it was a Saturday night and before the war she had led a busy social life. She still did, I suppose, if her theatre party was any indication, but I didn't have anything to lose. The alternative was to go back to my flat and look at the walls till it was time to go to bed.

Expecting her not to be home, it came as a surprise when she answered door almost as soon as I rang the bell. She looked at me as if she was surprised, too, the expression soon replaced by one of mild irritation.

'Harry,' she said quite tonelessly. 'What a lot we're seeing of you recently.'

The 'we' was the royal pronoun and didn't announce the presence of anyone else. I deduced as much from the fact she had expected someone else when the doorbell rang. But Julia was too well-bred to conduct a conversation on the doorstep and she stepped aside to let me in. We went into the drawing room.

'I'd offer you a drink but I'm expecting a friend any moment.'

And I could see she was dressed for an evening out, even if there was something more restrained about her evening wear than I remembered from before the war. Perhaps it was the lack of jewellery. She wore none except for a pair of discreet earrings and a simple string of pearls. Ostentation had gone out of fashion in much the same way as Jew-baiting had.

'I'll only stay for a second,' I assured her. 'It's just I was wondering how you happen to know Maurice Coveney.'

For a second she seemed nonplussed. That disconcerted me as I'd rarely seen anything disturb the surface of Julia's *sangfroid*.

'Maurice? Why do you ask?'

'I was just curious. The man he brought with him—'

'The fellow in that jacket?'

'His name's Jekyll.'

'I don't recall.'

'I happen to work for him.'

She raised a plucked eyebrow. 'Small world, isn't it?'

I waited for an answer to my original question but when it showed no sign of putting in an appearance went on:

'I was wondering why Jekyll was here and who Coveney might be.'

Julia reached for a cigarette from a box on the table and lit it with a lighter I remembered from when I lived there—a Dunhill gold-plated affair that looked like a petrol can and at a crime scene would have qualified as a blunt instrument. She blew a stream of smoke into the air above my head so as not to fog the few feet between us.

'Maurice Coveney? Surely you've met before? His wife was a good friend of Helen.'

'Penny's mother?'

'They were at boarding school together. Became friends. Helen used to holiday with Marie-Louise's family. She was killed in an air raid four or five years ago.'

'I heard that,' I said.

'Did you know she was coming back?'

This time my *sangfroid* took a knock. For a second I thought she was still talking about Coveney's dead wife and that perhaps Julia had taken up spiritualism.

'You mean Helen?'

'Of course I mean Helen. Reggie needs to see to his business interests.'

As far as I was aware Penny's father's business interests before the war had consisted solely of having his name on the board of several large companies. I didn't know he actually *did* anything.

'When?' I asked. 'The transatlantic passenger service hasn't started again yet. There's the troopships, but even if they manage to get a berth they're not going to find that very comfortable.'

Julia waved her cigarette in the air, leaving a little trail of smoke like one of the new jet aircraft.

'Oh I don't think they've set a date yet. I'm sure Penny will let you know.'

I sensed a certain vicarious pleasure evinced in Julia's tone and assumed she was looking forward to the prospect of me meeting my in-laws again.

Helen and Reggie Forster had scuttled off to America on the outbreak of war. They had wanted Penny to go with them—an invitation which although not specifically voiced had obviously not extended to me. Not that I would have considered it. I was ambivalent about Penny's going, though. Although there was an air of rats leaving a sinking ship about it, since it was my wife's safety being discussed I hadn't let moral scruples get in the way of a decision. Not that it had been mine to make and not that Penny took up the offer. She said her place was with her husband and so, only a little reluctantly, I agreed with her. That was shortly before I joined up and, after training, was posted overseas.

'They're well, I suppose?' was about all I could think to ask Julia.

'Reggie has a heart condition. Nothing serious.'

I resisted the obvious rejoinder. But it was hardly surprising news. Reginald Forster had been flirting with a heart condition for years, eating and drinking too well and too often, his only exercise as far as I knew getting in and out of his chauffeur-driven car.

Before the war he had toyed with the idea of standing for parliament. He had the money and the connections but as the political situation in Europe deteriorated he found himself on the wrong side of public opinion. He had been involved with the Anglo-German Fellowship, a pro-Nazi society that promoted closer ties with the Third Reich and had lobbied for a similar government here. The first time I met him he asked if I was related to an Ernest Tennant, some banker who was secretary of the Fellowship, and soon lost interest in me when I said I wasn't. Similar societies had closed when the nature of Hitler's regime became apparent, but the Anglo-German Fellowship soldiered on until 1939 when, I suppose, the allegiance of its membership began to come under scrutiny. In the end even Reggie resigned, issuing a statement, I recalled, about being "no longer able to tolerate Hitler's anti-Semitic laws and the German government's aggressive policies".

That had come as a surprise to me. In private he was forever ranting about the Jews and Hitler's heroic stand against Jewry's capitalist conspiracy. Somewhat rich, I had always thought, as most socialists would have looked upon Reginald Forster as an archetypical capitalist. I hadn't been politically minded then, nor am much more now, but at least before the war one knew who one's enemies were and it didn't usually turn out to be some East End tailor or music hall comedian whose name happened to be Cohen or Bloom. But there are two sides to every coin and the one thing going for me as a son-in-law was that Reggie was able to tell his friends that at least I wasn't Jewish. Having them back wasn't going to be an unalloyed joy.

The doorbell rang again and Julia stubbed her cigarette out, looking at me pointedly. I didn't follow her down the hall. One man leaving as another man entered might seem too much like a shuttle service. So I waited until she brought her caller into the drawing room and, to my surprise, he turned out to be an American. He was forty-something, short greying hair and well-groomed in an expensively tailored suit. Good-looking, he conducted himself with that laconic ease many Americans possess. A birthright in the home of the brave and the land of the free, perhaps. My surprise was compounded when she introduced him.

'Harry, this is Benjamin Tuchman.'

He didn't look Jewish but there was no escaping his name.

'Harry is Penny's husband,' Julia told him, presumably so there could be no misunderstanding.

'Ben,' said Tuchman as he shook my hand and cast an eye over my uniform. 'Still in, Harry?'

'They'll remember me sooner or later and let me go,' I said. 'I thought you lot had all gone home by now.'

'I like it here,' Tuchman said, giving Julia the benefit of a wide grin. 'Besides, someone's got to keep an eye on the boys we left in Germany.'

'Last time I saw them,' I told him, 'they were doing all right by themselves.'

We carried on in this style for a minute or two until I saw Julia getting restless and said I had to be leaving.

Unlike her brother-in-law, I had never found Julia to be overtly anti-Semitic, although like all her class she couldn't help the odd casual display of prejudice; that was bred in the bone and generally manifested itself through unthinking slights and rudeness. It was one of the things I first liked about Penny: that she didn't seem to have inherited the attitude.

I discovered this the first day I went to the house as a lowly police constable following a break-in. Jewellery had been taken. Penny and her parents were there and when an assessment of the value of the stolen items was required, Penny's father told me I could get one from the Hatton Garden jeweller who had appraised the gems for insurance. The man happened to be Jewish and Reginald Forster made a pointed remark upon the fact—something along the lines of the jeweller's race being untrustworthy and the possibility of his having fingered the house for the raid, no doubt hoping to buy the loot for less than he had valued it. Penny had protested at this only for her mother to tell her not to contradict her father. To her credit, Julia had supported Penny and said the idea was ludicrous; only spoiling her defence by adding that even though the jeweller was Jewish she had always found him to be honest.

As she walked me to the door I was hoping for her own sake that Julia had learned to curb her comments in front of Tuchman.

My first impression of him, however, was that if she had not, he would be quite prepared to tell her so.

'He seems like a nice chap,' I said as I opened the door.

She glared at me, assuming sarcasm I suppose.

'He is, Harry,' and added, deliberately lowering her voice, 'and I like him. So none of your wisecracks please.'

'Wisecracks?' I said with mock surprise. 'Julia, you're already learning the lingo.'

But I didn't count that as a wisecrack.

14

Sunday June 23rd 1946

Sunday morning I heard voices, looked outside my door and found Ida talking to Sam on the stairs. Whether he was on his way out or coming home I couldn't say, although he wasn't carrying a bag marked swag. He nodded to me cheerfully and carried on up to his flat. Coming home, I supposed. I suspected Stan had forgotten I'd asked him to tackle Ida about Hendrix so I asked if she could spare a moment.

She was wearing a rather moth-eaten pullover on top of a faded flowery dress and when her face brightened it didn't seem to matter. There was no longer much sign of the battering she had taken from her husband and, since I'd managed to find some tea, she sat at my kitchen table while I boiled the kettle. She was smiling in an innocent, girlish way that made me think she was probably young enough to be Stan's daughter.

'Settled in?' I asked.

'Thank you, Captain Tennant. It's nice here.'

I crossed Blackburn off my list of places to visit, set the pot to brew for a few minutes and put a loaf of bread on the table. Next to it I placed a jar of jam Penny had brought up from the country the first time she'd come to see me. Ida stared as if it were the Koh-I-Noor diamond. I got her a plate and cut her a slice of bread.

'I've got some marge,' I said, offering her the spread.

She put a little margarine on the slice then carefully took only enough jam to bring a blush to its face.

'Go on, take some more,' I told her. 'It's damson. My wife brought it up from the country and I don't really care for it.'

'You're married?' she asked, taking a bite and smearing jam across her chin.

'She lives with my mother.'

'In the country? I'd like to live in the country.'

I poured the tea. 'You told Stan you'd been visited by someone from Arnold Poole's battalion. Do you remember if he gave his name as Major Hendrix?'

'That's right,' she said, her mouth full of bread and jam. 'Major Hendrix. He asked me about Arnie and his sergeant. What was his name?'

'Kearney.'

'Sergeant Kearney, that's right. He told me Arnie's dad sent him round since Arnie used to write to me regularly. I told Sergeant Woodruff because of the letters.'

The "Sergeant Woodruff" surprised me. But it might have been she was being formal because I was Stan's commanding officer.

'Can you remember anything about him?'

'Like what?'

'Oh, I don't know. What he looked like, for instance?'

She stopped munching long enough to give it some thought. Then she sipped her tea. She wrinkled her nose and shrugged. 'Like an army officer.'

'Tall, short? As tall as me, say?'

'No not as tall as you, Captain Tennant. Quite short, really, now I think about it.'

'Moustache or clean-shaven?'

'Clean-shaven. And he had a little round face, if you know what I mean. Perhaps I shouldn't say it but I thought he looked a bit odd.'

'Odd?'

'It was his nose mostly. A bit like a dog's.'

I tried to think what a dog's nose looked like. Every shape under the sun.

'*How* was his nose like a dog's?'

'Squashed in,' said Ida.

'You mean like a Boxer or a Bulldog?'

'No, smaller. One of those small ones.'

'A pug?'

'Is that what they're called? And his hair was brown and sort of wavy. I remember thinking it looked a bit long for an army officer.'

She seemed to have been quite observant although when I tried to picture all the parts together I ended up with a dispirit mess.

'Did he speak with any sort of accent?' I asked.

She giggled. 'He sounded funny.'

'In what way funny?'

She shrugged again. 'Like in the pictures.'

'Like the movie stars speak, you mean?'

'Not the Hollywood stars. I mean like the British actors. You know, posh, but not quite natural.'

When I enquired as to what Hendrix had asked her, she said she couldn't remember exactly. Mostly about the other men on Arnie's carrier, Sergeant Kearney in particular, she thought. It had seemed a bit odd to her, she said, since as he was from Arnie's battalion she assumed he'd already know all about him. But she hadn't asked because her husband was due home any moment and was worried about what he might think.

'You didn't tell him about your letters?'

Ida blushed. 'I gave them to Sergeant Woodruff. He was nice to me and Johnny—that's my husband—he never liked me keeping them.'

'But you didn't think to give them to Hendrix.'

'No. Perhaps I shouldn't say it, but I didn't like Major Hendrix. You won't tell anyone that, will you?'

I assured her I wouldn't, then asked how she was managing, half-suspecting that Stan might be helping her out with money.

'I'll have to get a job,' Ida said, 'but they're not easy to find.'

'What did you do in Blackburn?'

'I worked in a factory during the war. But we all got the sack when the men came back.'

'There are factories in London,' I said, although I supposed the same thing applied.

Everyone had wanted women to do their bit and take on factory and agricultural work while the war was on and the men were away, but it was a different matter now they were back. Labour was cheap and jobs were scarce. Attitudes had changed, too, and all those women who had worked in service before the war had found a freedom they might never had dreamed before the conflict. Most weren't prepared to go back to the sort of servile work they had done before as a matter of course. Witness Julia's problems, I thought to myself. But that didn't help Ida. Nor Stan if he was helping support her. But maybe he looked upon it as part of a master plan. I couldn't help but feel sorry for the girl, escaping the clutches of one man to perhaps fall under the control of another, decent man though Stan Woodruff was.

She jumped up suddenly and said, 'Ooo, what's the time? I'm being shown the London sights today.'

It was gone eleven. I started to clear the table and pushed the jar of jam towards her.

'Take it. I won't eat it.'

Ida looked at me doubtfully then swept up Penny's jam, clutching the pot to her moth-eaten pullover. She smiled shyly as I saw her to the door. Washing up, I couldn't help thinking what a different proposition Ida from Blackburn was to the oddly confident, Rose Kearney from Ballydrum.

~

Despite the office presumption that we were Colonel G's right hand, he rarely told us what his left hand was doing. So—in a spirit of equitability—when Jekyll dropped in unexpectedly on Monday afternoon, I didn't tell him about Henry Gifford from Special Branch.

When I got back from an early lunch I found him leaning over Susie's desk, talking to her in a voice so low I couldn't catch what he was saying. Peter, who had been on the telephone all morning was adjusting the pins in his map again, taking no notice.

Jekyll straightened up as I came in, nodding to me. I waited, assuming he had some particular reason for being there since we'd only seen him the previous Friday, but he merely asked how the investigation was progressing, as if we had spent the whole weekend in the office.

I made a general comment about waiting for people to get back to us before asking, while trying to sound as off-hand as I could, how he had come to be at Julia's the weekend before last. I had been meaning to ask when I'd joined him for a drink at the Rag, and again on Friday, but the appropriate opportunity never seemed to turn up.

It was obvious he didn't care that it had turned up now, glaring at me indignantly as if I'd breeched some rule of social etiquette. With Susie and the others present, though, he wasn't prepared to be as rude to me as he might had we been on our own.

'A meeting,' he replied curtly. 'Sir Maurice happened to be running late and suggested we talk in the car on his way to his engagement.'

And having now given me an explanation he apparently felt bound to justify the way he had been attired.

'Coveney asked me in for a drink. Had I known it was a formal evening, naturally I wouldn't have accepted. Not dressed as I was.' His Scots nose wrinkled as though he'd just been presented with an over-ripe haggis. 'Rather bad form on Coveney's part, I thought.'

'I don't suppose anyone noticed, sir,' I said, suppressing a smile.

He turned his glass eye on me, no doubt suspecting impertinence.

'Of course, I was surprised to see you there. I had no idea the hostess was your aunt.'

'Wife's aunt actually, sir.'

'So Coveney said.'

'My wife and I lived at the house for a few months when we first married.'

'He said as much. A friend of the family, isn't he? I had assumed you'd met before. Not at the wedding?'

By his tone, I took this to be some reverse impertinence and recalled how Coveney had looked down his nose at me. I suspected the man might have told Jekyll what sort of wedding it had been. Whatever he and Coveney had met to discuss, I had the feeling I had been tacked on under "any other business".'

'No,' I said. 'It was a quiet wedding. We were married at a registry office.'

The fact was, neither Penny's family nor mine had been present. Apart from Julia, that is. And she hadn't really wanted to be there. Having a civil wedding service had been just another stick Penny's family had used to beat me with—one they shared with my mother in this case—despite it having been Penny's idea to get married at a registry office. She maintained she couldn't face one of those elaborate society weddings and, since I was just a lowly policeman and Penny's father had refused to pay for the affair, I was only too happy to agree. Reggie's motive had been to make Penny think twice, of course; it was only afterwards, once I found out how the rest of her family felt about me, that I had begun to question Penny's motive.

But Jekyll was right, Coveney hadn't been at the wedding but it was odd how I had never heard of him before or since. True, I didn't see much of my in-laws before the war—and consequently their friends—even so it seemed surprising that no one had mentioned him, Coveney's wife having been such a good friend of Penny's mother. I wondered suddenly what Penny was in the habit of calling him: Uncle Maurice? If so, it would hardly qualify him as a potential suitor. Equally, if he *did* have designs in that direction, I could hardly believe that Penny's mother would entertain the idea. Then I have found that the upper-classes have a different perspective on that sort of thing: their children, like their pets and their livestock, are often viewed as commodities, particularly useful for alliances and breeding programmes.

My conversation with Jekyll having died a natural death, he had turned to where Peter was still playing with his map. I looked over their shoulders as Peter pointed out the Château de Maltot to Jekyll. But the blood-red pin denoting where the carrier and Dabs' body had been found was no longer there. It had travelled slightly north-east and was now stuck in the middle of a wood bordering the River Orne.

'You've moved the carrier pin,' I said

Peter glanced over his shoulder. 'I had the wrong château. The fighting at the Château de Maltot was pretty fierce and I was thinking on Friday that if Kearney's carrier had been destroyed nearby *someone* would have seen it. But I went through both the Hampshire's and the Dorset's War Diaries for the day but no one mentioned it. 7th Hampshires' B Company was here, you see—' and he pointed to the edge of Maltot village closest to Caen. 'They got nearer the river than the rest of the battalion and must have been under severe pressure. It occurred to me that some of them might have crossed this road here, to Feuguerolles-sur-Orne, looking for cover in the wood perhaps.'

'But how do you know there was a château in the wood?'

'I got on to 43rd Wessex Division. They put me on to the 129th Field Ambulance who recovered the bodies. It's what I should have done in the first place, of course. They confirmed there was a building here—' he gestured to a small square on the map in the centre of the wood. 'The 43rd said that it was known as a château but wasn't a particularly grand house. Nothing but a ruin when they got there, or course, but not a *château* in the strictest sense of the word. But the French often allow themselves some latitude in these matters.'

So much for the French, I thought. I assumed that was what he had been doing on the telephone all morning.

'I was called Château de Hêtres, apparently,' Peter said, 'Hêtres being the French for beeches. I assume the wood is a beech wood.'

I took his word for it, Peter's French being far better than mine. Then the significance of the name dawned on me and I began to laugh. Peter and Jekyll both looked at me as if I'd lost my senses.

'Château de Hêtres,' I said. '*Strandhaus*, as Werner Richter called it. Beach house...*The Beeches*...? A play on words. At least there was one German in Normandy with a sense of humour.'

Jekyll didn't appear to know what I was talking about but Peter offered up the ghost of a smile. It wasn't much of a joke but I don't suppose there was too much else to laugh about during the Normandy campaign. What it did show was that Richter and the rest of Müller's platoon had been at the Château where Kearney's carrier had been found.

Grand house or not, according to the 43rd Division it was now a ruin. But then most towns, villages and farmsteads fought over following the invasion had been left in ruins. It made me wonder, assuming Richter was right, what the owner had been doing there, in the middle of a war zone. If they had had any sense, anyone left in the area would have evacuated themselves before the fighting came their way. But perhaps the owner had had no choice; and if the Gestapo were with him, as Richter had maintained, the man might well have been under arrest.

'I can't see,' Jekyll said to Peter, 'that confusing the châteaux is going to make any material difference. It's still down to the 25th SS-Panzer Grenadiers, isn't it?'

'Probably more so, sir, as the Château de Maltot was held by Frundsberg—10SS-Panzer-Division—not Hitlerjugend.'

'I've requested a copy of Obersturmführer Müller's file and anything further held on SS-Mann Richter and SS-Unterscharführer Vogel,' I put in, just so Jekyll would know I hadn't been sitting on my hands while Peter had been doing all the work. 'Ideally I'd like to interview Müller myself. In the meantime, though, we'll keep searching through the files we hold for anything relevant.'

'Well, if you need any further authorization to expedite the matter,' Jekyll said, taking my arm and steering me towards he door, 'just contact my office.' We were through the door and at the top of the stairs before he added, 'I shan't be making my usual Friday visit this week. I have to go to Scotland.'

'Very nice,' I said. 'Leave is it, sir?'

'Business. But at least I'll have an opportunity to see my people. I doubt I'll be back before the weekend.'

I noted he said "people" rather than "family". We still weren't sure if Jekyll was married or not. Susie was confident he wasn't and, in a twist on Jane Austen, was convinced a laird in possession of a grouse moor must be in want of a wife. She hadn't yet turned up for work in brogues and tartan, but I suspected she might have them on hand in her wardrobe.

At street level Jekyll stopped. 'Have a report for me when I get back, will you?'

He tipped his forefinger to his cap and I threw up a salute then watched him walk smartly down the street to his car.

'Colonel G's off to Scotland,' I told them back in the office. 'He won't be in Friday. That will give us a week to come up with our corroborating evidence. We've got his authorization to G-up anyone who's slow responding to requests.'

'G-up,' said Jack, putting the kettle on. 'Very dry.'

'Not for me, Jack,' said Susie, picking up her bag. 'I'm out for lunch.'

I went back to my desk. After a couple of minutes Jack came in with the tea, sat down and began pecking at his Remington again, like a novelist in the grip of his muse.

'I don't suppose there's any chance our Major Hendrix has called back?' I asked.

Jack merely shook his head, more miserly with the spoken word.

A fattening file marked Joseph Dabs sat on the corner of the desk. I leafed through it again and found a photograph I hadn't seen before.

'Where did this come from?'

Jack glanced at the photo and back at his typewriter.

'No idea.'

'Find out, will you?'

He muttered and went next door.

The photograph showed a well-dressed man in a suit and hat standing in front of a portico entrance to a building. Next to him was a woman in a short jacket and pencil skirt. They were young and, judging by the clothes, the photo had been taken some years before the war. She was smiling attractively for the camera. He was not. On the back was written: *For Billy: A terrible beauty.*

A terrible beauty I knew to be a line from a W.B.Yeats poem, although that was as much as I knew. Was Billy William Kearney?

I lit a cigarette and blew a couple of smoke rings. If Jekyll expected to be in Scotland for the whole week, I began to wonder what I was going to do while he was gone. I'd seen everyone I could; Rose had disappeared and Hendrix never appeared. Peter and Stan would be busy chasing the Hitlerjugend, Peter having suggested he go through the transcript of Meyer's trial to see if it threw up any familiar names. He would enjoy that, reading pages of legal testimony, although personally I couldn't see that it would advance things materially. We'd already added Meyer's tainted name to the mix, heaping more opprobrium upon the former general, and that was clearly enough for Jekyll. Even so, I still had a nagging suspicion there might be more to it.

I leaned across the desk towards the open door. 'Stan!'

A second later he looked around the jamb, the sort of a questioning expression on his face that his namesake, Laurel, usually wore whenever he'd done something to exasperate Oliver Hardy. Given his battered nose, though, the quizzical look wasn't as humorous.

'Boss?'

'The Barnado's homes? Any progress?'

'Susie's still ringing round to see which one Dabs was at.'

'All right. I want you to go back to the Wiltshire battalions. The ones involved in Operation Express. They should have a record of precisely who first found the carrier. I want as much detail as possible.'

'I'll get on to them tomorrow.'

'And see if anyone has any idea what it was doing so far outside the village...if there were other bodies found in close proximity... If so, on the road or in the wood, fine. But it just seems a bit odd to me that Kearney and his men were out on a limb like that by themselves.'

That left me at a loose end. I should have made a start on the report Jekyll said he expected on his desk upon his return, put the whole thing down as another SS crime, except that there were still some things that didn't fit that scenario. They may not have had any bearing on the outcome—that it was probably SS-Unterscharführer Otto Vogel, or his officer, Müller, who executed Dabs and, in all likelihood, Kearney. But the actions of the odd Major Hendrix and the fact that Rose Kearney had done a moonlight flit kept interfering with the report I was writing mentally in my head.

I would have liked to speak to Rose again but had no idea where to find her. And somehow her absence also made the week ahead look suddenly very empty.

I smoked, mulling it all over, thinking about what Stan had said about leave. I heard Susie come back and, in that instant, made an uncharacteristically impetuous decision. I'd kill two birds with one stone.

I stubbed out my cigarette and went into the other office. Susie was on the phone so I waited until she finished.

'A rail warrant for Liverpool,' I said to her as soon as she put the receiver down.

'And I thought you were waiting to ask me out to dinner,' she said. 'Who's the warrant for?'

'Me.'

'When?'

'Soon as possible.'

'What's in Liverpool?'

'The ferry to Ireland.'

15

Tuesday June 25th 1946

Tuesday morning, after packing a bag and leaving my uniform behind, I stopped at my bank to cash a cheque where they assured me that the Irish Republic still accepted sterling as currency. I still had the joint account with Penny that we had opened when we married. When I'd been posted overseas I'd arranged for my pay to go straight in, all but for running expenses. Penny had had her own money—an allowance from her father—although I had insisted we live on what I earned. When she moved down to live with my mother she had still drawn on our account and had done so until she seemed to have decided that our marriage was over. I told her—in a rather formal letter I regretted as soon as I posted it—that until she remarried I still had an obligation to support her. What she did with the money, I had no idea. I assumed her father still paid her allowance, so she was hardly likely to be short of funds. I only hoped she wasn't giving it to my mother or brother. I had never asked, not wanting to know the answer.

What was left in the account was enough for me to live on—provided I was frugal. The ferry fare and travelling expenses, though, would make a hole in my funds. I might have argued that the rail warrant was necessary for the investigation, even if I would have had a hard time making Jekyll swallow it, but expecting expenses on top of it was out of the question.

Despite making a reasonably early start, by the time I'd been to the bank then found the station, the train to Liverpool was delayed and I was too late for the Dublin ferry. I took a room in a cheap hotel, caught the early ferry the next morning then bought myself a map so I'd know where I was going. I'd never been to Ireland before, never been anywhere further than Wales until they shipped me off to North Africa, and I didn't know what to expect. I'd served with enough Irishmen to get an idea though. They had mostly hailed from Belfast or Dublin or one of the other cities, and the towns were fine, they'd said. I'd even heard them call Belfast the second city of empire when there wasn't anyone from Glasgow or Manchester around to contradict them. But they usually dismissed the rest of the country as a priest-ridden backwater. A priest-ridden backwater of empire once, I suppose, and now—the south at least—a priest-ridden backwater of the Republic.

A gazetteer I found in a bookshop revealed the presence of two other Ballydrums in Ireland, one in County Mayo and another in County Longford, although these were only townlands, that odd geographical division of land peculiar to Ireland. My Ballydrum lay on the other side of the Wicklow Mountains and to get there I'd have to take a bus to a town about twenty miles south of Dublin called Newtownmountkennedy, then catch another into the mountains. Looking at Ballydrum on the map there didn't seem to be much there except a couple of lakes and a lot of empty space. Little wonder, I thought, that William Kearney had got out when he could. The mystery was why his sister, Rose, had stayed so long.

At the bus depot I joined the queue to buy a ticket. Getting to the window I found a grim-faced bespectacled man with the look of a raptor who might have passed for Eamon de Valera if you were lucky enough to catch the First Minister of Ireland on one of his sunnier days.

'Newtownmountkennedy, please,' I asked, trying to stress what I thought were the proper syllables in the town's improbably long name.

The man stared back at me. '*Amháin nó ar ais*?'

'I'm sorry?'

'*Bailie O'gCearnaigh*,' he said. '*Amháin nó ar ais*?'

We regarded at each other for a while before I pushed a ten shilling note across the desk.

'Newtownmountkennedy,' I said again.

'*Bailie O'gCearnaigh*,' the ersatz De Valera repeated, and for the first time his expression changed. The line of his lips firmed. '*Amháin nó ar ais*?'

I heard the woman in the queue behind me mutter and before I could say Newtownmountkennedy again she pushed past me and stuck her face through the ticket window.

'For the love of God, man, he's said where he wants to go so why not give him a ticket?'

'*Amháin nó ar ais*?' De Valera persisted.

She turned to me. 'Do you want a single or a return?'

'Single,' I said.

She looked back at De Valera. 'You heard.'

I collected my ticket and change and stepped away from the queue, wondering which bus stand I needed but not inclined to ask.

'You'll be wanting the Wexford bus,' the woman from the queue said, tucking her own ticket into her handbag. 'I'm taking it myself.'

I followed her to the appropriate stand and waited while she checked the timetable and then her watch.

'Ten minutes,' she said and, glancing back the way we'd come, added, 'It's like an affliction from God. Some men as soon as they hear an English accent lose everything but the Gaelic.'

Her name was Mary Flaherty and she lived in Newtownmountkennedy, having been up to Dublin where her married daughter now lived. A stocky, genial woman, she was full of talk and banter and I thought wouldn't have looked out of place gutting fish with a gaggle of her kind on some port quayside.

'Ballydrum, you say?' she said when I told her where I was going. 'Now what would you be wanting in Ballydrum?'

I told her who I was and that a man named Kearney had died in Normandy. Ballydrum was where his family lived.

'Well,' she decided, 'the British Army's not as black as they're painted if they're after sending someone to a place like Ballydrum just to tell some poor woman her son's been killed.'

I didn't tell her that Kearney's mother was already dead, nor that my journey wasn't a wholly altruistic exercise. But that was fine by Mary Flaherty who wasn't really interested in me or the reason for my visit anyway, preferring to spend the hour or so it took to reach Newtownmountkennedy telling me what a fine marriage her daughter Mauraid had made and how well her son-in-law was doing in haberdashery. Stepping down from the bus she told me where to catch the one for Ballydrum and that I wouldn't have to wait more than an hour.

'And you'll be getting the ticket from the driver,' she explained, 'and I don't suppose he'll be wanting the Gaelic from you.'

I thanked her and carried my bag to the junction she indicated, sat on the bench by the stop and lit a cigarette.

If Mary Flaherty was surprised at the lengths the British Army was prepared to go over one dead Irishman, it was no less pronounced than my own surprise by my decision to go to Ballydrum. I had no idea what I expected to find out: Kearney's mother was dead and his sister presumably still in London; any other family—if Rose was to be believed—would be less than keen to speak to a member of the former oppressing caste. I'd already had a taste of what their attitude might be on entering the country when I'd got off the ferry at Dublin. Despite being careful to wear civilian clothes there was no disguising my passport and the *Garda*, or whoever it was who guarded the country, had wanted to know precisely what the nature of my business in the Republic was. I told them the truth, that I was looking for relatives of a man named Kearney who had gone missing in Northern France. If they were curious as to why I was going to so much trouble over one absent sergeant, they didn't say, just noted down in a large ledger all the details I had on the missing man, as if for some future reference

There had been a vindictive campaign in the new republic after the Great War against Irish nationals who had volunteered to fight for Britain, and I wondered if the same thing was happening now. The Garda weren't giving anything away, though. Not beyond a general demeanour of hostility and mistrust, that is.

Then again, they might simply have been bored and were looking for something to do. As usual, most of the traffic was still going in the other direction.

~

The bus drove west through a patchwork of green and gold, the road rising as we approached the Wicklow Mountains. It was cooler than it had been in Dublin and ahead, above the dark granite outcrop of the hills, grey cloud shrouded the higher peaks. The road was little more than a narrow track, the bus rattling as it struggled with the climb and the fields giving way to heath, upland grass and blanket bog.

Not wanting to waste my time while in the bookshop in Dublin, I'd read a little about the Wicklow Mountains. The area, it seemed, had been a centre of resistance to the Norman conquest and, thereafter, had remained a thorn in the side of whoever had subsequently ruled at Westminster. Those left of Wolfe Tone's uprising had taken shelter there in 1798. It had been Tone who'd originated the strategy of rebelling against the British government while they were engaged in a foreign war. We were fighting the French at the time and Tone had expected French support which had never come. But we'd all been there, I suppose. As a strategy Tone's stance was militarily sound although, unfortunately for him, guaranteed to gain the support of only those from whom he already had it. In those circumstances everyone else tends to damn you as a treasonous hound. The Irish rebels tried it again at Easter in 1916, with much the same result, only this time Westminster confounded its own folly by executing the leaders and so swaying public opinion—at least in Ireland—in the other direction.

Back in Tone's day they'd built a military road through the Wicklow Mountains to suppress the rebellion. But building roads hadn't been of much use in suppressing the IRA. After independence, the Irish had been left to do that for themselves and hadn't proved much better than the British at the job. By then it seemed that somehow the ideal had become subordinate to the action; as when the Fenian Brotherhood had murdered Cavendish and Burke in Phoenix Park. Both men had been supporters of Home Rule. But that hardly mattered once terror had become an objective, and blood became an end in itself.

~

Ballydrum when I reached it was even smaller than I had thought it might be and it wasn't hard to imagine why Kearney had left. The main street ran into a huddled collection of drab cottages then ran out again into the bog on the other side. There was a church, a pub, two or three small shops and an air of abandonment, as if all the residents had long-since joined the Irish diaspora. Getting down from the bus I hesitated outside the pub, but it was already early afternoon and if I was going to catch the only bus back that day I couldn't afford to waste my time. I turned around and headed towards the church.

It was silent as the tomb inside and almost as dark, and it took my eyes a minute to adjust to the gloom. Then I saw an old lady sweeping between the pews near the altar who told me I'd find Father O'Dowd in his vestry. He was younger than I expected and quite unremarkable, my conception of Irish priests proving less than immaculate. It had been coloured, no doubt, by Hollywood's irascible Barry Fitzgerald and the muscular Pat O'Brien. O'Dowd bore no resemblance to either and seemed equally surprised to see me, but then perhaps he wasn't used to visitors. Given his age, I thought it unlikely he was going to remember William Kearney unless he was from Ballydrum himself.

'Kearney?' he repeated when I told him who I was and why I was there. 'No, there's no Kearneys live around here. There used to be, I believe, but that was before I came to this parish.'

I thought I detected just a touch of wariness in his reply. It might simply have been self-consciousness as I had caught him smoking in his vestry and he had quickly taken the cigarette from his mouth and held it in his long and bony fingers out of sight at his side. The smoke was curling up in the air between us though, which was something of a give-away and finally, perhaps reluctant to waste a good cigarette, he gave me an apologetic smile and took a drag on it.

'A bad habit, I know, but God loves a sinner as they say and it often helps to have something in common with your parishioners. Smokers to a man although I know some of my good ladies don't always approve.'

'You wouldn't know if one of those Kearneys happened to be named William?' I persisted. 'I don't know exactly when he would have left but I should imagine he was probably quite a young man still.' I showed him the photograph of the man I assumed to be Kearney I'd found in the file.

Father O'Dowd studied the couple standing in front of the columns for a moment before shaking his head.

'No, but then I never met the family. The father was a farmer and as far as I know had just the one daughter.'

'Her name wouldn't have been Rose, would it?'

He took another pull on the cigarette. 'No, that would have been Cathleen, rest her soul. I only know because the poor girl's buried in the churchyard here.'

He lowered his voice and bent towards me as if there might be a third party listening at the door.

'There was a bit of a to-do about it, I believe. But Father Byrne—he was my predecessor—insisted on her being buried in consecrated ground and there weren't many people in this parish that would go against Father Byrne's wishes.'

'And she never had a brother?'

'Not to my knowledge.'

'And the father and mother?'

'Both dead...mercifully,' he added after a second.

It was obvious there was some sort of story here even if Father O'Dowd appeared reluctant to divulge the details. Whether the matter had anything to do with William Kearney was another matter.

I asked if there was anyone in the village I might be able to speak to who remembered the Kearneys.

'The elderly lady I saw in the church, perhaps?'

O'Dowd straightened up, his face freezing in what, under other circumstances, I would have described as puritanical horror.

'Now I wouldn't advise that course of action. Best let sleeping dogs lie, as they say. It's not a subject that's talked about here and I only know as much as I do through tittle-tattle. I'm not one to pass that sort of gossip along, you understand.'

'Of course, father,' I agreed. 'It's just I've come a long way and I'd hate to leave without following up any lead, no matter how tenuous.'

O'Dowd regarded me steadily for a second or two before stubbing out the remains of his cigarette.

'Then you should speak to Father Byrne. He knows all about the sorry business. I don't think it can have anything to do with this William Kearney you're looking for, but Father Byrne will know.'

'Is he still in the village?'

'He lives at the seminary now. Retired but still able to give the young seminarians the benefit of his experience and teaching.'

'And where is the seminary?'

Father O'Dowd gestured beyond the vestry door. 'Through the village on the main road. You can't miss it.'

'Do I need to take a bus?'

He chuckled. 'I'm afraid you came in on the only bus going that way. But you can walk there without any trouble. It's no more than five miles.'

16

According to Father O'Dowd's description, the seminary catered to both ends of the religious life, training the next crop of young men taking holy orders and providing a retirement home for those closer to discovering if they'd backed the right horse. I found the place easily enough as it was the only building there was, standing in the middle of a windswept wasteland several miles beyond Ballydrum. The gloomy Victorian pile sat cast against a grey Irish sky like an affront to the barren peat bog around it. So isolated even the devil might have thought twice about finding mischief for idle hands. Then perhaps that had been the point for those who had built it.

A suspicious-eyed housekeeper answered the door and informed me that the fathers were having their tea. When I said I'd wait she relented sufficiently to allow she might be able to find a cup for me as well. Calling to a thin drab of a girl in a grubby housecoat whom she addressed as Sheilagh, she instructed her to take me through to Father Byrne. I followed along a dank corridor to a large room where a shaft of milky sunlight issuing through a pair of French windows made little impression on the dismal interior. Half a dozen priests in identical black garb sat around the room like a flock of elderly rooks stunned into silence. Several empty chairs spoke of either attrition or vacancies, depending upon one's optimism, although neither view offered much in the way of assurance. Sheilagh, studiously avoiding eye contact, pointed out Father Byrne, and I picked up one of the empty chairs and set it next to him. He looked frail, stooped even in a sitting position, and didn't raise his head as I sat down. At his side a cup of tea stood untouched on an occasional table and his eyes were fixed on a point on the threadbare carpet halfway between his chair and the door. Looking at his grey, patchily shaven face, I began to suspect that Father O'Dowd had sent me on a round ten-mile goose-chase to interview a man in his dotage rather than talk about the Kearneys himself. But after a second Father Byrne stirred himself from his reverie, turned a pair of inquisitive eyes on me and bade me a 'Good afternoon,' with startling heartiness.

I explained who I was and that Father O'Dowd had suggested I visit him.

'Did you bring the pony and trap?' he asked.

'I walked,' I said.

'Pity,' he replied. 'I don't get out of this place much and it looks like a nice afternoon for a drive.'

While walking there, I personally hadn't thought the afternoon had that much to recommend it, although compared to being confined to the dreary seminary I dare say it had its attractions.

Father Byrne reached a palsied hand towards his tea and managed to bring it to his mouth without spilling too much.

'So what's your interest in Patrick Kearney?' he asked once the cup was safely reunited with its saucer.

'*William* Kearney. It's William Kearney I'm trying to find out about. And his sister, Rose.'

'Different family, then,' said Byrne. The Ballydrum Kearney was Patrick. He had a brother, Sean, but he went to America once their father, old man Kearney, died. His name was Brian. Patrick was the eldest and so took over the farm. It wasn't big enough to support two families, you see.'

'And Rose?'

'Patrick's daughter was named Cathleen, God rest her soul. And her mother was Mary. Mary died when Cathleen was just a child. There was no Rose in the family.'

I took the photograph out of my pocket and passed it to Father Byrne. He fumbled for a pair of spectacles then peered at the image on the creased photo.

'Now would you look at that,' Father Byrne said. 'And you say Father O'Dowd didn't tell you what happened?'

'No. He said something about village gossip and not wanting to repeat it.'

'I'm sure he did.' Father Byrne's pale lips compressed tightly as if to trap a comment he'd prefer not to articulate. 'But you still want to know, I suppose?' he said.

I wasn't sure that I did. I had a five-mile walk back to the village and with a good chance of missing my bus back to Dublin at the end of it. I supposed if I left immediately there was a chance I might flag the thing down on the road if I saw it, but otherwise I'd be looking for a room for the night and Ballydrum hadn't struck me as the most accommodating of villages.

'If it's not relevant...' I said.

'Oh, it's relevant all right,' Father Byrne said, 'and you'd be better hearing it from me rather than from some slack-mouthed village gossip. Though I can't see that it'll help you much.' He tapped a finger against the photograph. 'He's dead, you say?'

'If that's William Kearney then he probably is. Although his body hasn't turned up yet.'

Byrne chuckled unexpectedly. 'Well there's some irony in that at least,' he said.

'How do you mean?'

Father Byrne shifted in his chair and finished his tea before going on. He glanced around the room at his fellow priests but none of them were paying us any mind.

'He was a Godless man, Patrick Kearney. His wife, Mary, was devout and so was young Cathleen as she grew up. But Kearney himself never cast his shadow in *my* church. After Mary died you'd see him of an evening in the village—he'd not step into church but had no fear of crossing the threshold of Casey's public house. He was wanting a new wife, of course, having worked Mary into an early grave. But there has always been a shortage of marriageable women in Ballydrum and Patrick Kearney wasn't going to find one in the pub. And he certainly wasn't one for spending money on looking further afield. Given the sort of man he was—a drinking man, I mean—it wasn't any great surprise that once Cathleen began to grow he should turn to her to slake his carnal appetites.'

Father Byrne pierced me with his cold gaze. My mouth had gone dry and I found myself looking towards the door and wondering where my tea was.

'I didn't know when it started,' Father Byrne resumed. 'Cathleen was a stoical girl, like her mother, and she gave no indication of what was happening at home. She attended Mass regularly, and Confession, and I wouldn't be breaking my covenant by saying no word of what she was having to endure passed her lips in my confessional.

'Things came to a head you might say when she caught the eye of a young man in the village named Willy O'Connell. And a decent boy he was too. At least that was the general opinion until it became clear that Cathleen was with child. Talk was, naturally, that Willy was the father and—despite what you might have heard to the contrary about the way we do things here—had we been able to arrange a quick marriage things would have settled down soon enough. But Kearney made it quite clear that he wasn't ready to marry Cathleen off. She was packed off to the city and Willy moped about the village, apparently innocent of knowing what had happened but now and then not above taking a drink or two himself. When he heard the gossip about Cathleen's condition—and him knowing he had not had knowledge of the girl, if you take my meaning—he put two and two together. He was a decent boy, as I said, and willing to take the child, but Cathleen was still under the age of consent. She needed her father's permission, you understand,

and Willy began making threats about what he'd do if Patrick Kearney didn't give it.

'Well,' Byrne said, bringing his hands together and casting his eyes briefly towards the ceiling, 'the matter was taken out of our hands. There were complications in the birth and the child was mercifully born dead. Cathleen only survived the infant by a few hours.'

'And Patrick Kearney?' I asked.

'The paternity of the child was common knowledge by then and he knew better than to show his face in the village. Willy went off to Dublin and brought poor Cathleen's body home. There was some talk of her not being buried in consecrated ground but the bishop saw things my way and we gave the girl a Christian burial.'

Father Byrne fell silent. I waited, failing to see the relevance in the story and beginning to feel I'd been short-changed.

'Was that the end of it?' I finally asked.

'Almost,' said Father Byrne, 'almost. As I said, Kearney wasn't welcome in the village and was rarely seen. Young O'Connell left, too, after the funeral. It must have been the best part of a month before anyone had occasion to visit Patrick Kearney's farm. There was no sign of the man except a half-eaten meal mouldering on the kitchen table. Some of his stock had been turned out to graze but his two pigs were still in their pen, hungry but not quite as starved as you might imagine. The Garda were called and after going over the place some bones and bits of material were found in the pigsty.'

'Kearney?'

'That's what the Garda said. They thought he must have had a heart attack, or the like, while feeding his pigs. Fell over and...well, a pig being an opportunistic creature... General opinion was he got what he deserved. God's justice if not man's.'

'Was he usually in the habit of letting his other stock out to graze?' I asked.

Father Byrne smiled but didn't reply.

'And Willy O'Connell?'

'He went to Dublin. I never saw him again although they say he used to come home to visit his mother now and then. He took an interest in politics, I heard. Not what I would have expected of Willy. From what I knew of the boy he had never shown an interest in his fellow man.' Byrne smiled again. 'But he was always kind to animals.'

He handed back the photograph, shaking his head.

'I don't know the woman.'

17

I didn't see the bus on my way back to Ballydrum. To all intents and purposes when I finally got there the village might well have been closed for a public holiday, only there was no bunting. No people either, and walking down the street I might have been forgiven for thinking the plague had swept through in my absence. Dusk had already crept out of the bog and into the village and most of the windows I passed were either shuttered or masked behind heavy curtains. No lights betrayed the fact anyone might be home. Only the local tavern showed a light and that was as dim as the proverbial Toc H lamp. There were two or three men drinking inside when I opened the door but my sudden appearance seemed to strike them dumb and I didn't even catch the stray word of Gaelic.

The landlord was a round beach ball of a man with a matching bulbous nose whose broken veins suggested a thoughtful habit of sampling his merchandise before chancing it on his customers. I ordered a whiskey, downed it while he watched and told him to fill it up again. I asked him to have one with me and his glass joined mine with an alacrity that suggested he kept several beneath the bar for just such eventualities.

'I think I've missed my bus back to Newtownmountkennedy,' I said.

He looked at me sympathetically. 'Ah well, since it went through at three o'clock this afternoon, you're probably right.'

'Is there anywhere I might get a room for the night?'

His face brightened. 'Well you'll be fortunate in that we have a room or two vacant just now. Nothing fancy, you understand.'

I assured him whatever he had would be fine.

Fine, though, might have been overstating the case. The iron bedstead and sagging mattress both had the look of having been christened long before my father had. But I'd slept on worse and there were times in North Africa when the room would have looked to me like a little piece of Irish heaven fallen to earth. The water in the stained tub down the hall was warm enough for a shallow bath and, not having eaten since breakfast, by the time I'd put on a clean shirt and underwear, I was ready for some dinner.

Dónol Casey, my genial host, boasted that Mrs Casey's stew and spuds was renowned the length of the Wicklow Mountains, although he didn't specify for what. In the event I wasn't disappointed. I took a pint of Guinness with it—Dónol informing me that the waters of the River Liffey, which the Dublin brewery claimed went into the stout, rose in the nearby mountains. And seeing his eyes twinkling as he banged the glass down onto the scrubbed table at which I ate—the famous Guinness head barely shuddering at the jar—I wouldn't have put it past him to have nipped out the back and added some from upstream to the barrel so as not to give the lie to the brewery.

'And to what do we owe the pleasure of your visit to these parts, Mr Tennant?' he asked as I wiped away my foam moustache.

'I've been visiting Father Byrne at the seminary,' I told him.

'Have you now? And how did you find the good father?'

'Well.'

'And missed around here, I'm sure.'

His other patrons had left and just the two of us remained in the bar. Casey helped himself to a glass of spirit from a bottle on the shelf and rejoined me at the table.

'Father Byrne wasn't above taking a drink himself now and again when the need arose,' he said.

'Oh? I thought perhaps he might have been teetotal. The evils of hard liquor and all that...'

'It's true he wasn't above preaching the occasional sermon on the demon drink, but there's many a slip twixt cup and lip as the saying goes,' and he raised his glass as if to demonstrate that he wasn't in the habit of making many.

'Father O'Dowd, though, now he's a different kettle of fish. Smokes like a trooper but has never crossed this threshold.'

The phrase brought back something Father Byrne said to me.

'I'm told a farmer named Kearney was once a good customer of yours.'

'Kearney?'

'Patrick was his first name, I believe.'

'Well, he would have been more my father's customer than mine but I recall him well enough.'

'And his daughter, Cathleen?'

'Now what's your interest in the Kearney family, Mr Tennant?' Casey asked, suddenly suspicious.

So I told him that I'd come looking for a man named William Kearney only to have Father Byrne identify the man I wanted as Willy O'Connell. I showed him the photograph.

'That's Willy O'Connell all right,' he said.

'I'm afraid he's probably dead,' I told him. 'I'm just tying up loose ends.'

'And what ends might they be?'

'A woman claiming to be his sister, Rose, came to London looking for him.'

'Rose O'Connell?'

'She called herself Rose Kearney.'

'Now Willy had no sister. He was an only child.'

'You're certain of that?'

'Didn't I go to school with him?'

'The girl in the photo, then? Would that be Cathleen?'

Casey peered at the photograph again. 'No. Too old. Cathleen was just a slip of a girl when she died.'

'What about O'Connell's mother, when did she die?'

'Well, let me think,' he said, draining his glass and pondering upon the question.

'Take one with me,' I suggested. 'Put it on my bill.'

Dónol skipped behind the bar once more and came back with two glasses and the bottle of whiskey. I took a nip, finding the barley in Irish whiskey more to my taste than Scotch.

'That'll have been just before your last war. Willy came back for the funeral. We had a few drinks together for old time's sake and he let on he was joining the British Army.'

'And how did that go down around here?' I asked.

'Well, between you and me, I didn't blab the news about. Although, given Willy's history there weren't too many in these parts that could have thought any the worse of him. I take it Father Byrne told you about Cathleen and the child?'

'Yes. So some didn't believe the father of the child was Cathleen's own father then?'

Dónol pulled at his bulbous nose with his thumb and forefinger. 'There were one or two who found it difficult to accept. But Patrick Kearney was an unpleasant man, in drink and out of it. It was no stretch of the imagination to believe him capable of that. It was more the pigs they held against Willy. Father Byrne told you about the pigs?'

'Yes. But he thought Kearney got what he deserved.'

Dónol arched his eyebrows wryly 'And so did everyone else. It's just that the man who went up to the farm that day was the local butcher. He'd been booked to slaughter the beasts and though he didn't find much meat on them that's what he did. It was him who called the Garda. He began to have suspicions, you see, when Kearney didn't come round chasing him for his money. The trouble was, it was a day or two before the story got around and by then most of us would have eaten the pork.' He laughed and raised his glass.

'I can't imagine what the gossips made of that,' I said.

'Now there's two sorts of gossip in a place like Ballydrum,' said Dónol. 'There's the gossip that comes across my bar and which I have pay for by loosening the tongue with the odd free drink. And then there's the sort that Father Byrne used to get for nothing, just sitting in that little box of his in the church. Of course, that sort never went further than the confessional, although those versed in these things—like Mrs Casey, I have to admit—can often infer the content by the nature of the lesson at Mass. Willy, though, not being a confessional man, left us all to work out for ourselves how he'd got even with Patrick Kearney.'

'Father Byrne told me he developed an interest in politics while he was in Dublin,' I said.

Dónol Casey pulled a face. 'Well maybe he did but you can't grow up around here without picking up a little of the history, not in these mountains. And with a teacher like Sean MacBride there was no getting away from it.'

'Who was he?'

'He taught in our local school. Some say he came here to keep his head down—he'd been a Volunteer before the Easter Rising, he said, but he wasn't involved in that. He always maintained he was a cousin of John MacBride who was in the GPO and shot for his trouble afterwards. But then Ireland is full of men who claim blood kinship to the Easter martyrs. Though I've noticed there aren't many who'll claim Roger Casement as family. Now I wonder why that might be?'

Dónol Casey gave me a sardonic wink and knocked back his drink. My knowledge of Irish history was as sparse as the Wicklow Mountains and I'd only known of Wolfe Tone and his dictum that "England's difficulty was Ireland's opportunity" from my brief visit to the Dublin bookshop. A view like that had made me wonder if Tone's hatred of England would have been enough for him to have overlooked some of the Nazi excesses. Like their extermination camps. But then I assumed William Joyce—Lord Haw Haw—had. We'd executed him too, I recalled, despite his being an Irish subject and technically beyond British jurisdiction. Not that I'd heard anyone complain at the time. It was always possible though that De Valera had raised an objection.

'He was one of those rifle-carrying poets, if you know the kind I mean,' Casey was saying and still talking, I assumed, about his schoolmaster, MacBride. 'Could never quite see through the flowery verse clearly enough to make out the colour of the blood being spilt. Forever quoting Padraig Pease, he was, a particular hero of his. And Yeats, of course. Claimed to have met Maude Gonne herself. Water off a duck's back as far as I was concerned, but he hammered the verse into us like the catechism.'

Casey threw back his head and began to recite:

'To know they dreamed and are dead.
And what if excess of love
Bewildered them till they died?
I write it out in a verse –
MacDonagh and MacBride
And Connolly and Pearse
Now and in time to be,
Wherever green is worn,
Are changed, changed utterly:
A terrible beauty is born.'

'It's still there, you see,' he finished. 'I suppose I'll take it to my grave.'

I turned the photograph over and pointed to the inscription on the back—*For Billy*: *A terrible beauty.*

'Ah well,' he said, 'maybe Willy took it to his grave, too.' His eyes turned a little wistful. 'He lapped it up when we were boys, Willy and our pal Dermot Kavanaugh. The Three Musketeers we called ourselves and we'd play out on the bog all day, acting out the Rising. Only I'd have to be the bloody Englishmen, of course, as Dermot would never sully his hands and Willy being his best pal would always do what Dermot did. It was Dermot that Willy went to stay with in Dublin—after Kearney told him he wasn't to see his Cathleen again.'

'Father Byrne told me he had a friend in Dublin,' I said.

'That'll be Dermot, all right. He might have been Sean MacBride's best scholar but he was no favourite of Father Byrne.'

'Didn't like his politics?'

'No, it wasn't Dermot's taking the same anti-clerical line as the old rebels that Father Byrne had against him. Like a lot of Irish priests the good father was never convinced of the efficacy of turning the other cheek when it was an Englishman who'd slapped you. No, it was something else altogether. You see, Dermot was something of a poet himself. No Yeats, of course. More Pearse, perhaps. I didn't think much of his poetry myself. Though Dermot did get one of his verses published in one of those small Dublin papers. But that was

Sean MacBride's doing and I always thought MacBride might have been of Dermot's persuasion...'

He looked at me slyly and quoted again:

'Like a god as nature dressed,
Made mortal by Great Ceasar's mark
On mounds divine and heaven blessed,
Proud David bears old Ériu's harp.'

I didn't understand what he was getting at and I suppose Dónol Casey could see from my expression that I didn't because he explained:

'It was about Willy O'Connell, you see—the poem. Father Byrne took its meaning right away and from then on he regarded Dermot as the devil incarnate.

'He was the smart one of us three, was Dermot. Our Aramis, which is odd in some ways if you know your Musketeers and take my meaning.'

I didn't but it hardly mattered to Casey who was filling our glasses again.

'There was always something Jesuitical about Dermot, to my mind. Single-mindedness, maybe. Or it might have been the obedience. He won a scholarship to the university in Dublin to study Irish literature.'

Casey winked at me. 'Sean MacBride's one success. You see we're an ignorant lot here in Ballydrum,' going on without giving me the chance for demurral, 'only the trouble was he'd been too successful. Along with the literature, Dermot swallowed all MacBride's politics too. That's when he started calling himself Diamaid Caomhánach, the Gaelic form of his name.'

As Casey pronounced it, it sounded much the same as Dermot Kavanaugh to me, except with a thicker tongue in his mouth which might just have been the whiskey.

Casey repeated it and laughed. 'He'll always be Dermot Kavanaugh to me, though.'

'Where is he now?' I asked, wondering if it might be worth talking to him about O'Connell.

Dónol Casey shrugged. 'He turned up, six months ago perhaps it was. Had a bit of trouble up north, I heard. I was wondering at the time if he hadn't come back home to keep his head down. Like old Sean MacBride. Too late for Sean, though. He'd died with the cancer a year or two before. Dermot put some flowers on the old fella's grave, though.'

'Did he say if he was still in touch with Willy O'Connell?'

'No, Dermot hadn't heard from Willy for some time. I told him I'd seen him back in about thirty-eight when he'd buried his mam. And that Willy said he was going to join the British Army. Just to see the expression on Dermot's face, you understand. Didn't turn a hair, though. Just smiled as if he could have guessed as much. Mellowed, I suppose. But isn't that the way of it? A lot's happened since King Billy met Seamus a Caca at the Boyne but it's the grave that takes us all in the end, no matter the colour.'

King Billy I was familiar with, being a nickname of William of Orange, but "Seamus a Caca" was a new one on me.

'James the Shite, as he's known around here,' Dónol explained. 'The name he earned for running away from the planters.' He gave a small shrug. 'But maybe the yellow streak ran in the family. They say his grandson, the bonny prince, didn't linger too long after Culloden either.'

'It could be,' I agreed. 'Charles the Second's bastard son, Monmouth, is supposed to have pleaded for his life on the scaffold.'

Dónol chuckled. 'You can't condemn a man for trying a little grovelling in the face of the axe, now.'

'Probably not,' I said. 'Then again, his grandfather, Charles the First, is supposed to have asked for a second shirt before his execution. It was a cold day and he didn't want the onlookers to think he was shivering through fear.'

Dónol emptied the bottle into our glasses.

'Doesn't that just go to show it takes all sorts to make up a family?'

18

Thursday June 27th 1946

The deck of the ferry on the return trip to Liverpool was crowded, mostly with passengers hanging over the rails making a contribution to the choppy sea beneath. I might have joined them had I anything in my stomach to donate, but feeling delicate after leaving Ballydrum that morning I had contented myself with cigarettes and a single cup of coffee. I'd been late getting into Dublin and had only just managed to catch the last ferry. The hangover, dogging me all day, had cleared a little by the time we reached Liverpool and the throbbing in my head had subsided to a tolerable ache. I remained queasy until I got my feet on land that didn't move beneath them, then gingerly tried a second cup of coffee and some dry biscuits at the railway hotel.

Once at the station I picked up a copy of the Lancashire Evening Post and read on the front page that it had been announced in the House of Commons that bread rationing was to be introduced on July 21st. That was something the government never had to resort to during the war and seemed to me now like a kick in the teeth in return for all the sacrifices made. But the weather was poor with a wet summer thus far, following on from a cold spring. That was their excuse, anyway. The wheat harvest looked as if it would be a fraction of that expected and I suppose we didn't have the money to import the stuff. Now we'd fallen out with Uncle Joe I presumed eating Russian wheat was more than we could swallow anyway; and perhaps the Americans wanted to charge us more for their wheat than they had for the broken-down destroyers they'd sent us at the beginning of the war.

I know I had a hangover but the news left me with a feeling of despondency. It was more than just bread. It was everything. The country was bankrupt. We'd lost most of what had been left of the Empire—India would be going her own way any day—and no matter how hard we might scramble to retain what we had once held in the Far East, the people we'd ruled there for a century had seen us humiliated by an Asian race and weren't about to invite us back. And who could blame them? Given the mess we had at home, they could hardly do worse by themselves. All that sort of thing was behind Britain now and we'd better accept the fact with as much grace as we could muster. It was a new world and the Americans and the Russians had emerged with the loudest voices. We had no choice but to listen to them.

All the same, the thought of it didn't fill one with a sense of optimism. Not this one, anyhow.

And on top of it Dónol Casey had given me more than a headache to worry about. Not that it wasn't uncommon for men to enlist in the army under an assumed name. There were many reasons they might have for doing so: escaping family commitments or debts; evading the law or simply wishing to make a new start. I imagined the man we'd known as William Kearney had had his reasons for wanting a new start although, if I had got the timings correct from what Father Byrne and Casey had told me, he had waited a long time to do so.

I'd visited the graveyard at Ballydrum before catching my bus back to Newtownmountkennedy that morning and had found Cathleen Kearney's grave tucked away in a neglected corner. Father Byrne had got his way and had buried the girl and her baby in consecrated ground, but he hadn't flaunted the fact in the face of his Ballydrum parishioners. There were no signs of flowers ever having been left on the grave and the now flat soil in front of the stone was hidden under a tangle of weeds and rank grass. The stone simply read, 'Cathleen Kearney' with her dates given as 1913 to 1931. Father Byrne had said the baby had been buried with her. Unbaptized, it apparently hadn't rated a mention. Conceived in sin, I supposed the consensus had been, and so not worthy of a Christian name. So much for the milk of Christian forgiveness.

William O'Connell, as I now had to learn to think of him, had enlisted in 1939 shortly after the outbreak of war. Cathleen had been dead eight years by then although I couldn't be sure exactly when O'Connell had decided to change his name, perhaps when he'd come home to bury his mother and look on Cathleen's grave again. After all, from that date on there was nothing left for him in Ballydrum.

I was catching the late train to London and thought if I could book a quick trunk call I might still catch someone at the office. The bank of public kiosks wasn't busy and I squeezed into one of the boxes and placed the call. I wanted to let them know I'd be back in the morning although not first thing; it would be a Friday but since Jekyll said he was going to be in Scotland I saw no need to hurry.

The call came back in a few minutes and when they rang I fed my money into the box and was put through. Jack answered and I asked if he'd heard anything from Colonel G.

'Not since you left,' he said.

'Any developments?'

'A Superintendent Gifford rang and left a number for you to call.'

'Did you tell him where I was?'

'Just that you'd be out of the office for a few days.'

He gave me the number and I asked the exchange for trunks again. A woman began banging on the glass to use the phone and I pushed opened the door and explained I was waiting for a long distance call from London. It didn't wash with her and I spent the next minute arguing the toss until the box next to mine became free. She pushed her way into it and glared at me through the glass until the exchange rang back and I was put through.

Jack had been cautious on my behalf and while the line went through its last clicks and buzzes I wondered whether to let Gifford know I'd been in Ireland. Given the sort of area I policed when I'd been on the force I hadn't been likely to run across anyone Irish unless you counted Lord Londonderry or the Countess of Carlingford, and not even Julia moved in *their* rarefied circles. I had had no experience of the problem that the Irish Republican Army had posed between the wars and knew nothing of the work Gifford might have done. Ignorance seemed not only the best policy but the only possible one for me so, by the time the operator told me my party was on the line, I had decided that if Gifford asked where I'd been it couldn't hurt to tell him. But only if he asked.

'I thought I'd let you know,' Gifford said when he knew who he was speaking to, 'that you won't be treading on anyone's toes. You're free to trace your William Kearney as far we're concerned.'

I thought that a typical reply as far as Special Branch was concerned. *I* was free to investigate but the way he put it didn't necessarily rule out the fact that they had an interest.

'Thanks,' I replied, counting how much change I had in case the pips went. 'Only now I've found out that Kearney's real name was William O'Connell.'

'O'Connell?' said Gifford, as if the name sounded familiar.

'He spent some time in Dublin from nineteen-thirty on. Had a friend named Dermot Kavanaugh who went under the Gaelic form of his name. May have been involved in politics.'

'And what would the Gaelic form of Dermot Kavanaugh be?' Gifford asked.

'I haven't a clue,' I told him, unable to remember what Dónol Casey had said. 'Ask one of your Fenian friends.'

'What bearing has this got on Kearney's disappearance?'

'O'Connell's disappearance,' I said. 'And I don't know the answer to that one either. I take it Hendrix wasn't one of yours then,' I added, trying to clear that up at least.

'Not one of anybody's as far as I can tell,' Gifford said. 'There's nothing on anyone by that name.'

I couldn't say I was surprised. I was beginning to have other suspicions as far as Major Hendrix went.

'That *is* who you were wondering about, isn't it?' Gifford went on.

'Yes,' I assured him, probably less convincingly than I sounded. I had used Coveney's name when I had first approached Gifford and still the man had not been mentioned. I wondered if Gifford had begun to smell the rat.

'Where does this leave the sister, Rose Kear—'

The pips went.

'I'm out of change,' I told him, broke the connection and swept what was left of my money off the top of the box. I stepped out of the booth and went off to the station buffet to wait for my train.

~

It was gone midnight when I got back to my flat. The tube had closed and the alternative was to walk from the station or take a taxi. I took the taxi, using the ride to calculate how much the trip had cost.

There was some post waiting for me and I took it upstairs and looked through it while I waited for the kettle to boil. I had had nothing to eat all day except the biscuits in Liverpool and found I was now hungry; but there was nothing edible in the flat beyond a stale half-loaf of bread and no means of toasting it without the risk of immolating what was left of the building.

I found another letter from Penny amid the assorted bills, and a note from my landlord accompanied by a notice from the local authority saying that they'd finally settled on a date for demolition. I thought twice about the toast then. But there was still the old girl upstairs and Sam the housebreaker, and now Ida to consider as well as myself. So I settled for going to bed on an empty stomach and hoped that Penny's news wasn't going to upset it further. She was coming up to town on the weekend, she said, and needed to see me. She'd be at Julia's on Saturday if I cared to call.

Lying in the dark, the street below quiet, all I could hear was the creaking of the building as if now—officially condemned—it had decided to give up the long struggle to keep intact. Would I get up if things around me fell apart, or would I stay in bed and give in to it all? I lay undecided.

Things around me had already fallen apart and I hadn't done much about that so far.

She *needed* to see me, she had written, and I considered whether her use of that particular adjective held more meaning than, say, her writing *wanted* to see me. *Needed,* I decided, was a less personal declaration than *wanted*—one somewhat akin in some way to the formal announcement that my home was about to be demolished. The phrase "if I cared to call" seemed to establish the required distance between us. In other words, as Jack might have said, it put the tin hat on it.

~

I felt better in the morning but still hungry. I did some shopping and cooked myself breakfast before going into the office. Over tea, I read through Penny's letter again. It was short and didn't go into detail and on rereading didn't seem as full of omens as it had the night before. Then again, the sun was now shining.

Susie was alone in the office when I arrived about midmorning although I could hear Jack pecking at his Remington next door. I wondered what on earth he found to type and if perhaps he *was* writing a novel after all—an account of his wartime experiences. The only trouble with those was that we all had them and no one was much interested in other people's.

Susie smiled brightly as I walked in.

'Did you find the Rose of Tralee, Captain?'

'No, but I did find out that William Kearney didn't have a sister named Rose. In fact he didn't have a sister at all. And Kearney's not Kearney. Kearney's O'Connell. Where is everyone?'

Her eyes widened and she lost the bright look.

'Stan's gone to Chelmsford to meet someone from 7th Hampshires.'

'Did he manage to speak with anyone from the Field Ambulance unit who recovered Kearney's carrier—'

'O'Connell,' she corrected. 'Yes, someone in Aldershot yesterday.'

'And Peter?'

'Something came up,' she said without elaborating further.

I gave her the photograph of Willy O'Connell and the notes I'd taken while I'd been in Ireland so she could put them in the Dabs file where I'd be able to find them again.

'Anything come in?' I asked as she looked at the photo.

She pulled a sheet of paper off her desk and held it out. 'Reply from the Home Office. Joseph Dabs is the only one they had anything on. Eighteen months for burglary in May, nineteen thirty-six. Conviction spent so no bar to conscription.'

'Nothing on the others?'

'No. But that was before Kearney became O'Connell. Do you want me to get back to them with a new request?'

'No,' I said. 'We've done channels. I'll find out another way.'

In fact I was hoping Henry Gifford already had that in hand. My mentioning Dermot Kavanaugh going under a Gaelic name would have sent him scurrying back to the Special Branch Registry. And even if O'Connell hadn't committed any offences of interest to Special Branch, that wouldn't necessarily mean he was unknown to them.

'Colonel G been in touch?'

Susie shook her head making her dark curls dance. 'What's he doing in Scotland?'

'Drinking scotch in an Edinburgh club probably,' I said.

The Remington fell silent and Jack put his head round the door. 'Ready for tea?' We nodded and he turned to Susie as he lit the gas ring under the kettle. 'Biscuits?'

'I was saving them for Colonel G.'

'Bugger Colonel G,' said Jack. 'He's not coming in, is he?'

'No,' I said, 'but he'll bugger me if I don't start on that report he wanted.'

'You paint the prettiest pictures,' said Susie.

'One thing while you were gone,' said Jack, rinsing our mugs under the tap. 'I found out in which camp SS-Obersturmführer Franz Müller was—'

'Is he still there?'

'In a manner of speaking,' Jack said.

'And what manner would that be?'

'He's buried there. Hung himself at Christmas. Got a letter through the Red Cross. Told him his wife and young daughter were killed when the Russians took Berlin. Didn't say how.'

I didn't want to know how. I'd already heard enough horror stories of the days after the city fell to the Russians to last me a lifetime.

'He's a dead end, then.'

Jack's face adopted its customary expression. 'You could say that.'

'What about Werner Richter?'

'Nothing as yet.'

'It's been a week, Jack. Get back to them, will you? Tell them I want a detailed report of Müller's death from the camp for our file. It'll give the clerks there something to do other than bully the POWs. And they still haven't told us why the original interrogation report isn't available.'

'They finally admitted an earlier request had been submitted for it and the thing was sent off two months ago.'

'Earlier request? Who from?'

'That's why they were stalling. According to them the request had been mis-filed and no one remembers who the report was sent to. They won't know who had it till it comes back.'

Someone of a suspicious nature might have seen a conspiracy in this—a missing request for a report that was unavailable, and the man it concerned conveniently dead, but I'd been in the army long enough to know that ordinary military circumstances were quite sufficient to confuse any otherwise straightforward issue.

'Kearney's not Kearney,' Susie said to Jack, breaking the intervening silence. 'Kearney's O'Connell.'

'And who's O'Connell when he's at home?'

'William O'Connell,' I said, 'so at least we got the William right. And home was Ballydrum. He left when his sweetheart died after having her own father's baby.'

Susie dropped the biscuit tin.

I ran through what I'd turned up. Susie's bottom lip trembled and she dabbed at her eyes when I said Cathleen was only eighteen when she died.

'We can't do any more until I hear from my Special Branch superintendent again,' I said, hoping I was right. 'So we'll pull together what we already have and see if I can't come up with something that'll keep Colonel G off my back.'

'There you go again,' said Susie.

I had to wonder what sort of mind lay behind that pretty face. 'Did Stan come up with anything at Barnado's,' I asked her.

'I've just been typing up his notes,' Jack said. 'I know how much you hate his handwriting.'

'Good of you to find the time between recording for posterity how you cleared Jerry out of the Middle-East.' Jack frowned but I didn't trouble to explain. 'That photo of Kearney,' I said.

'O'Connell,' Susie corrected.

'Did you find out where it came from?'

Jack began fiddling with the tea mugs. 'Came with his battalion records, I think,' he muttered.

'Battalion records?'

'When they sent them over last week. They also sent his personal effects. The stuff he left behind when he was sent to France.'

'What personal effects? First I've heard of them. Did we get the effects of the rest of the crew?'

'Not Burleigh's or Poole's,' said Jack, stirring the pot. 'They went to the families.'

'Robert Burleigh's didn't,' I said. 'At least his wife said she didn't get anything.'

'Didn't leave anything behind then,' said Jack. 'Dabs didn't, apparently. And being a Barnado's Boy, he hadn't registered any next of kin, neither.'

'So why have we got Kearney's?'

'O'Connell,' said Susie once more.

'O'Connell, neither,' said Jack.

'Neither what?'

'Registered a next of kin.'

'What about Rose?'

'You just said she wasn't his sister after all.'

'I know. But *we* didn't know that then, did we? How come we didn't pick that up, Jack? We thought he had a sister and he says he's got no next of kin?'

He shrugged. 'Well, if he didn't have one, Kear—O'Connell's going to put down no next of kin.'

I stared at him, wondering if he was being deliberately obtuse.

'If someone turns up saying she's his sister,' I tried again, 'and he says he's got no next of kin...'

'Perhaps it was assumed they were estranged,' Jack said, looking down at the tea and not at me.

'*I* don't remember assuming anything of the sort,' I said.

'Sorry, Boss,' he finally muttered. 'My cock-up.'

I took my tea into the other office and sat at my desk. Had I known that Kearney/O'Connell had registered himself as having no next of kin I might have been able to find out who Rose really was when I met her in the *Minstrel Boy*. Then maybe I wouldn't. No one else she contacted had picked up the fact Kearney didn't have a sister. And, as I recalled, she had had an answer to everything; a *plausible* answer given she was lying through her teeth. I wondered where she fitted in, although couldn't see how it could have any bearing on the carrier even if I found out. It was a careless slip, though, and I spent the next couple of hours going back through all the information we had gathered to see if there were any other anomalies we had missed. I looked at what Stan had gleaned from Barnado's as well.

He had managed to get a photograph of the boy from the Barnado's records although Dabs couldn't have been more than eleven or twelve when it was taken. He looked a beggarly little kid with spiky, uncombed hair and resembled nothing as much as a dishevelled rodent. Maybe by the time he took to burglary he grew out of it, although at that age he seemed an unlikely candidate to become a companion for the sharp-dressing Arnie Poole. Ida said she didn't take to Dabs when he came up on leave with Poole, so I slipped the photo into my pocket to show Ida when I next saw her—just to double-check we had the same man. Dabs might have been only a kid when it was taken but his was the sort of face that would never change much, the sort he was going to have to spend the rest of his life with. Not that it turned out to be a very long life as it happened. And the face did change in the end, rearranged by the bullet that had entered the back of his skull.

19

'Been busy?' I asked Peter when he came in after lunch.

'I spoke to one of the 7th Hampshires' officers. He had to come up to town so I thought I'd take the opportunity. I'm not sure he was of much help.'

'I don't suppose he remembers any of them?'

'Jupiter tore the heart out of the battalion. I got the impression he remembers too many of them. One thing he could tell me was that as far as he was aware there were no other suspicious deaths. Apart from Dabs. Not all dead accounted for, though, so Kearney wasn't alone.'

'O'Connell,' Susie piped up from behind her desk.

I told Peter about it.

'Do you think it's relevant?'

'What, exactly?'

'That he took his girlfriend's name.'

'It depends why,' I said.

'Does it?' Peter replied. 'With respect...'

Peter was a great one for respect. It was his lawyer's training, no doubt. I suppose—like the rest of them—he had been taught to follow the letter of the law, even if that meant sometimes letting justice go hang. It was the sort of attitude likely to stick in my craw.

'Whatever reason he had to enlist under the name Kearney is neither here nor there,' Peter insisted. 'Our brief is to establish whether or not a war crime has been committed. And if it has, if possible establish who might be responsible.'

'Which German unit, you mean.'

'Naturally.'

'But supposing it wasn't the Germans? Suppose Kearney was presented with a good opportunity to disappear again? He'd done it once.'

Peter scratched his head and indicated the shelves around us, files full of the testimony of witnesses and the statements of participants that pointed to German guilt.

'The evidence is overwhelming,' he said.

'And we're spoilt for choice,' I agreed. 'With just what we've got to trawl through here, we could spend the rest of our lives uncovering every mean act committed. Or every panicky decision made on the spur of the moment. Nine times out of ten these men we are trying to link to crimes would have led normal, decent, law-abiding lives if the war hadn't happened.'

'But it did,' said Peter.

'And does that excuse it, boss?' Stan asked, having walked in and caught the end of the conversation.

'You made good time,' I said.

'Started early. So, does it?'

'No,' I admitted, 'but you know as well as I do what's going to happen a year or two down the line. The big fish will have been netted. They'll hang some, like they always do, and give the rest prison terms that in four or five years will be commuted. The tiddlers, the kind of people we're chasing, won't matter by then. We'll have been wound up and all this stuff,' I indicated the files, 'will end up in some archive somewhere and probably never looked at again.'

'Not our decision,' said Stan.

'No, and I for one won't lose any sleep over it.'

'What's your point?' said Peter.

'My point is, why did *this* particular file end up on our desk?'

'Colonel G brought it,' Susie said.

'I said *why*, not how. And someone gave it to him to give to us. Haven't we got enough files to trawl through without another, if it's just the same old story?'

'Well,' she said, 'maybe it isn't.'

'Precisely.'

Susie and I looked at each other but I wasn't sure she had got the point.

'It's the policeman in him,' Jack said, finally favouring us with his presence. And I knew *he* had the point. It wouldn't have surprised me if he hadn't got it before I did.

'The policeman?' asked Susie.

'Jack means Harry has a suspicious character,' Peter told her.

'Well we all know that,' she said.

'*Has* not is,' I said.

'You think,' Peter said, 'that the object of the exercise is for us to pin the deaths of Dabs and Kearney on the Hitlerjugend.'

'That seems to be Jekyll's object,' I told him. 'But I'm not sure that's why we were given the file.'

'So you think something else happened,' Susie said.

'I think someone else *thinks* something else might have happened,' I told her.

'Tea?' said Jack, his answer to anything confusing.

'And you think Kearney's background might be relevant,' said Stan.

'O'Connell's might,' I said.

'Point taken,' said Peter.

But Stan had missed the revelation that William Kearney was really William O'Connell, so while Susie explained it to him, I said:

'Let's keep calling the man Kearney. To avoid confusion.'

'Well,' Susie decided, taking the teapot from Jack, 'Colonel G's not going to be pleased, not if we come up with an answer he didn't want.'

'That's why we're not going to give him one,' I said. 'At least not yet. We're not going to tell him I went to Ireland either.'

'I wrote you a rail warrant to Liverpool,' Susie reminded me. 'Won't he want to know why you went there?'

'I'll tell him an uncle died,' I said. 'And I'll give you the money to cover the warrant for the petty cash.'

She turned her big brown eyes on me, blinking. 'Did you tell lies when you were a policeman, too, Captain?'

'Only when I appeared in court,' I said.

~

Over tea I outlined the way we were going to proceed: Peter would continue concentrating on the 25th SS-Panzer Grenadiers as we now knew that SS-Obersturmführer Franz Müller's platoon was at the château. Müller and Vogel were dead, but the diarist, SS-Mann Werner Richter, as far as we knew wasn't, and we needed to find out which POW camp was holding him. Assuming he hadn't been repatriated already. Yet at the same time I didn't want to lose complete sight of the other possibilities that Peter had suggested earlier: 2SS Das Reich, Gotz von Berlichingen and 1SS Leibstandarte may have arrived in the area too late to be the culprits, but units of 9SS Hohenstaufen and 10SS Frundsberg were still on-hand.

Jack and Susie could do Peter's ringing round for him and handle the paperwork—until I needed one of them to type up my report to Jekyll, that is. In the meantime I wanted to get back to Gifford and see if he knew anything about O'Connell's past. The man had already changed his identity once and, before I was willing to let the 25th SS-Panzer Grenadiers carry the can, I wanted to be sure he hadn't done it again.

'You don't need my input anyway,' I told Peter. 'I do bugger-all around here as it is. Just keep me informed so I can put anything that'll keep Colonel G happy in the report.'

'What about me, boss?' Stan asked.

'First you can tell me what the man from 129th Field Ambulance said.'

We went into my office and Stan brought a sheaf of notes with him. Susie came in with our tea while he was sorting them into order.

'You know who the woman in that photo is, don't you?' she said.

'What woman?'

'The one with O'Connoll formerly known as Kearney. After all that next of kin fuss with Jack,' she said, waving the photograph I'd given her to file in front of my face, 'I took another look.'

'Still known as Kearney,' I said. 'And no, I've no idea. The people I showed it to didn't know her. I know it's not Cathleen, though.'

'Look at it again,' she said, handing me the photograph and a magnifying glass.

I focussed the glass on the woman's face. Having been told to look, I saw now there was something familiar about her, something in the sharpness of the features...something in the way she was looking at the camera.

'It's—'

'The Rose of Tralee herself,' said Susie triumphantly. 'Younger, but try to picture her the way we saw her, without make-up.'

At the time I'd taken Rose's lack of cosmetics to be the consequence of a country upbringing. Looking at the Rose in the photo, it now seemed to have been more a matter of tactics.

'Well done, Susie,' I said. 'I would never have noticed if you hadn't spotted it.'

'You want to pay more attention to women, *Captain.*'

'That's odd,' I said to Stan after she bounced back into her office, 'my wife always accused me of paying them too much attention. So, learn anything of interest?'

'I spoke to a bloke from D Company 4th Wilts. Mostly he just told me what we already had in the file. He remembers the carrier because of Dabs. Thought by the look of it an anti-tank gun had done for the carrier and that it was odd two of them were burnt and the third wasn't. When they looked closer they saw why.'

Stan took the cigarette I offered, lit it and inhaled.

'He said the road was a gravel track and the carrier had been pushed out the way. It was July and the two bodies in the carrier had already been more or less cooked. Another two weeks sitting in the vehicle hadn't done them any favours. Dabs wasn't as bad but...' he shrugged. 'The stretcher-bearers with D Company HQ buried them where they found them which is standard procedure. They usually stay in the temporary graves until their own battalion Orderly Room Sergeant can arrange a proper burial. Knowing it was a four-man carrier they looked for the extra man in the immediate area, including the house.'

Stan sipped his tea then dragged on his cigarette and raised his eyebrows in what I assumed was supposed to be a significant manner.

'Well?'

'They found a grave at the back of the house. Whoever had dug it hadn't made much of a job but at least they'd taken the trouble of putting a stake in as a marker. They naturally thought it might be the fourth man, but when they dug the body up it wasn't wearing a uniform. It had been partially burned but not as badly as the men in the carrier and what was left of the clothing proved to be civvies. They made sure, though, and found French ID papers on him.'

'That was all in the file,' I said. 'But they *were* sure it wasn't Kearney?'

'They were satisfied it wasn't.'

'Did they get a name from the papers they found on the body?'

'Civilians weren't their responsibility, so no.'

'And no other sign of Kearney?'

'No.'

'That it?'

'Not quite.' Stan stubbed out his cigarette. 'Apparently, when the 4th Wilts men came to temporarily interring the bodies, they found Poole's and Burleigh's ID discs on the floor of the carrier, not round the men's necks. They weren't sure which man was which. You know how careful they have to be, taking down the information on the disc and where the body's buried. So a note to that effect was left for 7th Hampshires Orderly Room Sergeant. And when the time came to exhume Poole and Burleigh for proper burial, blood tests were made to make sure which was which. I got this from the 7th Hampshires' Orderly Room Sergeant himself whose job it was to ID their own battalion's dead from the lists of missing.'

'But they were sure the two were actually the bodies of Poole and Burleigh?'

'Yeah. As sure as they could be at the time. 7th Hampshires' blood tests matched the ID discs. They're interred in the War Graves

Cemetery in Bannerville-la-Campagne, east of Caen. That's near Sannerville.'

'That it?'

'One more thing. The Orderly Room Sergeant gave me the name of the man from B Company who'd been able to visually identify Dabs. He'd been on Kearney's carrier before Operation Jupiter...' he glanced at his notes, '...name of Barker. That's why I was in Chelmsford this morning. He said the body wasn't a pretty sight but he was sure it was Dabs.'

'Did he happen to know Kearney too?'

'Yeah. Reckoned he was a bit of a loner. Good man, he said, but in the habit of keeping to himself. This Barker got his stripe just before the landings and was switched to another carrier. Burleigh took his place. He said he wasn't sorry to switch except it pissed him off that he had to leave Burleigh his PIAT. He didn't have one on the carrier he went to. If he'd stayed, of course, he reckons he'd have been toast like the rest of them.'

'Barker knew the other two, Poole and Dabs?'

'Yeah. Didn't care much for either apparently. One reason he wasn't sorry to switch vehicles. Reckoned Poole being a corporal was too full of himself. Only a lance-jack but apt to act like he was in command of the carrier. Kearney was always having to slap him down.'

'Dabs?'

'He said Dabs was a thief. Stuff was always going missing and a lot of the men blamed Dabs for it. Though no one was ever able to catch him at it. Between you and me Barker said he wasn't surprised someone put a bullet in his head.'

'What kind of stuff went missing?'

Stan shrugged. 'Nothing of any particular value. Just personal stuff. That's what annoyed them.'

'Official complaint?'

'No. Barker said some men gave Dabs a working over just before Jupiter. Nothing serious. Not enough for him to get excused duty. He seemed uncomfortable telling me about it and I got the idea Barker must have been one of them. Probably felt guilty afterwards when he had to identify Dabs' body.'

'I don't suppose one of them did it because of the thefts?'

'Nah,' said Stan. 'Just talk.'

'Did this Barker say if Poole and Dabs were close?'

'Not especially. Dabs was always trying to ingratiate himself. Didn't work with Kearney, but Poole wasn't above having Dabs do his skivvying for him.'

'Was Barker's carrier anywhere near Kearney's on the advance?'

'West of it. Once the Panzers opened up, though, he reckoned there was no telling what was going on. A round fell short of his carrier and flipped it over, otherwise he thought they would have caught it like Kearney's lot. Barker and one of his other men were injured.'

Jack came back and resumed abusing his Remington.

'Anything else?'

'Nothing definite,' said Stan. 'Someone told Barker a carrier was reported crossing the road towards the wood sometime mid-morning. No one could say if it was Kearney's, though.'

'Any other sightings?'

'No.'

Jack's phone rang.

'All right, Stan,' I said. 'Good work. Give Jack your notes and he'll get them typed up.'

Jack exchanged a few words down the line then held the receiver towards me.

'Superintendent Gifford.'

20

Ida opened the door and seemed oddly disappointed to find me standing there.

'Captain Tennant,' she said, 'I was expecting—' then didn't tell me who she was expecting. Stan, I supposed. I almost told her I'd left him at the office, that we'd all worked later than we had intended. But it was none of my business and instead I took the photograph Stan had found of Joseph Dabs out of my pocket and showed it to her.

'Recognize him?' I asked.

'It's a boy,' she said.

'If he was a few years older...?

She scrutinized the photo taking it back into her room so as to hold it by the window.

'It's Joe Dabs isn't it?'

'That's what I was hoping you'd say. It was taken when he was a boy in the Barnado's home. It's the only one we have and I wanted to be sure it was him.'

'He's got that same pinched face. Cruel, if you know what I mean.'

I hadn't thought of it being cruel, just rather weasel-like. If you drew whiskers on him he wouldn't have looked out of place in the cast of *Toad of Toad Hall.*

'You didn't like him did you?'

'Not much, but I only met him that once.'

'Were they good friends, Arnie and Joe Dabs?.

'No,' she said. 'I don't think he really liked him either. They were in the same unit, that's all. He sort of latched on to Arnie.' She gave me the photograph back. 'I don't suppose there's any chance it wasn't Arnie's body in the carrier is there?'

'No, not really Ida. Sorry.'

'I just...' she stopped and sighed. 'I've thought him dead all this time so...' she shrugged and smiled at me.

'Any luck with a job?' I asked.

'Not yet.'

Thinking of Julia, I said, 'I know someone who might need help around the house once or twice a week—cleaning and dusting, that sort of thing...I could ask if you'd like?'

'Would you?' she said eagerly. 'I'd be ever so grateful.'

'I can't promise anything.'

I remembered the letter I'd had from the landlord about the building being demolished. Ida wouldn't have got one, of course. The owner never showed his face from one month to the next and would have no idea she was there. The rent was always collected by an agent and I'd told her to keep her door closed when he came around on Friday evenings. Now, no sooner than she'd settled in, they'd decided to tear the place down. Not any time soon, perhaps, but I thought she'd better hear the news from me rather than read it from some notice posted on the front door.

'Knock it down?' she said, her pretty face falling as if in concert with the flats. 'Where will you go?'

The threat had been hanging over the place so long it had ceased to hold much meaning for me. I hadn't given any thought as to where I'd go and was quite touched that Ida's first concern was for my welfare.

'I've no idea,' I said.

She looked so despondent that to cheer her up I said I'd make enquiries about the work right away and left her standing in the middle of the shabby room like a condemned prisoner in an already condemned cell.

I went downstairs and telephoned Julia.

'Harry,' she said tonelessly when she answered.

I told her I'd had a letter from Penny and asked when she expected her to come up to town.

'This evening. Didn't she say in her letter?'

'No, only that she wanted to see me. Well,' I amended, '*needed* to see me, to be exact,' still wrestling with the semantics of the thing.

'She didn't tell me what it was about, Harry, if that's what you're asking.'

'That's all right, Julia. I suppose I'll find out. Another reason I called though...' and I told her about Ida who was looking for work if she still needed help in the house.

'Who is she?' Julia asked rather tartly, as if she thought Ida might be some girl I'd just picked up in Soho.

'She's a nice young kid,' I assured her. 'She was doing war work but lost her job now the men are coming back.'

'Does she have references?'

I sighed loudly enough for her to hear me. 'Only those I give her, Julia.'

'Well,' she said grudgingly, 'if you're recommending her...'

'I'm not an employment agency, Julia,' I replied just as tartly. 'She's looking for work and you said you couldn't get staff... I was just putting two and two together.'

'There's no need to snap my head off, Harry! I'll be in tomorrow morning if she can come at ten for an interview. I'm not promising anything.'

I told her Ida would be there then went back upstairs to let her know.

'Just look presentable,' I said, giving her Julia's name and address, 'and be yourself.'

Ida fetched the two dresses she'd brought with her from Blackburn and held them up for me to choose. Neither was likely to threaten Julia's idea of the natural social order so I pointed at the green one. It matched Ida's eyes.

~

Back in the flat I looked for something to eat. My bread was stale although with the news of rationing I couldn't bring myself to throw it away. Cutting a couple of slices, I fried it in some dripping that didn't look particularly mouldy and chucked in the few other bits and pieces I had handy.

Gifford had said he wanted to see me in the morning. He hadn't told me why, but when I said I had a photograph of William O'Connell, he asked me to bring it with me so I assumed he'd dug up some Fenian connection. Or perhaps something on Dermot Kavanaugh. I was to be at a café in King's Cross at nine.

That left me with a free evening. Having had no shortage of these since getting home, one might have thought I'd have developed some strategy to deal with them. But I hadn't. So, as usual, I turned on the radio to see what the BBC had to offer.

The All-England tennis championship at Wimbledon had started at the beginning of the week—the first time it had been staged since the war—and I caught the tail end of the day's results. I used to play a bit when I was in the police but hadn't kept it up. I was still interested although none of the competitors' names were familiar from those I recalled from before the war. After the tennis results there was a piano recital followed by a choice of comedians—Arthur Askey on the Home Service or Eric Barker on the Light programme. In the mood I was in I doubted if either would amuse me. Later though, after nine, there was a programme about the atomic bomb that seemed more likely to strike a chord.

~

It rained again overnight, and at dawn as I lay half asleep I could hear the faint roll of thunder like distant artillery. I began drifting through an unpleasant dream that I was back in North Africa and, when I finally woke up, found I was late for my meeting. By the time I eventually located the café down one of those narrow side streets off the lower Caledonian Road, Gifford was waiting for me.

He was sitting at a table by the grimy window with a white enamel mug in front of him, one of the kind that are always chipped. The colour of the tea in it was a deep muddy brown and reminded me of the River Po where we crossed it moving north during the Italian campaign. A glance at the chalk board behind the counter offered few options so I asked for a cup myself and took the chair opposite him. He watched me without speaking, a lugubrious expression pulling at his face like gravity.

Feeling chirpy, I asked, 'How's tricks in the secret police?'

He sipped his tea, looked as if he was going to reply, then didn't. I passed the photograph of Kearney and Rose in front of the columned building across the greasy table. Gifford glanced at it.

'That's Kearney,' I said. 'Or rather, William O'Connell. The woman is the one who posed as his sister.'

Gifford brought it closer to his face.

'Probably Rose O'Shaughnessy,' he said.

'Her name *is* Rose then. Not a complete liar.'

'I did say probably.' He turned the photo over and saw what had been written on the back. 'Yeats.'

'The poem is "Easter 1916",' I said.

'Appropriate enough. They're standing in front of the Post Office in Dublin.'

'Is it?' I took the photo back and studied the ionic column behind O'Connell and O'Shaughnessy. 'That was the centre of the rising, wasn't it?'

'The building was gutted,' Gifford said. 'They rebuilt it in the twenties.'

'So, when do you think this might have been taken?'

'Difficult to say. Certainly before January thirty-nine. Seán Russell became IRA chief of staff in thirty-eight. He began planning a bombing campaign here. They made several raids on munitions stores both north and south of the border, then the IRA Army Council declared war against Britain. That was in January of thirty-nine. The campaign began a few days later. O'Connell and Dermot Kavanaugh were involved in one of the Belfast munitions' raids about eighteen months earlier. They got a tip-off though, and the police and troops were waiting for them. One man was shot dead and the two others were caught. O'Connell and Kavanaugh—or Diamaid Caomhánach as he was calling himself then. Kavanaugh was convicted and got twelve years.'

'What about O'Connell?'

'He was the man who provided the tip-off. He turned King's Evidence.'

Astonished, I could think of nothing to say.

'Kavanaugh was lucky,' Gifford said. 'In a raid on the Magazine Fort in Dublin in December thirty-nine, the IRA stole the reserve ammunition of the Irish Army. The RUC found two and a half tons of it a month later in County Armagh. After that the Irish parliament introduced the Emergency Powers bill, reinstated internment and military tribunals and executions for IRA members. If they'd sent Kavanaugh back south he'd have been shot.'

'And O'Connell?'

'Part of the deal for his giving evidence against Kavanaugh was that he only got three months. He served that in the Scrubs. If this is your man Kearney then he changed his name when he got out and enlisted.'

'Would they have taken him if they'd known who he was?'

Gifford shrugged. 'We were conscripting everyone. But if they had known a nod from us would have been good enough.'

'Where does Rose O'Shaughnessy fit in?'

'She was born in Londonderry. Went to the university in Dublin and presumably met O'Connell and Kavanaugh there. She wasn't on the raid, though how much she knew about it is another matter. Her name came up in court as a known associate of Kavanaugh and O'Connell but she has never been charged with anything.'

'How long did Kavanaugh serve? A friend of his I spoke to said he saw him a few months ago.'

Gifford's nose twitched. 'Did he? And where was that?'

'Ballydrum in the republic. Where he grew up.'

Gifford grunted and his lips pursed sourly. 'He did five years. Down the road in Pentonville. He escaped on VE-day. They probably forgot to lock the doors while they were out dancing in the street. There's been no word of him until now.'

He reached into an inside pocket and took out an envelope. He passed it across the table.

'That's Kavanaugh. Or Diamaid Caomhánach, as he likes to call himself.'

I slipped the photo out of the envelope. It was the usual police mug shot, the kind that could make Errol Flynn look surly. Kavanaugh may not have been born with Flynn's advantages but it didn't seem possible he looked as desperate in real life as the photograph suggested. A snub nose like a lump of putty lay in the centre of a small round face. He was clean-shaven and had bad skin below wavy hair that stood upright off his head as if he'd just had a fright. I remembered what Dónol Casey had said about him—how as a boy Kavanaugh had fallen under the spell of their schoolmaster and the supposed romance of the Easter Rising. Now, no longer a schoolboy, there was a vindictive look in his eyes, as if he'd just been roughed up by the Royal Ulster Constabulary and was staring at several years in prison without benefit of poetry.

'Seen him before?' Gifford asked.

'No,' I said. 'I don't know him. Can I keep it though? I want to show it to someone.'

'Rose O'Shaughnessy?'

I put the photograph back in the envelope along with the one of Rose and Willy O'Connell.

'She's gone,' I said. 'What do you think? Were they looking for O'Connell to dispense a little IRA justice?'

'Kavanaugh certainly. Who knows about O'Shaughnessy? O'Connell and her used to be an item, as the newspapers are fond of putting it.'

'Is that right?'

'And he gave evidence against Kavanaugh, not against O'Shaughnessy, remember.'

~

When I got home I picked up the phone and started to dial Julia's number to see if Penny had arrived, then changed my mind. While I hesitated I looked at the numbers that had been scribbled on the wall by the phone, several of them by me. They reminded me of the phone at the house where Rose had stayed in Claremont Street. It seemed to me that, together with Kavanaugh, she must have been plotting revenge for some time. Dónol Casey had told Kavanaugh that O'Connell had joined the British Army and somehow, despite his change of name, they had managed to track him down. Perhaps they had done it through the army lists, managing to persuade someone at Kearney's battalion to give them the names and home details of the rest of the carrier crew. Given that Kavanaugh had escaped from prison and was in hiding, I presumed, it must have been Rose who had done the leg work. I was impressed by how far she had got. I would have co-opted her into my section any day.

I went upstairs and knocked on Ida's door but there was no reply. I wanted to show her the photo of Kavanaugh. It seemed too improbable that a third person was also looking for Kearney.

Apart from Ida and Rose, the only other person who had met Hendrix was Edna Burleigh. The market in Deptford High Street was in full swing when I got there. Stalls and barrows lined the length of the road, crowds bustling between them. There were vegetables and fruit from the fields of Kent on offer as well as a bewildering variety of other goods: pots, pans, plates and cutlery; bicycles and car accessories and, on one stall, faded bolts of material that looked as if they had lain like the contents of Ali Baba's cave undisturbed since the beginning of the war in some forgotten lock-up.

Edna Burleigh lived south of the market in a part of Deptford which like the rest of Lewisham had suffered badly in the Blitz. Gutted buildings, stark against the sky like fleshless fingers, stood as a reminder of the Luftwaffe raids. And, once they had been beaten back, of the V1 had V2 rockets that had followed. The overnight rain had coated everything with a gritty film of grime. Weeds and shrubs had taken hold amid the rubble and greened the slopes and valleys of pulverized masonry. Bees, like ragged formations of aircraft, buzzed among the dandelions and buddleia; butterflies fluttered from bloom to pendulous bloom.

Some kids were playing amid the rubble, excavating holes with long sticks and looking for what they could find. They swarmed over ruins like the residents of Berlin had when battered household goods were still to be found amid the devastation.

The terrace of grimy back-to-backs all looked the same to me as I walked up and down trying to find Edna Burleigh's door. I knocked on one that looked familiar and waited and suddenly Edna Burleigh's snotty-nosed little girl appeared as if I had just rubbed Aladdin's lamp.

'Mum's not in,' she said, looking up and squinting at me.

I bent towards her. 'Do you know where she is?'

'Yeah, cos I do.'

'Are you going to tell me?'

'Are you my Dad?'

Her open mouth showed some missing teeth. A patch of something sticky on one of her cheeks was smeared with dirt. She was frowning, waiting for an answer.

'No,' I said, 'I'm not your Dad.'

'Johnny says he dead.'

'You'd better ask your Mum,' I told her.

'She's not here.'

'Where is she?'

She pointed to the next house. The front door was open and she darted inside. A moment later Edna Burleigh emerged and looked at me vacantly until I reminded her who I was.

'You told me when I came last that a Major Hendrix had visited you. From the Graves Commission?'

'That's right,' she said warily.

I took Gifford's photograph of Dermot Kavanaugh out the envelope and showed it to her.

'Is this him?'

She peered at the photo, then at me and scowled.

'What's the game? This looks like a police mug shot. What you playin' at?'

'Is this the man who called himself Major Hendrix?' I asked again.

'Looks a bit like 'im,' she decided. 'The nose mostly. This one's younger and 'e's got more 'air.'

'But it could be him?' I persisted.

'Could be. But I ain't sayin' it is.'

I thanked her and took back the photograph.

'He wasn't an army officer. He was someone who used to know your husband's sergeant, William Kearney.'

'I thought he was killed along with my Bob,' she said.

'Missing,' I said. I thanked her again and turned to go.

'Is that it?' she called. 'Why did 'e say 'e was an officer if 'e wasn't? That looked like a police photograph. What if 'e comes back?'

'I don't think that's likely,' I assured her.

'Oh yeah? What if 'e does?'

I took out a piece of paper and wrote down the office phone number. 'Ring this number and ask for me. My name's Tennant.'

Walking down the street I wondered if I should have given her some more money; if she had been expecting it. I was conscious all the while of her watching me go, her little girl gathered close as if now there were new dangers to consider.

I rang Julia from a call box, expecting her or Penny to answer. Instead a vaguely familiar northern accent announced:

'Miss Julia Parker's residence. Who's speaking please?'

'Ida? Is that you?'

'*Captain Tennant,*' she squealed. 'It's me, Ida. I got the job.'

'So I see,' I said. 'Is everything all right?'

'It's ever so nice here,' she said. 'And Miss Parker has been very kind to me. She said I could start straight away and even gave me some clothes to wear.'

I imagined Ida in a French maid's costume like a character out of a west-end farce. But somehow I doubted even Julia would be that crass.

'Is Julia there? Or Mrs Tennant?'

'Please hold the line,' Ida said, sounding as if Julia had spent the morning teaching her what to say when people called. A moment later Julia came on the line.

'Harry?'

'Hello Julia? Is Penny with you?'

'Here, yes, but she can't come to the phone just now. She'll see you this evening if you're free.'

I wondered if she was being sarcastic.

'Shall I come round?'

'Ben Tuchman will be here. You met him the other evening?'

'I remember.'

'We thought it would be fun if we all went out together. There's a new place just opened, near Wardour Street. We could have dinner and go on somewhere afterwards. What do you think, Harry?'

I had been thinking it would be more fun to take Penny to the pictures. The new Hitchcock film, *Notorious*, was playing and Penny had always liked Cary Grant. Besides, sitting in the cinema precluded conversation and might have prevented us from saying things we'd later regret. Julia and Tuchman being with us might serve the same purpose although I thought I could smell a plot. Not one likely to be as well-constructed as Hitchcock's perhaps, and, unlike those in the pictures, one it was difficult to see having a happy ending.

'If that's what Penny wants to do,' I said. 'What time?'

'Seven?'

'Seven, then. Ida worked out all right, did she?'

'Yes, Harry, I'm sure she's going to be fine. Unfortunately she told Penny how I found her.'

'Why "unfortunately"?'

'Because *you* found her.'

'So?'

'Oh, Harry,' Julia sighed with irritation. 'We'll see you at seven o'clock,' and rang off.

I spent the rest of the afternoon browsing through some of the west-end shops. If Penny was up for the weekend I decided it couldn't hurt to look my best. My army uniform was getting a bit shabby and it would only be a reminder, if she needed one, that I'd been missing for the past few years.

I might have found a costumiers and hired a police constable's uniform for the weekend. But perhaps that would have been seen as trying too hard. The last thing I wanted was to appear obvious.

~

According to Julia the club hadn't been open long. A dimly lit basement smelling of fresh distemper and damp, it boasted a dozen tables, a band and a small dance floor. They were playing the Charlie Barnet favourite *Skyliner* as we walked in but the band's brass line was too thin and lacked the necessary impact. On the other hand, glancing through the menu it was obvious the place must have a black-market supply of food. What was on offer could only have looked good to Londoners starved of anything other than Spam and carrots for the last six years. I suppose being in the army Tuchman and I had fared better than those at home, although judging by the way he grappled with his slice of beef when it arrived, Tuchman was probably more used to having his meat separated from its leather hide before being served. But he didn't complain. Nor enquire, I happened to notice, whether the meat was kosher when he ordered. Not that I had any reason to suppose him to be Orthodox, or even practising, which at least gave Julia some room to manoeuvre. I caught Penny's eye as the meal was served as we had once been attuned to that sort of thing, on occasions often able to tell what the other was thinking. She avoided looking at me now, however. I suppose had this been a Hitchcock film, the camera would have moved in for a close-up at that point and everyone would have been able to tell the moment had significance. But it all went over my head for a while longer.

I believe Tuchman sensed something was up and, rather than make him feel uncomfortable, the situation seemed to afford him some wry amusement. All part of our British quaintness, perhaps. But finally, when it became obvious even to me, rusty as I was, that Penny had some sort of grievance, I guessed that we were out with Julia and Tuchman so that Penny and I would not have to be alone together. Even then, while Julia was very fond of Penny, I doubted she would have been willing to ruin her evening with Tuchman just to rescue Penny or spite me, so I gathered there was more afoot than my usual run-of-the-mill differences with my wife.

We had finished dinner and ordered another drink when Tuchman suddenly sat upright and stared at Julia as if she had just kicked him under the table.

'Penny,' he said with admirable aplomb, 'would you like to dance?'

They excused themselves and glided across the empty dance floor to the strains of Irvine Berlin's *Just the Way You Look Tonight*. Tuchman was a good dancer, I noted, although I wouldn't have expected anything else. I nodded in their direction.

'Shall we?' I asked Julia.

She regarded me sourly. 'Hardly Harry. I remember what a rotten dancer you were. I don't suppose you've improved.'

'Not much opportunity,' I replied, although I recalled there had been the odd club or two in Berlin where a brief shuffle around the dance floor was the usual prelude to other diversions. I toyed with the stem of my wine glass for a moment then said, 'Is there something up?'

'Well of *course* there is,' Julia said. 'What do you expect?'

'I haven't a clue,' I told her.

That brought another disdainful look.

'For an ex-policeman you've always been oddly deficient in *them*. Ida?'

'What about her?'

'Did you really think it was a good idea to suggest I employ one of your girls? I mean, if I hadn't been *desperate* I wouldn't have considered it. To be honest,' she added, flicking cigarette ash carelessly on the tablecloth, 'it never crossed my mind you'd be quite so callous. Not until Penny told me you're supposed to be looking for her brother...'

I began to laugh. Julia became indignant.

'What are you laughing at?'

'Ida? You seriously thought—'

'I fail to see what's so funny,' she snapped. 'She's a very pretty girl. Or would be if she dressed properly.'

I watched Penny and Tuchman on the dance floor. Having broken the ice they'd now been joined by two or three other couples. I stood up, dropped my serviette on the table, and crossed the floor. I tapped Tuchman on the shoulder.

'May I?'

Penny glowered at me but was too well-bred to make a scene. Tuchman grinned. I put my arm around Penny's waist and took her hand, promptly leading off with the wrong foot. She winced.

'Sorry.'

'You still haven't learnt to dance,' she complained.

'I haven't had the opportunity to practise,' I said.

She muttered something and gazed over my shoulder.

'For someone who said they needed to see me,' I said, 'you've not got much to say for yourself.'

'Are you surprised?'

'Nothing surprises me anymore, Penny. Julia just told me you've taken exception to Ida.'

She made to pull away from me but I held her firmly. We stumbled through a few more steps before she said:

'Well? She's the one with the missing brother isn't she?'

'If you remember,' I said with overt patience, 'that woman was Irish. Even the tone deaf couldn't mistake Ida's accent for Irish. This one was engaged to one of the other men killed in the carrier. She married someone else who, it turns out, knocks her around. Stan, one of my men, paid him back in kind. Ida left her husband and turned up here.'

'She told me she'd moved in next to you,' Penny replied sullenly.

'That was Stan's idea, not mine. She had nowhere else to go. The only reason there's room in my building is that the place is falling down.'

'So she's with this Stan, is she?'

'I'm sure Stan would like to think so. But he's old enough to be her father.'

'You found her a job,' she said, managing to make what had been an altruistic act sound more like a criminal one.

'Julia needed help and Ida needed work. As simple as that.'

Julia and Tuchman whirled past us.

'He seems like a nice chap,' I said.

'Julia's very fond of him.'

'I hope he hasn't got a wife and family back home. What does he do?'

'He's attached to the US State Department or something. He's a colonel, actually.'

'Perhaps I should salute next time they pass.'

'Don't be ridiculous,' she said.

To change the subject I said Julia had told me Helen and Reggie were coming home.

Three months into our marriage I came to the conclusion I couldn't keep referring to them as Mr and Mrs Forster. I didn't care to call them mum and dad any more than they would have wanted me to, so in the end I settled for their Christian names. They didn't care much for that, either, but fortunately I never saw that much of them.

'I'd like to see your father's face when Julia introduces Tuchman to him,' I said to Penny.

'Why?' Then she realized what I meant. 'Oh,' she said, 'I don't suppose they think *that* way anymore. Not after everything that's happened. Not when you realize what having those attitudes led to.'

Everyone had seen the newsreels of the Nazi concentration camps playing in the cinemas at the end of the war. There had always been rumours about what the Nazi government had been doing to the Jews and those who had opposed them, but it took seeing film of the atrocities to bring it home. It was still news now, what with the war crimes trials dragging on and with executions scheduled.

But instead of pressing the point, I said something conciliatory to Penny about her parents. Conversation between us had become like crossing a frozen pond. It paid to watch out for thin ice rather than charge ahead heedlessly as I used to be in the habit of doing. I'd got into deep water so often before that now I had learned to tread carefully.

The band segued from a waltz into *In The Mood* and some of the couples around us began to jitterbug or jive, or whatever they were calling it now. Any attempt at the dance on my part generally resembled all-in wrestling and usually resulted in a tangle of twisted limbs. Penny, knowing me of old, turned back to our table. We passed Julia and Tuchman who were throwing themselves into the dance like a pair of adolescents.

'Was Ben at the house the other week when you went to the theatre?' I asked as we sat down.

'No, he met us there. Why?'

'I don't remember seeing him, that's all. As it happens I was talking to Maurice Coveney. I had no idea he was an old friend of your parents. You've never mentioned him to me before.'

'Uncle Maurice? Of course I have. You've met him, surely.'

'No, never.'

'Well, I've certainly spoken of him. He married Aunt Louise after her first husband died. I never knew *him*, of course. He was killed in the first war. They'd only been married a few months.'

I had to admit that "Aunt Louise" had a familiar ring to it.

'Was she the French one?'

'Yes. You see? She was Mummy's best friend at school.'

It came back to me then. Mainly because at the time there had been some lascivious story about Penny's mother, Helen, and the brother of her school friend. I'd found it difficult to believe at first. I couldn't remember how the subject had come up—some off-hand remark I had made to Penny about her straight-laced mother probably. I was not as careful then about skirting thin ice. Penny had taken exception to the remark, I seemed to recall, and to demonstrate how wrong I was about her mother told me the story about how when Helen was a girl before the First War, spending her summers in France at the home of a school friend, she had had an affair with the friend's elder brother. They had been in love, Penny assured me and it was assumed they would marry, although they had never been officially engaged. The boy had volunteered at the start of the war and shortly afterwards had been posted as missing, presumed dead. After several months Helen met Reggie Forster and married him. It was more than a year before she learned that her friend's brother was alive and in a German POW camp and by then Penny had been born.

To look at the prim and proper Helen I knew, the story was difficult to believe. But Penny had got it from Julia who had known about the affair at the time. Penny, of course, swore me to secrecy on pain of exclusion from the marital bed.

'I still can't believe you've never met him,' Penny insisted.

'Coveney? Well, I haven't. I only mention it now because when I met him that evening I thought he was interested in you.'

'Interested in me? You don't mean— Don't be ridiculous, Harry! Sometimes you can be so dense,' and she began to laugh.

'I jumped to a wrong conclusion,' I said.

Her laughter began to fade. 'What you mean is that now I'm the one who's jumped to a conclusion.'

'But I would never have called *you* dense,' I said. 'Were you jealous?'

'No!' she protested. Then looked at me sheepishly. 'Well, all right, just a little bit perhaps.'

There was more that could have been said, but with thin ice all around I decided to leave it at that.

'I'll be nice to Ida,' Penny promised. 'But not to the other one, the Irish one.'

'Rose? It turns out the fellow wasn't her brother after all, and that they were both mixed up in the IRA. So I doubt I'll be seeing her again.'

'Just as well by the sound of it,' said Penny. Then she rounded on me as she remembered something. 'I wrote to you about Aunt Louise being killed in an air raid so I know I've told you about the Coveneys.'

'Did you?'

I honestly couldn't remember. I may have been told although letters had a habit of going astray overseas.

'Mummy wanted Aunt Louise to stay with them in Connecticut. At least while the bombing was on. Uncle Maurice couldn't leave because of his work at the Foreign Office and Aunt Louise wouldn't go without him. Mummy was devastated when we wrote to tell her auntie had been killed in a raid. They had been friends since they were girls.'

'Who were friends?' Julia asked, a little breathlessly and catching the end of the conversation as she and Tuchman returned to the table.

'Mummy and Aunt Louise,' said Penny. 'I was telling Harry that Mummy used to spend her summers at their château in France.'

'I used to be so envious,' Julia said to Tuchman. 'They said I was too young to go. Then the war started and Helen married. My first visit wasn't until Marie-Louise and Maurice were married. You were still a child, Penny, so I don't suppose you remember.'

'Not then,' said Penny.

'It was a lovely old house,' said Julia. 'Maurice told me it was all but destroyed during the invasion. Such a shame. It stood at the end of a long wooded drive and was named for the beech wood it stood in.'

My throat constricted. 'Whereabouts in France?' I croaked.

'Normandy. Near Caen. The Château de Hêtres.

21

'*Hêtres* is French for beech trees, of course,' Julia prattled on as my glass went over, red wine spilling across the tablecloth.

I began dabbing at the spreading stain with a napkin.

Penny glared at me. 'You're so clumsy.'

Tuchman righted the glass and refilled it from the bottle. I picked it up and took a long pull at the wine, the hairs standing on the back of my head.

'What did you say the house was called?' I said to Julia.

'The Château de Hêtres. Such a shame. Of course Claude, Marie-Louise's brother, had inherited the estate after their parents died. Though he lived in Paris mostly. He was killed during the invasion.'

I became aware that Penny was watching me and put a hand over hers.

'Life can be so unfair,' Julia went on. 'The war taking both Claude and poor Marie-Louise. Didn't Maurice have to identify his body?' she asked Penny.

Penny, still alert to my reaction, glanced at Julia.

'Sorry,' she said. 'Identified who?'

'Maurice,' Julia repeated. 'He identified Claude's body.'

'Oh. Yes. But that was a long time after, surely...'

'Claude and Marie-Louise were the last of their line,' said Julia. 'Well, except for Jeremy, I suppose.'

I asked who Jeremy was.

Julia lit another cigarette, inhaling deeply before blowing a stream of smoke to one side of the table.

'Maurice and Marie-Louise's son. I dare say he's inherited the estate now. What's left of it, if there is anything. There was no land apart from the house as far as I know. Nothing that might provide any income.'

'It's going to be a while before farming can start again,' Tuchman stated with what wasn't quite a *non sequitur*. 'They'll have to clear the ordnance first.'

'What's ordnance?' Julia asked.

'Bombs,' I said. 'Ben means the unexploded variety.'

'He'll sell, I suppose,' Penny said.

Julia agreed with a murmur. 'You know your mother was quite sweet on Claude once, before she married your father, of course.'

Penny glanced at me. I knew she was thinking of the story she'd told me about Helen's affair, worried probably that I might say something and let Julia know that I knew.

'Your father and Claude became great chums, of course,' Julia went on. 'Although Marie-Louise did once tell me that Helen was the reason her brother never married.' She flicked ash towards the ashtray, adding with a wry smile, 'Actually I'm not sure how true that was. Claude had something of a reputation as a ladies' man, you know. He propositioned me once.'

'Well if he couldn't have one sister...' I suggested.

Penny elbowed me forcefully.

I winced. 'Did they keep in touch with Claude once the war had started?'

'I don't see how they could,' Penny said. 'Not with France occupied by the Germans.'

'She could write from America, surely. Until they entered the war, anyway,' said Julia. 'Wasn't it your mother who told Claude that Marie-Louise had been killed? When was that... nineteen forty-one?'

'March,' said Penny.

'Well, there you are. That was a long time before America came in.' She laid her hand on top of Tuchman's as if to demonstrate that it was a question of historical fact, not an aspersion upon America's tardiness. 'There was nothing to stop anyone in America corresponding with France, surely? Not if they were neutral at the time.'

'None at all,' said Tuchman who'd said nothing since his comment on ordnance.

'But that wouldn't be right,' said Penny, as if it was a question of loyalty. 'Mummy wouldn't do that.'

'Your father would,' I said, regretting the remark as soon as I voiced it.

Penny glared at me.

'We're getting a reputation as Johnny-come-latelys,' Tuchman intervened, smiling as he said it, although I got the impression he was less than comfortable with the subject.

'I don't see why,' Julia persisted. 'It's not as though Claude was *German*. Why shouldn't Helen write to him if she wanted? I don't suppose he wanted the Nazis there any more than the rest of France did.'

I might have given Julia an argument about French ambivalence to the German Occupation but I'd already spoken out of turn once.

'After America entered the war it was a different matter, of course,' said Julia. 'When was that, Ben?'

'December eighth, nineteen forty-one,' Tuchman said, although he wasn't smiling any more. 'The day after Pearl Harbour.'

'Of course it was.' Julia patted his hand again. 'Better late than never.'

A slightly pained expression crossed Tuchman's face and before Julia could get herself into deeper trouble, I asked:

'What was Claude and Marie-Louise's family name?'

'Pellisier,' said Penny, stifling a yawn. 'Sorry. I'm not used to late nights. In the country we're usually in bed by ten.'

She looked sideways at me as if expecting another tasteless remark. I pretended not to notice.

'Perhaps you'll take me home, Harry. You don't mind, do you Julia?'

'It's past my bedtime, too,' I said rising.

Tuchman got to his feet. Julia was eyeing us suspiciously, no doubt wondering if she might find Penny and I in our old room when she got home. But Penny's thoughts weren't running along those lines unfortunately. And since I could tell they weren't, I wouldn't have minded staying a little longer and finding out more about Coveney's brother-in-law, Claude Pellisier.

But the topic had died a natural death so we said our goodnights, leaving Julia and Tuchman at the club and catching a taxi back to Julia's house. Outside, Penny told me to take it on, gave me the briefest of pecks on the cheek and asked me to call her in the morning. Before I could stop her she slipped out of the taxi and was running up the steps and letting herself into the house.

'Clerkenwell,' I told the driver, sinking back into the seat.

~

The definition of chance depends upon one's theology, I suppose. It's a word under which both benign providence and malign fate can masquerade; where the concept of a guiding hand or—more sinisterly—predestination abnegate any need for explanation.

But a cynic like me requires answers.

Like chance, a definition of happenstance is an event that might have been arranged and yet is, in reality, accidental.

A cynic might argue that coincidence is the reverse.

~

Although it was late there was a light under Ida's door and I felt a sudden impulse to apologise to her for any slight Penny may have given earlier in the day. I thought I heard a sound inside and stopped to listen. It might have been the radio except by that time of night the BBC was off-air. Then, as I stood there, the light went out and I heard nothing more.

Lying on my bed unable to sleep and despite what I had learned from Julia, I found myself wishing I had taken Penny to the cinema after all. Moonlight filtering through my ragged curtains cast a silver glow over the room, washing it with a sheen of unreality that masked the tawdry verity. In that light the place looked almost presentable. I supposed it was the kind of view of life that we all—and not only Susie—looked for when we went to the cinema. We sought the glossy unrealities that film gave us; not the dust and the dirt and the grime of everyday life. Perhaps we were trying to avoid the truth of how we had to live now the war was over. For most people the experience had been hateful, terrifying and devastating. And yet for some it had been a thrilling escape from everyday existence—like the celluloid world. Now it was over I wasn't sure anyone was prepared to go back to what they had been before.

After a while these thoughts and the evening slid imperceptively into that half-conscious state one has between sleep and wakefulness, when weightless perception slips the tethers that keep one anchored in reality. On the edge of sleep, deviant imagination has its own priorities and, like surrealist film, unreels images of its own choosing.

The château near Caen came to me, shimmering opaquely through the moonlight. People I did not know yet could strangely recognize floated past me like ghosts down the long corridors of the house. I saw two young girls playing in and out of inter-connecting rooms, while in the shadows an older boy watched on silently. Uniformed men appeared and somehow, in the trance of dream, I could understand what was happening. As if I had been given the key piece to a once-incomprehensible puzzle, I found myself able to slot each element into an apprehensible whole—a whole that encompassed the château and Kearney, the carrier and its crew...even the elusive Rose. While I dreamed it all made perfect and knowable sense and, having understood, I fell into the deep oblivion of consummate sleep.

In the morning, waking, I could remember little of it. Only that briefly I had had an answer and now, the more I stretched to retrieve it, the further it receded. Until finally, as I became fully conscious, the memory vanished altogether.

~

It was early but I got up and made myself a breakfast with egg powder and milk. Feeling at a loose end until I could telephone Penny, I had a blitz on the flat and cleaned up.

By ten o'clock when I knew Penny would be up even if Julia might still be in bed, I went downstairs to the phone in the hall. She answered surprisingly quickly although any hope that she had been waiting by the telephone for my call was quashed when she said:

'Did you forget something?'

'No,' I replied, 'I don't think so.'

'Harry?'

'Who did you think it was?'

'Julia. I've just been speaking to her. I thought she forgot something and rang again.'

'Isn't she with you?'

'No,' she said, 'she didn't—' and stopped abruptly.

'Didn't come home?' I asked. 'I could have stayed over then.'

But Penny didn't take the bait.

'Don't tell her I told you, Harry.'

'Not a word,' I assured her. 'You're on your own?'

'Julia just rang to invite me out to lunch. At the Savoy.'

'I was hoping we could do something together,' I said. 'I take it the lunch invitation didn't extend to me. Will Ben be with you?'

'Yes,' Penny said, 'and she didn't exactly say I *wasn't* to bring you...'

'Nor that you should?'

'No...and it *is* the Savoy. I don't often get the opportunity these days.'

'Afterwards?'

'All right. Where shall I meet you?'

Even in London there were limits to what one could do on a Sunday afternoon, but there was always a walk in the park. I arranged to meet her near the Savoy at two-fifteen.

It was ten-fifteen just then and I had four hours to kill. I'd already filled my cleaning quota, didn't have the patience to sit still listening to the radio or read a book, so decided to go into the office and, finally, make a start on the report for Jekyll.

I took a bus and walked rather than wait for the Sunday tube service. The sun felt warm when it broke through the cloud and I was experiencing an unusual optimism. It might just have been the weather or perhaps a reaction to the fact I was meeting Penny later and that we had managed to get through an evening without arguing.

I realized I was beginning to re-map the ice on our mutual pond. Before the war I'd had a pretty good idea of where I could tread and where I could not, even if I did not always heed the warnings. Some subjects screamed *thin ice*, mostly those concerning her parents. It wasn't that I had been overly critical—by my lights at least—it was more that my responses had been a reaction to their criticism of me. Penny had been well aware that aspects of their behaviour warranted criticism but still felt bound to defend them. It upset her when I pointed out she was defending the indefensible.

Her friends—those that had predated our marriage—had been another bone of contention. By and large, I had found them an insufferable lot. I daresay they thought much the same about me, only then of course I didn't consider that possibility. I tried to remember if Jeremy Coveney had been among their number. He would have been two or three years younger than Penny so I supposed not. I certainly couldn't recall ever having met him. Those I did meet—the men at any rate—had figured pretty low in my estimation even before being introduced. I saw things differently now. The war and the year since had changed me. I could now see that back then I had had a chip on my shoulder. I had been conscious of the social difference between myself and Penny's circle and had reacted boorishly. The wonder was that Penny had ever put up with me at all. The irony now was that having mellowed and for the most part rid myself of the chip, Penny and I were no longer together. Perhaps she had liked the raw and diffident young policeman better than the man I had become. He was gone for good, though, lost somewhere between North Africa and Berlin, and Penny seemed unable to adjust to the man who had replaced him.

The office seemed a somehow alien place when empty. It was its default status, I suppose, and capable of making me feel like an outsider. There was an overwhelming silence despite the muted hum of traffic on the street below. It was a silence compounded by the lack of Jack's Remington and of the hiss of the ever-boiling kettle; of Peter's peremptory requests and Stan's grunted replies. Even the air seemed bereft without Susie's scent. What my contribution to the schema was I couldn't say. I had brought that in with me, I suppose, and could never more sense its absence than I would ever recognize its presence.

I put the kettle on hoping its familiar hiss would chase away the metaphysical aura that seemed to have surrounded me ever since I had got out of bed. Perhaps it had been the dream of the château and that the certain knowledge I had gained was now no more than a memory of certainty. Then I realized I was slipping back into the metaphysical and still procrastinating over the report.

I stood with my tea in front of Peter Quince's map. The flag indicating the position of Kearney's carrier was a short distance from the outline of a building that had to be the Château de Hêtres. Julia said the château had been destroyed but that wasn't surprising as it had been in the middle of a battle. Little survives under those circumstances and I supposed, like Caen itself and most of the nearby villages, it had been pulverized. Anywhere that afforded shelter for troops or concealment for guns would have been pounded by the opposing artillery. Particularly local châteaux or other large buildings that were liable to be commandeered as Staff HQs or command posts. It made them prime targets. I often wondered how the French had felt about their liberators, effectively destroying everything in their path in order to free it. Yet we had been welcomed by joyous crowds, many of them perhaps the same people who four years earlier had accepted the arrival of the Wehrmacht. All of which, I suppose, at least said something about what life must have been like under the Occupation.

I wondered if Claude Pellisier, Marie-Louise Coveney's brother, had accepted the arrival of the Germans with equanimity. He had fought against them in the Great War, according to Penny, but then so had Marshal Pétain. Pellisier hadn't had a chance to welcome the liberators since Julia said he had been killed during the invasion. And although I would have liked the opportunity to ask exactly how and when, the chances were he had died in similar circumstances to his sister; perhaps in an air raid in Caen.

I was still staring at the blank sheet of paper that was supposed to be Jekyll's report when I remembered from the entry in SS-Mann Richter's diary for the day Müller's platoon arrived at the château that the owner was there when they arrived. The man Stan had spoken to from the Field Ambulance unit had told him they'd found the body of a French civilian buried in the garden. If that was true it was possible it had been Pellisier's body. Richter had also said there had been Gestapo officers present. Perhaps Dabs hadn't been the only man at the château on the wrong end of a war crime.

I assumed Coveney would know the details. Penny had said he had identified Pellisier's body, although quite how, after the length of time that must have elapsed, I couldn't imagine. Given the man's attitude towards me when we met, however, I doubted he'd appreciate me asking him questions about it. I might be able to persuade Penny to do it for me, though.

As long as the subject didn't turn out to be thin ice.

I finally spent two or three hours on Jekyll's report, going back over what we knew from various sources. Susie had already begun to put some of it together in readable order. Going through it again, it now seemed to me that William Kearney turning out to be Willy O'Connell was something I'd do well to leave out for the present.

O'Connell's involvement in a raid on a Belfast barracks for arms proved a curious and interesting development—as was his turning King's Evidence—and although it suggested Dermot Kavanaugh and Rose O'Shaughnessy were looking for him in order to exact some sort of revenge, they couldn't possibly have had anything to do with Dabs' death. It might have been a powerful motive for O'Connell wanting to disappear, admittedly, but Kavanaugh was still in prison at the time, even if it wouldn't have taken a lot of imagination to predict what Kavanaugh would do once he was out.

Believing that O'Connell was prepared to kill his comrades to facilitate his escape, though, was still a stretch: a barely credible, and unreasonably drastic, solution to a problem that could be solved in other ways. And as Peter had already pointed out, if that's what he did he would surely have left his identification discs on one of the burnt corpses.

Despite considering the alternative possibility of it not being O'Connell but one of the others whose body hadn't been found, I hadn't turned up any reason for Poole, Burleigh, or Dabs to want to disappear either. Dabs had been visually identified and so, of the four, I was confident it was O'Connell's bones which were waiting to be discovered at the bottom of some muddy ditch in Normandy.

I put as much in the report while leaving O'Connell as we had originally found him—in the innocent guise of Sergeant William Kearney.

Afterwards I sat at my desk, feet up, smoking. My conclusion was the sort of thing Jekyll wanted to hear and so I assumed he'd be pleased enough to pass the report back to the place from where it had originally come.

I should have been pleased, too. Yet looking down at the small sheaf of papers that made up my considered opinion on the business, it seemed they were more eloquent in what they didn't say rather than in what they did.

I listened to the clock tick and watched smoke rings float over the report in the dusty office air, looking for answers that weren't there.

22

Sunday June 30th 1946

Penny was waiting outside the Savoy.

'I thought we could walk through Trafalgar Square and down the Mall to the park. Or is that too far for you?'

'No,' she said. 'I walk everywhere now.'

'Doesn't George still have the car?'

'We don't use it unless we have to.'

George was thin ice so I didn't enquire further. We walked along the Strand. The centre of London had its share of damage. There were gaps in the buildings here and there, much like the gaps the bombs had left in people's lives. I'd known one or two people who had died in air raids and supposed that Penny did too. She'd had a wide circle of friends before I met her.

I thought about Jeremy Coveney again and asked her if I had ever met him.

'Jeremy? I don't think so. He was still at school or had just gone up to university when we got married. He joined up shortly afterwards, anyway. I know he was overseas when his mother was killed. What made you ask?'

'Nothing really,' I said. 'It's just an odd coincidence. This business with this carrier crew I've been looking into...'

'The Irish woman and the IRA?'

'That turned out to be a red herring,' I said. As were my suspicions about Arnie Poole and Joseph Dabs. 'They've got nothing to do with it.'

'So you said last night. What's so odd about it?'

'They were killed near Caen. Pretty close to your Aunt Louise's old house.'

'Château de Hêtres? That is odd. What a strange coincidence.'

'Isn't it?'

'We were only talking about Uncle Claude over lunch,' she said.

'Oh?'

'Ben spent time in the area before the war. He was wondering if he knew the house.'

'Is that likely?'

'I wouldn't have thought so. It was a bit out of the way. And it wasn't the sort of house one imagines when one thinks of French châteaux. Not one of those grand houses the aristocracy owned before the revolution. It wasn't somewhere you'd visit, anyway. Not like the local big house, the Château de Maltot.'

'That was closer to the village, I suppose.'

'Uncle Claude's house was in the middle of a wood. One wouldn't pass it on the way to somewhere else. There was only the drive leading to it and a track at the back down to the river. After Aunt Louise married Uncle Maurice it was never much more than a weekend place for Claude. Mummy always loved it, though, and went back whenever she could.'

'Do you happened to know where Claude was killed?' I asked casually.

'I'm not sure. Mummy wrote to tell me but not the details. I suppose she got it from Uncle Maurice. I did ask him once but he doesn't like to talk about it. Too upsetting. First Aunt Louise and then Claude...'

Past Admiralty Arch we walked down The Mall and into St James Park. Although no longer being exhorted to Dig for Victory, the allotments that had been part of Churchill's campaign were still there—a small fraction of the parks and common land that had gone under the plough to supplement the country's food supply. During the war allotments had sprung up all over the city. The moat at the Tower of London had been transformed into a market garden. Even the Kennington Oval had been dug up. Cricket would return soon, I supposed, but the scars on the land would take longer to heal. Much like the human scars left after people's lives had been dug over; even the superficial ones like those Penny and I carried.

We talked of inconsequential things as we walked around the park, and I became more conscious of what Penny was not saying than of what she was. She might have still been considering my brother's offer of marriage—assuming he had had the good manners to ask rather than to take the matter for granted. It had already occurred to me that she might have wanted to see me this weekend to tell me so. I could have told her of my own continuing love, except I wasn't sure how sincere I could have made it sound. And, given her nature, it was possible such a declaration would have the unwanted effect of pushing her into a precipitate decision. One I wouldn't like. Despite a reputation for selfishness—of which I'm sure my mother had spent the war reminding Penny—I actually wanted the best for her, and for her decision to be her own. I was well aware that George and my mother would be lobbying for her to divorce me, but I could do little about that. All I could do, I realized, was to let her see what kind of man I was now and allow her to make her decision based on that.

We came out of the park by Victoria's statue in front of Buckingham Palace. Guardsmen stood at the gate resplendent in red tunics and busbies as if nothing had changed. The palace had been hit during an air raid although the damage hadn't been extensive. I hadn't been in London on VE day, of course, when the crowds had gathered outside the palace gates and the Royal Family and Churchill had waved at them from the balcony. I'd seen the newsreels of it later while in Berlin, and had wondered at the time if Penny had been in the crowd. I'd like to have been there myself—to have experienced that great wave of euphoria—of happiness and satisfaction, joy and hope—which even so must have been tempered by a sense of regret and sadness at the human cost of it all. Not to mention a sense of trepidation for what the future might hold. This last feeling I had experienced myself while watching the film of the celebrations, wondering what would happen now.

As she had always seemed able to do, Penny read my thoughts.

'Have you any idea what you're going to do, Harry?'

'What, the flat you mean?' I asked, obfuscating while knowing exactly what she meant. 'When they pull down the building?'

'That, yes, but I mean after. Or were you planning to stay in the army?'

I laughed. 'I don't think they'll want me. We'll have to keep troops stationed in Germany I suppose, to keep the Russians out. And I imagine there'll be a bigger standing army than we had before the war. But I can't see them letting me stay in. Not and keep my commission at any rate. It would be back to the ranks for me and I don't think I'd like that.'

'Now you've tasted power, you mean?' She may have been teasing but it was not without having an edge to her voice.

'Not exactly,' I said a little stiffly.

'Back to the police then?'

'Same thing would apply. Would you want to be married to a beat policeman again?'

'After everything that's happened?'

I wasn't sure if she meant the war or what had happened to us while we'd been apart.

Walking north, Penny slipped her hand into mine. We didn't speak for some time. We found a tea room open and shared a pot and a slice of cake. When we finished I asked her if she would like to do something else or go home.

'I'd like a drink, actually,' she said.

'The pubs won't be open for a couple of hours.'

'Don't you have anything in the flat?'

'Some gin,' I said.

'That'll do.'

~

I felt an odd sense of trepidation, trying not to take things for granted like my brother George.

'Where does Ida live?' Penny asked when we reached my floor. I gestured to Ida's door and Penny put a playful finger to her lips as we passed.

In the flat her eyes wandered around at the meagre rooms as if she was mentally totting up what my life had amounted to.

'It's not so bad,' I said. 'Places aren't that easy to get.'

'Didn't your pay go up when you were promoted?'

'Even so...'

I took the bottle of gin from the kitchen cupboard. It was half full, mainly because I didn't like gin without a mixer and I never seemed to have any mixers.

'The money you send me...' began Penny. 'I don't spend it.'

'Why not? That's what it's for.'

'It's mounting up. If you want it back...'

I took two relatively clean glasses out of the sink and gave them a wipe. Penny sat at the kitchen table.

'Leave it for now,' I said.

I poured gin into the glasses and Penny picked hers up, raising it towards me.

'What shall we drink to?'

'Better times,' I said.

'Better times,' she echoed and knocked it back in one, shivering slightly and grimacing.

I recalled our wedding night when, both nervous, we had sat in our room above a pub in Devon after the train journey down from London. There had been some talk—grudgingly expressed as I remember—of Penny's father paying for us to go to France for our honeymoon. Perhaps at the Château de Hêtres although I don't remember. In any case, I wasn't going to be beholden to Reggie

Forster, so we'd taken a room in a pub in North Devon. We'd arrived after an uncomfortable train journey and discovered we were suddenly shy with each other. I'd had some limited experience but was still unsure as to whether Penny was a virgin or not. We had held back during our brief courtship, not through any lack of desire but more from the want of somewhere decent to express it. My digs were out, as was Penny's parents' house. And Julia made sure she never gave us the opportunity at her place. We could always have taken a cheap hotel room, I suppose, although—inexplicable to me now—at the time both of us had wanted more for each other than that. Overtaken by the moment, we had often gone as far as possible wherever we had happened to be, and so once at the pub in Devon it seemed odd to find ourselves so unaccountably nervous.

That room with its creaking floorboards and awkward sloping ceiling couldn't have differed much from a cheap hotel, I suppose, but by then we were married and it no longer seemed to matter. We had bought a half-bottle of brandy in the bar below and drank most of it before we had settled our nerves. Then, after that first halting coming together it became difficult to keep us apart. For the week we were there we rarely left the room, except to eat and take the occasional breath of fresh air.

Now we were back in a room cheaper than either of us could have imagined and I was nervous again. Only this time it was because I was unsure of Penny's intentions. She took a second glass of gin, shivered less and managed not to grimace.

'Not as good as the brandy,' she said, managing once more to read my thoughts.

'No.'

She stood up and looked out over the kitchen sink at the rubble beyond the window.

'I thought I needed to get drunk but I don't.' She came over to where I sat. 'Can we try again, Harry, or is it too late for us?'

I pulled her towards me, my voice muffled against the softness of her breasts. 'I've never thought it was too late.'

~

About eight o'clock we got up and went out for something to eat. Penny had lunched at the Savoy but I'd had nothing since the powdered eggs I'd eaten for breakfast. We went to a small place I knew that served a decent meal despite the shortages and didn't care that we weren't dressed for a Sunday evening. That sort of thing didn't seem to matter as much as it had before the war; social standards along with many people's morals had slipped in the intervening years. Maybe both would come back one day although, till then, people seemed to be making the most of their absence. We ate and afterwards I took out two cigarettes and lit them, passing her one. She grimaced again but was laughing now as well.

'It's not one of those horrible Capstans, is it?'

'No. There's nothing to these, just like fresh air... Well, fresher than London air anyway.'

'Tastes cheap,' she said, inhaling.

'That's their selling point.'

'If it's so bad why do you stay?' she asked.

'If what's so bad?'

'London air.'

'It's where I work. I'm still in the army, remember? I can't do much else till they let me go.'

'Have you applied to be demobbed?'

'Not yet.'

'Why not?'

'Because I was co-opted into Jekyll's section. Anyway, I still don't know what I'm going to do yet.'

'What do you *want* to do?'

'I don't know.'

When I was younger and trying to decide on a career, unlike most people who didn't have the luxury of choice, I had disappointed those around me by choosing something they thought inappropriate. It hadn't worried me at the time as I'd always thought that if I hadn't joined the police I would never have met Penny.

Of course, voluntarily joining the army had been another matter.

'Something will turn up,' I said.

'And what about us?'

'We can live on what I earn.'

'In that flat of yours?'

'No. They've decided to pull it down so I'll have to find something else. Something better this time, I promise. I'll start looking straight away.'

'And in the meantime?'

'I'm sure Julia will be pleased to have you if you don't want to live at the flat.'

'What about your mother?'

'I can't imagine even Julia would be willing to take her as well.'

'You know that's not what I mean,' she said.

'Telephone her,' I suggested. 'Tell her you're not coming back.'

'And George?'

'Tell him, too.'

'It's not as easy as that.'

'I'll do it for you if you like,' I offered.

'You'd like that, wouldn't you?'

'I'd just as soon not talk to them at all. But they'll have to know sooner or later.'

'Later, then,' said Penny. 'Let's keep it between ourselves for now.'

'If that's what you want. But you'd better ring Julia and tell her you won't be back tonight.'

'I can't,' said Penny. 'I'll have to go back.'

I was about to insist but the memory of how our disagreements had a habit of escalating into fights stopped me. I looked at my watch. It was already past ten.

'Well,' I said, 'if you want to be back by midnight we'd better get started.'

'It's not *that* late already, surely?' she said.

'No, but you remember how I always liked to get to bed early on Sundays' I said. 'And if I've got to get up again to take you home we'd best turn in now.'

'Harry!'

~

It was almost midnight by the time I got Penny back to Julia's house. I said goodnight at the door then saw a taxi pull up at the kerb. Julia and Tuchman climbed out, Julia saying goodnight to Tuchman then hello to me.

'Have you and Penny settled things?' she asked, looking through her handbag for her keys.

'We've made a start,' I said.

'I'm glad to hear it, Harry. That girl deserves some happiness.'

I doubted Julia and I would agree on what might or might not make Penny happy, but decided it was up to Penny to break the news to her. I said goodnight and raised a hand to Tuchman, who was still waiting by the taxi.

'Can I drop you anywhere?' he asked.

'Only if it's no trouble.'

We got into the taxi and Tuchman waved the driver on.

'I'm glad I ran into you, Harry. As a matter of fact I've been meaning to have a word. What about a nightcap before you turn in?'

The taxi turned into Belgrave Place and crossed the square towards Hyde Park Corner. We went through Piccadilly and five minutes later were in Wardour Street, not far from the club we had visited the previous evening. Tuchman signalled the driver to stop. It was Sunday night and everything looked closed, but a dim light shone over a basement door across the road and Tuchman led me down the few steps. There was no number or sign but Tuchman knocked and the door opened. A man in a dinner jacket greeted him by name.

Perhaps Tuchman was used to clandestine bars from the Prohibition years in America although inside I found no riotous party, just a smoky basement with a few comfortable chairs and small tables. The walls were decorated with cartoons from sporting magazines and photographs of sportsmen—boxers mostly. I recognized Bombardier Billy Wells in the classic fighting pose, fists up and looking up and under at the camera.

The man in the dinner jacket gave Tuchman a pen and he signed the book that lay on a table.

'For guests,' he explained. 'Handy place if you want a drink out of hours.'

I'd seen few drinking clubs while in the police before the war although I didn't know this particular one. Mostly, drinking clubs was all they were. Others might offer gambling, and in some you could order a girl along with your whisky and soda—not on the premises usually, but at an address on a note slipped beneath the coaster of the drink you were served.

Tuchman chose a table in a corner away from the other drinkers and ordered a scotch and soda from the waiter. I asked for a glass of beer, dry from an evening of unaccustomed exertion.

'The thing is Harry,' he began once our drinks arrived, 'I've kind of got myself into a ticklish situation.'

My first thought was that he was married, having a little fun on the side whilst in London, and had somehow compromised himself with Julia. But that wasn't what he said.

'Back in civilian life I'm a lawyer. When the war came along I was with a New York firm.'

He made the war sound like a bus he'd been waiting for.

'Did you volunteer?'

'It seemed the right thing to do at the time.'

'At the time?'

'Don't get me wrong, Harry. I've no regrets on that score.' He raised his glass and peered at the scotch as if he might find a goldfish swimming there. 'I came over in forty-three. I went through France with Patton. When we got to Germany we found the concentration camps. You see any of those places, Harry?'

'Dachau,' I said. 'I happened to be with one of your units at the time. We got there a couple of days after it had been liberated. What I saw was bad enough.'

Tuchman nodded slowly. 'I'm afraid a few of our men lost their heads at Dachau. Some of the guards still there were shot out of hand. It shouldn't have happened but given what they found it's difficult to blame them.'

I didn't blame them at all. The stench of the place had been difficult to get out of my nostrils. Unlike anything else I'd ever experienced, the smell had a habit of coming back to me for months afterwards, bringing with it images, like photographs, each one seared into my brain. I remember a siding with railway trucks parked up and left, the living having been locked inside and abandoned to die of thirst and suffocation. The Americans were still burying their emaciated bodies when I first saw them—men and women like twigs with barely enough flesh on their bodies to cover their bones. Someone had had the idea of rounding up the local civilians to show them exactly what bestial depths their blessed Füehrer had reduced the German nation to. They'd been handled roughly but at least they'd lived. Not like the camp guards who hadn't managed to get away.

'We'd heard the rumours, of course,' Tuchman continued, 'but nothing prepares you for sights like that. I don't know if it was worse, my being Jewish. I guess probably not.'

He looked across the table at me, perhaps wondering if I might have a point of view on the matter. I didn't say anything and he went on:

'Are you familiar with The United Nations and the War Crimes Commission? The organization hasn't been formally established yet but it'll be structured along the lines of the old League of Nations. This time with some teeth hopefully.'

'I've heard about it,' I said, not bothering to add that I suspected it wouldn't turn out to be any more effective than the League of Nations had been.

'The objective of the Commission is to investigate allegations of war crimes committed by Nazi Germany and its allies. But perhaps that goes without saying. Much the same sort of work as you do, I imagine. Only we have a wider remit. Well, you know the score.'

I did, but I was surprised that Tuchman knew I did. Penny had a vague idea of what my job entailed and I supposed it was she who had told him.

'Penny told me you were attached to the State Department,' I said.

'Justice Department, actually. I was obliged to join them before I could be co-opted into the War Crimes Commission. It's what I tell people if I'm asked what I do.'

'It must make things simpler.'

'As I understand it, Harry, your area is solely military. The Nazi extermination programme cast a wider net than that, of course. The Party created a vast organization. A complete bureaucratic machine.'

He smiled although I couldn't see where the humour lay in what he was saying.

'And fortunately for us they were wonderful record-keepers. What is it about the Germans, Harry? Something in their psyche that makes them so punctilious and ordered? What do you think?'

I didn't know what to think. I had never known. It had become plain to me right from the start of my section's investigations that if one could get hold of the huge array of files and records kept by both the German civilian and military authorities, there was rarely any need to seek further evidence. They convicted themselves through their meticulous book-keeping.

'Well,' I said, as Tuchman seemed to be waiting for some sort of opinion, 'it seems to me that after they passed the necessary laws in the thirties for what they intended to do—the racial purity laws and the like—they gave their actions a semblance of legality.' I paused, staring into my glass for the words to express what I wanted to say. 'No, more than a semblance. It *was* legal. From their point of view. Not morally justifiable, of course, but technically legal. Perhaps that's why they felt bound to keep records when later, no matter how outrageous became the things they did in the name of their ideology, they could always refer back to their laws. Perhaps they thought that was enough to persuade the German population that *everything* they did was legal. Persuade themselves, too, perhaps.' I shrugged, trying to explain what, until then, had been no more than vague concepts. 'I don't know. Perhaps keeping a legal framework and records became an extension of the process. Even though what they were doing was reprehensible, by their lights it was nonetheless legal.'

'Good point,' said Tuchman. 'But does that cover the actions of, say, the Einsatzgruppen?'

'The murder battalions? No, of course not. But that's war. Trying to apply a framework of law to war has always seemed to me a pointless and hypocritical exercise.'

'An odd point of view for someone in your line of work,' Tuchman said.

'Perhaps,' I agreed, 'but you know what they say about those who write the history.'

'All right, let me ask you this. Do you think that it was the belief that what the Nazis were doing was legal that persuaded the majority of the population to go along with what was done in their name?'

I had no idea what had persuaded the German population to follow Hitler. His oratory...his charisma...? That's what some have said. But I'd been struck by neither. I hadn't been there, of course; nor was I German. What I did know was that had I been Jewish I would have taken the Nazis' dehumanizing propaganda and murderous campaign of liquidation as personal. Which, of course, is exactly what it was. Perhaps Tuchman was capable of more detachment than I. Or perhaps he was better at hiding his feelings.

But he was waiting for a reply so I tried to formulate one.

'Once they'd eliminated their most vociferous opponents, perhaps you're right. They silenced the socialists and the communists and anyone else who might have stood up to them. After that, any people left who still disagreed with the Nazis probably thought it best to keep their heads down.'

'All that is necessary for the triumph of evil, is that good men do nothing?' Tuchman suggested.

'That sounds like a quotation,' I said.

'Edmund Burke, I think. But it seems to fit the bill in this case. At any rate, more pertinently than when it was used back home before the first war as an argument for Prohibition. I wonder what Burke would have made of that?'

'I've no idea,' I laughed. 'I suppose it depends on whether Burke was a drinker. Philosophy isn't my strong suit. I don't claim any understanding of my fellow man or the nature of the universe.'

'It seems to me,' said Tuchman, 'some things are beyond understanding.'

I knocked back the last of my beer. 'Like why we're having this conversation? Why are we having it, Ben?'

Tuchman grinned.

'I told you, I've got myself into an awkward situation.'

'Julia?'

'Yes, in a way. Although my problem is Claude Pellisier.'

23

I signalled the waiter for another round, my mouth still dry. Tuchman wasn't helping. He waited until the drinks arrived and the waiter left again.

'It was a British initiative. The Commission, I mean. That's why your people have taken the lead. Claude Pellisier's name came up in Caen when we started looking into the deportation of French Jews to the death camps.'

'From Occupied France?'

'From the occupied territory *and* from Vichy. You won't find many Frenchmen willing to admit it now, but the Nazis didn't have any trouble finding willing collaborators. In fact, France was the only occupied country that passed its own laws for the deportations. All the Germans had to do was sit back and let the French authorities get on with it.'

Judging from Tuchman's expression he had taken French perfidy personally.

'It's no secret, of course,' he went on, 'that a great number of Frenchmen in positions of power were ambivalent about the Nazis from the beginning. Just look at how quickly they were defeated. It's a sad truth that many of the officer corps simply deserted their men in the face of the German advance.'

'Rather ironic,' I commented, 'that the French said of Dunkirk, that the British were willing to fight to the last Frenchman.'

Tuchman smiled but it was little more than an automatic response. Yet I knew how much truth there was in what he said. The relationship between the British and the French had been an ambiguous one for much of the war. Their capitulation in 1940 had, to say the least, been precipitous and there were those at the time who had preferred to blame the British for leaving them in the lurch at Dunkirk rather than their own High Command and politicians for the surrender.

That one hundred thousand Frenchman had also been evacuated to England seemed to have been conveniently forgotten. Although perhaps that was just as well; we had ferried them back in short order to ports further west along the coast just in time for the French surrender. Those that weren't killed found themselves in labour camps or, later, shipped east to work for the Germans.

'To be fair,' I said, 'we had our own share of enthusiastic supporters of Nazi Germany before the war. I often wonder if we would have come out of it smelling any better if Britain had been occupied.'

'Don't sell yourselves short, Harry,' said Tuchman. 'The point is, you weren't. And you weren't because you fought. There were opportunities to come to a negotiated peace, but unlike the French, Britain didn't take them.'

I wasn't going to argue. At least we hadn't had to resort to the expediency of rewriting history. Had the French Resistance been able to call upon the number of men who, once the Germans were on the run, came crawling out of the woodwork, brushing off their old medals and uniforms, the battle might have been over a couple of years before it finally was. It all went a long way to explain General De Gaulle's attitude: a proud man having to paper over the shame of his country in order to instil some of his own pride in a shattered nation. I didn't find it difficult to sympathize although, like many others, it did stick in the craw to see so many old collaborators stepping up as tardy saviours of *La Belle France*. But truth has a habit of exhuming itself sooner or later and, in my opinion, in the case of the worst offenders, the sooner the better.

'I understood Pellisier worked in Paris,' I said.

'Between the wars. When he was trying to make a political career for himself. After the fall of France he took up a post in Caen.' Tuchman picked up his glass, held it a moment but didn't drink. 'First it was Socialists and Communists...trade-unionists and the like who were rounded up. Many of them were sent to the camp at Natzweiler-Struthof. A lot of common criminals, too, although—like the Germans—the French soon found their sort were useful for doing their dirty work. The *Milice*, in Vichy for example. After they'd dealt with their political enemies it wasn't long before they turned their attention to the French Jews. And as we were saying earlier, the Germans kept meticulous records and they liked their French underlings to do the same. With what documentation has been found and the corroborating evidence of witness testimonies, we're able to identify some of the French civilian administrators who were only too happy to assist the Gestapo in Jewish deportations.'

'And you're certain Pellisier was one of them?'

'There doesn't seem much doubt about it,' Tuchman said.

He wasn't drinking but I needed one and took a long pull at the glass. It was the kind of development which beyond setting the record straight wasn't likely to do anyone any good. Myself included.

'I can see that it's an unfortunate turn of events,' I said. 'But Pellisier wasn't exactly family, was he? And I don't suppose any of them have any idea of what he was doing. Have you spoken to Julia about it?'

'I was waiting to see how things developed. To be honest, Harry, I've only just got involved in Pellisier's case.'

'Before or after you met her?'

'Before,' he admitted. 'Although I'm not sure that's relevant.'

'Let's hope Julia agrees,' I said. 'What is it you want me to do? Since I'm here, I take it you want me to do something.'

He smiled with that easy American charm which no doubt left Julia weak at the knees. She may have exhibited a frosty veneer at times, but the war and had turned us all upside down and worn thin our social distinctions along with our morals. I wouldn't have gone as far as to suggest she was to be had for a chocolate bar and a pair of nylons, but a New York lawyer with charm and looks wouldn't have had to resort to the American PX, Jewish ethnicity or not.

'If possible, Harry. I'd like you to stay away from the subject of Claude Pellisier. He wasn't involved in any crimes against the military as far as we can see. Not the British or American anyway. It might be prudent if you can see your way to steer clear of any awkward questions you might have felt you wanted to ask. At least, where Julia and her family are concerned.'

I got the impression he expected me to protest because he went on quickly:

'I know Penny's your wife and you've this investigation. I understand the Bren gun carrier was knocked out not far from Pellisier's château. But the man's dead so it's not as if he can be brought to trial. Reports will get written and filed away and the chances are no one will be any the wiser. At the moment though, it's a little awkward. And not just for me personally. You understand, I'm sure.'

I was beginning to. But just how *much* I was beginning to was a different matter. What Tuchman knew about my investigation into Dabs' death and Kearney's—or O'Connell's—disappearance was something else again. I didn't see that Pellisier's conduct during the war could have any bearing on it, but his collaboration would certainly be embarrassing for Penny's family and for Maurice Coveney. But what he had said suggested some disingenuousness on his own part. He didn't want me asking awkward questions yet, according to Penny that afternoon, he was not above asking them himself.

'I have to admit,' I told him, 'that I thought you looked a little uncomfortable yesterday evening. I assumed it was because of what Julia said about how long it took for America to enter the war. But it was because the conversation had got round to Maurice Coveney and his wife.'

'You're right, Harry. But I couldn't really admit to knowing about the family, not without saying why. Coveney being Pellisier's brother-in-law.'

'He helped with the identification of the body, didn't he? There's no doubt about that, I suppose?'

'No,' Tuchman said with a degree of certainty I hardly shared. 'Coveney happened to be in Paris with a British Foreign Office delegation shortly after the liberation. It seems while he was there he tried to find out what had happened to his brother-in-law. That was why he was asked to identify the remains found in the château.'

'I'm surprised the body was in any condition to be identified.'

'Photographs,' said Tuchman. 'It appears the body was buried initially by German troops occupying the château. Your people dug it up assuming it was a British soldier's grave then buried it again. The local authorities didn't seem to have much doubt that it was Pellisier so they re-interred it in the family vault. Even so, they took some photographs as a precaution. Pellisier had a birthmark on his right buttock, apparently. Quite distinctive, like an inverted triangle with one serpentine side. The body had been burned and was badly decomposed but by luck the birthmark was still identifiable. Coveney was pretty confident the remains were Pellisier's.'

'Call me suspicious,' I said, 'but given the body had been dug up more times than a dog's bone I would have found that a tad fortunate.'

Tuchman agreed. 'We do check these things, of course. Nothing is taken at face value. Once the war started going against them many of the people who'd been involved in the deportations and death camps began making provision against future prosecution.'

'How?'

'They simply disappeared. They had alternate identities ready and escape routes prepared. Of course, we've no idea if Pellisier had arranged anything although that might have been why he was at the château. Picking up personal belongings...? Who knows? It might be that he was simply caught out by the speed of the advance.'

I was on the point of telling him about the Gestapo officers who had been there with Pellisier, then changed my mind. I wasn't sure why, perhaps because throughout this business I had been a step behind the opposition and now succumbed to a miserly impulse to keep something back myself.

The club had emptied and the waiter and the barman were cleaning up. We finished our drinks. Out on the street Tuchman found a taxi and dropped me near my flat.

'I hope you don't think I've spoken out of turn,' he said as I climbed out.

'Not at all, Ben,' I assured him.

We shook hands. As I watched the taxi drive away between the rows of rubble that formed my street, its lights swept over the dark shape of a car parked several yards along the road.

The taxi disappeared, plunging the street back into darkness. No lights showed from the parked car and, turning to the door of my building, I didn't give it a second thought.

In the flat, I put the kettle on. I wasn't tired, having dozed for a couple of hours next to Penny earlier in the day. Tuchman's revelation that Claude Pellisier had been involved in Jewish deportations complicated matters. On the face of it, my carrier being found on the drive of Pellisier's château was no more than coincidence, and it would probably explain Coveney's interest in the matter. But that was on the face of it. As it was, I was not looking forward to Penny finding out that her Aunt Louise's brother was a Nazi collaborator; worse, that he had helped send Jews to the death camps. I didn't suppose Tuchman was looking forward much to telling Julia either.

With Pellisier dead there might be no reason for them to know. Telling them wouldn't do anyone any good. And yet I felt somehow uncomfortable about keeping it from them; from Penny in particular. Despite Tuchman's denial, I wasn't convinced that his befriending Julia hadn't been a deliberate move. He hadn't exactly told me that it had been no more than a coincidence but, if that was what it had been, it was one too many as far as I was concerned.

Deep in thought I didn't hear a sound until there was a knock at my door. It was well past two in the morning and I was hardly accustomed to receiving calls even during social hours. It first crossed my mind that it was Penny coming back then, somewhat conceitedly, that it might be Ida. Odd how a little sexual success goes to a man's head, vanity a hungry beast apparently prepared, it seemed, to feed on any scrap thrown its way.

I had started to open the door before I consciously considered any other possibility, and sensed rather than saw the person standing in the hall. I had completely forgotten the car parked along the street.

Even after the lifting of the blackout my penny-pinching landlord was still unwilling to spend money on light bulbs for the hallways of a condemned building, and with the door only partly open the dim light from my kitchen was too weak to illuminate the corridor. But, before I could open the door wider, I caught the astringent smell of something oddly familiar, a scent that brought back memories from before the war.

'I know you won't mind me calling on you this late, Captain,' said the teasing voice with its familiar Irish lilt. 'But when you gave me your address, you did say any time. So here I am.'

'So you are, Rose,' I said, opening the door wide, half-expecting in the weak light to see someone standing behind her. She was alone though and as I stepped back to let her in said, 'You don't mind me using your first name, do you Rose? After all, Kearney's a bit of a misnomer now, isn't it?'

She was as stylishly dressed as any woman could possibly manage in our straightened times and I realized I probably wouldn't have recognized her had I passed her on the street. The scent I had caught was from hair lotion, still clinging to the permanent waves she had curled into the brown lacklustre hair which had made her look so drab. What surprised me most though was how she was made up. Not artfully or excessively, but with a competence that made the most of her features; features until then I'd not realized she'd possessed. She was the girl in the photograph again, older now perhaps, but for those whose tastes ran beyond the bland, one who had grown almost beautiful.

She stepped past me, taller now too; almost my own height in her heels.

'Now, I've heard you've been visiting Ballydrum, Captain. I suppose you were disappointed with the place. Billy always said there wasn't much to it if you discounted the peat bog. I've never seen it myself, but then you know that by now.'

I shut the door and thumbed down the latch. Rose noticed and appeared amused.

'We'll not be interrupted if that's what you're thinking. Not unless you're expecting someone else? The girl again? Or the American?'

'You seem to know a lot about me, Rose,' I said. 'The girl's my wife.'

She raised a pencilled eyebrow. 'It's married you are? And living in a dump like this on your own? You're a man who keeps a surprise up his sleeve.'

'I'm not the only one.'

She looked over the meagre room, eyes wandering across the battered settee to the kitchen, through the open door to the bedroom. She glanced at the settee again and sat at the table.

'I've just made some tea,' I said, 'if you'd care for a cup?'

Her eyes widened and she smiled. 'Now isn't that the English all over? They never forget their manners. Even when they're sticking a gun in your face in some Dublin basement or other.'

I poured her a cup and she took a little powdered milk.

'So you've a wife,' she said, stirring in the milk powder. 'And here's me thinking you and the army tart you brought with you to Kilburn might be having a thing together. Or maybe you are?'

'Susie?'

'ATS Blake, I seem to remember she was. And too sharp for her own good. I saw her looking at my nail varnish and said to myself, "Rose girl, you've slipped up there."'

'She thought there was a man in the flat, too. That'll have been Dermot Kavanaugh, I suppose.'

'Now you don't want Diamaid to catch you calling him Dermot,' Rose advised, sipping her tea. 'Diamaid Caomhánach it has to be or he's likely to blow your head off. Especially if it's coming out of an English mouth.'

'Dónol Casey told me he'd changed his name. I heard he's a desperate character.'

'Casey the publican? Friend or no friend, Diamaid won't like to hear he's been blabbing.'

'Well I'm not telling him,' I said. 'Are you?'

She smiled again. 'You're a cool one, Captain, and no mistake. But Diamaid didn't change his name. He just says it the way it's supposed to be said.'

'When he's not Diamaid Caomhánach is he still posing as Major Hendrix?'

'No,' said Rose, 'he had a good run in that part but I told him he was pushing his luck thinking of meeting you as the Major. Grieving widows and sad little girlfriends are one thing, but I told him a British army officer was a horse of another colour. I said if you knew where Billy was I'd get it out of you quicker than his play acting would.'

'You're not bad at play acting yourself.'

She beamed at me. 'Well, it's decent of you to say so, Captain. I've always thought I had a little talent in that direction, treading the boards so to speak. It's how I met Billy, after all.'

'You're not going to tell me Willy O'Connell was an actor?'

'No, and we'll call him Billy if it's all the same to you. I never liked "Willy". Too many connotations of little boys, if you know what I mean. And Billy was no little boy, Captain, I can assure you of that.'

'What was he if he wasn't an actor?'

She glanced wistfully at her cup. 'Ah, Billy could have been anything. But it was his nature to be nothing much at all. It was Diamaid Caomhánach who brought him along to our little theatre group at University College. That's Dublin, Captain. I'm a university girl, now would you have thought that?'

'I'm sure you could have been anything, Rose,' I replied, echoing her own words.

'Are you flattering me, Captain, or like Billy suggesting I could be nothing much at all?'

She waited but I wasn't about to fall into any of Rose's girlish traps.

'A theatre group? Is that where Diamaid got his taste for acting?'

'He's a better actor than he is a writer, I'll say that. He'd written a play and was looking to our group to put it on for him.'

'I thought he was a poet.'

'That's the blabbing publican again, I suppose. Well, Diamaid had tried his hand at poetry but between you and me, he was no hand at it at all. He could recite a ballad, beautiful and no mistake, particularly with a drink or two inside him. But penning it himself wasn't a talent the good Lord blessed him with. And his play wasn't any great shakes, either. I've always said you can forgive a man for being ugly if he's got the streak of an artist inside him, but poor Diamaid doesn't have even that. Just the ugliness. Billy now, he was beauty.'

'So the blabbing publican told me,' I said.

'Well, I don't blame him for that. One for attracting the girls was Billy. And the boys, too, only he was the kind never to notice the fact. Just as well or he wouldn't have spent so much time in Diamaid Caomhánach's company.'

'You mean...?'

'Let's just say Diamaid's preferences are more Oscar Wilde that William Butler Yeats. Not that he could afford to try anything on with Billy. Billy's mam brought him up with strict ideas about that sort of thing. It's one reason he did what he did when he finally realized how things stood with Diamaid. Well, you talked to the priests, I'm told, and they always say it's a mortal sin.'

'So the blabbing publican keeps in touch, does he? Where is he now? Diamaid, I mean. In the car?'

Rose's red lips curled in a smile. 'No, I told him I would see you on my own. Do things my way. Much more pleasant and less messy. If you know what I mean?'

I thought I did and didn't care to think too long about it.

'And you think I know where Billy is, is that it?'

She dropped her eyes again.

'Well, I'm thinking he's dead,' she said softly. 'And I'm thinking you think he's dead, too.'

'Yes, I think he's dead,' I said, looking at the brown waves of her hair. 'I never told you but Billy's ID discs were found on the body of a dead German. Taken as a souvenir, probably. So if one of the bodies found by the carrier wasn't Billy then he's somewhere near. A lot of men were killed during Operation Jupiter. That was the name of the operation he was on. Did you know that?'

Rose looked up, eyes moist, and I wondered if it was play-acting like the rest.

'We found out a lot. Diamaid had all the details Billy had sent his mam—the regiment he'd joined and the name he was serving under. The name of the little waif of a girl he couldn't get out of his head.'

'Dónol Casey said Billy told him he was thinking of joining up when he came home to Ballydrum for his mother's funeral. Not that he was already in.'

'Now you shouldn't listen to publicans, Captain. They're an unreliable breed. Billy was already in the army by then. Though that wasn't the sort of thing you'd blab about in Ireland. They gave him leave to bury his mam.'

'You did well tracking him,' I said. 'And the other men's families. Always one step ahead of me.'

'Well, we had a good start and you just had my letter.'

'Whose idea was that?'

'Diamaid's. We'd got so far but no further and he thought if you lot knew anything more you might tell Billy's poor orphaned sister and put the dowdy little Irish woman out of her misery. But I knew it was a risky game. You're a suspicious lot, you English. Too shifty for your own good.'

'Not like the open-hearted Irish,' I said.

Rose laughed. 'Now I'll be really sorry if Diamaid decides to kill you, Captain.'

'That's what he's got planned for Billy, I suppose.'

'Yes, he has. And if he can't shoot Billy then you'll have to do. It seems to have eaten in to him and I'm thinking he'll carry on killing now until someone kills him.'

'Do you want to kill Billy too, Rose? What's eating into you? Not jealousy over dead Cathleen?'

'No, not the girl. And if you know our real names you must know he betrayed us.'

'Betrayed Diamaid,' I said. 'Not you.'

'No, not me. Not in that sense anyway. But he shouldn't have done it and he did, and had to leave afterwards. That was betrayal enough.'

'You couldn't go with him?'

'And me betray Ireland? Now what sort of patriot do you take me for?'

'I'm not sure how I'd take you at all, Rose,' I said.

Her eyes widened suggestively and she laughed again.

'What *do* you mean, Captain? What would that little wife of yours think if she could hear you?' She got up, smiling coquettishly, and trailed her fingers along my shoulders as she passed my chair. 'Or is she one of your demure English roses and wouldn't take your meaning? We've all heard back in Ireland what milksops your English roses are.'

I stood up and she paused at the door.

'Perhaps Captain,' she suggested, 'you should try an Irish rose sometime and see the difference.' She undid the door latch. 'And I'll be telling Diamaid you believe Billy is dead. Although whether *he'll* believe it is another matter. If he does I'd watch my back. He's a wild one, is Diamaid. A desperate man. He might have been an Irish Villon if only he'd had the knack of the poetry. Maybe then I wouldn't have looked at Billy O'Connoll. Ugly or not, it might have been Diamaid Caomhánach I loved.' Her eyes flashed again. 'For all the good *that* would have done a girl.'

24

Monday July 1st 1946

I stood at the window after Rose left. Down in the street I heard a car start and drive away. After a while I looked at the clock. It was well past three. I would have to be in the office in a few hours. But I didn't go straight to bed. Instead I took my revolver out of the cupboard, broke it down and cleaned it. Then I pushed six bullets into the chamber, closed it and slipped it back into its holster. I left it by the bed. I was going to have to change my habits.

~

Monday was always a quiet day in the office. After the weekend, coming back to the realities of missing and dead men, of the nature and the casualties of war, it always heightened the contrast between us and everyone else. Out there life had moved on. Slowly, perhaps, but things were changing. Men and women were out of the services and although life was hard with the rationing and the shortages and the other consequences of the war, there was a sense that they could see their way ahead. Us? Well, we were still looking backwards, picking over the horrors. Still immersed in what most other people were trying to forget.

For my own part I felt quite buoyant. Some sort of resolution with Penny had been achieved and, as long as I didn't fall through some unexpected thin ice, it looked as though I was going to be a married man again. It was what I wanted—at least, I think it was—and it promised to be an island of stability in an otherwise unstable future. Walking into the office, however, soon took the shine off of my optimism.

I was late, but even so the place felt more subdued than was usual for a Monday morning. I detected an air of coolness between Susie and Peter who, having had to work closely together, had achieved a greater degree of interaction than was required by the rest of us. But their exchanges sounded terse and brittle. I glanced at

Stan to see if he had detected it, but he merely stared back morosely and said:

'You fixed Ida up with a job, then?'

'Yes, lucky really. Penny's aunt was looking—'

'Domestic service?' he bit back scornfully, as if I'd forced Ida to join the Waffen SS. 'She's better than that.'

'It's hardly indentured,' I told him, wondering why it put his back up. She told me she needed work. She can always pack it in if something better turns up.'

'That's not likely the way things are, is it?'

I was about to say, if that were the case, it was as well she had any sort of job at all, but his sullen expression told me to drop it.

'She's moving in there,' he persisted.

'What, into Julia's house?'

'Parker, is that her name?'

'Yes.'

'She's moving in there.'

I picked up a handy file and pretended to look through it. I supposed after all the trouble he'd gone to in finding Ida somewhere to live, he'd expected a little more gratitude from her. Moving into Julia's house would put a crimp in his being able to drop by, no doubt. Not that I blamed Ida; who'd want to live in a semi-derelict hovel when they could live in Belgravia? Even if it was in domestic quarters. Stan wouldn't see it that way, of course, and had obviously made his mind up to blame me. As if Ida didn't have a mind of her own. What did surprise me was that Julia had acted so quickly. But if Ida suited her, I assumed she wasn't about to risk losing the girl by letting her out of her sight.

I hoped finding a new place for Penny and myself to live would prove as easy. It wasn't going to, of course. Decent flats in London were hard to come by and getting more expensive by the month. I would have to start going through the ads in the evening papers and visiting letting agents and it occurred to me that I might have enlisted Susie in the task if she hadn't been sitting stiffly erect in her chair and looking about as approachable as an irritable Medusa.

I turned towards my own office, glancing at the file in my hand and realizing it was a breakdown of Operation Jupiter casualty figures, the dead and the missing. Peter had compiled it from numbers supplied by the relevant battalions and reading through it brought me back to the matter in hand.

The Second Battle of the Odon, as those operations to the south and west of Caen were coming to be known, had been especially brutal. Some men Peter had spoken to who had had experience of the trenches on the western front in the Great War had even compared it to that horror. The number of casualties showed how desperate the fighting must have been. The assaults on Hill 112 and the Château de Fontaine, and the house to house fighting in Éterville and Maltot had been particularly fierce.

With the figures in front of me in black and white I had to ask again what was so special about Kearney's carrier? The area was littered with knocked-out armour; burnt-out tanks and M10s, and all the other paraphernalia of mechanized warfare. Even though we hadn't come across another, I suspected even finding a body with a bullet in the back of the head wasn't an isolated instance.

I dropped the file next to the report I'd written for Jekyll the day before and was about to ask Jack to type it up for me when I saw him sitting motionless in front of his Remington staring at a blank sheet of paper. He was making no effort to despoil its virginal purity.

'What's the matter? Muse deserted you?'

He pushed his glasses up his nose. 'Got a letter this morning notifying us of the exhumation.'

'What exhumation?'

'That's what I wanted to know.' He passed me the letter. 'It's from the Home Office.'

There were two sheets. The first was from some Home Office department and dated June 26th stating that the *avocat général's* office in Caen had acceded to a request for the exhumation of a body. A cemetery and plot number followed. It then noted that a copy of the *avocat général's* reply had been enclosed and that copies of both had been forwarded to Colonel Jekyll's office.

I looked at the other sheet. 'It's in French,' I said.

Jack threw me one of his long-suffering looks. 'I noticed that. I got Peter to translate it for me.'

'And?'

'It says what the other letter says. That the Caen advocat general's office, or whatever it's called, has agreed to the exhumation of the remains of one Claude Pellisier, originally buried at the Château de Hêtres and since re-interred.'

'Who requested an exhumation?'

'I assumed you did,' Jack replied petulantly. 'Without telling me.'

'But I haven't got the authorization for that.'

'*I* know that. But you know what you're like for cutting corners and getting round things...'

I didn't know any such thing but now was hardly the time to argue the toss about it.

'Then I get a phone call asking if I got the letter—'

'Jekyll?'

'That's what I assumed,' said Jack. 'But no.'

'No what?'

'Not Jekyll. This was some geezer called Bryce.'

'Bryce? Who's Bryce?' And although the name sounded familiar I couldn't for the life of me place it.

'Search me,' said Jack.

'Bugger,' I said. 'What was he, army?'

'Didn't give a rank.'

'Didn't you ask? Did he sound army?'

'You mean did he order me around? No. But he left a number. Wants you to get back to him. Says you'll know why.'

'Why should I know why? You sure that's what he said?'

'His very words,' said Jack, reaching for the phone. 'Want me to call him?'

I thought for a moment then said, 'No. Chain of command. Get onto Jekyll's office and see if he's there. If not, find out where he is.'

Jack pulled the blank paper out of the Remington and with great deliberation screwed it into a ball and dropped it into his waste basket.

I looked at the letter from the Home Office again. June 26th had been the middle of the previous week. I didn't suppose that Jekyll would have got his letter any sooner than we got ours and even if he had he had been in Scotland and wouldn't have seen it until he returned. It was just the sort of thing guaranteed to bring him storming up the stairs to our office—unless Jekyll had ordered the exhumation himself.

The only reason for an exhumation that I could think of was that someone suspected the body wasn't Claude Pellisier's after all. And if it wasn't, the chances were it belonged to William Kearney. I doubted Jekyll would have asked for an exhumation given his orders to hurry things along; besides, as far as I knew, he didn't know anything about Pellisier, not unless Coveney had told him. So, assuming the French weren't conducting their own investigation, that just left Ben Tuchman. When we spoke the previous evening he told me it was accepted that the body found at the Château de Hêtres was that of Claude Pellisier. So either the exhumation was nothing to do with him or he wasn't telling me everything. Of the alternatives, I couldn't help but favour the latter. According to the man from the 4th Battalion of the Wiltshire Regiment Stan had spoken to, the body had been badly burned. What with that and having spent two years in the ground here and there since, I found it surprising there was going to be much left to work with. I wasn't a forensic pathologist, though.

While Jack rang Jekyll's office, I lit a cigarette and tried to remember where I'd come across the name Bryce before. It had been recently, I was sure, and I wondered if it had anything to do with Ireland.

Jack put the phone down and shook his head. 'Not been in his office since last week.'

There were other numbers where we could sometimes reach Jekyll so I told Jack to try them.

The thought of burnt bodies sent me back to our file on Dabs and the carrier and I sorted through it for the crew's medical files. The blood group of both Burleigh and Dabs was recorded as O-positive—the most common grouping—while Arnie Poole's blood was B-positive. That group was found in less than 10 percent of the population. This information had been stamped on their ID discs. But because the discs of Poole and Burleigh had been found on the floor of the carrier, not on the bodies, which body was which had been determined by the 7th Hampshires Orderly Room through blood tests prior to final burial.

I was satisfied that both 4th Wilts and 7th Hampshires Orderly Room had done everything they could in identifying Poole and Burleigh. Of the other two, Joseph Dabs had been identified visually as well as by discs but there'd been nothing of William Kearney found at the scene to ID. His discs, of course, had been found later on the body of SS-Unterscharführer Otto Vogel. According to Kearney's medical files, his blood group was A-positive—not quite as common as that of Burleigh and Dabs but still found in over 30 percent of the population. Up till then, though, we hadn't had a body to compare the record with. Now it seemed we were going to get one.

Going back through the notes from Stan's interview with 4th Wilts, I began to wonder how the ID discs belonging to Poole and Burleigh had ended up on the floor together. It seemed entirely possible that the cords holding the discs around their necks had burned through in the carrier fire, although if that were the case I would have expected the discs to have lodged in what was left of their clothing or fallen into their laps. They might have become dislodged when 4th Wilts had removed the two bodies from the carrier, of course. But since the reason men wear discs in the first place is for accurate identification in case of death or—in the case of injury—the necessity for a blood transfusion, those charged with the work of handling bodies and the marking of graves are as meticulous as possible. And even assuming the discs *had* fallen onto the floor of the vehicle, the configuration of carriers and the compartmentalized seating arrangements, made the chances of them ending up in the same place improbable.

That left the possibility that the discs had been taken off the bodies at some point and not replaced around the necks but just tossed back into the carrier. And if this is what had happened, logic suggested—since the discs had been through the fire—that the burning of the bodies had been deliberate.

Jack put the telephone down again. 'No go,' he said.

I took an address book out of the desk drawer and tossed it to him. 'Try his flat.'

Going back over it again, it seemed to me that the only circumstance I could think of that would fit the facts was that Poole and Burleigh had either been already dead, but not burned, when the ID discs were taken off their bodies, or they were *not* dead but had perhaps been taken prisoner. In either case the discs had to have been put back in the carrier before it was destroyed—which now looked like an act designed to obfuscate. Peter had suggested the weapon used was likely to have been a *Panzerfaust*—literally a "tank fist"—a single shot recoilless anti-tank weapon, or the smaller *Faustpatrone*; possibly even the carrier's own PIAT. All were portable and could be operated by a single soldier. Whatever had destroyed the carrier, the unpleasant conclusion drawn from this latter scenario was that if Poole and Burleigh were prisoners before their discs had been taken off them, then they had been killed in cold blood before being burned. This meant that not only Dabs' death had been a war crime but their deaths as well.

Jack banged the telephone receiver down with a finality that suggested he was sick of using it. 'Want me to try his club?'

The clock on the wall stood at 12.30, nearly lunchtime. The frosty atmosphere next door hadn't thawed appreciatively so I decided to try the Army and Navy in person.

'Give them a ring. Have him paged and if he's there tell them to let him know I'm on my way.'

~

At the Army and Navy Club the man on the desk frowned, remembering I suppose that he had already received a phone call on the subject. He told me they had paged the colonel without result and didn't believe he had come in since. Nor did he appear willing to check further. Under other circumstances I might have puffed myself up and made my uniform more conspicuous; but uniforms didn't impress at the Rag being their bread and butter, so I merely asked for Jekyll to be paged again. He wasn't keen but, after all, they were there to do as they were told. While one of the boys trawled through the various rooms calling out for Jekyll once more, I hung around the lobby.

Colonel G walked in while I was waiting.

'Harry?' he said, obviously surprised. 'I didn't know you were a member?'

I threw him a salute. He might have been off-duty and there for lunch but I was still hard at work. He touched a finger to his cap in return but was in the process of taking the thing off anyway.

'I called your office, sir, but they said they hadn't seen you.'

'I got back late last night. Thought I'd have a spot of lunch before going into the office. You might as well join me now you're here. Was there something in particular?'

I gave him the letter concerning the exhumations and well as what I had on the men's blood groups.

'We received it this morning. If you haven't been to the office, you won't have seen your copy yet.'

He read it quickly, including the French. His face, grim at the best of times, seemed to solidify like setting cement.

'Who ordered the exhumation?'

'I thought that might have been you, sir.'

'Have you been back to them?'

'I thought it best to consult you first, sir. Corporal Hibbert's been ringing round trying to find you.' I was about to add that we'd had a phone call on the matter from someone called Bryce, then thought better of it. If Jekyll hadn't ordered the exhumation, in his present mood I didn't want to complicate matters.

He read the letter again, grunted with what could have been irritation or merely hunger pangs, then stomped off still clutching it. Towards the dining room, I assumed, and having been invited to lunch I followed meekly behind.

Jekyll told a steward he wanted a table and stopped at the bar for a whisky and soda. The barman looked at me so I asked for a brandy. I hoped it might settle my stomach. Once the drinks were in our hands I tentatively began to outline the conclusions I'd come to earlier concerning the confusion over Poole's and Burliegh's ID discs, laying the onus heavily on the 25th SS-Panzer Grenadiers as I did so.

'One of the oddest things,' I added as casually as I could as I finished, 'is that the château where the carrier was found belonged to a friend of my wife's family. A man named Claude Pellisier. Sir Maurice Coveney was his brother-in-law.'

I watched for a reaction but if he'd been connected to a seismometer it wouldn't have registered a ripple on his whisky and soda.

'I am aware of that.'

'You knew?'

'Of course I knew, Tennant,' he snapped. 'Why do you think I was with Sir Maurice at your aunt's house the other evening?'

'Right sir,' I said, wondering why, if he knew, I'd had to find out for myself. I tried to recall what I had overheard them talking about. I couldn't, but did remember something else. Coveney's secretary had been there. *His* name was Bryce.

The steward told Jekyll a table was ready and asked if he would like to choose his wine. Jekyll asked what they were serving at lunch and then, ordering something I'd never heard of, we followed the steward into the dining room. The table was by the window overlooking the street. Down below us traffic roared by as if petrol had just gone off-ration.

Returning with the wine the steward uncorked the bottle and dashed a little in Jekyll's glass. He ran his beak over it, sniffed and sampled it and told the steward to serve it. I took a sip and wondered why people bothered with the ritual. But then I've never paid what that bottle probably cost and decided Jekyll was entitled to a little theatre for his money.

A bowl of thin soup arrived and I sifted my spoon through it looking for something substantial.

'Obersturmführer Franz Müller,' I said, breaking a bread roll in half and wondering if it was the last I'd see if bread went on ration in a couple of weeks. '25th SS-Panzer Grenadiers. His platoon was at the Château de Hêtres around time Dabs was shot.'

'I remember,' said Jekyll. 'Richter's diary.'

'Unfortunately Müller hung himself in his POW camp. I've requested a copy of his file but I'm told it's unavailable.'

The empty soup bowls were taken away and two plates of indeterminate meat and vegetables took their place.

'What about Richter?' Jekyll asked, poking an exploratory fork at the meat and looking mildly surprised when it didn't fight back.

'We still haven't established in which camp he's being held. As soon as we do, I'd like to interview him. Under the circumstances I'd like to hold on to my report for a couple more days.'

Jekyll grunted once more. 'Anything else?'

'Nothing concrete,' I said.

He seemed preoccupied and, after we had danced around the subject of the carrier and its crew for a while longer, I considered whether or not to tell him of Kearney's IRA involvement. But I couldn't really see there was much more mileage in that angle so I decided there was no point in pursuing it.

Jekyll asked about the team back at the office and how ATS Blake was shaping up. In an attempt at humour, I said shaping up was the least of Susie's worries. But my wit proved as weak as my soup and Jekyll, obviously not amused, became uncommunicative. We finished lunch more or less in silence and in the end I left him to his brandy and his coffee in the club lounge. Outside, despite the petrol fumes, I found the atmosphere easier to breathe.

~

I spent the rest of the afternoon enquiring of letting agents for anything available at a rent I could afford. As the general consensus seemed to be, not much, I started to figure how long we could manage if we used the money I'd been sending Penny, and which she said she hadn't spent, to subsidize the rent. With luck, we might swing a year before it ran out and I thought that by then something else might turn up. What I didn't factor in was the allowance she got from her father as I'd still just as soon starve in a garret than be beholden to Reggie Forster.

As a principle, that was all well and good, except I couldn't see Penny happily starving alongside me. Nevertheless I marked off two or three flats to take a look at then dropped by the office before going home.

The atmosphere wasn't any better than the one I'd left in Jekyll's club. I was going to ginger up Jack to find out in which camp Richter was being held but found he had already bailed out, leaving some poor excuse behind him to cover his retreat. I left a note about Richter on his desk then followed his example. Stan threw a last accusatory glance in my direction as I left and, getting back to my flat, I thought I'd better check to see if Ida really had moved out. Her door was ajar and so I walked in. She'd left the room clean—or as clean as it was possible to get it which was a damn sight cleaner than she'd found it—and seemed to have taken little more than her battered suitcase with her. The bed and the stove and the few other bits and pieces Stan had taken the trouble to find for her lay abandoned, leaving the room looking like the set of a failed stage play. Poor old Stan had backed the production but had lost his investment, left in the dark when they'd switched off the lights.

I was still wondering what I'd say to him in the morning when I heard a noise behind me. I don't know if I really expected to see Caomhánach there but I was almost as surprised to see it was Sam, the housebreaker from the floor above.

'She's gone,' he said.

'Yes. Found a job,' I told him.

'I thought I might have that cupboard if no one else wants it.' He gestured to a small cabinet with a Formica top and sliding glass doors that Stan had found for Ida.

'I'm sure that'll be all right,' I said. 'Ida won't need it.'

'No,' said Sam.

'You know they're pulling this place down?'

'Yeah. I got the letter.'

'What about the old girl at the top of the stairs?'

'Mrs Randall? She's going to her niece in Sussex.'

'Oh, right,' I said. 'Mrs Randall.' I'd been there for almost six months and hadn't even learned her name. 'You fixed up?'

'Got a few irons in the fire,' he said. 'You?'

'Looking into it.'

'Right,' he said, rubbing his hands together and making a move towards the cabinet.

'Need a hand?' I asked.

'No, I can manage.'

And since I assumed he was used to moving property out of one place and into another, I left him to it.

25

I telephoned Penny that evening. Once past my mother, I told her I had made enquiries with several agents and had a couple of flats to view.

'Do you want to come up and look at them with me? We'll have to be quick because they don't stay empty long.'

I could tell by her tone she was prevaricating. 'I can't get away at the moment.'

'You haven't told them yet.'

'I've got to pick the right time,' she said.

'Right for who?'

'Whom,' she said.

She had always done it, corrected my grammar. At first it had amused me. After a while it had worn thin and she had made the effort to stop herself doing it.

'I don't see the problem,' I said.

'You wouldn't. You don't like them.'

'They're my family,' I said. 'My prerogative.'

'Speaking of families,' she said, 'a man came to see me about Mummy and Daddy.'

For a moment she sounded like a little girl but just then I didn't find that endearing.

'Perhaps,' I suggested, without thinking first and putting a foot straight through the ice, 'the Labour government have decided to make everyone who left the sinking ship renew their citizenship before they're allowed back.'

'That's a hurtful thing to say!'

I'd deliberately not called them rats but I suppose that's what she thought I was thinking.

'I'm only joking,' I said. 'What did he want?'

'To know if they'd sold the house or had bought any other property. Stupid questions like that. He asked if I knew when they were coming home.'

'I thought they'd rented the house out.'

'So they did.'

It was a big place in central London and had come through the war unscathed. Rather like Reggie Forster himself.

'I suppose it's just bureaucracy,' I said.

'I don't see what business it is of anyone else's.'

'You know what this government is like. They probably want to make sure your father pays all his taxes.'

'It's criminal,' she complained.

'No, not paying them is criminal,' I said. 'And if they're coming back he'd better get used to the fact.'

When she didn't reply I said:

'These flats then? What do you want me to do?'

'You'd better look at them by yourself, Harry. You know what I like.'

I might have remarked that there'd been a time when I did but I'd done enough damage for one evening and was running out of change anyway. I said goodbye and hung up. I started back up the stairs then changed my mind and went out.

It wasn't late although with the present run of poor weather we'd had, the heavy overcast and drizzling rain, it seemed more like autumn than a summer evening. I walked around aimlessly for a while then went into a cinema. The main feature was *And Then There Were None* with Walter Huston and Barry Fitzgerald, the man who often played the part of an irascible priest. I'd missed the first half but went in anyway. The girl in the ticket booth smiled at me and said I could go in cheap since I'd missed so much. The film was about a group of people stranded in a big house on an isolated island getting themselves killed one by one. About ten minutes in I realized it had been made from an Agatha Christie book I'd read. I couldn't remember who'd done it, only the trick of how, and I couldn't concentrate anyway. My mind wandered back over my conversation with Penny and I began to think she was having second thoughts about living with me again. Then I wondered why anyone would contact her about her parents. I couldn't help thinking about Diamaid Caomhánach and his pretending to be Major Hendrix and wished I'd asked Penny what the man had looked like.

Ugly according to Rose, but there were many kinds of ugly. If it was Caomhánach wanting to get at me for some imagined offence I'd caused him—other than the obvious offence of being an English army officer—I didn't want him near Penny. I decided to ring her again and get a description. Then it occurred to me that if it wasn't Caomhánach but a genuine enquiry about Helen and Reggie Forster, whoever the man was might have been to see Julia, too.

As I got up to leave there were just two of them left alive on the island, the young girl and a man, attracted to, and yet wary of each other. They were scrambling over the rocks on the beach unsure of their footing. Like me and Penny, I couldn't help thinking. Like Penny and *I*.

It was dark and gone ten when I reached Julia's house, late for a call but I rang the bell anyway. Ida answered.

'God!' I said, 'she hasn't got you working at this hour, has she?'

For a moment Ida looked as if she was going to cry.

'It's all right, really,' she whispered. 'I don't mind. I had the day off yesterday.' She let me in then said, 'They're in the sitting room. I'll announce you.'

Tuchman was with Julia. They were sitting side by side on the sofa. Tuchman got up and we shook hands. Julia looked less welcoming.

'Harry,' she said in that usual tone of hers.

I apologised for calling so late and glanced at the door to make sure Ida had closed it behind her.

'The girl needed a job, Julia,' I told her, 'not a prison sentence.'

'You might know about the latter being a policeman, Harry,' she replied mordantly, 'But I think I know more about domestic service.'

'Don't you mean servitude?' But I could see I was making Tuchman uncomfortable so I raised a placatory hand and said, 'That's not why I'm here. I spoke to Penny on the phone this evening and she said someone had been to see her asking questions about Helen and Reggie. Has anyone been to see you?'

'Drink, Harry?' Tuchman asked at the drinks cabinet. 'Another, Julia?'

'Please, Ben,' she said.

'Just an Indian tonic, if you have one,' I told him.

'As a matter of fact,' said Julia, 'there has.'

'Can you describe him? Short? Ugly...round face, snub-nose?'

'You sound like one of Ben's detectives.'

'I read detective stories,' Ben said, handing me the tonic. 'The hard-boiled kind. Julia finds the fact endearingly American.'

'She never found it endearing to have one living in her house,' I said.

Julia took her drink from Tuchman. 'You were a uniformed constable. There is a difference.'

'I suppose there must be,' I said. 'I never got to slap the girl around.'

'Who's the ugly snub-nose, Harry?' Tuchman asked.

'An Irishman named Diamaid Caomhánach. He's an IRA gunman who's been impersonating an army officer.'

'Well,' said Julia tasting her fresh drink, 'you certainly choose your company.'

'Is he dangerous?' Tuchman asked.

'It's this carrier business. One of the men in it betrayed Caomhánach to the police and he wants to kill him if he's still alive.'

'And is he?'

'No, I don't think he is.'

'If it's any consolation,' said Julia, 'the man who came to see me was neither Irish nor ugly. One might have described him as seedy. Nothing a decent suit of clothes and a little grooming wouldn't have improved. He could have been almost as presentable as you, Harry.'

'I'll take that as a compliment,' I said. 'I was going to ring Penny again and ask her to describe the man. It doesn't sound like Caomhánach so I'd rather not. There's no point in worrying her.'

'But why on earth did you think he'd be interested in Helen and Reggie?' Julia asked.

'He's not. Caomhánach's interested in me. At least he is if Kearney's dead.'

'Who is Kearney?' Julia sighed.

'He was the sergeant in command of the carrier. His real name was O'Connell.'

She still seemed mystified. 'And if this Kearney is dead why would the Irishman be interested in you?'

'Thwarted ambition,' I replied, preferring the vague to the melodramatic.

She laughed. 'We've all been there, darling.'

'One other thing,' I said, as if it was nothing more than idle curiosity. 'That chap Bryce I met here the other evening. Do you know him well?'

'What chap Bryce?' asked Julia.

'I think he said he was Maurice Coveney's secretary.'

I was aware of Tuchman's eyes on me but kept mine on Julia.

'Oh, him. Young man with those spectacles. He brought Maurice's evening dress over. Typical of Ronnie to ask him in for a drink. *He* doesn't have to pay for the stuff. Drinks quite enough by himself without handing it out to all and sundry.'

'Has Bryce been with Coveney long?'

'I'm not familiar with Maurice's office arrangements, Harry, although in this instance I do happen to know he hasn't. Maurice used to have a female secretary until her sweetheart came home and she ran off to marry him. Maurice told me he would employ only men in future as marriage doesn't tend to go to their heads as it does with girls. Why the interest?'

'Nothing in particular,' I said. 'He rang my office this morning, that's all. Said he wanted a word.' I glanced at Tuchman. 'Don't know what about.'

Tuchman's face remained impassive. For a moment I considered asking to speak with him on his own and telling him I'd received a letter about Pellisier's exhumation. But apart from not wanting to arouse Julia's curiosity, I didn't want to play all my cards in front of Tuchman. Instead, I finished my tonic water and said I'd leave them to it. Julia rang the bell for Ida to let me out—as if I wasn't smart enough to find the front door by myself.

'Thank you, Ida,' she said while pointedly looking at me. 'That will be all for tonight.'

Ida bobbed and took me down the hall.

As she opened the door she said, 'Tell Stan for me I'm sorry, will you, Captain Tennant?'

It closed again before I was able to ask sorry for what. But on reflection I didn't really want to know.

~

I was in the office early the next morning but even so Jack was in first.

'Did you see the note I left,' I asked him.

'What, the one about Richter?'

'We need to find him.'

'Then you'll have to go to Hamburg,' he said. 'Didn't you see *my* note?'

'What note?'

'I left it on your desk. They got back to me while you were in Ireland.' He began sorting through the mess of papers on my desktop. He pulled one out and waved it at me. 'Here. Richter was repatriated in August forty-five.' He grinned unpleasantly. 'His wound turned septic and they had to take his leg off. As soon as he got back up on his foot they told him to hop it.'

'Very good, Jack,' I said, finding less humour in it than Jack obviously did, 'but you might have checked to see if I'd got the note.'

He looked offended. 'I can't do everything around here. Oh, and that Gifford bloke rang after you'd gone yesterday.'

'Do you mean *Superintendent* Gifford?' I asked, wishing Jack could show a little more respect for rank even if any hope of discipline had long since evaporated.

'Yeah,' said Jack. 'He's the one. Wanted you to meet him today. Same place as last time, he said. Twelve o'clock.'

I took the same place to be the greasy café off the Caledonian Road. The thought of the tea there made me queasy so I put our kettle on and looked in Susie's biscuit tin to see if there was anything other than crumbs. There weren't and I sent Jack to the shop down the road to see if they had anything we could have with our tea. While he was gone I flipped through our burgeoning file on the Bren Gun carrier. The Irish connection had been a red herring, achieving little apart from putting Diamaid Caomhánach on my tail, and if it wasn't Caomhánach asking questions about Helen and Reggie Forster, that left only Tuchman's investigation into Claude Pellisier's collaboration. Assuming, that is, Reggie wasn't wanted for fraud or tax-evasion. Something I wouldn't have wholly discounted. But barring that, I couldn't imagine what bearing Reggie and Helen might have on Pellisier's crimes and would have assumed that if the questioner *had* been connected to Tuchman, he would have found some way of letting me know the previous evening at Julia's.

The others arrived while I was still looking through the file. The frostiness between Peter and Susie seemed to have thawed although I no longer detected that frisson between them which had suggested to me that they had something going on. Stan, however, seemed as morose as ever so I thought twice about passing on Ida's message.

An apology is one thing, but one that carries with it the suggestion of finality wasn't the sort of thing I thought Stan was going to welcome.

'Jack not in?' Peter asked. 'Do you know what he did with that letter from the Caen *avocat général*?'

It was still in my pocket from my visit to Jekyll's club. I fished it out and gave it to him. Peter gave it to Susie who had just settled in behind her desk.

'If you can book the call for me, Susie,' Peter said, 'I'll speak to them. Just get them on the line, if you will. Is that all right?'

'Sure,' she said brightly. 'It'll probably take a while though.'

'That's all right. Whenever you can manage it.'

International calls had been suspended just prior to the outbreak of war and had only recently been reinstated. As trunk calls within the country often took an age to be put through due to the demand, I couldn't imagine how long a call to France might take.

Jack walked in with some stale buns, moaning about the fact they were all he could get. Which at least made a pleasant change from the exaggerated politeness with which Peter and Susie were treating each other.

'Take them or leave them,' said Jack. 'I had to queue for fifteen minutes just to get these. Want me to toast them on the ring?'

'What do you want with the Caen *avocat général*?' I asked Peter.

He blinked at me in his scholarly fashion. 'You remember in his diary Richter said that when the platoon arrived at the Château de Hêtres there were Gestapo there with the owner? Now everyone assumed that the body they dug up in the garden must have been the owner of the house since it was dressed in civilian clothes and carried French ID.' He glanced down at the letter from the *avocat général's* office, '...name of Claude Pellisier according to this.' He shrugged. 'Well, where the SS or the Gestapo are involved we all jump to conclusions. But if the French are going to exhume him again, it's obvious they're having second thoughts about it being Pellisier. Which means the body might well turn out to be William Kearney after all.'

'We're not jumping to another conclusion, are we?' I said.

Peter looked non-plussed. 'Why else would they write to us if they didn't think it was Kearney?'

'So what do you want to talk to them about?'

'If the blood group of the body is A-positive, it could be Kearney. And I thought if there was a record of this Pellisier's blood group on record somewhere and he was also A-positive, it might be that Kearney was murdered to fake Pelliser's death.'

'Why?'

'I've no idea,' he admitted. 'But the body was burned and in civilian clothing. With French ID...? It's a possibility don't you think?'

'The body was also identified as Pellisier's from a birthmark,' I said.

'Ah,' said Peter. 'I didn't know that.'

And the only reason he didn't was because I'd not told him. Not about that, or about Pellisier and his collaboration. It was true I had only found out about Pellisier's connection to the Château de Hêtres and Penny's family myself over the weekend, but I still might have mentioned it to Peter.

On Sunday night Tuchman—however politely—had suggested I stay away from asking questions about Pellisier. So far I'd complied. But Tuchman hadn't asked Peter. Nor could it be said that I'd led Peter to the Frenchman. He'd followed his own nose.

'So you already know about him?' Peter asked. And although I couldn't detect any trace of grievance over the fact I'd failed to pass information on to him, it was there nonetheless.

'Colonel G does,' I replied, not exactly answering his question.

'Should I pursue it?'

'By all means,' I said. 'Although even if the blood group of both men does turn out to be A-positive it won't be conclusive. It occurs in about thirty percent of the population. There's a one-in-three chance they will be the same anyway.'

'One in nine,' said Jack, who'd been listening while passing out the buns. 'That's the thing about odds...one in three for each man but for them *both* to be the same you have to—'

'And it won't mean the 25th SS-Panzer Grenadiers didn't kill him,' I said to Peter.

'Or the Gestapo,' Peter concluded. 'What do we know about Pellisier?'

'Is that the time?' I said, looking at the clock on the wall and stuffing a bun in my mouth. 'I've got an appointment. You'll let me know what the Caen *avocat général* has to say, won't you Peter?'

~

Fortified with tea and toasted buns, stale as they were, I took the tube a couple of stops and walked to the café to meet Gifford.

Run-down for decades, the area around Kings Cross was a well-known red-light district. The cheap housing had made it a mecca for successive waves of immigrants since well before the war and Göring's Luftwaffe had done it no favours since. It hadn't been my beat when I'd been a copper but I knew it from the second-hand market on the Caledonian Road which had been notorious for selling stolen goods. I'd been there on several occasions on the lookout for property stolen in my area, but it wasn't the sort of place anyone would go for high-end goods. Besides, the local villains had a nose for the police, even in plain clothes, and green as I was they generally knew I was coming before I'd decided to go there myself.

During the war it had been a natural hive of black market activity and still was now. If you wanted anything off-ration, or anything generally unobtainable, the market in the Caledonian Road was the place to get it. Turning towards the café, I wondered if that might be why Gifford favoured the place; perhaps not for black market goods, but for something less tangible, something passed not by hand but by mouth.

Avoiding Peter's questions had made me early and Gifford wasn't at the café. Patrons came and went and I found an empty table easily enough. The tea didn't look to have improved appreciably so I tried a mug of what they described as coffee. When it arrived I found it wasn't easy to tell the difference. Or from what the stuff had been made from, for that matter. Acorns, judging by the taste. Or an old bottle of Camp coffee someone had turned up on a bombsite. Whatever its origin, like their tea it reminded me more than anything of the mud I'd swallowed as we'd worked our way up the boot of Italy during the winter campaign.

I didn't notice Gifford arrive until I found him standing over my table. He had a chameleon's ability to blend into his environment. He put his enamel mug down next to mine. The brew in them looked identical.

'Anything on Caomhánach?' I asked as he sat down. When he shook his head I said, 'Rose O'Shaughnessy came to see me.'

I could tell that got his attention by the way one of his eyebrows rose slightly.

'She admitted that Caomhánach was my Major Hendrix. But I already knew that. I showed that photo you gave me to some of the people he talked to. They identified him.'

Gifford didn't say anything. He lifted his tea and took a swallow. To his credit his expression barely changed.

'I'm pretty sure Kearney—O'Connell, that is—is dead. I told Rose as much. She doesn't think Caomhánach will believe it. A difficult thing to prove. One of my men is working on the angle that the body in the Château de Hêtres wasn't Pellisier's at all but Kearney's.'

I watched Gifford's face. As with the tea, he gave no indication what I said was hard to swallow. He didn't reply and I took that as indication enough. I had mentioned Coveney's name the first time I'd phoned him. But not since. Nor had I ever told him anything about the Château de Hêtres or Claude Pellisier. If he'd not known what I was talking about, at the very least I'd have expected some expression of curiosity. Instead, he reached into his jacket pocket and pulled out another buff envelope.

'More photos?' I asked.

'No,' he said, dropping it on the table between us and speaking for the first time. 'It's what you've been asking for. It's the full transcript of Franz Müller's interrogation.'

I must have looked surprised.

'That's what you wanted, isn't it?'

'Yes, but how did you know? And how come you could get it when I couldn't? You're not army.'

'No,' he said, 'but then it's not an army problem.'

'Isn't it?'

He regarded me with an expression that could have been disappointment. 'Why do you think this particular file landed on your desk?'

I shrugged. 'I could say it's because investigating war crimes is what we do. But as far as this business goes even I don't believe that.'

'Didn't you ever wonder why anyone was interested in the death of Joseph Dabs and the disappearance of William Kearney? How many other men were summarily executed or went missing during the Normandy campaign?'

'I don't know,' I said. 'But the Hitlerjugend's 25th SS-Panzer Grenadier Regiment was right on the spot when Dabs was shot. We already knew they didn't take prisoners. I assumed someone thought it would be nice and easy to pin this one on them too. It's what my colonel wants and I just do as I'm told. And if it wasn't them, there were plenty of other SS units in the area we could hold responsible.'

Gifford gave a mirthless chuckle. 'You do as you're told, do you? What about when you saw Jekyll at your wife's aunt's house? And when you discovered this carrier of yours was found outside the Château de Hêtres? A place owned by the brother-in-law of your wife's uncle?'

'Not a blood relation,' I said, as if that had anything to do with it.

'Somewhere your mother-in-law spent her holidays as a girl...'

'All right,' I said, 'I admit I've always thought the business a bit odd. I did wonder why I was given it, and why whoever passed it to my colonel thought I might be able to turn up something they couldn't. Don't ask me what. Particularly since Tuchman—I assume you know who Ben Tuchman is?—warned me off asking about Coveney's brother-in-law since it might be embarrassing for the family...'

Then it dawned on me just what Gifford might be suggesting.

'Is that why I got it? Because of the Forster family? Or Coveney? What is it, the old boy network covering each other's backs again? Did they think that because of my family connection I'd do as I was told? I thought we got the file because it was the sort of thing we did, spend our days trawling through testimony like *that*,' and I pushed the envelope containing Müller's interrogation back towards him. But the table top was sticky from someone else's breakfast and the thing didn't move more than half an inch. 'Anyway, since you've already got it, what did you need me for?'

Gifford pulled out a pipe and started thumbing tobacco into the bowl.

'Don't go off half-cocked. Read the file first, although you won't find it as useful as you thought you might.' He pushed the envelope back to me again, struck a match and lit the pipe. 'And Tuchman's interested in Pellisier. We have another angle.'

'And what's that?'

'Read that first.'

He let out a cloud of smoke, like a locomotive ready for the off, then got up. He fished inside his pocket again and dropped a slip of paper on top of the envelope.

'If you need to get in touch use that number. And keep your eye open for Caomhánach. He's not stable.'

'That's what Rose—' I started to say, but Gifford was already walking away.

26

Tuesday July 2nd 1946

Susie was alone in the office when I got back. Stan and Jack hadn't yet returned from lunch down the pub; Peter was off somewhere following his nose.

'You and him all right, Susie?' I asked.

She looked at me in that way she had, blinking as if she was short-sighted with a small wrinkle creasing her brow. Cute in her way but she'd copied it from Betty Hutton and hadn't got it quite right. Before this she'd tried imitating Lauren Bacall but was neither tall nor sultry enough to pull that one off.

'I thought I detected an atmosphere, that's all.'

'We're okay.'

'Spoken to Caen yet?'

'All the lines are booked. Might not even be today.'

In my office I took the envelope Gifford had given me, still feeling out of sorts after talking with him. First it was Jekyll wanting me to hang the murder of Dabs on the SS and now Gifford, too, it seemed. Just so some influential peoples' connection to a German collaborator didn't come to light.

I pulled out the transcript of Müller's interrogation. We rarely received original files but if the document was important enough it would have been replicated by Gestetner, a stencil cut on a typewriter from the original with as many copies made as were needed. Something really important might be Photostatted but we rarely dealt with anything of that nature. Müller's testimony was a carbon copy of the original typed interrogation, and probably a copy of a copy at that.

Given that thousands of POWs needed to be interrogated, the army couldn't run to stenographers and the interrogator himself would have had to make notes as he went, in whatever fashion suited him. These would be typed up later, a process that left a great deal of room for misreading and typographical errors. I don't know if the army Intelligence Division deliberately used substandard carbon paper but there seemed to be something unstable about it. Either it was too light to be legible or smudged at the slightest touch. I'd read thousands of the things and sometimes I thought I'd never live long enough to get the ink off my fingers.

Müller had been captured in the Falaise Pocket in August 1944—at the same time that Vogel's body had been recovered. Since Müller served with 25th SS-Panzer Grenadiers, he was of special interest. Brigadeführer Kurt Meyer, then commander of the 25th SS-Panzer Grenadiers, had used the Ardenne Abbey for his regimental headquarters and, after it was liberated on July 8th 1944, the body of a young Canadian officer had been discovered. At the time of Müller's interrogation the bodies of the other Canadians murdered in the abbey had still not been found. By the time they were, in the winter and spring of 1945, Müller was dead.

Reading the transcript, I found that during the interrogation Müller was asked repeatedly about Lieutenant Fred Williams, the Canadian whose body had been found in the abbey. Each time Müller denied any knowledge of the incident, stating that at the time of the massacre his company wasn't at the abbey. It appeared Müller had a good memory for dates, always able to remember being somewhere else when questioned about a particular event. On the other hand, his memory didn't seem as good when asked about the names of his comrades. His excuse was that during the last month or two before his capture, the 25th had taken heavy losses and had continually received drafts of new men which meant he hadn't got to know them well. Of those he could remember, it seemed to me they often bore suspiciously common surnames. But then his own—Müller—or variations upon it—was perhaps the most common German name of all, so I was probably looking for duplicity where none existed.

As Gifford had warned me I didn't find the transcript as useful as I had hoped. There was no reference to SS-Mann Richter and his diary nor to Müller's platoon having been at any château near Maltot on July 10th.

I went through it again, deciding obstinately that I'd do things my way. I made a note of the names of men in his platoon he had remembered—the dead SS-Unterscharführer Otto Vogel being one of them. Then I pulled out the copy of Richter's diary we had and added two or three more names.

Stan and Jack came back from the pub and I put the report aside for Peter to look at.

Jack, seeing me with my feet on the desk and blowing smoke rings asked, 'Busy?'

'I've just been through the full transcript of Obersturmführer Franz Müller's interrogation.'

Jack dropped into his chair and gave a beery belch.

'Where did you get that?'

'Superintendent Gifford.'

'Well, well. The prerogatives of rank, I suppose. So, are we getting somewhere at last?'

I told him what was in the report. Jack listened attentively. 'The answer's no, then.'

I heard Peter come in and called him through. He put his head round the door, an oddly bland expression on his usually intelligent face. I tossed him Müller's transcript and he caught it awkwardly against his chest. I told him what I'd told Jack.

'We want to find anyone who might have been with Müller at the château.' I gave him the list of names I had made. 'If we really want to know what happened, it's the only way we're going to find out.'

Peter read the list.

'Schmidt...Klein...Hess...Neumann...Hartmann...?' He looked at me doubtfully. 'There must be dozens of men with these names who served in the 25th SS-Panzer Grenadiers.'

'Pity there's not a Featherstonehaugh,' said Jack.

I smiled at Peter. 'Susie said your Caen call is going to take some time to put through.' Meaning, of course, it gave him time to chase up the Neumanns and the Schmidts.

'I'm putting a letter in the post to them tonight in case I can't get through to anyone,' Peter said. 'But I won't be holding my breath.'

'It might be worth asking around to see if anyone has compiled a roll of men in the individual 25th SS-Panzer Grenadiers companies. Get Stan on it as well.'

'So where do we go if we can't find a Klein or a Neumann who was with Müller at the château?' Jack asked. 'Want me to write up that report you wrote for Jekyll? We can suggest Müller or the Gestapo were responsible, and dump it back in his lap. Müller's dead and we ain't going to identify the Gestapo men, so it's not as if they're in any position to object.'

'It's what Colonel G wants,' I agreed. 'I told him yesterday I needed a couple more days to track down Müller's file, for what that was worth. But if that's as far as we can take it, so be it.'

'That's what I like about the army,' said Jack, feeding a fresh sheet of paper into his Remington. 'When you don't know anything push it higher up the chain of command for someone else to worry about. I'll do a draft then. If there's anything I can't remember or don't know, I'll ask my superior officer.'

'God knows what you're going to do when you have to think for yourself on civvy street, Jack.'

He grunted and started hitting keys. 'Never said I couldn't. It's just that in the army other people like to do it for you.'

I couldn't fault that argument so didn't try. I lit another cigarette as Susie came in with our afternoon cuppa.

'So you're giving Colonel G your report at last,' she said.

'Those cute little ears of yours should have been requisitioned as radar dishes,' I told her.

She smiled sweetly. 'Finally given up on the Rose of Tralee? Is she nowhere to be found?'

'Didn't I tell you? She found me the other night.'

Susie's eyes widened. '*No*.'

'And very different she looked, too. She'd permed her hair and was wearing make-up. She asked after you. In a manner of speaking.'

Her eyes narrowed again. 'And what kind of manner was that?'

'I wouldn't care to repeat it.'

'Bitch. Was her so-called cousin with her?'

'No, I'm glad to say he wasn't. He's a desperate man according to Rose.'

'That'll make two of them then.'

'Oh, I should imagine Rose does all right.'

'Careful Captain,' said Susie. 'Sleeping with the enemy can get you shot.' And she flounced back into her own office, leaving me to reflect upon the possibilities.

I changed my mind about Jekyll's report again and told Jack to hold off. I'd only seen him the day before and he wouldn't be in to the end of the week. That would give Stan and Peter at least a couple of days to see if there was any chance of turning up one of Müller's comrades. It was a tack I realized I should have tried earlier, but I had been hoping for more from Müller's interrogation. The moral seemed to be, never wait for what you hope for; grab what you can get first.

Jack let out a long sigh and pulled the paper out of the Remington again.

I wondered if I ought to let Ben Tuchman know that it was possible Pellisier wasn't dead. There was always the chance he had instigated the exhumation himself, but if he hadn't I assumed Tuchman would want to set the bloodhounds back on the Frenchman's trail. I really couldn't believe he hadn't considered the possibility already but that was all beyond our remit—unless it had been Pellisier himself who had shot Dabs and possibly Kearney. Not that I thought that to be very likely; not with the Gestapo and a unit of SS on hand, men who took to that kind of thing with the avidity of fat men in a bun shop.

If Pellisier wasn't dead, though, I couldn't help thinking it was going to leave Coveney open to some scrutiny. He had identified the man's body and despite it all being a bit too close to Penny's family for my liking, I decided to let Tuchman know anyway. His reaction would be interesting if nothing else. And I could still say without bending the truth completely out of shape that *I* wasn't the one asking questions about Pellisier. It was going to make me a lot happier if I could leave him to explain to Julia and Penny what it was all about if the need arose.

Drinking my tea, however, I began to speculate about Coveney's identification of Pellisier's body. The corpse had been badly burnt, by all accounts, although apparently not sufficiently to obscure some sort of birthmark by which Coveney had been able to identify him. Albeit by photograph. Perhaps Coveney, like everyone else, had supposed the body to be Pellisier's since it had been found in Pellisier's château. Even so, dead or alive, talk of Pellisier's collaboration wouldn't be the sort of thing Coveney would care to have bandied about.

Then I remembered the phone call Jack had taken from the man called Bryce. I hadn't got back to him but if this Bryce was the one I'd met at Julia's and was Coveney's secretary, it seemed likely he'd have been instructed to find out how much we'd discovered. A cynic might surmise that once Coveney got wind of what Pellisier had been doing in Caen, he'd be keen to see that his dead wife's brother should remain regarded as dead. Coveney may not have been a politician himself, but he was high enough up the bureaucratic ladder to think like one. And in my experience, as with politicians expediency runs in civil servants' blood like an additive. Having Pellisier charged with war crimes wasn't going to reflect very well upon him. If I'd read Gifford right it might be that it had been Coveney who had engineered my getting the Dabs' file in the first place.

But, as I say, that would be a cynic's view.

~

Towards the end of the afternoon I toyed with the idea of ringing Bryce back and pumping him for information under the pretext of allowing him to pump me. But that could wait and, since it was almost time to knock off, I took Stan down the pub for a drink instead. He'd already had a couple at lunchtime, I'd noticed, which hadn't helped his morose state of mind, but he wasn't an aggressive drunk, just a self-pitying one and I was familiar enough with that breed myself to have some sympathy for him.

'Let her settle in for a week or two,' I suggested over a pint. 'Ida's a bright enough girl. She'll soon find her feet then maybe you can take her out on her day off.'

Assuming Julia ever gave her one.

Stan didn't look convinced. But at least he was no longer blaming me for the situation.

'You can't hold it against her for moving out,' I said. 'After all, the place is little better than a slum and they're going to pull it down soon anyway. She would only have had to find somewhere else. Now she's got a job as well as somewhere to live.'

Stan muttered into his beer. 'I suppose so.'

'I'll give her your number and she can give you a bell once she's settled in. How about that?'

'If you like,' Stan agreed, as if I had a preference in the matter.

'Good.' I said to settle it, not at all sure Ida would call him but at least leaving the ball firmly in her court. As opposed to mine where Stan could take a kick at it whenever he felt down.

We drank up and I put him on his bus before taking the tube to Hyde Park Corner. I didn't have a phone number for Tuchman, nor an address. The only place I knew he frequented was the drinking club in Soho and I had no idea how often he could be found there. That left Julia although I would have preferred not to have involved her.

When Ida opened the door I gave her a slip of paper with Stan's number on it.

'In case you need help with anything, Stan said,' I lied. 'Just give him a ring.'

She tucked the note into the pocket of the maid's uniform Julia had been so thoughtful to supply, then led me to the drawing room and announced me.

'It might be easier,' Julia commented dryly as I walked in, 'if I had the bed made up in your old room, Harry. It would save all this coming and going.'

She was sitting in an upright armchair by the window, reading a book by the light of some rare afternoon sun.

'Actually it was Ben I wanted to see,' I said. 'But I don't know where to find him.'

'As gallant as ever, Harry.'

'Although it's always a delight to see you, Julia.'

She put her book aside. 'As a matter of fact he's due in twenty minutes or so. You might as well stay and have a drink. I'll have to ask you leave after you've seen him, though, as we've plans for this evening.' She spoke to Ida who was still hovering by the door awaiting instructions. 'Mix us a couple of martinis, please Ida,' she said. 'Dry for Harry, I should imagine.'

Ida carefully measured gin into two glasses and followed it with Vermouth. Julia watched like an instructress in a domestic science class.

'I've been teaching Ida how to mix drinks. It's a useful skill to possess. It will set you in good stead for the future, Ida.'

Ida bobbed dutifully and brought the drinks to us on a tray.

'How thoughtful,' I remarked. 'You can always get a job in a pub, Ida, when Miss Parker gets too much for you.'

Ida hurried out of the room, embarrassed. Julia scowled at me.

'I do wish you wouldn't say that sort of thing in front of the girl, Harry. But then you've always allied yourself with the servant rather than with the served.'

Had I thought it would do any good, I would have told her that the world had changed. The only wonder was, she hadn't yet found out for herself. Perhaps it had been the slow accumulation of shifts and alterations that had masked how different everything was now. And forever would be. But even Julia could no longer expect the old privileges to remain. Penny's parents, Helen and Reggie, were going to find things noticeably more egalitarian upon their return. America might have the reputation of being the shining democratic light of the world, but money spoke louder there than it did almost anywhere and I doubted if living there had changed their lifestyle much at all. They had probably spent the war years ordering a bunch of coloured servants around.

Julia lit a cigarette. 'You seem rather pensive, Harry.'

I admitted to thinking about Helen and Reggie. 'Any news yet on when they're coming back?'

'They managed to get a berth on the Queen Mary. They leave New York on the twenty-ninth.'

'This month!' I hadn't realized it would be so soon.'

'The Queen is taking war brides to Canada. Halifax, Nova Scotia, then sailing to New York. Can you imagine it? What on earth do all those girls think they'll do in the backwoods of Nova Scotia?'

'I doubt they'll be obliged to build their own log cabins, Julia.'

She turned away, remarking, 'Sarcasm doesn't suit you, Harry. I don't know why you persist in employing it,' making it sound like an itinerant peddler I occasionally engaged for an odd job here and there.

'Penny tells me you are going to live together again.'

'Well, once we've found another flat,' I admitted.

'Are you sure this will be the best thing for her?'

This display of concern for Penny's happiness was, as was the case with her sister Helen, a view observed from their own perspective. When focussed upon me, I was to be found somewhere on the outer edges of visibility, a thing of small consideration seen through the wrong end of a telescope. I no longer felt any need to defend myself, although it was one more reminder that some things hadn't changed and that all the old arguments we had played through before the war would have to be rehearsed once again. As it happened, I was spared having to reply as the doorbell rang and a moment later Ida announced Tuchman. He kissed Julia on the cheek and shook my hand. Julia, with surprising percipience, said she would leave us alone to talk.

Tuchman mixed himself a drink. 'Something up, Harry?'

'Claude Pellisier,' I said. 'I know you asked me to steer clear but something's come up with this carrier business that I thought you'd better know.'

'Okay, shoot.'

I gave him what I presented as Peter's theory that the body in the château might have been Kearney's and that the French were going to exhume the body.

'I don't know if they can prove the body is Kearney's, not after two years in the ground, but it does leave open the possibility of Pellisier still being alive.'

Tuchman toyed with his glass. 'You haven't mentioned this to anyone beyond your office?'

'No. Pellisier isn't my concern. Even if I was sure he was at the château when Kearney and his men arrived, it's hardly credible he killed Kearney and Dabs himself. And if he did, there'd be no way to prove it without a witness. I'm satisfied it was a unit of the 25th SS-Panzer Grenadiers who killed the men. But since they found Kurt Meyer guilty of what was a massacre and still didn't hang him, they aren't going to hang Pellisier or some SS man for a couple of British Tommies, even if they could pin their deaths on them.'

'They've probably got enough on Pellisier to hang him anyway,' Tuchman observed.

'Well that's a different matter,' I said. 'Kearney and Dabs were casualties of the conflict, even if they did die in cold blood. Far worse things happened than that. The things Pellisier did, for one. But that's not my concern. I just thought I ought to let you know.'

I knocked back what was left of my drink and stood up.

'I'll let myself out. Say goodbye to Julia for me, won't you?'

~

Out on the street, although the longest day had passed no more than ten days earlier, I felt I could already sense the shortening of the summer evenings. Perhaps it was the cloud which had drifted up, obscuring the sun by which Julia had been reading; perhaps it was my mood.

I felt oddly empty. I hadn't eaten since the buns Jack had bought that morning but it wasn't hunger. It was a sense of deflation, as though all the impetus of the last couple of weeks had leaked away, leaving me hollow. We'd got closer to a conclusion than I might have expected. Yet it didn't bring anything in the way of satisfaction. At least not for me. The ghost of other possibilities seemed to hang over it still. There was the life Robert Burleigh might have come home to live, with his wife Edna and his two children; not a comfortable or prosperous one, probably, but one at least which might have held the capacity for improvement. It would have been life, anyway. Not the long struggle Edna Burleigh now faced alone with two kids to bring up. Ida, I suspected, was well out of a union with Arnie Poole although he might have changed. There was always the old adage of what a "good woman" could achieve, although personally I doubted she would have made much of an impression on the man Poole had become. I suspect Joseph Dabs—had he lived—would have been destined for a life in and out of prison.

That left William Kearney—or Billy O'Connell. I couldn't help thinking of him as someone apart. What might have become of him had he managed to stay out the vengeful reach of Diamaid Caomhánach? Perhaps together with Rose...? The wistful fondness she evinced whenever she spoke of her Billy made me doubt that she could have pulled the trigger on him if she'd ever found him. But perhaps I was being sentimental.

I wondered if I was somehow equating the chance they had lost with the one I still might have with Penny. Yet that sentiment, even as I considered it, was in some manner bound up with the feeling of emptiness I was experiencing. The fact that the investigation into Kearney's carrier seemed to have ended outside the Château de Hêtres, brought it too close to home. The connection with my wife's family now hung over it all like an ominous cloud, if a cloud I had decided I could leave to Tuchman to dispel.

Or so I thought.

27

Thursday July 4th 1946

Late Thursday afternoon Peter appeared in the doorway looking unusually pleased with himself.

'What are you grinning about?'

'We've got one of Müller's men. SS-Sturmmann Karl Hess. He's presently in POW camp 65.'

'You're sure? How did you find him?'

'You were right. There is a muster of 25th SS-Panzer companies but not a complete one. And, as we expected, there were several names that matched those we got from Müller and Richter. None fitted the bill, though. Anyway, I left that with Stan and tried a different tack.'

He paused. For dramatic effect, I suppose.

'Well?' I finally asked.

'Swedish Red Cross. It occurred to me their lists might be better than ours. Persuading them to help wasn't easy so I got Susie to sweet-talk one of the male clerks. She's a revelation. Just don't believe anything she tells you.'

'Where's Camp 65?'

'Setley Plain in Hampshire.'

'All right, get on to them and tell them we want to interview Hess. Only they're not to tell him we're coming.'

'Already done. They're expecting us tomorrow.'

'Tomorrow is Friday. Colonel G's day.'

'Stan can handle him,' said Peter.

So we left Jekyll to Stan. Susie was to find something decent to go with the colonel's tea and Stan was to sweeten it with a spoonful of how well we were doing and how we'd managed to trace one of the men who'd been in SS-Obersturmführer, Franz Müller's platoon. I thought it might be going a little far to state categorically that this Hess was there when Kearney's men were killed so I told Stan to imply as much without actually saying so and to leave Jekyll to infer the rest himself. If we had the wrong Hess at least we'd have the weekend to come up with a plausible excuse for the error.

The next morning we took the train to the nearest station to POW Camp 65, which turned out to be Brockenhurst, in the New Forest. On the way down I belatedly took the opportunity to tell Peter what I knew about Clause Pellisier's background, omitting the fact he had been known to my wife's family.

'I got this from my Special Branch contact,' I explained as if I just learned it.

Peter frowned. 'What interest would Special Branch have in a French collaborator?'

I then had to spin him a story about how Special Branch was in touch with an American from the War Crimes Commission who was interested in Pellisier. Peter nodded although I suspected he hadn't swallowed it. He didn't ask anything else, though, so I left it at that and, after a minute or two, began gazing out of the window at the passing countryside.

I'd never been to the New Forest before and was somewhat bemused to find there were hardly any trees, just hundreds of acres of heath; gorse and bracken and heather just coming into bloom, painterly daubs of mauve and russet brown amid a dozen shades of green. It had me humming Duke Ellington's *Mood Indigo* until a sideways glance from Peter shut me up.

We were met at Brockehurst station by a car from the camp. The village looked pleasant enough, with crooked-gabled redbrick houses and a few thatched cottages, even if the whole was somewhat spoiled by the railway and the level crossing that dominated one end of the hamlet. A corporal was leaning against an Austin 12 in the gravel car park, smoking and watching the women who had got off the train. When he saw us he threw down the cigarette and up a salute which turned out to the smartest thing about him; the rest of him was all creased tunic and trousers, scuffed boots, and skin that looked as if it hadn't seen the ablutions for a week or two.

'Corporal Givens,' he announced. 'Sent to escort you to the camp, sir.'

We climbed into the back of the Austin and Givens swung it out of the car park and bumped it over the railway lines of the level crossing.

I studied the back of Givens' grubby neck then caught his eye in the rear-view mirror. 'Do you know Sturmmann Karl Hess, corporal?'

'Hess, sir? Yes sir.'

Peter had mentioned the camp had its own theatre and I wondered if Givens was in the habit of giving a music hall turn on Saturday nights.

'What's he like?'

'Like?'

'You know he was SS?'

'Yes, sir. We don't have many of that sort here. We've got a camp on the Isle of Wight where they sometimes put the SS till they settle down. I think that's where Hess was for a few months. We used to have Eyeties here at first. Soft bunch. To be honest we could never see much harm in them. Jerry's a different matter but most of those we got were just soldiers doing what they were told. We don't have any that were involved in the sort of thing you see on the newsreel at the pictures.'

'They keep them in the camps up north,' I told him.

It was a fact, although I didn't know exactly why. The hardliners and recalcitrant POWs, the died-in-the-wool Nazis, the malcontents and trouble-makers—the outright dangerous—had all been restricted to camps in the north of the country. Out of sight and out of mind, I suspected. That was usually where you found the SS POWs; where I might have expected to find SS-Sturmmann Karl Hess.

'Any trouble from him?' I asked Givens.

'No, sir, not as I'm aware. Does his work. Does what he's told when he's not doing his work.'

'What work do the prisoners do?'

'Forest work mostly, sir. Felling and clearing. There's a saw mill close by and some of them work on the local farms or do gardening. But only one prisoner to a property, thems the rules. And no fraternizing, of course.'

'Of course.'

'Different with the Eyeties. After a while you almost forgot they were supposed to be prisoners. We had to call them "co-operators".'

'Not the Germans, though.'

'No sir, not the Germans.'

The camp lay a couple of miles outside the village, south on an arrow-straight road cut through the heath. Rows of Nissan huts flanked four or five low redbrick buildings with concrete paths between the huts. There were no goon towers, gun emplacements or machineguns, just a barbed-wire fence strung around the perimeter. Low enough to hurdle if the cookhouse wasn't over-generous with the bread and potatoes, and you felt like a wander round the blasted heath. It was a phrase Shakespeare had often favoured and I daresay if we'd brought Jack with us he could have quoted a line or two from Lear or Macbeth to complement the scene.

The car stopped at the gate and Givens spoke to the guard. The prisoners we saw beyond certainly didn't look underfed. One of the perennial complaints of the public was that German POWs were better fed than our own civilian population. As there was still a couple of hours until lunch I told Givens we'd eat in the canteen before we left, to see if it was true.

They had SS-Sturmmann Karl Hess waiting for us in one of the redbrick buildings, sitting at a table in a makeshift office with a guard at the door. Almost as if our interest had suggested that he might be worth keeping an eye on. In the room leading to it one of the camp officers was sitting on the edge of a desk, chatting to an NCO, a lance corporal, leafing through paperwork and adding an occasional signature. He looked up as Givens showed us in and introduced himself as Lieutenant Nugent. He must have been forty, with a ruddy face and folds of allied fat that bulged over his shirt collar, lending him the impression he was quietly asphyxiating. Not the man to hurdle the wire after decamping POWs. He didn't waste any time in letting us know he was new to the camp and was expecting his discharge papers any day. Conveying an implication, I assumed, that if we discovered something nasty in Camp 65 it would have nothing to do with him.

He looked concerned all the same. 'War Crimes unit? Anything we should be worried about?'

I was noncommittal. 'An enquiry into a man he might have served with. We've nothing against Hess.'

Nugent relaxed. 'I've looked over his file. He spent time on the Isle of Wight. That would have been because he was SS. Behaviour was regarded as good, according to them. He's been no trouble here.' He glanced at the lance corporal as if seeking corroboration. The corporal ignored him.

Nugent offered me Hess's file and I passed it to Peter. We followed him into the small office and SS-Sturmmann Karl Hess jumped to his feet as we entered. He saluted but didn't offer the stiff-armed Nazi greeting and accompanying cry of *Heil Hitler* that many diehard SS men habitually gave anyone from a British officer to a tea lady. I returned his salute and in my rusty German told him to sit down again. Nugent hung in the doorway a moment, shifting his weight from one sturdy leg to another, until finally saying, 'I'll leave you to it then.'

We waited until he closed the door before sitting down. Peter opened Hess's file while I watched the man.

I had been prepared to find him young—many of the Hitlerjugend had been recruited straight from their youth brigades and still might have been two or three years from leaving their teens. Hess I judged to be around twenty and had managed to keep a youthful bloom about him; smooth unblemished skin marked only by traces of a fair fuzz that was still struggling to become a beard. His hair was blond and swept back from his forehead. Beneath was a square, good-looking face with a straight nose and firm jaw and lips. The model of a Nazi Aryan, I suppose, the kind Leni Riefenstahl's lens might have lingered over while filming *Triumph des Willens*. Only Hess's eyes suggested he might have seen more in his twenty years than one might have wanted. He was using them to watch us in return, his handsome if somewhat bland face warily alert.

We began by confirming Hess's details as logged in the file. Peter's German was of the academic style, learned in school and university and was a little dry, like his lawyerly training. He'd spent some family holidays in Germany as a boy, he'd once told me, but didn't seem to have picked up much in the way of colloquial speech. My German, on the other hand, was little more than colloquialisms, picked up mostly in beer halls and on the streets.

Hess nodded and answered in the affirmative to most of what we said. His name was Karl Hess and he was an SS-Sturmmann—that is a Lance Corporal—in the 25th SS-Panzer Grenadier Regiment, Hitlerjugend. He had been captured, like Müller and many others, from the 25th SS-Panzer Grenadier Regiment, in the fighting around the Falaise Pocket in the middle of August, July 1944.

'Do you speak English?' I asked him as Peter paused to consult the file.

A slight frown marred the perfection of his Aryan brow. 'Little English. Guards' speak..."Be quick. Pick up this...move that. March, left right, left right..."' He smiled as though it was amusing.

'Wir sprechen Deutsches,' I told him, then to Peter, while still watching Hess, 'Ask him about Obersturmführer Franz Müller.'

The smile faded and Hess's eyes became guarded again.

Peter asked and the German's eyes flicked from Peter to me as if uncertain which one of us to address.

'*Franz Müller? Es gab viele Männer namens Müller.*'

'SS-Obersturmführer Franz Müller,' Peter said again. '*Fünfundzwanzigste Panzergrenadiere.*' He laid a notebook and pencil beside the file, picked up the pencil and held it poised over a blank page.

Knowing how Peter would handle him, I was able to follow most of the dialogue: some phrases and words familiar; others, like jigsaw pieces, to be slotted in where they fit.

'Obersturmführer Müller,' Peter continued in his precise German, watching Hess steadily, 'has testified to that fact that you were a member of his platoon.'

Hess's mouth twitched and a little colour came into his pallid Germanic features. 'Now I remember Obersturmführer Franz Müller, yes.'

'On July 10th 1944 the platoon was ordered to a house known as the Château de Hêtres, a kilometre to the east of the village of Maltot. Do you remember the Château de Hêtres?'

'The date again, please?'

'July 10th, the day the 25th SS-Panzer Grenadiers evacuated Caen.'

'You say Obersturmführer Müller has told you this?'

'Yes. Now we would like to hear what you have to tell us. Do you remember the Château de Hêtres and what happened there on that day? July 10th?'

'It is not easy to remember,' Hess replied. 'A day two years ago...things happen and you forget. If you can tell me what Obersturmführer Müller has said, I might be able to recall this château.'

'Have you had any contact with Obersturmführer Franz Müller since you were taken prisoner?'

Hess nodded. 'We were in the first camp together for some weeks, yes. It was not easy. They...some of the men...they still acted...' he cleared his throat. 'Our senior officers, *SS officers*, they expect us to behave as if we are still in combat. I did not think this way.' He straightened in his chair. 'I am a prisoner. I think for me the war is over and Germany cannot win.'

Peter glanced at me. I nodded.

'Obersturmführer Müller is dead.'

Hess's licked his lips.

'He committed suicide. Something to do with his family in Berlin.'

'He had a wife and daughter in Berlin.'

'They died.'

Hess became sombre. He looked down at the table for some time.

'This is not good news,' he eventually said. 'Obersturmführer Müller was a honourable soldier. He served on the eastern front where our regiment was almost destroyed. If Obersturmführer Müller has told you, I will also tell you what I remember. What exactly is it you wish to know?'

'Müller was your Obersturmführer?'

'Yes.'

'Among the other men in the platoon, there was an SS-Unterscharführer named Otto Vogel—'

'Vogel was killed before we were captured,' Hess said.

'We are aware of this. There were also men in the platoon named Neumann, Schimdt...Klein...Hartmann...?'

'All, yes.'

Peter noted Hess's replies in his book. I glanced down at the shorthand he used, a scrawl that looked like Arabic to me.

'And you recall the evacuation of Caen and the Château de Hêtres?' Peter continued.

'We had been told to hold Caen but our Brigadeführer knew we could not. We were ordered out of the city. To wait in reserve at a village to the south...'

'Maltot.'

'I did not know the name. Units of the 10th SS-Panzer Division, Frundsberg, were holding the front. We were told a reserve company of the 22nd Battalion had taken over a house in the woods. When we arrived we found they had been ordered into the village where the British—' a smile passed fleetingly across his lips, '—where you were attacking in strength. We were told to hold the house until the arrival of 9SS-Panzer Division, Hohenstaufen.'

'Do you recall seeing Gestapo officers and a French civilian at the château?'

Hess appeared to give this some thought. I wondered if he was considering the advisability of a denial. But before he could make up his mind Peter said:

'SS-Mann Werner Richter was a member of the platoon, was he not?'

'Richter? Yes, Werner was a comrade.'

'In his diary Richter states that there was a Frenchman as well as Gestapo at the château when the platoon arrived.'

'Werner wrote this in his diary?'

'Yes.'

'And you have talked to Werner?'

'Richter has been repatriated.'

This seemed to surprise Hess. 'We have heard that some men have been sent home but only the sick and the wounded.'

'Richter was among the wounded.'

Hess nodded thoughtfully.

'The Gestapo and the French civilian?' Peter prompted again.

'Yes, the Gestapo I remember. Two of them and the Sicherheitsdienst Hauptsturmführer.'

I sat up. 'An SD capt—'

Peter's knee nudged mine beneath the table and I shut my mouth.

'This Intelligence officer...' Peter said evenly, '...the captain. Do you remember his name?'

'I did not know his name,' Hess said.

'And what rank had the two Gestapo men?'

'I do not know. They were not in uniform and I didn't speak to them.'

'But the officer from the Sicherheitsdienst, he was a captain?'

'A hauptsturmführer, yes.'

'They had brought a military escort?'

'No,' said Hess. 'Perhaps they had come with the reserve company of the 22nd Battalion who had moved up to the front. I do not know.'

'They had no vehicle?'

'Yes. A Kübelwagen. I saw it in front of the house.'

'How many men were in your platoon?' Peter asked, switching direction.

'At the house? Only a few. We had suffered much in the fighting for Caen. There were only ten or eleven of us left.'

'Names?'

Hess frowned. 'Unterscharführer Vogel, Mann Huber, Mann Lehmann, Mann Krause...Werner Richter, as you know. Neumann, Schmidt, Hartmann...but this you know. There was one other who had just joined us but he was killed shortly after and I do not remember his name.'

'All Hitlerjugend?'

'Yes.'

'Weapons?'

'We had our rifles and pistols. A machinegun and also a faustpatrone. You know the faustpatrone?'

'Anti-tank weapon,' said Peter.

'Yes, anti-tank.'

'Tell me about what happened when you reached the château. Was there anyone other than the SD captain and the two Gestapo men there?'

'We had been told there would be a company of Frundsberg there as I have said, but they had already moved up to the village. The Tommies had crossed the river at dawn that morning and were in the village by the time we got to the château. You could hear the fighting...tanks, rifles...artillery. The house had been shelled.'

'Did you encounter any British forces before you reached the château?'

'No. Not at first.'

'You say the château had been shelled. Was it badly damaged?'

'Not badly.'

'Was it burning?'

'No, I think not. There had been a small fire, from the artillery perhaps. But it was not burning when we arrived.'

'What did you do when you arrived at the château?'

'When we arrived we wanted to eat but Obersturmführer Müller told me to take three men and the machinegun and the faustpatrone back down the drive. It was about two hundred metres long with two bends. He told me to set the MG up in the trees where we could see anyone approaching. I chose the first bend where we had a good field of fire.'

'And the other men? What did they do?'

Hess shrugged. 'Obersturmführer Müller told Richter and two others to set up an observation post along a track at the back of the house. This was narrow and led to the river. He remained at the house where there were outbuildings to fortify.'

'At this point you believed you were to stay and occupy the château?'

'Yes, Obersturmführer Müller told us we would be relieved by Hohenstaufen—9SS-Panzer Division.'

'And the Frenchman? What was he doing?'

'I did not see the Frenchman then. Only later.'

I stood up. Hess followed me with his eyes. I opened the door. Nugent and the guard had gone but the corporal was still at his desk.

'Can you organize us some tea? Three mugs?'

The corporal looked as if he hadn't quite caught what I had said. 'What, for the prisoner too, sir?'

'If you can.'

I went back to the table and sat down again.

'Tell me about the British Bren gun carrier,' Peter asked Hess.

The German's eyes became vacant.

'The Bren gun carrier wasn't there when you arrived, obviously. But it was when you left. Obersturmführer Müller has already told us this. We need confirmation. That is all.'

Hess looked down at his hands while I looked at Peter, wondering if he was as prepared to lie as barefacedly in a British court when this was all over and he finally became a barrister.

'Müller told you this?'

'Before he killed himself,' said Peter. 'And we have Richter's diary as well. What we need is to have the story from your perspective.'

'But I wasn't at the château.'

'No, but you were on the drive when the British Bren gun carrier arrived.'

Hess gave a sigh, glanced at his hands once more. 'We had just set up the machinegun when we heard the sound of a tracked vehicle approaching. I signalled to my men—

'Which men were with you?'

'Lehmann, Neumann and Krause.'

'Go on.'

Hess faltered. 'There was a bend in the driveway. I signalled my men not to fire until the target was close enough. When it came around the bend in the road we saw the vehicle was a British Bren gun carrier. There were four men in it, the one beside the driver had a Bren gun.

'Four men in the vehicle?'

'Yes.'

'What happened next?'

There was a knock on the door and Hess hesitated. The corporal came in with three mugs of tea. He set them on the table and I pushed one towards Hess.

'*Danke*,' he said and picked it up.

'What happened next?' Peter asked again.

Hess drank some tea before resuming. 'When Lehmann saw the carrier he fired the faustpatrone.'

'You destroyed the vehicle?'

'Yes, but Lehmann fired too quickly and his aim was bad. The vehicle swerved to the side of the drive. Neumann had already opened up with the MG.'

'The machinegun?'

'Yes. The driver and one of the men in the back were killed. The sergeant with the Bren gun was slumped in the front.'

'But he was alive?' I asked.

'Yes. But he was wounded by the faustpatrone.'

'Was the carrier on fire?'

'At that time just a little.'

'And the fourth man?'

Hess shook his head. 'No, he was lucky. He was not injured.'

'What happened then?'

'We waited to see if other vehicles were following. Tanks, we thought, maybe infantry...'

'Were there?'

'No. We heard nothing except the sound of fighting in the village.'

'Did the two men still alive surrender to you?'

Hess glanced at me again. 'If Obersturmführer Müller told you this, then you must know...'

'We need to hear your version of events.'

'*Befehl*,' said Hess. 'You understand this?'

'Orders,' said Peter. 'Yes, I understand.'

'My rank is SS-Sturmmann. It was my job to do as I was ordered by my superior.'

'We understand this,' I assured him.

Hess sipped his tea, licking his lips. 'So,' he said after a moment, expelling breath like a sigh. 'Two men are dead. The driver and one man in the back. The radio operator, I think. The one in front—the sergeant who carried the Bren gun—was wounded.'

'And the fourth man?'

'He was on the ground. He had put his arms over his head.'

'But he wasn't injured?'

'No,' said Hess. 'Frightened. He was not a brave man.'

'What did you do?'

Hess put his mug on the table. 'We disarmed them.'

'What weapons did they carry?'

'A Bren gun, a rifle and an anti-tank gun. The kind you call the PIAT. There was also a radio but it had been hit by the MG.'

'What did you do with the two captured men?'

Hess cleared his throat. 'I left Lehmann and Neumann with the carrier. Mann Krause and myself returned to the château with the prisoners to report to Obersturmführer Müller.'

'You say the sergeant was injured?'

'He had a few burns to his face and hands from the faustpatrone.'

'What happened when you reached the château?'

'The one whose name I cannot recall was guarding the door. We took the prisoners inside. Obersturmführer Müller and Unterscharführer Vogel were in a ground floor room with the SD hauptsturmführer and the Frenchman. This was the first time I saw him.'

'But you knew he was French?'

Hess shrugged. 'The manner of his dress. But he spoke good German.'

'Did you receive the impression that he was under arrest?'

'Arrest? No, not at all.'

'What were they doing? The Frenchman and the others?'

'Sorting through papers. The Frenchman and the SD hauptsturmführer. They examined them and some they handed to the two Gestapo officers who were burning them in the fireplace.'

'They were burning the papers?'

'Yes.'

'Did you see what these papers were?' I asked Hess.

'No.'

'How did they react when you brought in two prisoners?'

'They became very nervous. They thought the Tommies had arrived. The Frenchman told the two Gestapo men to burn all the rest of the papers and began talking urgently to the hauptsturmführer and Obersturmführer Müller. Then Müller told me to take the prisoners into another room and await orders.'

'Did the prisoners say anything?' Peter asked.

'Not the sergeant. The other was trembling and speaking quickly. I could not understand but I could see he was frightened. The Tommie sergeant told him to be quiet.'

'How long did you wait in the other room?'

Hess shrugged. 'A few minutes...'

'And then?'

'Obersturmführer Müller came in. He looked at the identity discs of the prisoners then ordered us back to where we had left Neumann and Lehmann. He said I was to collect the identity discs off the dead Tommies in the carrier and bring them back to him.'

'Did he say why he wanted them?'

'To note the identification of the men, he said.'

'Was that normal practice?'

'I do not think so.'

'You did as he asked?'

'Yes. Krause and I went back to the Tommy vehicle. It was burning now. Lehmann and Neumann were complaining as the bombardment had started again and artillery shells were falling nearby in the wood.'

'Did you take the ID discs off the men as you had been ordered?'

'With the vehicle on fire it was not so easy but Krause got the ID discs off and I told him to take them to Obersturmführer Müller.'

'But he had told you to bring them, is that not the case?'

'I stayed with Lehmann and Neumann.'

'Why?'

'Because they needed their NCO with them.'

'What happened after that?'

'Krause was gone maybe ten minutes. When he came back, Unterscharführer Vogel and one of the prisoners was with him.'

'Which one?'

'The frightened one, not the sergeant.'

'He was uninjured?'

'Yes.'

'Vogel said Obersturmführer Müller had ordered Krause to put the discs back on the men in the carrier and that we were all to return to the house immediately.'

'And did Krause put the identification discs back on the two bodies?'

Hess glanced at me then back to Peter.

'The vehicle was burning fiercely by this time. We could not get close enough to replace the discs around the men's necks. There were cans of petrol ready to explode.'

'What did you do with the discs?' Peter asked.

'Krause threw them onto the bodies. I knew they would not burn and that their comrades would still be able to identify them.'

'What were Vogel and the prisoner doing?'

'They were standing by the side of the road. Unterscharführer Vogel told us to go back to the house.'

'And did you?'

'Yes.'

'And the prisoner?'

Hess shook his head. 'No.'

'Did you hear the sound of any shots from behind you or from the château?'

Hess shook his head. 'We heard only the sound of artillery and rifle fire in the village. Then the fuel cans exploding in the Tommy vehicle.'

'What happened when you got back to the château?'

'Obersturmführer Müller told us to form up by the truck and to wait.'

'How long did you wait?'

'A few minutes.'

'Did Vogel join you?'

'Yes.'

'Did you see either of the two British prisoners again?'

'No.'

'Did you ask what had happened to the sergeant and the man you left with Vogel by the carrier?'

'No.'

'Were you ordered not to speak of what had happened?'

Hess looked surprised. 'No, not at all.' He had answered Peter but was looking at me. 'This was not necessary. It was war. It is regrettable but sometimes it is not possible to take prisoners. As soldiers we understood this.'

'And afterwards? Did Unterscharführer Vogel or any of the others speak of what had happened?'

'There was little time to speak of these things. We were expecting the Tommies to arrive any moment. The SD hauptsturmführer and the Gestapo were anxious to leave. Obersturmführer Müller ordered us into the truck and we left by the track to the river.'

'Did you see the SD hauptsturmführer and the Gestapo men leave the château? Did you see the Frenchman leave?'

Hess shrugged. 'They were not in our truck. I assumed they followed us in the Kübelwagen.'

'But you didn't see them?'

'I was sitting in the front cab. I could not see behind.'

'You didn't see the Kübelwagen again? Later perhaps?'

'As we crossed the river,' Hess said, 'we met units of the 9SS-Panzers moving up. There were tanks and trucks and men everywhere. I did not see the Kübelwagen again.'

28

Friday July 5th 1946

By the time we had finished with Hess, the camp staff had eaten. That left us with several hundred POWs as lunch companions, in my view a prospect too soon after hostilities not to interfere with digestion. So we skipped the canteen and I told Corporal Givens to drive us back into Brockenhurst. There would be a two-hour wait for the train although we found the Rose and Crown was offering pigeon pie and local ale in compensation. Finishing what I regarded as the first decent meal I'd eaten in weeks, I began to realize why Penny looked so healthy on her rural regime.

Over a second pint, Peter read back to me from his arcane shorthand in order that I had understood all of what Hess had told us.

When he finished, Peter snapped his notebook shut and slipped it into his pocket.

'There is some discrepancy with what Richter wrote in his diary,' he said. 'But Richter didn't give much away so I don't suppose it's important.'

I lit a cigarette. 'I got the impression Hess knew more than he admitted. Perhaps if we'd made it clear Dabs' death had been the point of the interrogation, he might have been more forthcoming.'

'Or clammed up altogether,' said Peter.

'You've been spending too much time at the pictures with Susie,' I said.

He looked mystified. 'Clammed up,' I said.

He smiled. 'The Americans weren't here long but they certainly left their mark.'

That made me think of Tuchman.

Peter said: 'We still can't be absolutely sure that the Frenchman at the château was Pellisier. But it certainly looks like the body buried in the garden was Kearney's.'

'Well Müller's men didn't bury it. Not unless Hess was lying to us. It's possible the Gestapo and the SD captain tried setting fire to the place before they left in order to burn the body and botched it because they were in a hurry.'

'We know 9SS-Panzers relieved the 10SS-Panzers and what was left of the Hitlerjugend around Maltot and Hill 112. Would they have tried to burn the château if they knew another unit was coming to take it over?'

'Perhaps they just tried to burn the corpse to prevent identification,' I suggested. 'Then when 9SS-Panzers arrived they buried the body in the garden. I don't suppose they'd want to keep stepping over a corpse while they were there. And they weren't to know he wasn't French remember.'

'And it was probably 9SS-Panzers who pushed the carrier off the road to clear the drive,' Peter said.

'But what was a captain in the Sicherheitsdienst doing there? The SD were Intelligence. Richter wrote in his diary that the Gestapo were at the château and I've been assuming the owner of the place was under arrest. At least I was until I found out Pellisier was a collaborator.'

'It's a pity we didn't know that sooner,' said Peter.

I finished my second pint and pushed the glass aside. 'All right. How did it go? After they abandon Caen, Pellisier decides it's time to clear out but first has to go to the château for some reason.'

'They were burning papers if we believe Hess. Some sort of evidence of what he'd been doing, I suppose.'

'Something he doesn't want our lot to find when they arrive? Something incriminating. Then Kearney and his carrier turns up.'

'Two live prisoners,' Peter said.

'And we know the Hitlerjugend aren't in the habit of taking prisoners. But are we to believe that on the spur of the moment Pellisier thought about leaving one of them to masquerade as his own body?'

Peter pursed his lips. It was a prissy, sort of old maid habit and one I'd often thought wouldn't gain him many admirers if he used it in front of a jury. I might have mentioned the fact to him except it wasn't the sort of thing one man could say to another.

'Perhaps he'd already considered doing something similar if the war started going against Germany,' he suggested. 'Although I would have thought that sort of thing would have been easier to arrange in Caen. After all, he could hardly rely on Kearney and his men turning up. Or that one of them would have the same blood type as his, if that was the idea.'

'Something we don't know yet,' I reminded him. 'Or how the man buried in the garden died. 'If he wasn't shot or bludgeoned, say, or if his blood group isn't the same as Kearney's, this hypothesis goes out the window.'

'Then what did they do with Kearney? We know now Vogel shot Dabs.'

'It had to be opportunistic, then,' I agreed. 'Otherwise how do you explain the business with the identity discs? And the way Hess told it, it does corroborate how they were found.'

Peter still didn't look entirely convinced, his expression suggesting he would need hard evidence to secure the conviction.

'Don't you think it was a bit soon for Pellisier to bail out?' he asked. 'For all he knew the Hun might have thrown us back into the sea.'

'Then nothing lost,' I said. 'He could turn up again, alive and well. And resume deporting Jews or whatever he was doing.'

'But to burn your own house down...?'

'There is that,' I agreed. 'Unless it was just the body they tried to burn; with a small localized fire.'

We batted it back and forth until the train was due and walked down the high street to the station. The afternoon was overcast and cool and a rain shower had darkened the redbrick houses of Brockenhurst and left pools of water on the road. The train was the express from Bournemouth to London and we got back to the office in time to find Stan locking up for the weekend.

'Colonel G wasn't best pleased,' he announced as he saw us coming up the stairs. He unlocked the door again and put the kettle on. 'Bit my head off as soon as I told him you wouldn't be back. Wants a report on his desk Monday morning.'

He passed me a note he'd left to that effect on Peter's desk. I screwed it into a ball and tossed it towards the wastebasket. It hit the side and rolled across the floor, stopping unsatisfactorily in the middle of the room.

'Anything else?' I asked.

'Only that he wants this investigation wound up. We've spent too much time on it already in his opinion. *And* he knows you went to Ireland.'

'How the hell did he find out about that? I didn't claim any expenses.'

'Susie had already put in for the rail warrant, remember?'

'I told her to say my uncle died,' I protested. 'I was going to give her the cash to cover it.'

'Did you?' Stan asked.

'I was going to,' I said.

'*Cuiusvis hominis est errare—*' Peter began quoting.

'Meaning?' I interrupted, only too familiar with his penchant for Latin aphorisms.

'*—nullius nisi insipientis in errore perseverare*,' he finished regardless. 'Anyone can err, but only the fool persists in his fault.'

'Going to Ireland wasn't an error.'

'I doubt Colonel G will agree.'

I muttered while Stan made the tea. Peter said he'd get his notes written up over the weekend so I had little option but to promise to rewrite the report to Jekyll and append Hess's statement on Monday. There didn't seem much else to discuss. I saw little for it but to take the report round to Jekyll on Monday morning and expect a bollocking for my trouble. Winding up the investigation wasn't the problem; as far as I could see we couldn't take it any further since we had found out—at least to our own satisfaction—what had happened to Kearney and that Vogel had shot Dabs. Even if nothing could be done about it.

Pellisier was another matter. If he *was* still alive he was the United Nation War Crimes Commission and Tuchman's problem. Or Coveney's. Not ours and not even Jekyll's. True, having Penny find out about him would be awkward but she could hardly blame me for having a fabricated uncle who committed war crimes.

When we'd finished our tea I thanked Peter and Stan and told them to call it a day. I picked up the ball of paper on the floor and binned it, then went into my office and found another note, this one from Jack, saying Abel Bryce had phoned again and left a number to call back. I wasn't in the mood to listen to Coveney's secretary tell me how awkward it might be for his boss if his brother-in-law was found to have committed nefarious acts, so I binned that note, too. Then I sat down and started writing the report for Jekyll.

~

It was well into the evening before I was finished. The dull weather promised an early twilight and I had one more cigarette while staring out of our window at leaden cloud. I wasn't particularly happy with the report—too many ifs and buts with only a likelihood to hang our premise upon. Worst of all was my attempt to justify the Irish trip, particularly as it had turned out to be a cul-de-sac. And, although tempted, I could hardly use the excuse that at the time Jekyll was in Scotland and therefore unavailable for consultation; my decision to go had been made almost as soon as the office door had closed behind him. Besides, it would have read as if I was expecting to be accorded equal latitude of action with a full colonel, a prospect as unlikely as Joe Stalin voluntarily giving back his half of Europe. The very suggestion would have been taken by Jekyll as kindly as a bull takes to being prodded by a sharp stick.

But I wasn't going to sit up half the night polishing nuanced phrases in the hope he wouldn't notice the bones beneath. Maybe it was the exasperation I felt, but for some reason I was hungry again, despite the pigeon pie I'd eaten at lunch.

I had no food in the flat and at that time of evening the shops with whom I was registered for my coupons were shut anyway. Besides, I didn't have my ration book with me. So I took the tube back to Clerkenwell and tried a new Italian restaurant that had opened recently. The menu was pasted onto the window, offering two kinds of pasta, garnished with a narrow choice of sauce.

It was a small place, squeezed between a milliner who had gone out of business and the butcher with whom I was registered for my meat ration. There were half a dozen tables inside, bedecked with the inevitable red and white check tablecloths and some old wine bottles with half-burned candles protruding from their necks. On the counter stood a wine rack and a few bottles, to give the place an Italian feel I supposed. A wiry Italian and his even stringier wife stood behind it, looking at me hopefully as I stuck my head round the door. I thought if they'd been able to bottle poverty and ruin they'd have better caught the flavour of the Italy I remembered.

I sat at a table and the wiry Italian came over, grey moustache on a sallow face and fingers like a claw-hammer. He had wine, he said, if I would care for a bottle and scurried off to fetch it. I dithered between the round spaghetti and the flat linguini until the wine arrived. Its dusty bottle and torn label weren't too encouraging but my appreciation of wine has never been enhanced by any knowledge of provenance. I asked for the linguini while he opened it and suggested he take a glass with me. Surprised, he shouted my order to his wife in Italian then drew out a chair and sat down.

His name was Mario Rossellino, he said, and assured me he had never supported Mussolini.

'Ten years before the war I am in London but we are interned like all the others.'

Some trace of his indignation still remained and I offered my sympathies.

He shrugged. 'The food they give us was lousy. Forgive me but the English, they cannot cook.'

'We prefer to eat,' I said.

'Italians do both.'

We shared a glass of wine and in a while his wife brought my linguini. Her name was Maria, which together with her husband I thought contributed to a pleasant euphonic symmetry. I was the only customer so I asked her to take a glass with us too as long as she didn't mind watching me eat.

She wiped her hands on her apron and sat next to her husband.

'I like to see people eat,' Maria said.

I could see she had been a good-looking girl when younger although now her face was lined and in repose held a hardness between the bones and the skin. A residue of whatever had happened to them while interned, perhaps.

I said I hoped that things would soon get back to normal now the war was over. 'Everyone needs to eat.'

Mario had reservations. 'It is not easy to get ingredients.'

I assured them it tasted all right to me and told Maria she was a good cook. She smiled and the hardness in her face fled.

A young couple came in and they both stood up. I poured myself some more wine and finished my meal. Mario brought me a glass of some fierce liqueur which, on top of the wine, left me light-headed. I paid, thanked them both and walked a little unsteadily back to Cowcross Street.

My building was in darkness and when I switched on the stair light nothing happened of course. I began feeling my way up the stairs holding the banister rail, still under the effects of the wine and Mario's liqueur and wondering if all those years of knowing my limit were behind me.

Mind distracted, I put the key in the lock, pushed open the door and was reaching for the light switch before becoming aware of some small alteration in the atmosphere. My senses started twitching...something familiar... But too late. I had turned on the light.

Even then it was a moment before my sluggish brain told me I was looking down the snout of a .38 automatic.

~

The nose of the gun lifted slightly, as if pleased to see me.

'You've been keepin' us waiting.'

I didn't know the voice but it had an Irish accent and even the innumerate, drunk or not, can usually put two and two together.

My first impression was that he looked like a boxer. Not the sportsman but the breed dog. Then I remembered what Ida had said and she'd been right, he better resembled a pug. His face was squat and ugly with a snout that rivalled the .38's.

Rose was standing behind him, looking even better by comparison, and with an amused smile playing on her red lips.

'Major Hendrix,' I said conversationally.

I was pleased by my self-control, although the effect was spoilt somewhat by my inability to think of anything further to add. Not that it mattered. I soon discovered that Diamaid Caomhánach preferred the sound of his own voice to mine.

'Sit down, Captain,' he ordered, waving the gun at me like it was the Irish tricolour on St Patrick's Day. He jerked his chin at Rose who came round behind me as I sat on one of the kitchen chairs. She ran her hands over my chest to my waist, bending over my shoulder so I could smell her scent, that change in the atmosphere I had been so slow to place. Her mouth was close to my ear and I could feel her breath hot against my face.

'He's not carrying a gun, Diamaid,' she said and I thought of how good intentions were shorter-lived than New Year's resolutions. My revolver was back hanging in my cupboard, clean now but just as useless.

I lifted my hands slowly. 'Do you mind if I take my tunic off and hang it up?' I asked. 'I'm suddenly very warm.'

Caomhánach shook his head. 'I don't think so, Captain. Keep your hands still. We won't be detaining you long, will we Rose?'

Rose glanced at the gun then at me and I could tell they didn't mean to leave me sitting comfortably by my kitchen table when they left.

'O'Connell's dead, you know,' I told him. 'The SS shot him in 1944.'

'So *you* say.'

I raised my hands. The automatic jerked nervously.

'It's a long story,' I said. 'They passed O'Connell's body off as a French collaborator who needed to disappear. I've no evidence but I've no reason to lie to you either.'

'When's an Englishman needed a reason to lie to an Irishman?' Caomhánach sneered.

But Rose needed to know. 'How'd they managed that? Passing Billy's body off as someone else?'

'Sorry Rose but they burned his body.'

Some last hope died in her eyes. I glanced at Caomhánach but there was nothing there to move his pug's face.

'What made them think it was the Frenchman?' Rose asked.

'The body was in the Frenchman's house. They'd dressed him in his clothes and we're pretty sure they shared the same blood group. Maybe there was more...I don't know. Anyway, his brother-in-law identified him. Said he recognized a birthmark but I think—'

'Birthmark?' Caomhánach stiffened. 'Where was it?'

'Where? What, you mean—'

'Where on his body, man? The birthmark, whereabouts on the body was it?'

'His backside,' I said. 'His right buttock.'

Caomhánach's features were as still as a china figurine. 'What did it looked like?'

'Like an inverted triangle, they said. Except one side wasn't straight. "Serpentine" was the word used.'

The Irishman's face, no longer frozen, was growing red. Beyond a blush, some inchoate rage was rising within him.

Rose looked at me but it was Caomhánach she spoke to.

'Like old Ériu's harp, eh Diamaid?'

I had heard the line before. I hadn't understood it then, in the pub in Ballydrum when Dónol Casey had recited a verse of Caomhánach's poem. Bad poetry, Dónol and Rose had called it. But just because the poetry was bad didn't mean it hadn't been heartfelt.

'Shaped like a harp?' I said, some of Dónol's words inexplicably coming back to me: '*On mounds divine and heaven blessed*...isn't that how it went?'

'Shut your mouth!' Caomhánach yelled. He jumped up, pointing the gun at me.

'He's dead,' I said again, realizing I'd already said too much. 'Isn't that the evidence you wanted? Killing me won't do any good. They'll know it was you. The police know you're in London.'

But Caomhánach wasn't listening. He came around the table and jammed the muzzle of the .38 against my forehead. I jerked my head back, feeling blood begin to trickle down my face. Rose began to rummage in her bag. I wondered if she was going to give me a last cigarette.

Caomhánach didn't seem in any mood to waste on pleasantries for the condemned, though.

'That bastard Dónol told you, didn't he?' He pressed the gun harder against my skull. 'I'll kill the swine, I will. If I'm too late for O'Connell then I'll shoot that other damn bastard when I get back. You too, you English—'

And I heard the shot.

I sat there for an instant, mouth open...eyes closed. Then he was on top of me, a dead weight that knocked me backwards in the chair, Caomhánach falling on top of me.

Beneath him on the floor unable to move, it was a moment before I realized he wasn't fighting. He lay, sprawled like a sack of potatoes on my chest. I heaved him aside and struggled to my feet.

Rose hadn't moved. But it was no cigarette from her bag in her hand. Instead she held a gun.

'I told you he meant to kill you,' she said.

'You shot him,' I gasped, incredulous and unable to stop myself from stating the obvious.

'Do you think I was going to let him kill Billy if he'd found him? It's why I came along.' Then she smiled and the spark came back into her eyes. 'But there's no need to thank me, Captain. For saving your life, I mean. You were going to thank me, weren't you?'

My wits returning, I moved to her side and took the gun from her hand. She didn't resist. She felt around in her bag again and this time came out with a packet of cigarettes. Her hand was shaking as she tried to take one from the pack. I put the gun on the table, reached for the cigarettes, took two and lit them.

She breathed the smoke in deeply, releasing it with a sigh. Her eyes met mine.

'So the blabbing publican told you about the poem, did he?' She gazed down at Diamaid's body. 'The poor sod was only a schoolboy when he wrote it. Their schoolmaster got it published in a Dublin paper. Once Billy realized what it was about he told me he used to tease Diamaid when they'd had a few too many. "An Ode to an Arse", Billy called it.'

I dragged on my own cigarette, eyes following hers to where Caomhánach lay. I was wondering if anyone had heard the shot; if anyone had called the police. They would have to know sooner or later. One way or another.

I picked up her gun again. It was a .22 calibre Beretta automatic—what the Americans disparagingly call a "pocket pistol". A dainty little thing, I'd seen enough of them in Italy to know they're only effective if the user knows what they are doing. Or happens to get lucky. Caomhánach was lying dead on the floor, his luck running true to form. Whether Rose knew what she was doing or had got lucky, I didn't know. But it had been lucky for me and I thought the least Rose deserved was another throw of the dice.

She watched as I examined Caomhánach. The bullet had entered from the side and into his heart, not through his back, thankfully. It was hardly perfect but it would do.

I wiped the Beretta clean with my handkerchief then knelt over Caomhánach. I prised his .38 out of his hand and replaced it with Rose's automatic, wrapping his dead fingers around the butt and trigger. Then I took hold of it with my right hand, making sure my fingerprints were on it, too. I left it lying by his side.

I stood up, Caomhánach's .38 in my hand.

'Get going, Rose. And be quick about it. They might already be on their way.'

She stared at me with genuine surprise. 'And what are you going to tell them?'

'That I shot him while we were struggling for his gun. I know the man from Special Branch who was after him. He'll accept what I say.'

I had no idea, of course, if Gifford would accept it or not. But Rose had shot Caomhánach before he had shot me and I owed her this at least. If I told them what really happened there was a chance she wouldn't hang. But she was an Irish Fenian and it would have meant prison however you looked at it. She deserved more than that.

I held out Caomhánach's .38. 'If I give you this,' I said, 'will you promise not to shoot anyone with it?'

She laughed. 'Now what's the point of me having the thing if I can't shoot anyone with it?'

Then she came to me, pulled my head down on hers and kissed me on the mouth, taking the gun from my hand. She placed her cheek next to mine.

'I've almost a mind to stay,' she whispered.

I pushed her towards the door. 'What will you do? Where will you go?'

She cocked her head a little. 'Perhaps I'll try America. Isn't that where all we Irish go when we're sick of our lives and are looking for a new one?'

'Then go quickly,' I told her. 'Do you have money?'

'Are you offering me money, Captain? Now what sort of girl do you take me for?'

'One after my own heart, Rose.'

I opened the door and glanced along the corridor. She slipped past me, looking back once before hurrying down the dark stairs and out into the night.

I waited fifteen minutes but no one came. Outside it was quiet; inside it was as deathly still as the corpse I was sharing the room with. When I judged she must be clear I went down to the telephone in the hall and rang the number Gifford had given me.

~

I got him out of bed, something he was none too pleased about. The first thing he did when he arrived was make sure Caomhánach was dead. Rose's shot had made a hole in Caomhánach's jacket and I could see from where I stood there was no powder burn on the material. If Gifford noticed he didn't mention it. For a moment he regarded me with a sceptical expression before going back downstairs to use the phone. In the hour it took for them to arrive I explained what had happened; how I found Caomhánach waiting in the flat for me and how I realized he meant to kill me.

'I didn't think I had much to lose so I jumped him at the first opportunity.'

I waited for a response. When it didn't come I said:

'We struggled for the gun and it went off.'

Gifford glanced at the blood on my forehead and at Rose's Beretta on the floor. He bent down and picked up a shell casing that lay under the table.

'And we'll find your prints on the gun, I suppose?'

'I assume so.'

He turned the casing in his fingers. 'Small calibre for a man like Caomhánach. More of a woman's gun.'

'Easy to conceal,' I suggested.

A van finally arrived, two men with a stretcher and a third man carrying one of those old newspaper cameras with the big flash. He was young, unshaven and dishevelled, as though like Gifford he too had been pulled from his bed. He looked oddly familiar. Then he took a shot of Caomhánach's body and blinded me with the flash. Dropping the spent bulb into a pocket of his coat, he screwed in a new one and took a second shot, looking over at me as if about to say something. Then he glanced at Gifford and seemed to think better of it. He followed the stretcher and Caomhánach out the door.

Waiting for the van and afterwards, Gifford and I had drunk our way through my week's tea ration. If he was tired he gave no sign of it.

'Did he mention the O'Shaughnessy woman?'

'The one who posed as O'Connell's sister? No, he didn't. Perhaps he just used her to get information about O'Connell. Are you still looking for her?'

Gifford seemed to consider the question. 'We've nothing on her,' he said eventually. 'The sooner she's back in Ireland the better as far as I'm concerned.'

I told him about the poem Caomhánach had written; about O'Connell and the birthmark on his buttock. I said:

'Isn't that how Maurice Coveney identified Pellisier's body?'

'There were some half-burned identity papers but it was the birthmark Coveney said he recognized.'

'How did he explain that? Was he in the habit of gambolling naked with his brother-in-law?'

Gifford cocked a sardonic eye. 'Swimming in the river near Pellisier's château. He said they never wore bathing costumes.'

'A stroke of luck.'

Gifford shrugged. 'How do you contradict him without evidence? The body in the château wasn't in good condition. They only had the photographs, Pellisier's clothes and ID—'

'And the blood type?'

'If they can type it. The body's been in the ground two years. But with or without it you'd still have to prove the birthmark was O'Connell's. How? Caomhánach is dead and even if he wasn't I can't imagine he'd be likely to volunteer information to help us. O'Connell's mother is also dead. There's Rose O'Shaughnessy, she'd know presumably.' He shrugged. 'But it would be her word against Coveney's and no one's going to take the word of an IRA sympathizer against a man in Coveney's position. And even then you'd have to prove Pellisier didn't have an identical mark.'

'How do you prove a negative?' I said.

'Exactly. Who's left to say the birthmark wasn't Pellisier's, that he didn't have one? His sister's dead and there's no other family. A lover perhaps, if you could find one.'

I said it without thinking.

'There's Helen Forster.'

'Forster's wife? What about her? Did they all go skinny-dipping?'

I tried to picture Helen stripping off and jumping in the river. The thought was farcical. At least it was for the Helen I remembered. But she had been a girl once, and younger when she had first known Pellisier than Penny was when I met her.

Gifford was watching me, waiting. I shouldn't have said any more but Gifford was the sort of man who could get things out of people they didn't even know they knew. At that moment just his silence and his expectation seemed enough. Besides, I was tired and hung-over. More to the point I didn't think I owed Helen and Reggie Forster a damn thing.

I sighed heavily, just to let him know I'd put up some sort of fight.

'As you seem to already know, when my mother-in-law was a girl she used to spend her summers at the Château de Hêtres. She apparently had an affair with Claude Pellisier. It went on over several summers. Of course, I can't say whether or not she ever saw him naked.'

'That would all depend on how and how often they did it and where,' Gifford said, cutting prosaically through any vestige of romance and getting down to brass tacks. 'If they were shy, or enthusiastic. You knew her, what's your guess?'

I wondered if he imagined I had some sort of inside knowledge simply because I was married to Helen's daughter. I did, of course, but was he thinking what I was thinking? Could one's appetite for sex be passed down from mother to daughter like some inherited predisposition? I had discovered early on what an enthusiastic lover Penny was. Neither demure nor in the least inhibited and I admit it had shocked me at first. Did Penny take after her mother?

'Who knows,' I finally answered vaguely.

'Who told you about it?' Gifford persisted. 'Your wife?'

'She got it from her Aunt Julia, Helen's sister. And I was told in confidence,' I added, far too late to do any good. 'Anyway, I can't imagine she'd ever admit to it.'

'But you're certain it happened? Did Forster know? I thought he and Pellisier were supposed to be chums?'

'I've no idea. You know what that class can be like. They think no more of bed-hopping than they do about a rubber of bridge. Perhaps he didn't know. Perhaps he didn't care.'

'When did it end, assuming it did?'

'She heard Pellisier had been killed in the war—the Great War, that is. She married Forster soon after. It was a year or more before she found out Pellisier wasn't dead but in a POW camp. At least, that's the story according to my wife.'

In fact when Penny first told me about it, I had wondered if the affair had continued after Pellisier had come home. Even briefly speculated whether Penny was perhaps Pellisier's daughter and not Reggie's. It might have explained how different Penny was in attitudes and prejudices to her father. But the timings hadn't seemed to work out and now it turned out that Pellisier had been even more deeply fascist than Forster.

'Anyway,' I said again, 'she'd never admit to it. Besides, she's in America.'

'Due back on the second of August, aren't they? Sailing on the Queen Mary?'

I wanted to ask how he knew but wasn't too sure I wanted to know the answer.

It was beginning to get light. Gifford looked at his watch and got up from the table. 'Hardly worth going back to bed now.'

'Don't you want me to make a statement or something?' I asked. 'There'll have to be an inquest I suppose?'

Gifford yawned. 'Caomhánach was a gunman on the run. No one is going to be surprised that he's turned up dead. All the same, it will be as well to keep this to yourself.' He paused at the door. 'Rose O'Shaughnessy. She'll probably keep her head down now but if you do see her you'll let me know won't you?'

I assured him I would. After he went I washed up the teacups and scrubbed at the bloodstain Caomhánach had left on the floor. By the time I finished that I decided it was hardly worth my going to bed, either.

29

Saturday July 6th 1946

Being a Saturday I slept in then later, bleary-eyed, went to the shops. Perhaps I was light-headed from the events of the previous evening but I had conceived some wild idea about baking my own bread. Since the news that it was to go on ration, though, it seems a lot of other people had become light-headed too and there had been a run on flour emptying the shelves.

Back at the flat I found a van parked outside and Sam from upstairs helping another man load furniture into the back. I thought he might be moving his ill-gotten gains until he explained he was helping old Mrs Randall move to her niece's place in Sussex. Out of breath from carrying an old Victorian sofa down the stairs, he collapsed on top of it and asked:

'Found anywhere yourself yet?

I admitted I hadn't while wondering why clambering up drainpipes for a living didn't keep him in better condition. But perhaps his modus operandi was picking locks.

'I've made a few enquiries,' I said.

'I've found a nice flat on the Ossulston Estate,' he said. 'Lucky to get it. And it's not far from the station so it'll be handy.'

The Ossulston Estate had been built on the site of the old Somers Town slum between St Pancras and Euston Stations about fifteen years earlier. I wouldn't have thought the area provided particularly rich pickings for burglary but since he said it was close to the station it might be that he commuted to his favourite haunts, dropping down into Bloomsbury, say, for his work. I supposed he knew his business better than I did.

I asked if Mrs Randall was leaving that morning, ready to lend a hand if need be. But they'd almost finished so instead I popped up and said goodbye to the old girl, none too sure as I wished her the best that she knew who I was.

I rang Penny that evening, briefly speaking to my mother before I could get her to hand over the phone to my wife.

'So,' my mother announced without preamble, 'you've managed to persuade Penny to move back in with you. You were always a selfish boy, Harry. I had hoped the army would teach you something of moral responsibility...'

She never had, of course. As she blamed the army for getting my father killed, she thought less of the institution than she did of me. But everything about my mother was selective, from memory to prejudice, and getting her to change her opinions was an alchemy as difficult as transmuting base metal. There was some more of the same until I heard Penny's voice near the phone and imagined the two of them having a struggle over the receiver. Nonsense, but Penny did sound breathless when she finally answered. I might have hoped that the prospect of speaking to me had taken her breath away but she soon disabused me of that notion.

'I was out in the garden earthing up our potatoes,' she said.

'Quite the country girl,' I observed.

'We've all had to muck in.'

I thought for some reason her tone was implying I hadn't been doing my share. As if fighting my way up the Italian peninsular hadn't been "mucking-in" enough.

I told her I was looking at some more flats in the coming week which, although not quite true, would be once I had fixed up some appointments.

'Well, I don't suppose there's any hurry,' she said. 'We could always wait till after Mummy and Daddy get back.'

Assuming for a second she was suggesting we move in with them, I was on the verge of saying something in reply that would have well and truly shattered the ice. Then I realized that even six years of war wouldn't have been enough to make her forget my reservations on that score.

'They're booked on the Queen Mary on the twenty-ninth this month, aren't they?'

'How did you know that? I only got a letter myself yesterday telling me their plans.'

'It must have been Julia,' I said. 'I was over there the other day to see Ben Tuchman.'

'I'm no longer sure *that's* a good idea,' she said.

'What, me seeing Tuchman?'

'Don't be obtuse, Harry. *Julia* seeing Ben Tuchman. He's apparently been asking her all sorts of odd things.'

My first thought was that she meant Tuchman had been making some peculiar requests of Julia—to suit some particular sexual peccadillo or other—but of course she hadn't.

'What sort of things?'

'About Mummy and Daddy before the war and how much they saw of Aunt Louise and her brother...'

I told her it was probably only curiosity and changed the subject. I said she'd be happy to hear they were going to knock my building down.

'I know. Ida told Julia. Now she's living in, it must be lonely for you in the flat.'

I wasn't sure what to make of that. Whether it was some sort of retroactive dig at Ida again or concern for my well-being. I might have told her I hadn't been lonely at all, what with Rose's visits and Caomhánach lying dead on the floor, Gifford and his men traipsing in and out, but there was no point in mentioning any of that so I shifted the subject again and asked how the garden was coming on. I had spent too many hours as a boy digging over a previous garden of my mother's to care, but suddenly there didn't seem much else to talk about. It kept her happily on the line, though, until I could decently tell her my money was running out and I'd have to hang up. I told her I'd ring again after I'd seen the flats.

~

The rest of the weekend dragged and by Monday morning I wasn't sorry to be back in the office. I felt a little nervous, half-expecting Jekyll to turn up any minute. But he didn't and by lunchtime I'd polished up my report and put it with Peter's typed account of our interview with SS-Sturmmann Karl Hess. By the time everything was finished it was well past the time Jekyll had said he expected the report on his desk and, preferring not to face him, I got Susie to drop it round to his office in New Cavendish Street. She seemed a little jumpy, as if expecting me to dress her down for submitting the monthly account with the rail warrant without clearing it with me first. But there was no point in rehashing that. I was in a better frame of mind than I had been on Friday, now fully expecting the fact of our having more or less solved the question of Kearney's disappearance to outweigh with Jekyll the price of a return rail fare to Liverpool. And, since we heard nothing from him for the rest of that day, I felt—not unreasonably—pleased with myself.

Which only goes to show how one erroneous judgement can lead to all sorts of complacent assumptions. A point well worth entering, I would have thought, into the army officer's handbook.

This particular officer saw the error of his complacent ways early the following morning when Jekyll turned up unexpectedly and dropped the bombshell upon us that our unit was to be wound up.

He made a little speech complimenting us on our "sterling work" over the past months, saying it was through our efforts that new evidence had been added to that already held against certain individuals—which all came as news to me. He told us we had until the end of the week to tie up any loose ends and to send all unfinished business over to his office so it might be reallocated. He was personally going to ensure, he added, that our papers were processed without delay so we might resume our civilian lives as soon as possible. To that end—and as a mark of the Corp's gratitude—there would be no need to return to our respective battalions, and we would continue to be paid until our demobilization became official.

To me it all smacked a little of what Susie's GI might have called the bum's rush, and Jekyll's gratitude little more than a lever to get us out of the door that much quicker.

I was thinking this as he wound up by asking, 'Any questions?' and, before waiting to see if there were, turned to me and added gruffly, 'A word in private.'

His tone hung ominously over the otherwise silent office as I followed him into mine and shut the door behind us. He didn't look inclined to sit, so I had little choice but to stand as well. He laid his attaché case on Jack's desk and pulled a slim file out. He handed it to me without comment and watched as I opened it.

There was only a single page of close-typed text and it didn't take long to read. After all, I'd written most of it myself, if in a different form. At the bottom I saw that Jekyll had already countersigned it. All it was waiting for was my own signature.

'You don't think it worth attaching Hess's statement?' I asked, looking under the single sheet on the off-chance I had missed something.

Since there was nothing in the brief report about Claude Pellisier, the SD officer or the Gestapo; no mention of blood groups or switched identities; I didn't suppose he did. But I thought it worth mentioning anyway.

'I'm aware the chances of bringing a charge is slim...' I went on, glancing up at him. But his expression—the kind you get by taking a chisel to lumps of Scottish granite—told me not to persist. To give myself something to do during what became a rather oppressive silence, I read the report again, spotting one or two uncorroborated assumptions I had missed the first time. SS-Unterscharführer Vogel having been found with Kearney's discs had now been credited with sole responsibility for his death and for the murder of Dabs. All mention of the rest of Müller's platoon had been removed.

What I finally said was, 'You've chosen to omit any mention of Claude Pellisier, I see.'

'You've provided no proof that this Frenchman who was allegedly at the château *was* Pellisier.'

'None,' I agreed, 'beyond the fact that the body buried in the back garden carried his ID and was identified as him by his brother-in-law.'

Colour rose in Jekyll's face which made something of a change from granite grey.

'Irrelevant,' he snapped.

'And the Sicherheitsdienst officer?'

'You only had Hess's word that he was there. The word of the SS.'

'I judged him a reliable witness,' I said.

Jekyll scoffed at that, as though my judgement rated somewhere below his opinion of Hess's word. I had come that far, though, and rather than accept a rout decided I might as well try and make some sort of stand.

'The point is, if we accept the body in the château as Kearney's then it can't have been Pellisier. Which means Coveney misidentified him. Whether in error or—'

'That, Captain Tennant,' he interrupted brusquely, 'is beyond your remit. You have no evidence beyond an SS corporal's testimony to back up this theory. Testimony you seem to hold in higher regard than the fact of Kearney's ID discs being found in Vogel's possession.'

I pointed out that one didn't necessarily contradict the other. 'What I have may be circumstantial, but there is the birthmark...'

'Are you calling Sir Maurice Coveney a liar?'

'I didn't call him anything,' I replied evenly. 'I never mentioned him in my report. Nor did I included him in my investigation.'

'And while we're on the subject of the investigation,' said Jekyll, 'who authorized that jaunt of yours to Ireland?'

'I used my initiative, sir. I was investigating Kearney's background.'

'Initiative?' Jekyll roared. 'You are fortunate I don't regard it as Absence Without Leave.'

I knew he had considered it as his tone capitalized the offence.

Not for the first time I thought how ironic it was that the value the army placed upon a soldier's initiative never really matched their desire to have men do what they were told.

But Jekyll hadn't finished. '...and as for this fantasy concerning IRA involvement...'—which I thought a little odd since I had never mentioned the IRA to him let alone included it in my report—'...are you seriously suggesting it had any bearing upon the events in Normandy?'

'Kearney's real name was O'Connell,' I replied evenly. 'His involvement with the IRA was peripheral but it did have a bearing on the case. The birthmark—'

'Birthmark again!'

For some minutes Jekyll's voice had been loud enough to carry next door and I could picture the others exchanging glances as they listened.

'All I required from you were facts,' Jekyll went on. 'Verifiable facts. All you've given me, Tennant, is supposition and innuendo.'

He snatched the file from my hand, slammed it on my desk and took a pen from his breast pocket.

'Sign it.'

I considered pointing out that naming Vogel as the man responsible for the murder of Dabs and Kearney was hardly a verifiable fact. But from the beginning Jekyll had seemed to have made up his mind as to what he wanted the eventual report to say, and nothing I'd done in the meantime had persuaded him otherwise.

I wondered what he'd do if I refused to sign. I was out of a job anyway—out of the army altogether—although I supposed there remained the possibility that he could have me court-martialled before my papers came through. That didn't seem likely as he wouldn't want to give me the chance to produce what evidence I did have, and I almost thought of seeing if he'd go that far. Until it occurred to me that an alternative was for him to have me broken to the ranks again. There were possible grounds for charges of disobeying orders and being absent without leave and I considered what all that might entail—not least the loss of a captain's pension.

And what did it matter anyway? If I *did* sign the thing it would make no difference. The report would be filed away and in all probability never see the light of day again. Besides, Gifford and Tuchman knew as much as I did about the business and would do whatever they thought necessary regardless of any doctored army report. Regardless of Jekyll. Regardless of me.

When it came down to it, signing was a matter of principal and a matter of morality, even if the exercise of either of these luxuries on my part wouldn't change a damn thing.

So I took Jekyll's pen and signed.

'I never wanted you in my unit in the first place, Tennant,' Jekyll informed me as I gave him his pen back. 'You came with a reputation for circumventing orders and I didn't think you'd be the kind of man I'd want on my team. I derive no satisfaction from having been proved right.'

I hadn't been aware I had come with any sort of reputation, but I didn't suppose it the best time to enquire about that, so, as he stuffed the file back in his attaché case and marched out of the office without another word, I didn't say anything either.

As the door closed noisily behind Jekyll and I emerged from my office, I said to the others who were looking embarrassed:

'He wanted some changes to the report,' and left it at that. I saw no reason for them to catch my flak.

~

We spent the rest of the week squaring up our files and sending any unfinished business over to the New Cavendish Street office. What was left we carried to an unused room along the corridor that housed some empty filing cabinets doing little other than gathering dust.

By Friday morning everything had been cleared away and our offices had taken on an air of desolation. I'd already had Jack make copies of my original report on the carrier and had taken these home. All that remained at the office were a couple of sacks of waste paper, the furniture and two typewriters.

At lunchtime I suggested we retire to the pub for a final drink together, locked up the office and the room where we had stored our files and gave the key to a rather subdued Susie to run round to Jekyll in New Cavendish Street. She'd been quieter than usual, not her bouncy self for the last few days, and though the others put it down to the break-up of the section, I wasn't so sure. It almost came as a surprise, after we'd been in the pub for three-quarters of an hour or so, that she turned up at all.

'Did you give Jekyll the key?' I asked her as Jack went to the bar to get her the rum and blackcurrant she favoured.

'He wasn't there,' she said, her new and uncharacteristic diffidence preventing her from looking me in the eye. 'I gave them to that secretary of his.'

'Absent without leave,' I quipped, but she didn't pick up the irony as she might once have done.

I raised my glass to everyone and announced, 'Well, that's it. We'll be civilians before we know it and will have to start working for a living.'

We toasted each other, talked a little about the last few months and said we'd keep in touch. Susie left first, making the excuse of a date that evening. She gave us all a peck on the cheek and left. Peter had an interview at a law firm on Monday morning, he said, and needed to bone up on criminal jurisprudence or some such, and bade us farewell. Stan said he was going up to Burnley to see his brother. He was thinking of starting out in the building trade and said there'd be a spot for Stan if he wanted. That left Jack and me. So I got another round in and asked him what his plans were. He pursed his lips and, unusually for him, kept them tight, just saying he was giving it some thought. Then, out of the blue he said:

'She's been transferred, you know.'

'Who's been transferred?'

'Susie. She not getting her papers. At least, not yet. She's been transferred to another section.'

'How do you know?'

'I saw the letter. Something called Section D. The offices are in Hallam Street.'

'Does she know you know?'

Jack pulled a face. 'Nah. I often open all the letters if I'm in first. Just slit them, you know, while I'm waiting for the kettle.'

I had noticed before how helpful Jack was like that, giving everyone a hand with their correspondence. Saving them time by opening their letters.

'When was this?'

'Last week.'

'Before Jekyll told us?'

'Yeah.'

'She say anything to you or the others?'

'No.'

We had another beer then Jack said he had to see a man about a dog so I had one more by myself and killed the rest of the afternoon in a cinema. When I woke up I found I'd killed the best part of the evening, too. I went home, exchanging I couldn't help thinking, a deserted office for a deserted building.

Before going up the stairs I rang Gifford's number. He wasn't there so I left a message to say I would no longer be contactable at the office. I was about to leave the number of the phone in the hall until it occurred to me that there was no one left to answer it there, either.

Lying on my bed in the dark I felt as if I must be at one of those points in life where everything is undergoing change. The odd thing was I felt no different at all. There was no sense of my being on the cusp of anything new. Perhaps I would begin to feel different over the weekend, yet I still suspected that come Monday morning I'd get up ready for the office and realize I had nowhere to go to.

30

Monday July 15th 1946

I met Penny on Monday at Paddington so found I had something to do after all. She came up to open her parent's house ready for their return. The place had been shut up since they had decamped to America. I suppose we might have used the house ourselves after they left but with air raids every night neither they nor I had wanted Penny in London. There had been some talk of renting it out while they were away although the Blitz just then had taken the edge off the London market. Later, when they might have rented it out to some of the military brass that gathered before the invasion, they had been put off by reports from friends of how the services treated rented accommodation. Consequently it had remained empty and there was the stale musty smell of disuse hanging in the hall when we unlocked the door.

The house appeared undamaged. We wandered from room to room, peeking under the dustcovers and into empty cupboards. In the half-light that seeped through the shuttered windows, everything seemed to be covered by that dust which spontaneously materializes in the absence of people. Wiping my finger along a shelf thinking the place was going to take some cleaning, I told Penny she might have difficulty in finding people prepared to go back into service.

'I don't see why,' she replied, 'people will still need work, won't they?'

'Yes, but domestic service may not be the kind of work they're prepared to do after what they've been through.'

'We've all been through it,' she retorted. 'It was the same for everyone.'

That wasn't quite true, particularly in Reggie and Helen's case. But I didn't think it politic to mention the fact.

'Where is everything anyway?' I asked her. There was still furniture in all the rooms, hulking silently under their covers like an ark full of Noah's specimens waiting to repopulate the world, but there was little else; no drapes or paintings, no rugs or china.

'Packed away in the cellar,' Penny said, and she looked through the keys on the ring and strode off down some back stairs to the kitchens. She threw the master switch on the fuse box in the corridor and led me through the kitchen door.

An array of pots and pans smeared with six years' worth of grime hung from ceiling hooks, as if the dust and grit exhaled from the bombed buildings had deliberately sought out undamaged property to demonstrate Penny's point on the egalitarian nature of war. She unlocked the cellar door and flicked on the light switch. A flight of steps led down into a gloomy cavern that hung with cobwebs and smelled of damp. Wine racks lined a wall and in the centre of the cellar packing cases were stacked four deep.

'I used to hate coming down here as a child,' she said, reaching for my hand.

'I don't blame you. This is the sort of place they're finding unexploded bombs.' I felt her stiffen and began to say I was only joking when I was forestalled by a rodent scuttling across the floor.

'Rats,' I said.

Penny shivered and retreated back up the stairs.

'I hope Mummy's Meissen is all right.'

'They won't eat that,' I said, 'although they might like to eat off it. You find a cultured strain of rat in this part of London.'

'Stop it,' Penny said.

'If I were you I'd get a firm in to unpack that lot. I don't suppose your mother did it herself when they put it away.'

'Broughton organized it,' Penny said, referring to the butler her parents had employed before the war, a man who had always regarded me as something one might find sticking to the underside of one's shoe.

'I'd forgotten about Broughton,' I said. 'What happened to him?'

'Oh, Daddy let them all go when they closed the house.'

She looked at me as if expecting some sort of comment on the loyalty of employers but by now I'd learned when to keep my mouth shut.

'Why are they coming back so soon, anyway?' I asked instead. 'I thought all the liners were still repatriating troops or shipping off war brides.'

'They are,' Penny said, locking the cellar door again. 'But all the troops and the brides are going the other way so it wasn't difficult to get two berths from New York to Southampton.'

'It's hardly going to be a luxurious voyage,' I pointed out. 'Ferrying a few thousand troops twice a month will have played hell with the furnishings.'

'The alternative was to wait until October when the proper service starts again.'

'I can't see what the hurry is. You're not going to get this place straight by the middle of next month even if you find the staff.'

'There's some sort of problem over their immigration status. Mummy said some men from the State Department came to see Daddy about it and all of a sudden he wouldn't hear of anything except packing up and coming home.'

'But they've been there six years,' I said. 'Why is there suddenly—'

'*I* don't know!' Penny protested. 'I'm not even sure Mummy does. Something to do with the war being over now. You know what Daddy can be like.'

That proved to be another opportunity for me to keep my mouth shut so we went upstairs in silence and checked through all the bedrooms and bathrooms.

My attempts to get Penny to linger in one of the bedrooms proving unsuccessful—an irritating coyness in the family home I remembered from our courtship inopportunely resurfacing, as if the ghost of her girlhood still haunted the house—I at least extracted a promise from her to come back to my flat later. But this was only on condition that I accompany her round a succession of staff agencies in the hope of recruiting the household servants her mother would expect to be in place on her return.

By five o'clock when the agencies closed we'd achieved nothing except to argue over some triviality and I took her back to Julia's, her promise to come to the flat forgotten.

I went home alone, which was probably just as well as I found Gifford waiting for me in the flat. He had let himself in. After twenty years in Special Branch I suppose it was a habit he wasn't able to break.

'I hope you brought your own tea this time,' I told him, putting the kettle on the electric ring.

He didn't reply, just pulled a half bottle of Navy rum out of his pocket and placed it on the table. I turned off the kettle and fetched two glasses.

'What are we celebrating?' I asked. 'My being unemployed, or have you got a promotion?'

'I saw a copy of the report you gave to Jekyll,' he said.

'Oh? If you want to see the original I've got one of my own here somewhere. Want to compare notes?'

Gifford poured two shots of rum. I picked up my glass and tasted it; I didn't really care for rum any more than I cared for scotch or gin but since I seemed to have become a drinker I knocked it back anyway.

'It doesn't matter,' he said. 'Tuchman has enough evidence now to reopen his case against Pellisier.'

'In Jekyll's opinion it's all circumstantial.'

'Not quite. There's something you don't know.'

'Just something?' I said. 'I was under the impression there was a lot I didn't know.'

Gifford stared across the table at me, face devoid of expression as if he was waiting until I had got what Julia called wisecracks off my chest.

'The men that first found the Bren Gun carrier...' he said.

'What, 4th Wilts, after they retook Maltot?'

'No. This was the same day the carrier was destroyed, July 10th.'

'First I've heard of it,' I said.

'I told you there was something you didn't know. It was early that evening just before they started pulling out of the village. Some platoons had got lost and communications were out. The Dorsets were trying to round men up to tell them to pull back. Some of them went into the woods and came across the carrier. They were led by a young second lieutenant, a man with a bit of nous about him, if you know what I mean.'

Given what I knew about the carrier and the proximity of the Hitlerjugend, I wasn't sure I would have characterized it as "nous".

'The two in the carrier were still burning but he thought the third man—Dabs—looked as if had been executed. He took his men up the drive to the château to investigate.'

Gifford sipped his rum. I poured myself another.

'He saw smoke coming out of one of the ground floor windows. As there wasn't any sign of German troops around he went inside to take a look.'

'I'm not sure I would have,' I said.

'He found a body in the room that was on fire and by the look of it thought it had been set deliberately to incinerate the corpse. There was a smell of petrol and the hands and head had been burned while the rest wasn't that badly damaged. His first thought was that whoever had done it had been in a hurry and botched the job. Instead of waiting around to make sure the whole place went up it looked as if they'd scarpered.'

'Just as well for your second lieutenant,' I said. 'Or he would have run smack into Müller's platoon and I'd have been looking into *his* execution.'

'Actually you wouldn't,' Gifford said. 'Because no one would have been interested if we hadn't known about what he found.'

'Found?'

'The circumstances made him curious. Dabs being executed and the attempt to burn the body in the house. He put the fire out and found some ID on the corpse—in the name of Claude Pellisier. Then he had a look around. He found some half-burned papers in the grate, which again he thought a bit odd being summer and as they'd set fire to the house anyway So naturally he had a rummage through them.'

'Naturally,' I said.

'There wasn't much left he could make out,' Gifford went on ignoring me, 'except that some were in English. More than that, several bore the stamp of the British Foreign Office.'

Gifford paused, watching for a reaction. I didn't feel like giving him the satisfaction of supplying one.

'He couldn't have had much time,' I said. 'The 9SS-Panzers were already moving up in support of the 10th's battalions in Maltot.'

'No, he didn't,' said Gifford. 'His men heard armour approaching so they had to pull out pretty sharpish. Lucky they weren't cut off. The lieutenant had already made a note of Dabs' ID but couldn't do anything for the other two as the carrier was still red hot. He did bring back the papers he found in the grate, though. It was afterwards he began thinking that whoever had set the fire hadn't really meant for the whole château to go up, just the body.'

'Sounds to me like he was the man you should have got to investigate Kearney,' I said. 'Not me.'

Gifford shook his head and for once allowed himself the luxury of looking pleased with himself. 'Not Kearney. Coveney. We discovered Coveney had been passing information to Pellisier. But *you* had to be the one to look at Kearney, see if you could establish it wasn't Pellisier's body. Call it a pincer movement. You knew the family. That's why you were attached to Jekyll; so your section would get the file.'

I found my glass was empty again. Gifford refilled it.

'I wasn't aware Special Branch had that sort of pull.'

'Not us. The people we answer to.'

'Jekyll told me he hadn't wanted me handling it in the first place,' I said.

'It was Sir Maurice Coveney that didn't want you handling it. He didn't want *anyone* handling it. But particularly someone who knew the family, who knew about his connection to Claude Pellisier.'

'I can believe it of Coveney,' I said, 'but you're not going to tell me Jekyll was complicit in leaking Foreign Office files to Pellisier? He may be a hard-nosed prick but he's not a spy. Never that.'

'Of course not. He didn't know what Coveney had been up to before the war. But he wasn't above helping him smooth things over afterwards, when asked to. Coveney didn't go into details but he told Jekyll something of his family connection to Claude Pellisier and how the Frenchman's action during the war might prove an embarrassment to him. He told Jekyll that if there was any way it could be played down, he'd be grateful.'

'Grateful?'

'The Coveney family have ship-building interests on the Clyde. There was to be a position in the company for Jekyll when he came out of the army.'

'Well, we've all got to look to the future now,' I said. Gifford's expression suggested some people might not have one. 'You said *before* the war. Did Coveney stop passing stuff once it started?'

Gifford emptied his glass but didn't pour another. 'Not immediately. Being a member of the Anglo-German Fellowship wasn't uncommon among that class before the war. Even after it started there were some who hoped for an accommodation with Hitler. It was when his wife was killed in a German air raid that he stopped.'

'So I assume he passed his stuff to Reggie Forster in America who sent in on to Pellisier from there.'

'Until America entered the war. But by then Coveney had had second thoughts. And by that time his son had joined up as well.'

'What happens to Coveney now? Have you got enough to arrest him?'

Gifford looked at his empty glass. 'Not my decision. Apparently it's been decided that a scandal wouldn't be in the national interest. The country needs to rebuild its industry and get back on its feet. There's no suggestion that the rest of Coveney's family were involved in his passing information and it's thought a court case might prove prejudicial to getting the shipyards back to work.'

'He gets away scot-free?'

'You could say *Scot*-free,' Gifford agreed, replying with what, if I hadn't known the man, I might have taken for a joke. 'They're taking a lenient view. Coveney never passed anything after his wife was killed when it might have done some real damage and as far as we're aware seems to have cut all his ties with Pellisier.'

'Until he was asked to identify his corpse?'

Gifford pursed his lips. 'I suspect he might have done that for the sake of his dead wife. She had been close to her brother. But he'll have to resign, of course. Although that's as far as it will go.'

'Resign?' I repeated a little caustically. 'Well, that's all right then. At least we'll both be out of work.'

'Which reminds me. There's someone who wants to meet you. Abel Bryce. Says he's got a bone to pick with you.'

'I've already met him,' I said. 'Coveney's secretary. He's been trying to get in touch—'

Whether it was Gifford being there, I don't know, but recalling Bryce, something else fell into place.

'He told me he met you at Julia Parker's house,' Gifford went on. 'He was none too pleased about you getting him out of bed to deal with Diamaid Caomhánach's body. He was late for work the next morning.'

'The man with the camera,' I said. 'Bryce works for you?'

'Not Special Branch. Bryce is MI5. They managed to put him in as Coveney's secretary. Bryce was the second lieutenant with nous who found the carrier. Made captain by the end of the war.'

'Not brigadier? I'm surprised. Why does he want to see me?'

'I'll give him this address.'

'They're knocking the place down,' I said.

'You'll hear from him before that.' He stood up and moved towards the door, leaving what was left of the rum on the table. 'One other thing,' he said, as if it had just occurred to him. 'You might prefer not to be there when the Queen Mary docks at Southampton. It'll be handled quietly but it might be better if you weren't there.'

~

I found a flat for Penny and myself a couple of days before the Queen Mary was due to berth. North of the Marylebone Road in a service block off the Edgeware Road, the building wasn't old but had had a bad war and was unfurnished and shabby—unlike Cowcross Street, though, in no danger of demolition. I took a lease on it and arranged for a painter to tidy the place up. Penny was still struggling to get her parent's house ship-shape and had little time to spare to worry about where we were going to live. I thought she might be upset about my not going down to Southampton to meet the liner but she didn't seem to mind. Julia was going with her and she wanted to get Helen and Reggie settled before announcing that she and I were getting back together. She hadn't written to tell them.

She said she'd try and ring me from Southampton once they disembarked and we agreed on a time. I said I'd wait by the phone in the hall for her call. I didn't know exactly what Gifford had in mind for Helen and Reggie when they arrived and thought it probably best I didn't, but I stood by the phone fifteen minutes before she was due to ring and stayed for an hour after, littering the floor with cigarette butts. Even after I knew she wasn't going to phone I still waited, taking the opportunity to jot down on paper all those telephone numbers I'd scrawled on the plaster over the last months. Even the number for Rose's flats in Kilburn.

Finally I gave up and walked down the road towards Kings Cross and bought an evening newspaper. I stopped in a pub and went through each page over a pint, not seriously expecting to find anything but compelled to look anyway. The next morning I waited until almost noon then rang Julia.

Ida answered with barely a trace of Blackburn leaching through her best telephone manner. In the background I could hear someone wailing and Ida dropped her voice as if not wanting to be overheard.

'Captain Tennant?' she almost whispered. 'Something terrible's happened.'

'My wife's there is she?' I asked.

'And Miss Julia and her sister. They took Mr Forster off the ship...'

'Can I speak to my wife?' I said.

'They're all in a terrible state, sir. He's been arrested!'

'I don't suppose Mr Tuchman's there, by any chance?'

'Yes. Do you want to speak to him?'

'Please Ida, if I may.'

The receiver was put down and I could hear muffled voices and the wailing still going on and a minute or so later Tuchman came on the line.

'Harry? If you hold for a minute I'll pick up the extension.' I heard him say something to Ida who must have come back to the phone with him and a few moments later he said, 'Harry,' again and I heard a click as Ida replaced the receiver in Julia's hall.

I could picture him in Julia's library, a large room with some comfortable chairs and decent books that nobody read. The library was hardly used and Tuchman would be able to speak freely there without fear of being interrupted.

'Ida said they arrested Forster,' I began before he could say anything else. 'How are they taking it?'

'Not well. Julia's sister had a fit of hysterics yesterday. She isn't much better this morning. Julia's being a trouper. She spent all yesterday evening on the phone trying to find someone with enough pull to get him released. Of course that's not going to happen, not immediately. She asked me if I could do anything, but under the circumstances...' his voice trailed off.

I put a toe in the water. 'Penny told me they'd already been questioned in New York. Something about their immigration status?'

'So I heard,' said Tuchman, 'although the story I got from Julia was that they were asking about Helen and Pellisier. Back before the first war? Know anything about that, Harry?'

It was then I realized just how disingenuous Tuchman could be. I couldn't be certain Julia had told him about the affair, but it was difficult to believe, given his interest in Claude Pellisier, that he hadn't ferreted out everything there was to know. Gifford's interest in Pellisier was marginal beyond the fact he was the recipient of Coveney's intelligence, which after the fall of France in 1940 could only have reached Pellisier through Forster. I had told Gifford about the affair and he might well have told Tuchman. Either way, the man already knew and one or the other of them had used the information. But since Gifford had got it from me, I could see that I was going to be the one left holding the baby. The only question was how long it would take for Julia to put two and two together and for the penny to drop. And for Penny to drop me.

'How's Penny taking it?' I asked.

'Upset, naturally,' he said, conveying a liberal use of understatement.

I asked him what had happened at Southampton.

'Gifford's men went on board with the pilot. It was all low key and as soon as they berthed they took him off through one of the crew exits. They let your mother-in-law disembark but she had to be helped ashore. I'm afraid the press were on hand to record the fact so you'd better expect some publicity. Julia's trying to keep it out of the papers but it's only a matter of time.'

'I should come over,' I said.

Tuchman didn't reply immediately. When he did it was obvious he was weighing his words.

'We've got Helen calmed down at the moment. It probably wouldn't do any good for her to see you. Not just now, Harry. Under the circumstances.'

'Tell Penny I called then, will you? And that I took your advice about not coming over.'

'Sure, Harry,' Tuchman said, and this time there was no mistaking that we both knew where we stood.

~

I rang again the next morning. Ida told me Tuchman wasn't there and that no one else was available to come to the phone.

By then I knew I was just going through the motions.

I tried once more later and this time Julia came to the phone. She said Penny didn't wish to speak to me. I asked why and a moment of icy silence followed before she said:

'How *could you* betray a confidence, Harry? You told them about Helen and Claude. It's unforgivable.'

I thought about suggesting that both her and Penny had betrayed it first and that Tuchman also knew. Even if Julia denied telling him I'd be planting a seed of suspicion which, if unlikely to grow there and then, might germinate later. But for now Julia would assume I was just trying to shift the blame and that would be how it would sound. It might even be the truth.

Instead I dissembled until she put the phone down on me. I went round there, of course, rang the bell and hammered on the door until Ida eventually opened it. The poor girl was shaking and close to tears as she told me she had been instructed to say I was no longer welcome at the house. I could have pushed past her, I suppose, had I thought it would have done any good. I knew it wouldn't so stood on the doorstep for several minutes after she had closed the door in my face.

Strangely, all I could think about at the time was that I was stuck with a lease on a flat I could no longer afford.

31

The day I moved out of Clerkenwell Abel Bryce came to see me with the offer of a job. They needed men like me, he said, with a police and army background who were dependable and not afraid to use their initiative.

He might have added with a suspicious nature and no family ties, but was decent enough not to mention either.

The youthful naivety I had seen in him when we'd first met at Julia's seemed subsumed now beneath a mature exterior, as if he had either suddenly grown older or had cast off a part he no longer needed to play.

'Think about it,' Bryce said, 'and come and see us.' He handed me a card with an address but no name. 'I think you might enjoy the work. We're all in it together since that Irish business, after all.'

If the comment was meant as a veiled threat, a reminder that I still had Caomhánach's death hanging over my head, he managed not to make it sound as such, and in his face I caught a flash of his former naivety.

The game, I suspected, came as second nature to him.

Would I have done what Bryce had if I had come across the Bren gun carrier outside the Château de Hêtres; found the bodies of Arnie Poole and Robert Burleigh in the burning vehicle and the corpse of Joseph Dabs nearby, shot in the back of the head? Would I have possessed the requisite initiative to search the house, the nous to realize things weren't quite as they seemed?

I didn't suppose I would but then we can't all be John Buchan characters.

'Did you hear about Maurice Coveney, by the way?' Bryce asked as he got up to leave.

'No,' I said, pocketing his card.

'Shot himself when Forster was arrested.'

'Did he leave a note?'

Bryce raised an amused eyebrow. 'No, and it wasn't us if that's what you're suggesting. We don't go in for that sort of thing as a general rule—just in case you thought we might. And no, no note. Hard on Coveney's son. He was quite innocent of any involvement. Spent his war in the Far East and had something of a tough time of it, I'm told.'

Hard on Helen, Julia and Penny, too, I couldn't help thinking after he had left. It seemed the men in their family—blood relatives or otherwise—were all destined to betray them to some degree or other. I was the worst in their eyes, of course; even if—in *my* eyes—the most innocent.

I didn't doubt that sooner or later Tuchman, too, would abandon them, but I found it difficult to feel much sympathy.

Some people—like Mussolini's mistress for instance—just couldn't back a winner.

~

I asked Jack to give me a hand moving my few things out of the Clerkenwell flat and into my new place. He had a friend with a van and I swapped some of the ration coupons I never used for the use of his petrol. Jack himself wasn't yet working—at least not officially—although I got the impression he and his mate were getting by quite comfortably one way or another.

He had heard from Stan in Burnley who was now working with his brother. There was no shortage of building work to be done, according to Stan, just a shortage of materials to do it with. I was able to tell him Peter had joined a law firm and then Jack told me Susie had left the section she had transferred into when Jekyll closed us down.

'I got the impression she was hoping Jekyll was going to marry her,' said Jack as we manoeuvred my old settee down the stairs.

'Susie and Jekyll?' I asked in amazement, almost dropping the thing on Jack who was several steps below me.

'Didn't you know?' he grunted, taking the weight. 'She knew she wasn't going anywhere with Peter so when Jekyll started sniffing around—'

'It does explain a few things,' I said, thinking of how Jekyll had known about my Irish jaunt and Kearney's IRA connections without my telling him.

'Anyway,' said Jack, 'it didn't pan out. He was on a promise of some high-powered job up in Scotland and she thought she'd be playing the laird's wife. The job fell through and now Jekyll's rejoined his regiment. He's apparently had to drop a rank to major.'

No Coveney, no job, I presumed, although I didn't say anything to Jack about it. For a world in which justice had been in short supply I found it gratifying to know that, now and then, someone got what they deserved. As opposed to what they wanted, that is. I didn't doubt Susie would bounce back; playing the laird's wife wouldn't have suited her any more than playing the vamp had. She might try being the girl next door only it always came out as more Betty Hutton than Betty Grable, and that sort of in-your-face bundle isn't every man's cup of tea. Not mine, at any rate, despite Susie's physical attributes.

~

I had been living in the new flat for about two months when I got a letter from Penny. By then her father had pleaded guilty to passing confidential material on to a foreign government— France—as opposed to an enemy power—Germany. At what I had thought to be a precipitously arranged trial, he was given a lenient three year sentence which led me to wonder if the judge hadn't been an old acquaintance from the Anglo-German Fellowship. But Gifford let me know the leniency of the sentence had been in return for Forster's cooperation in tracking Claude Pellisier down to his hideaway in upper New York State where he was living under an assumed name as a French Canadian.

Given all this, and the fact that Forster had lost a great deal of his wealth in America in risky stock speculation, I half expected Penny's letter to be a contrite admission that she'd been wrong in supporting her family. Instead she wrote that she would be seeking a divorce and would expect me to do the decent thing. It recalled the conversation we had had in the Clerkenwell flat when I'd asked her if she expected me to take Rose to a hotel to furnish the grounds. I thought while reading her letter that instead of Rose she might now suggest Ida for the role, until she mentioned in passing in the final paragraph that Ida had left Julia in the lurch. The girl had run off, she wrote, with that postal worker who had lived in the flat above me.

She meant Sam, of course, who I'd caught once or twice in Ida's flat and had always suspected of being a housebreaker.

It was then I remembered Sam had told me he had found a flat near in Euston and I finally worked out what Penny meant by his being a postal worker. Euston Railway Station is from where the overnight post office sorting trains operate and while I had been thinking his work was burglary, his unsocial hours were spent sorting letters on the Night Mail.

Had I not been amused by this revelation I might have thought Penny's letter a cold piece of correspondence. But at least she had spared me news of my mother and brother, George. And later, upon reflection, I concluded that Penny hadn't sounded particularly bitter. It was the sort of assessment that might lead an optimist into reading into it the possibility of a future reconciliation.

But perhaps I'm not an optimist. My reading was the realization that neither Penny nor I were the same people we had been when we were married. It had hardly been uncommon for couples to drift apart during the war, even those who had not been forcibly separated as Penny and I had. And although I had returned to England thinking I wanted things to go back to the way they once were, in reality what I wanted was that things be as they had once been, only now fitted to the man I had become. But of course it wasn't only I who had changed, and any dynamic would have to accommodate the change in Penny, too.

Given time, Penny and I might perhaps have grown used to each other's new personalities, perhaps fallen in love all over again; but there hadn't been the time. There had been too many other things going on, too much standing between us. A tragedy, I suppose, but a very small one when measured against the great tragedy that had been playing out all around us.

Almost everyone has had to learn to let go of something or someone they had once known; to learn how to cope with different circumstances within a different world. You could look back with regret and stay within your own pool of self-pity, or you could dust yourself off, turn your face to the future—no matter how uncertain—and embrace it. The world is full of what-ifs and what-might-have-beens and the thing to do is to not be content dwelling upon them; to accept what had happened and to strive towards the what-might-yet-be.

A decent enough philosophy, I suppose, but one not always easy to live up to. It is one thing to look at the world and the events of the past decade and count oneself as fortunate to have got through it; unlike those whose lives had ended abruptly, unjustly, and in millions of cases, unspeakably. Yet it is still difficult to entirely ignore oneself, even when faced with the generalizations that encompass the world. We are egocentric creatures, as much as we might practise selflessness and strive for empathy. Great events and ideologies wash us this way and that but it is the small eddies and tides that catch and spin each of us individually that concern us most deeply.

It is good then if, once in a while, we are granted the opportunity to see for once beyond our own petty concerns and, with a selflessly glad heart, be able to take pleasure in the fortune of another.

~

To claim I hadn't thought about Rose Kearney occasionally wouldn't have been the whole truth. And any pretence it might be because she hadn't used her real name, equally disingenuous.

So it was one dank November evening a year or two later when, seeking escape, I took refuge in a cinema.

Sitting cocooned in the dark, looking up at the screen—my mind wandering as it often does these days and thinking of things other than the film—I was shocked to suddenly see Rose standing in front of me, larger than life and smiling at the man who held her in his arms.

I recognized her immediately, even though they had changed her hair and the way she wore her make-up. But they couldn't change her eyes. And, when she looked down on us in that dark audience, still smiling, it was her eyes I remembered most of all. I felt she was looking at me in the way she once had. And I found myself smiling back at her. Sick of the life she had been living, Rose had found herself another. And the thought of that gladdened my heart, helping to warm it against the cold years ahead.

Printed in Great Britain
by Amazon